LUCY SUSSEX was born in Christchurch, New Zealand and lives in Australia. She works as a researcher at LaTrobe University and also as a freelance author and editor. Currently her day job is writing a newspaper review column. Her writing has been published internationally, and in a variety of genres.

She has been a judge for the Tiptree award, and a writer-in-residence at the Clarion Writers' Workshop. In addition she has edited four anthologies, one crime and three science fiction. Of these, *She's Fantastical* (1995) was shortlisted for the World Fantasy Award. She has won Ditmar and Aurealis awards, and been shortlisted for the International Horror Guild Award, and the Kelly awards (crime). Her work has been translated into Japanese, Polish, Czech and Russian. Her first adult novel was *The Scarlet Rider* (1996). Her *Women Writers and Detectives in Nineteenth-Century Crime Fiction: the Mothers of the Mystery Genre* was published in 2010 (Palgrave-Macmillan). In 2011 she was awarded the Peter McNamara Award for Science Fiction. *Matilda Told Such Dreadful Lies* is the fourth collection of her short fiction.

MATILDA TOLD SUCH
DREADFUL LIES

MATILDA TOLD SUCH DREADFUL LIES

THE ESSENTIAL
LUCY SUSSEX

$T\approx$
$p\approx$ Ticonderoga
publications

In memory of Joanna Russ and Peter McNamara

Matilda Told Such Dreadful Lies: the Essential Lucy Sussex
by Lucy Sussex

Published by Ticonderoga Publications

Designed and edited by Russell B. Farr
Typeset in Sabon and Minion Pro Condensed

A Cataloging-in-Publications entry for this title is available from the National Library of Australia.

ISBN   978-0-9807813-6-6 (hardcover)
        978-0-9807813-7-3 (trade paperback)

Ticonderoga Publications
PO Box 29 Greenwood
Western Australia 6924

www.ticonderogapublications.com

10 9 8 7 6 5 4 3 2 1

*I would like to thank Russell B. Farr,
Ticonderoga, Delia Sherman, Deborah Klein,
the editors of the previously published stories in
this book, the various writing groups who have
critiqued me over the years, Damien Warman
and Marianne McNamara, for a nice surprise at
Easter, and the greater skiffy community for their
long-standing support.*

CONTENTS

INTRODUCTION

DELIA SHERMAN

When Lucy asked me if I'd write an introduction to this collection of her short fiction, I jumped at the chance.

Part of my enthusiasm was pure opportunism. After the wonderfully gender-and-genre bending "My Lady Tongue" came out in 1988, I considered myself a Lucy Sussex fan, and combed the usual SF and fantasy magazines for more. But the vagaries of publishing kept many of her early stories out of USAian markets, and my search languished until 1996, when she submitted "Merlusine" to Ellen Kushner and me for our "music and magic" anthology, *The Horns of Elfland.*

We were blown away. We know Louisiana and Cajun music—I have relatives there, I've written things set there, and at the time, we were going to Cajun dance nights every week. And she'd got it all exactly right—the history, the speech patterns, how the music makes you feel and how it fits into the culture. Not only that, she'd seamlessly knitted in the French legend of the serpent-bride Melusine as well as dealing with such vexed political themes as racial identity and class in the American South.

And it was a good story, too.

We took it—of course we took it. And if we'd sold the ballad anthology she wrote "Matilda Told Such Dreadful Lies" for, we'd have taken it, too. Because it's got that same blend of folklore and history and political consciousness and characters you'd like to have dinner with (even when they aren't human) that "Merlusine" has, and while still being completely different.

Over the years that followed, her stories popped up here and there in my reading landscape, and I always greeted them with cries of joy. But until I sat down with the stories chosen for *Matilda Told Such Dreadful Lies*, I'd never read so many, nor had the opportunity to read them all in one gulp. I saw themes and patterns I couldn't see before, saw the range of interests and styles of which she was capable, and was blown away all over again.

There is much in Lucy's stories to enchant. Their structure, for example—the way they layer history and character and narrative like the layers of color in an oil painting, each layer contributing its bit to the depth and subtlety of the finished story. In "Albert & Victoria," climate change, New Zealand mythology, the tension between the protagonist and her estranged husband and her old friend, the ways in which tourists engage with the country they're visiting, all come together, piece by piece, into an extended meditation on identity and magic and the gods of the land, with a strong flavor of outdoor adventure and a side of romance.

As you may be able to tell, Lucy has a free and easy way with genre. Is "Mist and Murder" a mystery story or a ghost story, a historical fantasy or science fiction? The answer could be "Yes," or "Not really," or "Kind of," or even "Who cares?" Her doll stories—"Frozen Charlottes," "La Sentinelle," "Matricide," "Something Better Than Death," draw from the forms and conventions of horror, urban fantasy, psychological thriller, and mythic romance, (among others) to generate multi-layered narratives in which history, human desire, human weakness, and evil, all play their parts. Even stories like "My Lady Tongue," "The Queen of Erehwon," and "Absolute Uncertainty," which sail fairly close to the shores of pure science fiction, carry a cargo that looks to our own cultural past and present as much as to our technological future.

As various as they are in subject and treatment, these stories have in certain traits in common that mark them as Lucy Sussex stories. They tend to take place in liminal spaces, for instance: between countries, between times, between states of existence. Two of them, "Something Better Than Death" and "Matricide," open in that most liminal and artificial of all locations, an international airport terminal. And if the terminal in "Matricide" occupies the space between life and death, well, so do several other stories, either physically or metaphorically—the ghost stories, of course, but also the stories in which illness or extreme danger momentarily releases her down-to-earth protagonists from the shackles of their own common sense. The knowledge the protagonists of "Kay & Phil," "Ardent Clouds," and "Matricide" gain from in these moments of freedom isn't always comfortable or encouraging, but it does bring them clarity.

Clarity—of thought, of expression, of understanding—is another earmark of a Sussex story. And no wonder. As a journalist, a researcher, and a historian, Lucy is a professional unraveller of mysteries, a bringer of light into hidden places, and of hidden or forgotten facts into the light. Take the indigenous mythology of her adopted Australia, for instance. In the interview with Timmi Duchamp included in the collection *Absolute Uncertainty*, she explains that "Maltilda Told Such Dreadful Lies" is an exercise in "interrogating the text" of that most iconic of Australian ballads, "Waltzing Matilda."

What this means in practice that that she deconstructs the familiar narrative of swagman, jumbuck, and billabong, putting it in the hands of a narrator who is both unexpected and absolutely authoritative. It's a fine piece of folklore and a fine send-up of colonial cultural myopia and self-importance. It's a political story in the sense that it takes an unexamined truth (that Australia is all about the experience of the European colonists) and examines it through the lens of history, psychology, and indigenous folklore. Oh, and it's very funny.

Wit and humor, in fact, is one of the elements that runs through even the most political and serious stories. "My Lady Tongue" is an explicitly and seriously feminist story that takes on (among other things) lesbian separatism, the problem with utopias, and sexual politics, both homo- and hetero-. Its narrator, Raffy, is extremely charming, louche, and, well, raffish. Raffy is always testing the boundaries of the Womyn Only ghetto/commune where she lives, which gets her into trouble in ways that demonstrate both the strengths and limitations of separatism, as well as just how outrageous a truly outrageous woman can be.

There are other recurring themes as well: history, and the way it bleeds into and influences the present is the most pervasive, but these stories also touch on the growth, endurance, or death of love between individuals, emotional vulnerability, the strength of women, the metaphorical and literal powers of natural phenomena like volcanoes and glaciers, the magic inherent in man-made things like dolls and books and fairytales. These are the ones that speak to me. The ones I've missed, I leave to you to unearth.

DELIA SHERMAN
JANUARY 2011

MERLUSINE

The Universal Mother, capricious in her invention, commits her errors and failures when matter is lacking, or when it is plentiful, or when she is on the point of shaping her Work, or when the faculty is disordered or defective. It is not a new thing in the world . . .

"Aiee Merlusine!"

It gets me in the throat even now, that ululation at the start of the old Cajun song, though I've played "Merlusine" hundreds of times. "Aiee Merlusine!" I voice in soprano reply, tapping my feet until the final triumphant chords of fiddle and accordion. My "Merlusine" is on tape, a copy of the original 78, a copy of a performance nearly half a century old, but still I rise involuntarily to lift the needle from the record. As I do, I almost see the rotating disc before my eyes, the spiral twisting ever inwards . . .

I live with helices: the double twist of DNA and the spiral scratch of old American folk records. In my thoughts they interwine, a triple helix. DNA plays a song to me, and it is "Merlusine".

. . . that men have seen the effects of the nature of a Monstrous child . . .

The next tape I would play is another version of "Merlusine", but it exists only in memory. The nearest thing I have to it is a CD by Heath and the Ramblin' Roses, *Live in New Orleans*. The Roses adulterate Cajun with soft pop and whilst not completely ersatz, they're too bland for my purist tastes. However Cajun acts so rarely tour Australia that I couldn't pick and choose; when a geneticist's conference coincided with Heath & Co's Queensland dates, I skipped the official dinner and went on down to Festival Hall.

Immediately I took a dislike to Heath. Firstly, because he wore MTV leathers and a silly headband, secondly because he thought an accordion made a good phallic symbol, thirdly, because although he'd got technique, in the sense of being able to play fast, there was no passion, no feeling behind those furious riffs. The rest of the band weren't such virtuosi—they played with a sense of fun rather than self-promotion, even managing some of the grit and sweat of the originals. So I did enjoy myself, even if I never came close to clapping.

Encore time, though, was different. The Ramblin' Roses trotted out into the spotlight with an additional player: a sixtyish man clutching a violin and blinking owlishly at the audience from behind bi-focals. He looked like a farmer on holiday; he looked like the Cajun musicians of the forties and fifties. Heath's fiddle player, a tall girl with a rope of black hair, grabbed the mike and cooed:

"Ladies and gentlemen! A special guest—Mr Gervais Boudville!"

I don't believe it, I thought. G. Boudville, who cut a couple of discs for an obscure Cajun label in the fifties and never was heard of again? He was marvellous then—but now? As if in answer the old man grinned like a maniac and launched into "Allons à Lafayette!"

Within a few bars he had proved he was the real thing, as intoxicating as a draught of swamp beer, both for the audience and the Roses. Suddenly the band were playing, not note for note, but with the true spirit of a vagrant, eclectic music, beginning with chansons de toile in medieval France, carried by settlers to Acadie in Canada, and from then down to Louisiana when the British evicted the French colonists. Did they sing as they travelled south, to drown out the pain of the forced march? And did their songs attract other exiles, African slaves, with their own tunes of loss? I have an image of black and white grouped around firelight as their two musics interbred, spawning heartfelt, passionate sounds: the French-Afro Cajun and the Afro-French Zydeco.

The transfigured band played "Le Two Step de L'Anse Meg", then "Tit Canard Mulet", while the crowd went bats. It took a full three minutes for the applause to die down after the third song, I know, because I clapped until my hands were sore. When silence finally fell in the hall, Gervaise grinned again, flourishing his bow.

Please God, I thought, not that I believe in you. Please let it be the A-side from his second disc, the nearest thing he ever got to a hit record.

"Aiee Merlusine!" sang Gervais.

Apotheosis.

. . . and the Philosophers say that in their day was born a child composed of three Natures . . .

My personal style is k d lang meets boffin, so when I went backstage that night, it was obvious I was not some bimbo with a taste for Cajun musicians. The tour manager was happy to believe I was interviewing for a campus radio show, publicity for this tour having been patchy. Shortly afterwards I was esconced in a back room, with a borrowed tape recorder and the rider: a proper cajun meal of red beans 'n' rice, jambalaya, and gumbo, set at one end of a long table, with several crates of beer at the other.

Bit by bit the Roses rambled in, first the guitar player, who had changed into a conversation starter of a t-shirt, emblazoned with "3rd Annual Baton Rouge Record Collectors' Fair". I'd been to the first fair, during my postdoc fellowship in the US, so we got on fine. The next musos in—the Roses' rhythm section—proved equally as fond of rare Cajun vinyl, and our conversation became so fevered that when Heath made his grand entrance he was completely ignored. It took the real star of the show to silence us as completely as if he had commanded:

"Taisez-vous!" (Shut up!)

Gervais strolled into the room with the fiddle girl, proud as a monarch crowned, proud as Clifton Chenier, late King of

Zydeco. On my tape of the "interview" all you can hear at this point is his padding footsteps, then an appreciative "Eh *bien*!" at the refreshments. Then, as if signalled, the band started babbling like a brook, so anxious to tell me the story that they interrupted, finished each other's sentences, and switched between French and Southern US at breakneck speed.

See, the fiddle player and the bassist had gone to this shopping mall, in that Surfers Paradise, y'all call it, in search of real *US* beer, and walked straight into good ol' Gerry Boudville, who'd been the 1 millionth customer at a Lafayette supermarché and so won a trip anywhere in the world he wanted which was L'Australie to see his fille, who'd gotten married to un soldat Australien, no the guy's a fighter pilot . . .

"Lucky find," said Heath. "Million to one chance, huh?"

I nodded. It's my professional joke not to call those odds astronomical but genetic, given the chances, say, of a 17th century Dutch ship, *The Gilded Dragon*, hiring in Cape Town a seaman whose inheritance included one of the rarest of genetic disorders, and when the ship was wrecked off the coast of Western Australia, this man surviving, going native, leaving descendants, so that hundreds of years later, local Aboriginals were diagnosed with a syndrome only found among the descendants of a 17th century Cape Town couple . . .

Had I believed in the soul, I would have bartered it for a find like that, or for this million to one meeting with Gerry Boudville. You can't have everything—and so, while we ate, I was content to question my Cajun hero.

"Why did you only make two records?" I asked in French.

"La claustrophobie." Not severe, I gathered, but enough to put him off playing in those little recording booths. He played a few dances after that, but his wife didn't like it much.

At that moment the fiddle player was feeding Gerry a spoonful of gumbo, her long dark plait dangling between his knees. I quite saw Mrs Boudville's point.

"Oh man," Heath said drunkenly. "With all your talent . . ."

The rest of the band went pink at this lack of tact, but Gerry wasn't fazed, merely remarking that playing the fiddle every night to his cows had tripled their yield. In the astounded silence after this anecdote I deftly introduced the subject of "Merlusine".

"You own a copy of the record?" said the guitarist. "Oh wow! I've only got a third generation tape."

"Shoulda been a monster hit," mumbled Heath.

Yes, I thought, "Merlusine" is Cajun classic material, but curiously nobody's even covered it since.

Gerry shrugged, unconcerned.

"It might have caused trouble," he explained.

"Why?" I said, puzzled, and then suddenly thought I had the answer. Most Cajun songs are little more than mating calls, lyrically embellished with references to dance and drinking, or Tante Nana's pistachios. "Merlusine" is unusual in its lyric, which is both bizarre and obscure. "Aiee Merlusine!" it begins, and then follows a tale of woe. Merlusine's pappy sold her to the carnival because she is a freak, with un tail de serpe, but everything will be all right (repeated many times, the chorus line) because somebody called Maurice is going to get her back.

"You mean," I said, "on religious grounds, because of Merlusine being the daughter of the devil, like in the medieval legend?"

Utter blank incomprehension appeared on Gerry's weatherworn face. "What sorta question is that?" asked Heath petulantly, obviously feeling too long out of the limelight.

"I don't know about her being the daughter of the devil," said Gerry. "Nobody said that when, after the record was pressed, I found out the tune I'd learnt from old Lou Charpentier—a great fiddler, but a greater drunk—had a story behind it. I thought it was just an old Cajun song. That's why the radio stations wouldn't play "Merlusine", because one grandson was a Sheriff, another Mayor, people to whom you didn't show disrespect. And, more than that, their father was still living, the youngest of Merlusine's children, a man who looked like you and me, with nothing to show that his mother was a snake-woman . . ."

And the hair on the back of my neck stood up and reached for the sky.

This was conceiv'd in the imagination and the fancy, and the Citizens of the town of Biseiglia in Pouille, which is a Province of the Kingdom of Naples in Italy, declare that this child was born of honest and respectable parents, the father being Pierre Antoine Consiglio, and the Mother Elizabeth Nastasia . . .

Once upon a time, and it was long ago that I heard these words, in the halting, French-accented voice of my grandmother, the young knight Raymond was hunting in the forest of Coulombiers, and met, as knights do, with adventure in the form of Mélusine, an eerily beautiful woman. He offered his hand at first sight; she offered him in return her beauty and her cunning mind, which would make his fortune. There was one condition—that husband should never see wife on a Saturday.

It must have soon seemed to Raymond an eccentric but very small price to pay. By trickery Mélusine obtained for him a generous portion of land around the spring where they had met, and by magic built a castle, Lusignan, with no more than a mouthful of water and three armfuls of stones. The couple settled down to family-making, with ten healthy sons born to them, great riches in patriarchal France, even if the boys looked a little peculiar: the heir, Geoffroi, had boar's tusks, another had three eyes, a third was furred like a bear, and the rest partook of freakishness in various degrees.

This mutant brood and the castle won not by inheritance nor battle, caused talk and not a little jealousy, to which the couple were blissfully oblivious. It was a spiteful relative of Raymond's who finally struck at his weak spot: that Mélusine, unlike other wives, had a day off each week, and wasn't this a bit suspicious?

At this point in Grandmère's narration, my disbelief ceased to be suspended, in fact fell crashing to the floor. Raymond had cheerfully accepted a magic castle and a boar-toothed heir without comment—it was surely rather late in the day for him to query his marriage compact. Had he never heard of killing the goose for its golden eggs? Probably not, my small girl self decided, given that Raymond himself was a character of folktale.

The suddenly jealous husband secretly followed Mélusine to the Lusignan tower where she spent her Saturdays, and there surprised her, as she bathed in the fountain fed from their forest spring. Did he scream as he realised her true, monstrous nature: a fine figure of a woman to the waist, and below that a serpent, covered with blue-green scales?

Peeping Raymond thus destroyed his marriage: Mélusine literally flew out the window, leaving the hearth and home she had created, not to mention ten eldritch boys. A broken home and a serpent in the family cupboard should have spelt disaster for the lads, but they did well by the standards of the time, fighting, sacking, marrying and begetting. One line of descent married into a little known family called Plantagenet, and thus four hundred years later the Kings of England carried traces of the blood of Mélusine, revelling in the self-description "Scions of Satan".

Grandmère showed me postcards of ruined Castle Lusignan and could even be persuaded, if in a very good mood, to unwrap from its tissue paper a fairing, from the nearby town of Font-de-Sé: a hard disc of shortbread, moulded with the image of a serpent-woman. "Voila!" she would say. "Here's proof of the story."

I didn't need any. Mélusine had taken hold of my imagination, so much so that when browsing in the Baton Rouge Record fair, I came across a 78 entitled "Merlusine," I paid the high price unquestioningly, purely on the strength of the name. And now I found the song was about another snakewoman, a Cajun, still within living memory.

It had always been on my mind that behind the story of Mélusine was perhaps no devilry, or faery enchantment, but simply some form of ichthyosis, a congenital skin disorder causing those afflicted to apparently grow scales. Stranger things happen in the world of teratogenesis, my professional specialty: the Elephant Man, for instance, or Maria Pastrana, furred like a bear and with two sets of teeth. I had researched these famous monsters as well as many lesser known but weirder others. Yet never could I have expected that by a million to one chance I would discover a second, researchable, Mélusine.

. . . who say that the cause of this Prodigious Child was Elizabeth going to wash linen on the Sea Shore, where there is a river abounding in Sea Fish and shell fish . . .

Cajun music and the DNA helix made an odd couple, but they promised to be as strangely fruitful as Raymond and Mélusine. It just took time from first bud (a letter to Ann Savoy, historian of Cajun music), to pollination (her ten-page reply directing me to other Cajun enthusists, collectors of Louisiana, local historians and genealogists, to all of whom I wrote) the dropping of the petals (the letters begetting others in truly Biblical fashion, to produce, after about three generations, enough evidence for me to write a research grant application) to tiny green fruit, which I date precisely to the moment I stepped onto a Louisiana porch and clasped the genetic matter of Merlusine in my bare hands, by pressing the horny palm of Huey Ponsonby.

He eyed me politely, but askance: I may have come from the underside of the world to see him, but I was a young woman and a University Doctor, two categories never before meeting in his experience. For my part I thought how little he looked a limb of Satan's stock, being a well-fed pensioner, who waddled, now that introductions had been made, back to his rocking chair, a genuine D. L. Menard. I perched on a stool, beside a table holding beers and two tape recorders—mine, and that of an amateur local historian, called, improbably, Turtle. He had collected me at the airport and driven me out to the farm for the payoff of being in on the interview.

There was a dead silence, broken only by the chirrup of crickets and a frog croak from the river (clearly recorded on the tape). Then Huey opened his mouth:

"Well, I don't know if I can help you much, after you comin' all this way too."

I indrew breath, not loudly, but audible enough that Huey's wife, a tiny, wizened woman, paused from placing pork rinds on the table to glance sharply at me.

"But you know the story," I said. "About your father Luke Ponsonby . . ."

"Everybody called him Mistah Luke," said Huey.

"Mister Luke, and how *his* mother was called Merlusine, because she was supposed to have a serpent's tail."

Mrs Huey, her head still turned towards me, hissed, a thread of sound:

"She had legs."

On the tape, her interjection is barely audible, and cut off by Huey, who proceeded to make quite a speech. He spoke softly, ponderously and extraordinarily slowly—I could have died of frustration just waiting for a sentence to finish. The gist was:

Yes, he knew the story. Even knew the song, too. His late brother Dwight (the Sheriff) got taunted with it in the schoolyard, and KO'd his tormenter. Thin-skinned, Dwight, like the also late Luke jnr (the Mayor). It got like nobody dared to mention Grandma around the boys. Consequently Huey hadn't thought about the story much for—oh—some sixty years. He really didn't think he could remember the details.

"But it all started here, didn't it?" I said. "Here on this farm?"

Turtle chipped in. "Title deeds show Alfred Fondecy bought the land 1870."

When I had first seen the name, in a letter from Turtle, I had thought: Font-de-Sé, near Lusignan, where my Grandmère's relatives had bought a country house. The surname was a possible, though unprovable link, with the historical Mélusine, assuming that the snakewoman disorder was hereditary.

"And he married his first cousin Marie, a girl of fourteen," Turtle continued. "But she died in childbed, leaving twin children, Marie and Maurice."

Huey's rocker creaked as he leant forward. "Twins, eh? You know more than I do."

I rolled my eyes in exasperation, and caught the gaze of Mrs Huey, who with a jerk of her head, indicated the door to the house. She slipped in; I waited a few moments, then followed, as Turtle reiterated his research—which I already had, via letter—to Huey.

Mrs Huey was waiting for me in her kitchen, standing in front of a graded row of cookie jars shaped like strawberries.

"I ain't puttin' my husband down to his face, but you're going about this the wrong way, Miz Professor-Doctor. Men don't remember family things—it's us womenfolk who keep pickle receeps, mend the christening gowns and pass stories down over the quilting."

I nodded, remembering Grandmère, whose French family I knew intimately, despite never having met any of them, and her husband, Grandad, a man whose surname I bore, but whose ancestry was a complete blank to me, for all he ever talked about was fishing.

"But Mister Luke only had sons, and as Huey's the only survivor, I have to interview him . . ."

"Mistah Luke, he was dying," she said urgently. "And he took his time about it. His wife had died years before, and the other daughters-in-law had houses full of babies, so Huey and I moved in here and I took over the nursing. Mistah Luke, he had things on his mind, and I was the only one listening."

"So tell me," I said. The taperecorder was running out on the porch, but I had notebook and pen in my pocket.

She folded her hands neatly over her check apron and began. Unlike her husband, she spoke quickly, sing-song, as if recounting a fairy tale. My notes are almost illegible, scrawled and abbreviated, but the first two words are: Monster Ogre.

Once there was a monster ogre, who treated his young wife so bad, she died, leaving two babies, one a boy, normal to the eye, the other a girl, perfectly formed, fine even, but with blue-green scales running from waist to toe. The father, ashamed, kept the girl confined in his house, though the boy roamed free, bearing for all to see the marks of cruel beatings. Come one day, when both children were thirteen, a carnival passed through the neighborhood.

"And it happened like the song says?" I asked. "Father sold daughter to the carny folk?"

"Reckon that's why the song got written," she replied. "To shame old Fondecy, once the neighbors realised his new buggy and suit had been bought with his own flesh and blood."

"Maurice talked?" I said.

A quick nod. "And then went after his sister. But what could a dirt-poor Cajun boy do? Couldn't buy back the star attraction in a raree show, could he? That would take real money. All he could do, Mistah Luke said, was hang around the carny, doing odd jobs here and there, waiting for a chance to make their escape. But Mistah Nathaniel, Luke's daddy, happened along first."

"A Knight in shining armour?" I threw in.

She started to shake her head, then stopped in mid-motion. For a long moment she hesitated, clearly chewing over words forthcoming, rapping her fingers on the table as if accompanying an inner agitation. The rhythm brought back to me a song called "Oh how she dances!", a ditty performed by James Luther Dickinson, Southern rock with the timeless quality I admired in the Cajun tunes. It has a spoken intro, the puff of a carny barker, but as I recalled the words they sounded strangely different.

"Ladies and gennelmen, discernin' customers! Right this way, right this way to see the greatest show of freaks on earth! See Elastoman, the contortionist, see Two Tons of Fun, the Fat Lady, see Princess Merlusine perform her spectacular snake dance!"

With the song echoing through my mind I was mentally transported to the outskirts of a small town at night, carnival lights, smells of candy floss and horse dung, pandemonium, following through the crowd a dandy young man in a white suit, smoking a big cigar. He paused, eyeballing a canvas awning, crudely painted with the image of a woman like a mermaid, except her tail had no fin on the end. Then he paid his quarter and strolled into the big striped tent.

Mrs Huey, in my improbable vision standing beside me, still in her neat apron amongst the disreputable carny crowd of over a century ago, shook her head reprovingly, finally decided on spilling the family dirt.

"Looks like a gennelman, doesn't he? Sure he had the money to buy Merlusine outa the carny, but it weren't from Christian charity. Mistah Nathaniel Ponsonby mighta come from a fine ol' Georgian family but he had the tastes of weird white trash, to marry a snake lady."

She shook her head again, and the vision vanished. We stood in the spotless kitchen, momentarily silent.

"He got thrown out of Ole Miss, that's what Mistah Luke said. Wouldn't tell me why at first, but when his wits went, out it came anyway. I ain't a-tellin' you, 'cos it ain't fit to repeat. Mistah Luke, he was a gennelman, but he had real bad blood in his family. That's why his mama sent him back here to claim his grandaddy's farm, so he'd be outa harm's way. I mean, outa the way of his brothers, the ones who were snake through and through."

I recalled Mélusine's alien brood, and was about to question Mrs Huey more closely but there came a holler from the porch: "Ruthene! More beer!" She bustled off, at the beck and call of her husband. I followed her out to the porch and was greeted by happy beery smiles from Turtle and Huey.

"We been having a real good time out here, guess we 'bout done your interview for you," said Turtle.

When I played the tape back later, it transpired Turtle and Huey had talked family history for just five minutes—Turtle dominating the conversation while Huey just sat, drank beer and listened. About all I learnt that was new was that Huey had a belch like a foghorn. Then they got onto catfishing, which occupied them the rest of the time I was in the kitchen.

Sitting in my motel room that evening, I used their voices as background ambience, while I examined photographs. I had taken polaroids of the old farmhouse, although it had been entirely rebuilt since Alf Fondecy's day, first by Mistah Luke on his arrival from Georgia early this century, after Alf's death, and subsequently by Ruthene and Huey. Then the inhabitants, Ruthene stripping off her apron to pose beside her husband, the pair stiff as boards, Jack Sprat and his wife, in reverse. The last shot was of Turtle, to keep him happy.

I laid these modern images aside, and opened an envelope of photos from the Ponsonby family album. Ruthene and Huey on their wedding day, dressed up to the nines, c. 1929, but clearly no more confident with the camera. Huey, a decade or so earlier, in company with the future Sheriff and Mayor, the three boys all wearing short pants and sullen expressions. Most interesting of all was a photo of a sweet-faced elderly man, Mistah Luke himself. Ruthene had provided these precious images just before I left, calling me back the length of the driveway to do so.

As we were, briefly, alone again, I made use of the time: "I have to know. When you said some of Mistah Luke's brothers were snakes through and through, what did you mean?"

She replied, as I'd expected: "Why, they had scales on 'em. But not as much as their mama."

So the snakeskin gene, though clearly recessive, *could* be transmitted through successive generations! Ruthene was covered in flour from piemaking, but nonetheless I hugged the faithful recording angel of a daughter-in-law.

. . . which she fancied she saw presently in her mind: this Woman, marvelling and ruminating on this, conceiv'd a confused idea of these Fish, and upon this Woman being known by her husband, this great Fancy of Fish influenced the birth of this Child, who was born with fish-like scales . . .

She had, though, missed one vital piece of information—precisely where in Georgia Nathaniel Ponsonby had carried his bride and brother Maurice, and from whence, a generation later, Mistah Luke had returned to Louisiana. However the deficiency could be remedied, possibly, by a visit to the only place named in her story: Ole Miss, more properly the University of Mississippi, alma mater of the Southern aristocracy.

But that could wait—it was Saturday, dancehall night for all true Cajuns. So we *allons au bal*, me and the Turtle family and had a high old time to the sounds of the Hackberry Ramblers, vintage Cajun, with not a band member under seventy. I waltzed and two-stepped to my heart's content, my best dance all night being with one Leesa Jane Thibodeaux, grandaughter of Sheriff Ponsonby. She was a big-haired, bosomy teen, the focus of male gaze in the dancehall—and of mine too, but for research almost as much as appreciation. As our legs, mine clad in linen trousering, hers in sheer nylons under a leather miniskirt, moved in unison to the music, I discreetly scanned the expanse of skin from her toes to upper thigh, which was interrupted only by a diamente shoe-strap. Alas, I found not a scale anywhere.

Sunday I declined the Turtles' invitation to attend church, and instead hit the Interstate in my rented car. Come Monday I was sitting in the office of the Mississippi University Archivist. A real historian this, genuine PhD, who sat looking at me over half moon glasses. If he was surprised to see a woman in a bow tie he didn't show it.

"You have only the name, a possible date of late last century and a home address somewhere in Georgia?" he said sternly.

My heart sunk as I nodded.

"Shouldn't be too difficult, then," he said, tapping on his computer screen.

To fill in the time between taps and bleeps, I said:

"What's a Georgian boy doing this far west? There were universities he could have attended closer to home."

Bleeeep!

"Speaking from my extensive knowledge of the young Southern male, I'd say he was being sent away from bad company. Often as not, the bad's within the boy, rather than an outside influence, but at least he's raising Cain at a safe distance."

He got up and strolled across to a huge card catalog, which filled one wall of the office. "I've computerized some of my indexes, but the rest are still on good ol' hard copy."

He opened a drawer, reached casually inside and retrieved a card.

"I think we may have your man here. Nathaniel Jefferson Ponsonby, from Columbine County, Ga., medical student 1884–7." He turned the card over, then, almost shockingly, snickered.

"Oh him! Thought the name sounded familiar. I gave a paper to the faculty coupla years ago, on the misdeeds of the frat houses, last century. Gist was, some things don't change. Nathaniel Ponsonby figured quite large."

He started making notes from the card onto a sheet of paper.

"Take this down the corridor, to my assistant, and she'll find you the relevant records. You're gonna have a fun afternoon."

Indeed. Mistah Nathaniel had been quite a hellraiser, to judge from his appearances in the Dean's disciplinary book. Cussin' and drinkin' were only to be expected; but there were other, darker offenses beyond college rites of passage. A divinity student had complained about Nathaniel's taste in room decor, which allegedly had included a shrunken human head from the Amazon. Nathaniel had responded that the head was from a mummified monkey, "sold to him, with tail of cod attached, as that mythical creature the mermaiden." Charge was dismissed, upon evidence from the Professor of Anatomy on the differences between monkey and human physiology.

Within a month he was in trouble again, over allegations he had borrowed a two-headed baby from the Medical Museum to display at his twenty-first birthday party. This time it was clear he had amassed a private freak show in pickle jars, from the evidence of the witnesses, who claimed to have noticed nothing unusual, well, no more unusual than normal, about Nat's rooms—those who could remember anything of the night, that is. I skipped a few entries, looking for the final enormity that had led to expulsion and had sealed Ruthene's mouth in a prim moue.

When I found it, I bit my lip, for like Ruthene I found nothing humorous about a freshman fraternity initiation involving sex with a piebald negress. The shock value, even after a century was considerable, and the stir it created at the time was obvious—even the handwriting of the Dean's secretary, recording the hearing, became stiff as if in outrage. What seems to have rankled most was the rather high price charged for the freshmen's privilege, and the fact that young Ponsonby was getting a cut of the proceeds.

"That's him," I said, closing the book with a thump and a small cloud of dust. "Couldn't possibly be two Nathaniel Ponsonbys with such bizarre tastes."

"Indeed," said the archivist, from the other side of the reading room. "He was certainly an original. I wonder what became of him. A latter-day Baron Frankenstein, perhaps?"

"No such luck. He settled down to family-making—with a woman who happened to be a latter-day Mélusine, complete with scales."

"Ah," he said, rubbing his glasses. "Now why does that surprise me not at all?"

. . . on his feet and hands; his Neck and his Face, like his Nature, are fair . . .

"Hurrah," I sang as I crossed the border into Georgia.
"Hurrah! We bring the Jubilee!
Hurrah! hurrah! the flag that makes you free!
So we sang the chorus from Atlanta to the sea
As we were marching through Georgia!"
Singing a Yankee song in Confederate country was probably a lynchable offence—but it was preferable to the prozac country on the rental car's radio. And I had already played my Cajun tapes to the point where repetition was threatening to dull pleasure, perhaps permanently; they were inappropriate anyway, since I was Partons de, rather than Allons à, Lafayette. So like a minstrel out of hell, I sped down the highway on wings of song, shutting up only when I had to stop at Bob's Gaso to buy a map, to try and find where in Georgia Columbine County was.

What I found instead was Nathaniel Ponsonby, a lawyer from Atlanta, announcing his intention to run for the Senate, via the medium of a giant TV set in which the sad-faced Bob appeared engrossed. I narrowed my eyes at the screen—there wasn't a great resemblance between this Nathaniel and the Lousiana Ponsonbys, but he did have Luke's arched brows and strong chin, features that were quite telegenic.

"Now what's that you got there?" said Bob.

I jumped—it hardly seemed he'd glanced away from the screen, the whole time I'd been in the station. Then, as he held out one huge paw, I deposited the precious photograph of Luke into it. In dead silence he compared the images.

"They's related," he said finally. "The old guy, he's Billy Carter, Dad Clinton, some kinda skeleton in the family closet?"

"Hardly. Mr Luke Ponsonby seems to have led a blameless life . . ."

Bob spat, into a spittoon crudely shaped, I saw, into a caricatured Jimmy Carter.

"But some of the family certainly didn't."

"Oh," said Bob, brightening. "That's all right, then." He nodded at the screen. *"Democrat!"*

. . . of a not disagreeable colour, and his Hair is fine and blonde, and below his neck, a black Hue is diffused all over his Body, which is somewhat hairy, pitted, and tousled like a scaly Fish . . .

Nathaniel Ponsonby was trying to be nice, with the resignation of someone practising for the terminal blandness of high office, but really he was unhappy about inviting me inside his plush Atlanta home. Australia meant only one thing to him, and that was Murdoch tabloids. His suspicion that I was a muckraking journalist in disguise was confirmed when I kept talking about hereditary disease.

"Not on my side of the family, Ma'am," he repeated.

I looked at this clean-cut young politico, and tried to imagine his ancestral namesake being a pimp for a woman patterned like a pinto pony, let alone snuggling up to scaly, Cajun legs. As I was cynically aware of the bones behind the whitest of political sepulchres, my imagination didn't have to work very hard.

"I'm afraid it is. I have eye-witness accounts"—a lie, since nobody I had spoken to had encountered a scaled Ponsonby—"that your great-great-grandma Merlusine had a form, possible never before described by science, of ichthyosis."

He saw a way out, and jubilantly pointed at a frame on the wall. "The family tree says her name's Marie!"

"That was her christened name. Merlusine was a nickname, possibly also stage name, after the snakewoman of medieval legend. Do you mind if I have a closer look at the tree?"

Before he could protest I casually unhooked the embroidered family tree from the wall, propping it on the walnut coffee table. "Ah, I see she and your ancestor Nathaniel had seven sons. Mind if I note the names and dates?"

"If you must."

I noted down the details in my notebook for Nathaniel jnr, Jefferson, Maurice, Raoul (d. young), Robert E. Lee (also d. young), Wendell and Luke.

"That's my work," said a female voice, dripping with Southern honey.

I looked up, and saw, in the doorway, what was obviously Mrs Nathaniel—nobody else would have been made over into a cross between Tipper Gore and Jackie Kennedy, complete with pink pillbox hat atop platinum tresses. But the eyes behind those baby-blue contact lenses were shrewd and her smile, as Nathaniel introduced us, etched laugh lines deep in her face.

"I do embroidery," she said, sitting down on the couch. "A harmless enough hobby"—with a meaningful glance at her husband.

"It's beautiful work," I said.

Nathaniel-the-many-generations-junior cleared his throat.

"Shari, hon, we have a *geneticist* here, all the way from Australia."

She took off her hat. "You've come about Granny Snake?"

Her husband went ashen.

"Nate, you're not denying the story?" She looked at him, exasperated. "Sooner or later we're gonna get questions, we can't hide the fact your family tree is . . . colourful."

I glanced down at the embroidery. Sure enough, she had used almost electric green wool for the leaves, and the trunk was a russet verging on orange.

"And frankly, I've been expecting anyday to have some newscaster recall that your distant cousin Braxton went to the chair."

I stopped copying names and dates and transcribed this interesting information.

"Not to mention cousin Harv . . ."

"Shari!" Nate said. She quietened, but only for a second.

"I heard all about Granny Snake when Nate and I got engaged. One side of my family came from Columbine county, same as

Nate's, and did I get the third-degree about that! His relatives were paranoid we might be related . . ."

"Quite sensible," I said. "Seeing as this skin disease appears to be linked to a recessive gene."

She nodded. "Made me think of the rule in the middle ages, where you couldn't marry a cousin even nine times removed. I majored in history, so I know about these things."

"The medieval lawmakers may have had the historical Mélusine in mind," I said. "Where this disorder apparently originated. Those sons of hers certainly showed signs of major genetic disruption—medical textbooks, they were. Thierri, furred like a bear, that's hypertrichosis, hirsuteness. The youngest, with three eyes, possibly a Siamese twin . . ."

She lifted one pink-clawed finger. "I just remembered something."

Several minutes later we were all in the attic, panting slightly and inspecting, in a dusty, Victorian frame, a C17th broadsheet I had seen before only on microfilm. It described one Bernardin Consiglio, a fish-scaled prodigy from Naples.

"Original," I said, after a while. "In good condition too. Where did you get this?"

"Guess it came from the big old house in Columbine county, before it got burnt down," said Nate.

Very likely, I thought, but did not say, it was part of the original Nathaniel's gallery of monsters.

"Do you have any more stuff like this?" I asked. "Heirlooms, family photos?"

"Not much. It all went in the fire . . ."

Shari replaced the picture, dusting her hands absently on her tight pink skirt. "Arson, wasn't it, Nate? All over inheritance, too. Maurice set the house on fire to spite Nathaniel II, but instead killed Wendell, his favourite brother. Not that it ever got proved in court, but everyone knew he did it."

"*Shari!*"

She pouted. "Nate, if you go into politics, your history belongs to the fourth estate. And I'd rather have sensational, safely-dead relatives than Whitewater anyday!"

The magnolia had metamorphosed from soft petals to hard steel. Nate took one look at his wife, swallowed, and suddenly started to co-operate.

. . . somewhat speckled with white, both the soles of the Feet and the palms of the Hands being white, human in form, but speckled with many Hues like the Turtle; he is ten years of age and is called Bernadin.

Oddly enough, a magnolia tree was planted overlooking the grave of Marie Ponsonby, beloved wife, loving sister, devoted mother, as the white marble attested, and flowers littered the triple memorial, which was also to Nathaniel I (in the centre) and Maurice Fondecy (on the left). Looking at the grave, I was struck by its resemblance to a king-sized stone bed. A little further away were the smaller, but still lavish headstones to Robert E. Lee, Raoul and Wendell, aged eight, fourteen and forty. Their uncle and father had lived to fifty and sixty-four, respectively; Granny Snake, as Shari had called her, had made it to seventy.

I crouched on the white paving, taking notes amid the sickly-sweet smell of decaying flowers. A succession of afternoon teas with Nathaniel's elderly cousins had laboriously established his line of descent, which had tended to small, sparse families of boys and utter respectability. No snakes here. Days spent in Atlanta libraries, examining old microfilmed newsprint, had revealed much more of the family history. Jefferson, the second born, had become a monk—no descendants there. Luke I knew was no snake; which left only Wendell and Maurice II as possible carriers of the snakeskin gene.

I pondered again the fact that the Ponsonby offspring had ranged from saintly (Luke and Jefferson) to demonic (Maurice and Wendell)—the clippings I had gleaned from the library were an extensive history of wild oats, even before the fire. Like father, like some of his sons, I decided, with the difference that Nathaniel I had, after arriving in Georgia with his bride, turned over a new leaf, becoming respectable.

Or had he? For the nth time I pulled out the envelope of photographs I had slowly extracted from the various Atlanta Ponsonbys. Largest of all was a group photo, family on porch, boys in knickerbockers grouped around the figures of two bearded paterfamilias, Nathaniel I and Maurice, one blonde, one dark, seated side by side. By Nathaniel sat a woman—but her face and hair were obscured by a sunbonnet, as she bent over the cradle where reposed the sleeping Luke. Other photos showed the boys in detail, an inscription on the back of one identifying Maurice II and Wendell. No mistaking it, these boys had a glint in their eyes ... but then, so did Mistah Nathaniel, even when settled down to family life.

Another photograph depicted Maurice and Nathaniel, younger and beardless, in a conventional Victorian pose of male amity. Or was it? Blond charmer Nathaniel gazing into the eyes of gorgeous gipsyish Maurice reminded me irrestistably of the more romantic gays in Robert Mapplethorpe's canon. The last photo, wrapped in tissue paper, for it was the only decent image I had of the Snakewoman, showed idyllic lovers, arm in arm on a porch swing— three of them, Nathaniel between Maurice and a dark beauty with a piquant, gallic face. Her eyes were sharply intelligent, her chin strong; I sensed here another steel magnolia. What had she made, I wondered, of a life of luxury with weird Nathaniel, after a deprived childhood, then adolescence in a carny? I somehow thought she had made the very best of it that she could.

Turning, I eyed the triple bed grave again. I was developing dark suspicions about these three, lying here together, in death as they had in life?

His Mother, dismayed at his monstrous birth, kept him Confin'd, Hidden and Unknown to all the neighborhood. She dipped him in Water many times, in order to make him shed his scales ...

"Those Ponsonbys, mumble mumble click mumble," said the old cracked voice on the tape, before bursting into an impish giggle. Zediya Atkinson pressed the pause button with one cocoa-coloured finger.

"Did you understand that?"

"Not what came after 'Those Ponsonbys.' I'm not good with Afro-American, particularly when it's that dialectal. And there's a lot of background noise."

"Gramma had this habit of clicking her false teeth. And she liked the TV on loud, all the time. I'm used to it, so I can interpret that she said: 'Those Ponsonbys, they was degenerates.'"

"I know that already."

I had gone looking for Chloe Pearl Atkinson, daughter of another Chloe, this time Chloe Mae, personal maid to Mrs Nathaniel I. Alas, I was too late, for when I knocked on the door of the little pink house in Rise 'n' Shine, an almost exclusively negro townlet, I found Zediya, sorting through her grandmother's personal effects. We made a quick trip in Zediya's station wagon to lay some flowers on the new, modest grave, and then returned to the house, and to a briefcase full of cassettes, records of a verbal struggle between a gossipy, contrary old woman and her descendent, an oral historian desperately in search of her Afro-American roots.

"When she got ornery she'd talk about the Ponsonbys, 'cos she knew I wasn't interested in whitefolks."

I eyed Zediya nervously, as I had when she had opened the door. She was an alarming figure of black pride with her heavy, clanking ankh pendants, Malcolm X badges, and the African batik that swathed her body, leaving only hands and face visible.

"And so justabout every damn tape has stuff about the Ponsonbys. You'll havta listen to all of them, I guess."

"Here?" I asked timidly.

"Well, you're gonna need me to interpret, least till you're used to the way she talks. And it gives me company, while I pack up here, even if it's white company . . ."

So began a very strange week. Rise 'n' Shine was too small for even a motel, but I found lodgings several blocks away with Mrs Snodgrass, the widow of a Baptist minister and a woman with an extensive collection of gospel records. That at least was a bridge across the melanin barrier, as our evenings were spent around the record player. It contrasted acutely with my daytimes spent in the formal front room of the pink house, solitary except when I called in the helpful/hostile Zediya to interpret. The time was fruitful, I grant that—I discovered a new musical enthusiasm, and first my notebook, and then a whole stack of index cards filled up with notes.

As I had suspected, Nathaniel, Maurice and Merlusine had lived very happily in a menage à trois for nearly thirty years. Three of the children had been affected by the snake gene: Raoul, who had died young, Wendell and Maurice II. They had only been scaled on the calf and foot, Chloe Pearl recollected. The prudery

41

of Victorians, and their total body coverage, had ensured the boys never went barelegged; similarly Chloe Mae was the only outsider to see underneath Merlusine's long frilled skirts.

Thus the secret had been kept, even in an era with intense, prurient interest in freaks. With Nathaniel as family doctor and Chloe Mae as midwife, nobody need look askance at wealthy, happy Mrs Ponsonby. Things got more difficult when the next generation grew up, and under the influence of Nathaniel's nature and nurture Maurice II and Wendell ran wild.

The Ponsonbys must have been endearing, I decided, for though Chloe Pearl cackled with glee at their misdeeds, there was affection in her laugh as well. I thought I had an answer, when she recounted how the wild, snakey boys had horsewhipped a Klansman (Zediya, for once, made approving responses to this Ponsonby tale). But then I realised there must be more to it, for both Chloes had kept in contact with the various branches of the Ponsonby tree, to the third and fourth generation.

Bit by bit I came to understand Chloe Pearl's speech, and had less call on Zediya for interpreting. My last morning in Rise 'n' Shine, she poked her head around the door whilst showing a real estate agent the property, but otherwise let me alone. Thus she did not see my complete Ponsonby family tree, a system of index cards linked with string, until I had finished it, and laid it out on the carpet.

"Oh!" she said, walking slowly round and round, inspecting my handiwork. I proudly explained how the snake effect was traced by a system of colour coding, red for Merlusine, dark pink for her affected sons, Maurice II, Raoul and Wendell. Braxton had only been snake an "itty bitty bit" according to Chloe Pearl; he got a pale pink card. Nobody else in the third generation had been affected; the fourth generation, Wendell and Maurice's grandchildren, was snakeless, although I had my suspicions about Cousin Harv. The only son of Braxton, he lived to break family and social taboos, culminating in the ultimate anti-American act of emigrating to Communist Russia. I had put a pink question mark on his card—he was certainly a snake, even if scaleless.

There was a long pause after I finished, then Zediya said: "You better pick this up before I stomp on it."

Because her tone meant business, I did, scrambling off the floor just in time before her temper gave way. Zediya had been placid the whole time I had been in the house—now she howled, aiming a clumsy judo kick at the pile of cassettes which scattered them to every corner of the room.

"I spent hours lissenin' to Gramma talk about these damn Ponsonbys, wishin' she'd tell me *my* family history, not some whitefolks'! You've got a full family tree here—yet I can't trace my kin beyond Chloe Mae! Where she was born, who she had Chloe Pearl with, what she did before she worked for the Ponsonbys, I don't know none of these things. You can trace your snake people back to France, maybe . . . but me, I got no roots at all!"

These last words were an impassioned shout, and in the silence afterwards we stood awkwardly, divided by an abyss of race and pain. When she spoke again, it was threatening:

"What you lookin' at, white gal?"

The batik had ripped with her kick, a thigh high split which revealed that the bare skin on her legs was particoloured. The sight sent a complex chemical thrill coursing through me: at one level erotic, so violent it was almost painful; at another level cold horror at this unprecedented reaction, when far less flesh had been revealed than with Leesa Jane; and thirdly, a jolt of pure pleasure in the part of my brain reserved for teratogenesis, for Zediya's enveloping robes had hidden a melanin deficiency. This black woman was a magpie, patched with white.

Trying to keep my voice steady, I said: "Did Chloe Pearl have skin like yours?" It had not struck me as odd before, but there had been no photograph on the grave, and Zediya had never volunteered a visual record of her grandmother. "And her mother, Chloe Mae?"

She nodded twice, the up-down gesture violent as a blow.

"Then I think I can tell you something about your family."

She looked at me opaquely, as she unfastened a badge from her turban and pinned the cloth on either side of the rip, holding it closed. With the ivory white against milky cocoa, that tantalizing contrast, concealed, I felt—a little—more scholarly and professional.

"If you go to the archives of the University of Mississippi, you'll find records of disciplinary action against Nathaniel Ponsonby I, in 1887."

Eons ago, it seemed, I had sat in the Ole Miss archives and wondered at Nathaniel's tastes in women. It didn't seem the least peculiar to me now . . .

"Mentioned in the proceedings is a an ex-slavewoman called Mary Pinto, yes, like the pony. He'd bought her out of a carny, as he did Merlusine. I think she's your great-grandmother Chloe Mae."

Her dark eyes were calm now, imploring more information. I wondered whether I should voice my suspicion that Chloe Pearl's interest in the Ponsonbys was precisely because they were *her* family, that the menage à trois had been à quatre, with Master Nathaniel and maid having, as was common in the C19th, an upstairs-downstairs baby. No, better stay with what seemed more certain, the records in Mississippi, sordid though they were.

Zediya listened to the tale of the frat house prank, then threw me out—just as I had anticipated she would.

. . . but God willed that he should be deemed curious enough by the State, a Child so monstrous, the most terrible thing the world has seen, to be portrayed in the state of Nature.

On the way back to Mrs Snodgrass' house, every tenth step or so ivory and chocolate cream would recur in my mind's eye, like a fetish, and in order to keep walking normally I would be obliged to concentrate hard on something unaphrodisiac, like Zediya's rage. Yet after a block even that was beginning to seem endearing, and the only solution seemed higher things: Gospel!

I was chilling out to the strains of "Will Hell Be Your Santa Claus?", when the phone rang.

"My name's Frank Thurwell from Decatur," said a basso profundo. "Miz Shari Ponsonby gave me your number. I rang Nate after I seen the TV news."

"We don't have TV here. My landlady says it's sinful."

He grunted.

"I'm a part-time Democratic party organiser. Nate I know, but I never realised he and Braxton Ponsonby were related, till some Republican asshole splashed it all over the news. See, my late father, he was a procrastinator, but even he had to die—"

I wondered where this was leading.

"—was pathologist for the State Penitentiary. I opened Dad's safe for the first time last month and got the fright of my life. There it was, together with notes towards a medical article that never got written."

The song had reached an accapella crescendo. I ground the receiver into my ear and yelled: "What was in the safe?"

"Why, this foot, in formaldehyde, labelled Braxton Wendall Ponsonby."

The track finished, and in the calm before the next song I said: "That's pretty weird."

"So's the foot."

The next song was "Blessed Assurance", and with precisely that feeling I asked:

"How much do you want for it?"

Ten minutes later I was driving to Decatur. Some hours later I began my return trip to Rise 'n' Shine, accompanied by the ripe, strange fruit of my enquiries—a glass jar, sitting on the back seat, padded in an old quilt and seatbelted to be on the safest side. Inside was a foot, adorned with the blue-green scales of a type of ichthyosis never before known to science. "Oh blessed be to God for procrastinators!" I sang to various old gospel standards, none of which quite fitted the words.

As if God didn't agree with this sentiment, the weather turned foul. I arrived back at Rise 'n' Shine in the middle of a thunderous shower, and was pulling up to Mrs Snodgrass' house when a figure in flowing batik waved at the car. I stopped, opened the door, and Zediya squelched in. Even through her general damp I could see she had been crying.

"I've got a buyer for the house," she said.

"Good," I said awkwardly. In her current state, Zediya was no Miss Wet t-shirt, nor threatening, but I was still wary of another embarrassing surge of desire . . . and of her temper.

"But that's not why I'm here. Found this after you'd gone."

It was a postcard with a Russian stamp: "Dear Cousin Chloe, Leningrad is swell. I've even met another American, of similar, right mind, and she is one fine girl. In fact, apart from telling you I'm still alive, though the rest of the family wish I weren't, I'm writing to say I'm getting married!!! To a great comrade from Louisiana, Belle Fondecy. Think from the name we must be related, but what the hell, we're in love!!! Long live the Revolution, Harv Ponsonby.

"It was the Cousin bit that made me cry," she said. "The more I pressed Gramma on my family, the more she'd talk Ponsonby. And I never"—here her voice slipped towards sob—"ever caught on."

"I guessed it, but didn't want to say. I thought you'd throttle me."

That drew a small, sad smile. "You thought right." The rain had eased slightly, and she opened the car door.

"Goodbye," she said. "I'm off to Mississippi in search of Mary Pinto."

I looked at the card, pondering Harv Ponsonby. He had undoubtedly known the family phobia of endogamy, of recessive genes producing another Granny Snake, but this had not stopped his ultimate act of defiance, in marrying a possible relative. I mentally calculated how much was left in my grant—enough to take me to Leningrad, once again St Petersburg? It might be greedy, but I couldn't give up the chance of possibly more strange fruit, living and fresh instead of preserved in formaldehyde. The thought of a Russian Ponsonby, a Boris or Marina, complete with scales, was irresistible. And so, while I was preoccupied with my Slavic Merlusine, Zediya slipped quietly out of my car—and I let her go without a word of thanks, or farewell.

Back at the Snodgrass manse, I let myself in quietly, for it was late. A light still burned in the living room, but my landlady slept, spread around her that evening's task, half-finished: the filling of a new album with old photographs. I bent over her, to turn off the light, and suddenly noticed, among the images of church picnics and Sunday schoolchildren, something familiar.

I picked up the photograph and examined it closely. At first sight it was unremarkable, a middle-aged negro woman, a small child in her lap. It was her gaze that had caught my attention, for she had the unmistakable Ponsonby glint in her eye; and then I noticed that on her neck, legs and arms were blotches, patches of white. Chloe Pearl, I guessed, hearing in my mind the wicked cackle on the tapes. Yet it was the child she nursed who transfixed me, a little girl, similarly pied, the cornrowed spikes of her hair black and white.

Zediya! and I sat down abruptly on the couch beside my sleeping landlady. I had been ungracious to her, even unkind—when the sight of her particolouration could literally make me weak at the knees. But this time I felt more than eroticism in the charge; for now I longed for her gruff speech, her anger, her dark pride . . . as I never had for any human being before.

I considered the blue-green scales on the foot of Braxton Ponsonby, then transposed them onto a living, female form, my hypothetical Russian Merlusine. It was no contest: although, as had perhaps happened with Mistah Nathaniel, teratogenesis had crossed my personal dividing line between passions purely intellectual and those physical, I really could not come at scales. With fondness and relief I thought of the bird in hand at Rise 'n' Shine, my difficult magpie, so angry that the gods of genetics had made a sport of her. Moving very slowly, so as not to wake Mrs Snodgrass, I crept out to my car again. The rain had ceased, and as I drove to the pink house, pools of water in the road reflected my headlights dazzlingly. But as I rounded the corner, I saw the little home dark behind its For Sale/Sold sign; moreover, Zediya's big station wagon was absent from its habitual spot in the driveway.

I paused, dumbfounded—then saw on the crest of the hill rising out of Rise 'n' Shine, where led the road to the Interstate, the red of taillights. Living as I had in this sleepy hollow, I knew how little traffic there was at night; the lights might be from a truck, or lovers-a-courting, but equally they could be Zediya's. I reached for a tape as I considered the matter, slotted it into the player, then pressed the accelerator down hard.

Raucous Cajun sounds filled the car as I sped out of Rise 'n' Shine, so that even poor Braxton's foot seemed tapping to the beat. I had made an ideal choice of song; the only possible soundtrack to my personal chase movie. Even if I had to pursue Zediya all the way to Mississippi, I would find her—though what I would say, once I did, was another matter. And I couldn't imagine what she might say to me.

A yes was, I had to admit, unlikely. But had not I been living in a world of million to one, genetic odds, ever since I had attended the Ramblin' Roses gig? My backseat companion, rocking in its formaldehyde, was surely proof of that. This investigation had led to a significant scientific discovery; and also a revelation on the level of personal genetics. It had been a long and strange chain of chance, a triple helix, that had drawn me half across the world. Was it too much to hope that my luck would hold for one last link?

"Aiee Zediya!" I sang.

KAY & PHIL

"I know that this may sound quite ridiculous but the writer had very much the character of a visitant."
— From a letter describing Katharine Burdekin.

Midnight, 1961, Point Reyes, California. Not a creature was stirring, except in the small cabin, its one lighted window like a wakeful eye. Suddenly that eye blinked—and standing before the bright curtain was a figure, tall and thin as a shadow puppet. It paused, huddling the folds of a long robe tightly to it, its head moving back and forth questioningly. From within the cabin, the noise of a book closing cut through the rural night like a pistol shot. The visitor nodded, and moved soundlessly towards the cabin door.

Phil called this place the "hovel," though it was really a haven, the place away from home where he wrote. Tonight, though, he was not seated at the Royal typewriter but lolling in the armchair, a pile of books at his elbow. He had Goebbels' *Diaries*, Alan Bullock on Hitler, *The Tibetan Book of the Dead*, anthologies of Japanese poetry, and on top, the black-backed twin volumes of the *I Ching*. You do too much research, his wife

Anne had said over dinner. Like heck, he had thought. Now he wondered if she was right. Maybe I should just go ahead with the book. We need the money, don't we? All those goddamned bills . . .

No, he thought. This has gotta be good. If I slip up anywhere, it'll show, and we'll have no sale then, no cash for the cars and the cat food and the kids' teeth.

Behind him, he heard the sound of a discreet, very low cough. He turned his head to see, standing by the door, what he at first took to be his mother. Dorothy shouldn't be here, he thought— last I heard she was on vacation. And why is she dressed in her nightclothes?

Then he remembered that his mother never wore pajamas, let alone striped flannelette ones such as showed through the slit in the mannish woolen dressing gown, nor plain slippers without heels. The tall, thin, elderly woman standing in front of the closed door was a stranger.

"Forgive me for interrupting you at your work," she said.

An English voice. It put him in mind of movie stars he had seen during the war years: Laurence Olivier, Vivian Leigh . . . those well-bred tones, ineffably polite. Almost without thinking, he stood, offering her his chair.

"No, no," she said, moving towards his desk. "The typing chair will do."

Phil started to say that the chair was currently occupied by Beulah, a little half-wild stray who lashed out at anyone who tried to pet her. But the woman merely scooped up the cat and placed her atop the desk, beside the typewriter.

"Oh," he said, finally speaking. For he knew then that his visitor was extraordinary, even beyond her appearing in his hovel in what was hardly visiting dress. Should he bow to her, kneel to her?

"Ma'am, who, or what, are you? Only an angel coulda got that close to Beulah and come away in one piece."

She smiled. "I'm not an angel. I'm Kay."

"Phil." He started to put out his hand, then withdrew, nervously.

"I'm not a ghost either," she added. "Although close to it, these last five years. I had what the doctor called an aneurysm. He said I wouldn't last the week, so I did, and more! But I've been bedridden all that time."

She crossed one leg over the other, a slipper dangling nearly off her topmost foot, and for the first time he noticed that her white, prominently veined feet were soft, without calluses.

"Being confined like that, one needs some form of compensation. So my spirit . . . wanders. I hadn't left England since the 1920s, well, not bodily. But in the last few years, how I've traveled! To Versailles, where I set a novel I wrote from my friend Margaret (an American, like you Phil), my friend Margaret's notes; to Berlin, where Margaret's husband reported on the Nazis for the *Guardian* newspaper; even to Sydney, Australia, where the cosmic finger first touched me and I wrote my maiden novel, in six weeks! That was the most time it took, with all my books."

She fell silent, but Phil made no response. Hesitantly, she said: "Please forgive an old woman for her ramblings."

"No, Ma'am—"

"Kay," she corrected gently.

"Kay, I was just thinking that writing as though God had tapped you on the shoulder is like my way of working. Night and day, at speed."

And *on* speed, he thought, but I can't say that to an old lady. You can't tell a Grandmom that you've been taking drugs to keep up your writing schedule, just to support that expensive habit, a family.

"I wrote that way," she said, nodding. "But no more, not since my illness. No more books. A relief, perhaps, since after the war my agent couldn't place a single work of mine . . ."

"Jesus!" said Phil, thinking of his own unsold novels. Then suddenly remembering whom he was addressing, he looked at Kay plaintively. If swearing bothered her, it didn't show in that lined, pale face. A little reassured, he said:

"I think . . . we have things in common."

"I could sense that."

"Sense?"

"A sixth, possibly even seventh, sense. You see, Phil, I was lying in my bed in Suffolk, under the best eiderdown, and suddenly I *knew* that someone was thinking about a novel of mine. That's rare these days—I've been quite forgotten. So I came to see who it was."

She leaned forward, scrutinizing his face. He tried to arrange it into something seemly, under the pressure of that intense gaze, but knew that it expressed only bafflement.

"Hey, I was just sitting here, thinking about all the books I'd read, in order to write just one of my own . . . and none of them—"

He gestured at the stack.

"—none of them were by a Kay."

"I was only Kay for two books," she said quickly. "For the rest I used all of my christian name. Katharine. Katharine Burdekin."

"Sorry, but it means nothing to me."

"I also used a pseudonym. War was near, and being anti-fascist could have been dangerous, for my family and friends." She was silent for a moment, then added shyly: "Very few people know this. I was Murray Constantine."

This is hell, thought Phil. She's an old lady, what's more she's a writer, so how can I hurt her feelings by telling her she's got the wrong guy?

It must have showed in his face, for Kay looked momentarily uncertain. Then she shot at him: *Swastika Night!*"

"Oh," said Phil. "I read that book ten, fifteen, years back. But it was by a man . . ."

"Murray Constantine. Me."

She smiled. Damn her, thought Phil, suddenly irate. How dare she bother me when I'm trying to work? He didn't even remember *Swastika Night*, apart from the title. But she had bent down and was examining the stack of source material.

"Ah," she said, straightening. "That nasty little man's diaries. Bullock's Hitler. Those I understand. But the Tibetan book?"

"I am creating a world," he said, "in which Germany and Japan won the war."

"As I did in *Swastika Night!*"

She's right! thought Phil. It's slowly coming back, that novel, and how it began . . . in a sorta Nazi Church, hundreds of years in the future.

"Kay, until now I had no conscious thought of your book."

"Subconscious, then. Never underestimate it."

"No," said Phil. "I never would." He eyed her nervously. Was he about to be accused of planning plagiarism? But her expression was thoughtful rather than angry.

"There would be differences in how we would envisage such a world," she said, swinging one foot. "You are fortunate to be writing well after the defeat of fascism. In 1936 it seemed an all too possible future. Now it is merely an alternative for you to toy with, fictionally."

Phil got to his feet, stung. "Hey!" he said. "I'm not playing with anything. I'm serious!" He gestured wildly, inarticulately, then froze.

At the tip of his index finger a window had opened up, as if one of his stepdaughters had snipped an illustration from a *National Geographic*, leaving a neat hole in the glossy paper, so that in flipping through the magazine he had found the page depicting the home of a Pilgrim father cutting to the following photo-feature on Tahiti. There, in his cabin, was a large square of bright blue sky, with a vapor trail across it.

"Aargh," he said, and snatched back his hand. The window remained, floating in mid-air.

Kay had arisen. "My fault, I'm afraid. Things like this happen when I go abroad. I suppose it's so improbable that a sickly old Englishwoman should wander via the astral plane that attendant improbabilities follow hard upon . . ."

She shuffled up to the square and gazed into it. "The view from an office," she commented.

Phil neared, and cautiously peeked over her bony shoulder. He saw a room obviously very high up, dominated by a glass wall, showing the San Franciscan skyline and the Golden Gate bridge. In the foreground was visible one corner of a shiny hardwood desk, and by the window hung a scroll, of beautiful paper, with Oriental characters writ large upon it. He smiled in recognition. "That's Tagomi's office."

"Tagomi?"

"He's in the book I'm planning."

She turned her head, and he saw a glint of excitement in those old eyes. "Shall we take a closer look?"

She reached out one hand to the bottom of the window, which moved downward at her touch, until it reached the floor. There it stayed, and Kay unbent, breathing heavily. Their feet, in Kay's slippers and Phil's sneakers, were only inches from the threshold.

"What does one do now?" she said, and Phil, without knowing why he did so, slipped his hand around hers. It was lukewarm to the touch and so dry he imagined that if she rubbed her hands they would sound like dead leaves on the sidewalk. Thus joined, they took a deep breath and stepped into . . .

Soft expensive carpet. It came as a shock, perhaps because it was so mundane. They disengaged, Phil standing still, Kay almost skipping to the window. "Why," she said, "it's like a picture postcard. 'Wish you were here'—with that bridge on the verso."

"It's the Golden Gate, in San Francisco," Phil said.

"I never went there. Is this much like . . ." She paused. "How it really is?"

"Like enough," said Phil.

"Beautiful," she said. "Very beautiful. What is that big structure there, to the left, the shell, with one side open?"

He made his feet move slowly across the carpet until he stood by her side, his nose almost touching the glass.

"Golden Poppy stadium," he said after a moment. "For baseball."

"How everything is golden, in this America!" she said.

"This Japanese America," he said.

She gave him a sidelong look. "I had that too," she said. "Not that I tried hard to imagine it. I concentrated more on Nazi Germany."

Phil was staring down at the view. Either the ships in the Bay were moving very slowly, or their engines had stopped, despite the long plumes of smoke from the funnels. And what about the cars he could see at the base of the building? They weren't parked, or in a traffic jam, yet they were immobile.

He glanced at his watch and saw the hands moving. It was 12:30 a.m., California time. What of the clocks here? He looked around, trying to find one, and noticed that seated at the desk was a small Japanese man.

"Tagomi!" he said, and heard a gasp, as Kay saw him too. Tagomi made no response; he didn't even seem to breathe.

"Is he dead?" That was Kay.

"I don't think so." Phil walked around the desk, stopping behind Tagomi. The Japanese was bowed over an open drawer, one hand inside it, arrested in the act of turning the key of a small teakwood box. Phil looked at Tagomi's wrist and saw that the smallest hand on the Seiko watch was still.

"We're beyond . . . time," he said.

"Or perhaps outside it, in this world of yours," said Kay. "Here, you are God."

"Gee, I suppose I am," said Phil. The idea scared him.

Kay joined him behind the desk. "What's in the box? Do you think we could have a God's-eye view?"

"If you must," said Phil. Open! he thought at the box. Tagomi's hand moved very slightly, completing the turn of the key, and reaching down Phil flicked the lid of the box back. There, on a bed of crimson silk, lay a—

"Cowboy gun," said Kay. "Like little boys have."

"It's a US 1860 Civil War Colt .44," said Phil.

"Really?" Kay sounded impressed.

"No," Phil admitted. "It's a fake. But Tagomi doesn't know that. The gun's a prized possession, to him and his Japanese friends. They collect authentic American artifacts."

"But you said it wasn't real."

"Well yeah, there's a flourishing trade in fakes by Americans, who sell them to the Japanese . . ."

"Then the Japanese must be stupid, to be hoodwinked like that," she said flatly.

"No, they're not stupid," he said, echoing her pronunciation, so that he said *stew-pid* rather than *stoo-pid*. "They're very intelligent and high-minded and civilized."

"In my book," she said, "I had one of the Nazis say the only mental characteristic of the Japanese was ape-like imitativeness."

"And what was the response to *that*?"

"That he was a little prejudiced, perhaps."

"A little? Listen lady, during the war I thought much like your Nazi. I punched the wall when I heard about Pearl Harbor and almost cheered when I saw the old Jap market gardener, who hawked vegetables up and down the neighborhood, dragged off to the internment camp. But then I met this Jewish guy, who'd been interned himself in China. He said there were no ovens in that camp. And, get this: when the Germans requested that the Japs turn their machine guns on the Jews, they refused!"

"I didn't know that," she said. "My only contact with the Orient was in the ports to and from Australia. I must admit that I didn't like what I saw."

There was a short silence.

"The Japanese would have had little contact with the Jews," she said. "Not enough to feel threatened, to incite xenophobia, the fear of the other."

"Fear of the other," said Phil, chewing over the idea.

"The person who is different from you. Who, by being so, makes you insecure, uncertain that your right is the divine right, as you believe. And if they will not be like you, they must be suppressed, confined, finally exterminated. That is what lies behind all racism and . . ."

Her voice trailed off. What was she about to say? thought Phil. Something important, I can tell that. But her gaze was fixed on Tagomi's outstretched hand.

"Phil, I don't want to alarm you unnecessarily, but I think your Tagomi moved a little, all by himself. Towards the gun."

Phil bent down and stared at Tagomi's hand. It was then he noticed how beautiful it was, the golden skin finely grained, the fingers long and tapering towards the well-shaped nails. I made that? he thought.

"I was always nervous of guns," Kay was saying, "even before I became a pacifist."

He glanced up at her, then back at the hand. In that instant, it seemed, something changed. While my attention was away, he thought, Tagomi started to reach for his trusty Colt. He doesn't like me here. He wants to lead a dull life, with that dumpy wife of his (on the desktop there was a photo of the woman, looking, in her kimono, like a bolster with a sash tied around it). He doesn't need Nazi hit men in his office, nor all the other things I've planned for him. So he's trying to shoot first and ask questions later.

He gazed at that round Oriental face, but found it inscrutable. If Tagomi can hear us, he thought, he's not letting on. But I'm not going to stay around and find out.

"Let's get outa here," he said, standing upright. Kay nodded emphatically. They clasped hands again, and without taking their gaze from Tagomi, stepped to one side of the desk and backwards—

They found themselves standing on the wooden floor of the hovel. Before them was the window. I gotta close it, he thought, before Tagomi comes gunning after us. But how?

"What did you do?" he asked, "to make it big enough for us to go through?"

"I'm really not sure. Does it make sense to say that I tugged on something that wasn't there?"

Phil put one finger to the bottom of the window. It didn't feel as if he was touching anything, but the vista snapped shut like a rollerblind.

Shocked, he released Kay.

She took a step sideways. After a moment she said: "In retrospect, I believe we imagined that man reaching for his gun. Like children alone in a dark barn. Did that shadow move? Ooh, it's the bogeyman!"

"Tagomi isn't a bogeyman," said Phil, feeling an urge to defend his creation. "He's one of the good guys. It'll almost destroy him to use his prized gun on the Nazis."

She clapped her hands. "What an original touch! Cowboys and Indians with the Reich! I would never have thought of it."

"Then it's not in your book?" said Phil, pleased.

"No." She gave an impish smile. "That is all your own work. But I'll tell you something that maybe, just maybe, isn't. In *Swastika Night* I had a Samurai who collected American traditional tunes. He preserved 'Shenandoah,' for instance. It seems to me that he is not so far away from your Tagomi and his friends, with their guns and their cowboy hats, I imagine, and fringed leather trousers."

No way, though Phil, am I going to tell her that Tagomi buys a Mickey Mouse watch. Because she'd laugh, and I swear, though she may be old and a woman and sick and half a ghost—I swear that I'd punch her as hard as I could.

"Okay," he said, to change the subject. "I'm not going to argue that one. It might be that the seed that made my Japanese collectors of American artifacts came from you. But if it did, then it was a pretty small seed. I'd have to see a lot more of your Nazi world to believe any sort of plagiarism."

"I wasn't suggesting that. More of an influence."

"Oh yeah? Prove it!"

She looked at him.

"You mean, conjure up one's book, like you did?"

"That's right, lady."

She put her head on one side, thinking.

"You became angry. So angry that your arms flailed out, pointing at thin air, which suddenly parted, showing the Otherworld. Phil, I doubt if I could do that. I was brought up to be genteel, by my parents, my governess, and the Cheltenham Ladies' college. Though I grew up to be something quite different from what they intended, the training lingers."

She closed her eyes.

"I cannot show anger. I will have to summon my novel, not unconsciously as you did, but by an effort of will."

She clasped her hands. There was a long silence, broken only by a distant owl hoot. Phil wandered over to Beulah. Her paws twitched; she poked out a sliver of rough pink tongue. He wished she'd let him pet her. Maybe, if he really worked on it . . .

He glanced over his shoulder at Kay, who was frowning in agonized concentration. Suddenly her hands unclasped, the palms moving apart jerkily, as if forced. Between them he could glimpse grey, formless matter. She was trembling now, the motion so violent that it seemed she would inadvertently crush what she held. He took two big steps across the room and caught hold of her wrists, steadying her. Slowly, their combined strength brought her imaginary world into the ordinary reality of his hovel.

He could see that this window was different from his, being fuzzy around the edges, showing not sky but heavy dark masonry and two or three unlit glass bulbs, cone-shaped, as if from an electric candelabrum. Her hands pulled further apart, and now he could see the false candles, and below them a metal wall bracket. It was cast in the form of a swastika.

Kay moaned, and her hands went limp. He drew her gently away from the window, which remained, no bigger than a trapdoor but solidly *there*, as had been the threshold into Tagomi's office. Still with her eyes closed, she whispered:

"It's such a sad world that I made."

Phil peered into it again. It looked more solemn, to him, like an Episcopal church, if you ignored the repellent shape of the bracket. "Hey!" he said. "Open your eyes."

She did. "Ah," she said. "Where I began. In Germany, in the 7th century of the Third Reich. We are looking into a Nazi place of worship, built in the shape of a swastika—"

Phil could remember that vaguely from the novel.

"—where a service is in progress." With an obvious effort, Kay dragged her gaze from the window and faced him. "Phil, back in your San Francisco, we became fearful that the Samurai Tagomi would shoot us down, despite his being a good man. Here, we will be intruding on a sacred ceremony, performed by men, who if not evil in themselves, are devoted to an evil creed. It will be particularly unsafe for me."

"You're afraid," said Phil. Damn it, hadn't it been dangerous for him too, back in Tagomi's office, a demiurge faced with his flesh-and-blood creation?

"No, I am merely recalling that we panicked."

She was staring at the window again. He too was increasingly drawn to it. I betcha anything there's music with the service, he thought. It's the best thing about the Germans—their sublime feeling for sound. I wanna hear the tunes, even though they're Nazi.

"This is your world," he said unkindly. "It's up to you to keep it under control, okay?"

Kay said nothing, merely ducked her head to the level of the window. She paused, then thrust forward, and the top half of her body vanished into the scene as if she were a horror movie ghost. Phil hastily grabbed the tail of her dressing gown and was half led, half drawn into the opening scene of a book that was mostly haze in his memory.

He found himself kneeling on cold flagstone, clutching an old woman's skirt. He released it and glanced around him. They were halfway up a flight of stairs; the only light came from a high, barred window.

He looked at Kay, who shrugged. "Down, I think. It's over twenty years since I was in this world."

He stood, and followed her down the steps to a small square space with two exits. One, presumably leading to the outside, had a thick wooden door, braced with metal, securely locked; the other a green velvet curtain, dependent from massive brass rings. Kay drew the fabric slightly away from one wall and yellow light fell upon her, gilding her fine white hair. She paused to peer between cloth and stone, then boldly pulled back all the curtain.

Revealed was another swastika candelabrum, lit this time, illuminating two human backs, stock-still in front of an elaborate keyboard. A church organ, thought Phil. Seated at it were the organist, a woman with mouse-brown hair, and a young girl, with the same drab coloring, a page-turner. Kay took a few steps forward; he followed. Now they were gazing over the musicians' heads, into a vaulted space, very high but narrow, though he could barely see the arched roof. Against the opposite wall was a kettledrum and, leaning over it, a burly figure, sticks poised to strike. There was a choir too, all in long, flowing robes, like gospel singers, their mouths half open, as if about to sing.

At the center of the building, where its four arms met, stood an aged and dignified man wearing a black cloak over a tunic as blue as the San Franciscan sky, with silver swastikas on the collar. Around him were the congregation, who had risen from simple wooden chairs, their mouths also agape.

"Frozen like that, they do look absurd," murmured Kay.

Phil knew ministers, and he did not doubt the calm authority of the man in black and sky-blue. What bothered him, though, was that the swastikas were accompanied by the flowing hair and beard of an old testament prophet. What is the guy, he wondered, a beatnik? The drummer was similarly hirsute, as were the choir and congregation. Bearded like hillbillies, the lot of them. The only exceptions were the children in the congregation, a very pretty blonde girl in the front row of the choir, and the sisters? mother and daughter? at the organ. He looked down at the two mousy heads below him and realized that he was in error: though the organist had hair as long as Anne's, *he* also sported a straggly goatee.

Kay goofed, he decided. The Nazis would never let their hair grow like that—they'd think it effeminate. But he could hear, barely above a whisper, her voice again.

"The old man is the Knight von Hess, the feudal leader of this district. I suspect that he may be rather like your Samurai Tagomi, a noble man in an ignoble system, although he himself would reject any comparison with the Japanese. It was he who compared them to apes."

Phil was looking at the congregation. "Who's the young man in the second row, with the broad, ruddy face and the protuberant blue eyes?"

Kay turned her head. "Clever you," she said. "That's Hermann, another main character."

"He sticks out because he's gawping at that chick singer. When the service is over, is he gonna ask Goldilocks for a date?"

"Goldilocks is a boy."

"The faggot!"

"They all are."

He stared at her. You may look like a sweet old lady, he thought, but hoo boy! you sure don't think like one.

"Is that the reason for the long hair?"

"No. Even before the war certain sections of the Nazi party were identifying with pagan mythology. I merely extended the concept to their religion and their personal appearance, having them bearded and tressed like Thor and Wotan. And . . .."

A slightly mischievous expression crept across her face.

"But perhaps I will let you see for yourself. If we could find a secluded nook in this church, somewhere where we could see without being observed ourselves, I might be able to start the action of the novel. I feel a curious desire to hear the choir, vile though their lyrics are. I should know—I wrote them myself."

"Behind the curtain?" said Phil.

"We couldn't see anything there. I wonder about the steps, though. Might they lead to a vantage point?"

Before he could reply she had answered herself. "Of course! How could I forget, not that I made use of it in the book. The Hitler miracle plays!"

"What?"

"They would have been performed in the church, and the scenes where Hitler and Goebbels are addressed by the Divine Thunderer, from Heaven where the heroes live, require *gods*. Upstairs!"

She darted out of the alcove, and her passage nearly smothered him in the voluminous folds of the curtain. He extricated himself and followed. She was nimble on the stairs, so much so that he worried for her. What if she has another an . . . whatever-it-is, here? he thought, as they passed the window with its comforting view of hovel and sleeping black cat. Will I be trapped in a Nazi world?

But he said nothing, and they came to a landing cum props room, heaped with horned papier-mâché helmets, wooden spears, even a breastplate, its gilt beginning to flake and peel. The room was closed on one side by another curtain, blue this time. Kay marched up to the slit in the center of the curtain and drew it aside a smidgen.

"Yes," she said. "I was right!"

Looking down through the lips of dusty blue cloth, he could see the choir, the congregation, and the grizzled head of von Hess.

"There's a platform out there," he said.

"Too visible. We will be safer behind the curtain."

She sat down on the cold stone, catching her breath. Phil did likewise, feeling vulnerable and wishing that they could be closer to their exit.

After a while Kay said: "You may find this strange, but I am not entirely sure how to get things moving."

"Concentrate," he said. "Or maybe snap your fingers."

He acted out his words, then regretted it, for the sound was fearfully loud in this quiet place. Kay smiled, cautiously lifted her hand, then repeated his motion.

Music. First there was an organ chord, deep and sonorous, then a roll on the drums, as loud as if Kay's Divine Thunderer were within the church. Phil looked down and saw that the Knight had turned towards the west of the building, with the congregation following suit. A massed choir of male voices sang out: "Ich glauben!"

"Their Creed!" said Kay, speaking loudly into his ear, for the singing soared towards the gods at awesome volume. They believe, Phil thought, they must really believe, to sing like that. That singer, the blond boy, what a pure soprano! It put him in mind of an angel, a Wagnerian angel. Pity about the tune though. And the arrangement. It sounded like the duller bits of Beethoven and Wagner shaken around in a barrel with some Bavarian drinking songs. This is supposed to be 700 years in the future, he thought. Surely German music would have progressed in that time. What about Schoenberg and the other avant-garde composers? Then he recollected that they had mostly been Jewish, and that the Nazis had abominated their work.

What were they singing about now? He caught the word "exploded," and on cue the organ and the drums cut in again, augmenting the sound to a thunderous roar. The figures below lifted their arms stiffly in the Nazi salute, and he felt a pang of distaste.

"What was that crescendo for?" he said into Kay's ear. She turned her head and, her lips almost against his earlobe, said: "Adolf Hitler, their Christ. They were saying he was not born of woman, but exploded from the head of the Thunderer."

It sounded crazy to Phil. He shut up and listened to the rest of the Creed, which contained some familiar names, with Stalin and Lenin execrated, Goebbels and Goering praised, bizarre in that mass-like setting. At the end the Knight turned back towards the east, and the congregation sat, the sound of their chairs on the stone floor jarring and discordant. There was a long silence, then the Knight, after a cough as polite and soft as Kay's, began to intone in beautiful courtly German. Phil mentally translated the words:

"As a woman is above a worm
So is a man above a woman."

What? he thought. That wasn't in the Nazi ideology. They were keen on *Kinder, Küche, Kirchen,* but I don't think they were misogynists. Hitler had Eva Braun. Goebbels was a womanizer. Most of the others were family men. Maybe it's got something to do with Kay making them homosexual. He turned, intending to ask, but she was intent on the service.

He said nothing, listening to that elegant voice that could make such bloodthirsty sentiments sound poetic. There was stuff now about race defilement—that figured, then something about Hitler and the Thunderer. Apparently they formed a Duality. While he was still trying to work that out, the Knight finished, coughed again, and saluted the congregation. The ceremony was over.

"Is that it?" he whispered to Kay. Below, the singers were moving out of their seats with military precision. They formed a neat bloc in front of the choir stalls, then marched in formation down the aisle. The drummer and the pair at the organ followed and, after a pause, the congregation.

He nudged Kay, still wanting an answer. She shook her head. The Knight, Phil suddenly noticed, was not among the marchers. "Where is the old man?" he asked, and she replied: "In the Hitler Chapel, resting. He has another service to conduct shortly."

At the same time Phil heard, from far below, shouting, of which he caught only the final imprecation not to dawdle. He sat back, watching the church empty, until only two brawny men remained, collecting the wooden chairs and stacking them against the walls. Then they too left. What now? wondered Phil.

He heard sounds below, shuffling and whimpers, and a body of people came slowly into sight, not marching, but straggling. They were all dressed in jacket and trousers of an ugly dun-brown, and their downcast heads were shaved.

"Jesus!" thought Phil, appalled at this mass of ugliness. The Knight had reappeared and was walking, shoulders back, white head erect, towards the mass of brown, which as he neared emitted shrill, terrified cries. Another bearded man, carrying a big stick, moved among the crowd; like a sheepdog, he brought them to a halt, a disorganized clump halfway up the church. When all stood still, he saluted the Knight and marched quickly out of the church. Far below huge doors slammed.

"I hadn't thought of it until now," Kay murmured, "but they could, in theory, while alone in the church with the Knight, tear him to pieces."

"You mean the ones with the shaved heads? Are they from a concentration camp?"

"They live in a cage, yes."

"What are they? Jews? Communists?"

"Listen to them!" said Kay. The Knight had stopped, yet the screams continued. Phil traced one of the thin sounds to a short figure, its naked head almost too big for its puny body. Why, that's a boy! he thought, then almost immediately spotted another, his head half-buried in the lap of an elderly adult. It's kids who are screaming, he realized, indignant. What's the old man think he's doing, scaring those little guys like that?

The form of what was unmistakably a pregnant woman, despite the shaved head, and the unfeminine, unflattering garb, caught his eye. Shouldn't she be sitting down? he thought. She doesn't look too good. He could distinguish other full-bellied figures in the crowd, and had started to make a count before he became distracted by the number of people who were weeping—children, the pregnant females, old folk, young adults, they were sniveling or sobbing or howling unrestrainedly.

He glanced at Kay and saw her eyes were damp. Embarrassed, he looked back down again and suddenly became aware that besides the factor of dress in common, all were narrow-shouldered and slight. Though none wore dresses or makeup, below him was a company of—

"Women," said Kay, and below her the Knight shouted: "Frauen!" Phil jumped at the sound of that deep voice, but felt, besides the physical reaction, a more profound shock. Kay was regarding him intensely again.

"Phil," she said, "didn't you remember the Women's Worship from my book?"

He hadn't, until now, because those shaven heads, that abject misery, had upset him so much that he had put *Swastika Night* out of his conscious memory.

"No," he said truthfully.

"You must have had some inkling from what von Hess said. Or from the men-only ceremony."

"I thought I saw some girls," he said, recalling the page-turner and a few beardless faces among the congregation.

"Immature boys," she said. "You sat through the service and never noticed the absence of women!"

She had an all too familiar look on her face. He had seen it on Dorothy, his mother; on Anne; and on his other two wives. It said: *Men!*

"That's right," he said aggressively. "But you confused me with the longhairs. Hey, what have you got, some sorta hair fetish? Why shave the women?"

"They can't be allowed to be beautiful," she said sadly. "Because they are only kept for breeding. They are worms, remember? A beautiful woman has power over men, and in this world women are powerless. The society depends upon it. This service reinforces the message, by telling them it is their sacred duty to be submissive and bear sons."

"You got one helluva warped vision!" he said. "I read all about the Nazis for my book, and they never put women in camps, unless they were Communist, or Jewish, or . . ."

"Feminists," she finished. "In 1932 Hitler suppressed the German organizations for women."

"Yeah, but they wanted to work outside the home and—"

He froze, thinking of the argument this remark would have provoked at home. "I didn't mean that," he said quickly. "But Kay, this stuff is paranoid. And I don't see how it can work. How do the Nazis make sure they all grow up faggots? Teenage boys go crazy about girls—they make holes in the walls of changing rooms, they . . ."

"Ssh," said Kay, suddenly very still herself. Phil glanced down again and saw only the Knight calmly addressing the women. "Relax," he said. "Nobody heard."

"But I can hear!" she whispered, and suddenly he understood: coming from the stairwell was the faint but unmistakable creak of a heavy door's hinges. It was followed by soft, ascending footsteps.

"Hermann once hid in the church when he was a lad, to sneak a look at the Women's Worship," she said. "He's well past that now, but some of the boys in the congregation wouldn't be. Even though the punishment is to be publicly shamed and beaten insensible."

"To the window!" said Phil, scrambling to his feet. She was having trouble rising, so he offered her a hand up, feeling again her dry skin and now the lightness of her body, as if her very bones were hollow. They started down the staircase, leaping and stumbling—

But they were too late. "Gott in Himmel!" said a husky voice, and they saw, halfway up the stairs, the young page-turner, transfixed by the window in front of him, the hole in his reality. He glanced above it, at Phil and Kay, and his spotty chin dropped even more. That man had a beard, but his graying dark hair was cut so close to his skull that he could have been a woman. And behind him was another man, venerable as the Knight, with a fine head of hair yet beardless as a boy! The big iron key he had stolen dropped from his sweaty fingers and clattered down the stairs.

"This wasn't in the book," panted Kay.

"I know, I remember it perfectly now. The noise that key's making! Von Hess'll hear! Kay, snap your fingers!"

She did, but without a sound. "I was never good at that sort of thing," she said apologetically.

Women weren't, in Phil's experience. He supplied the sound himself, but of course nothing happened.

The boy saw movement in the window, and the mask of a small black cat appeared, only inches, it seemed, from his face. It showed sharp teeth and hissed noiselessly at him. He took a step back, then ducked. Phil paused only long enough to yell: "Get outa the way, Beulah!" and made a mad dive at the window.

He landed in a heap, not at the bottom of the stairs, but on a wooden floor. Seconds later Beulah inflicted a set of deep scratches on the back of his hand.

"You're risking a trip to Naziland!" he growled, then felt a slipper in the small of his back. "Oh I'm sorry," said an English voice, and Kay stepped into the hovel.

"Get rid of it!" he said. She obliged, putting both hands around the gap, through which, as he rolled aside and stood, he could see the boy, fleeing down the stairs lickety-split.

"I hope he doesn't hurt himself," said Kay.

"I couldn't care less," was Phil's reply. Kay was exerting herself, pushing at the space. "You need help?" he asked, but she shook her head firmly. The veins on her neck stuck out, her face reddened . . . and slowly the window dwindled between her palms. She brought her palms together in the gesture of prayer, then relaxed with a flourish, as though washing her hands of the Nazi world.

There was a long silence, during which he returned to his armchair and just sat, drained. Kay remained standing, looking very old and ill.

"Why?" he said finally. "Why make the Nazis treat women like that? It's . . . horrible."

"It's not so far removed from the real situation of women throughout the centuries," she said. "And the germ of it is present in the Nazi writings. I believed when I wrote my book, though not many agreed with me, that the Nazis were capable of exterminating the Jews. And after that, what next? The Nazi system fed upon hate, it needed an enemy. Why not the oldest?"

"The oldest?" he repeated, thinking: I don't hate women, although I don't get on with Dorothy, and things with Anne aren't so good now . . .

She sighed. "I was married once."

"I've done it three times," he said glumly.

"You amaze me. After I left my husband, I made sure that I never again lived with a person of the opposite sex. It's too hard, Phil, being with someone who is human, like you, but oh, so different!"

Is it ever, thought Phil.

"We fear the other, who is not like us but is necessary for the continuance of the race. If not for that, I suspect men would have exterminated women long ago."

"That's too dark, Kay," he said. "I can't accept that. I think we'll hafta agree to differ there."

"As we do with our separate visions of the fascist world?" she said.

"Yeah!"

They shook on it. Her hand felt ethereal, as if a gust of wind would blow her spinning up into the air. She can't stay here much longer, Phil realised.

"I'm glad I dropped by," she said, the words incongruous, the sort of talk he associated with women's tea parties. "Your book looked most interesting. If I live to see it published, I'll ask my companion to buy a copy for me."

If it's published, thought Phil, but merely said: "Thanks."

She smiled. "And I think I did, just a bit, influence you."

"Yeah," he said. "I guess I was thinking about the book, before you came."

"Goodbye," she said, but made no move. She's the guest, Phil thought, and she wants me to escort her outside. So he got up and opened the door for her; she stepped out into the Californian night.

"Thank you, Phil, for showing me your book."

"And thanks for showing me *yours*. Goodbye, Kay."

She turned and began to walk away, so he closed the door. That was one weird lady, he thought, with relief. He could hear the faint flap of her slippers, one step, two steps . . . then silence.

He flung the door open again, but saw only country darkness. "Kay!" he shouted, but there was no answer. Feeling acute loss, he shut out the night.

Wonder what she looked like when she was young, he thought. From her eyes and brows, she had dark hair. I like that on a woman. She might even have been beautiful.

His gaze fell on another dark gal, Beulah, who had settled herself in his armchair. "Watch it, cat," he said. "I could take you by the tail and cast you into a Nazi church service."

The fuss that'd cause, Beulah falling, claws out, and hissing, into the midst of those poor downtrodden women.

"Or into the office of a good friend of mine, Mr. Nobusuke Tagomi."

At the thought of Tagomi his head turned, and he contemplated the space in the hovel where the first window had been. He put out an arm, pointing at the non-existent space. Nothing happened. He repeated the action, more forcefully, but got the same result.

He turned again, to look at the typewriter. Jesus, I'm tired, he thought, but sleep can come later. He walked over to the desk, opened the top drawer, and took out a small bottle. There were two pills left. He gulped them down without water and took the cover off the Royal typewriter. Then he spent some time searching for paper, which he placed within easy reach of his typing chair. He sat down and rolled the topmost sheet into the machine.

I gotta get back to Tagomi, he thought, but without Kay, there's only one way I can reach him. It's not as spectacular, sure, as pointing at the air and watching the fabric of the world roll down, but it's tried and true. Here I go!

He began typing his novel.

MY LADY TONGUE

Honeycomb, my honey, sweet Honey Coombe. I love her so much I daubed her name on the biggest white wall in the ghetto and round it a six-foot heart. The paint was shocking pink, and it dribbled, when I so wanted my ideogram to be perfect! She passed by that wall everyday, but unfortunately so did others, and that was how the trouble started.

"Vandalism!" That was the Neighborhood Watch, our ghetto guards. I was minding my own business, thinking of Honey, but cat curious I followed the groups of womyn drifting towards the clamour. It was only when I was in the main square that I realised the offence was mine. Ah well, I'd brazen it out—I'm nothing if not brazen.

There was a crowd in the square, which included the off-duty Watch and most of the powers-that-be in Womyn Only. One of the most dignified of these Elders was actually atop a step ladder inspecting my splash.

"Honeycomb," she announced to the groundlings as if every womyn jill of them couldn't already read. "Possibly male reference to our genitals?'

"Ishtar!' cried the Watch Chief. "They got in this far?' There was a horrified mumble from the masses.

"Tsk tsk sleeping on the job," I said, just loudly enough for the Watch to hear and not pinpoint me. Zoska, who'd reared me, came forward trailing her youngest.

"Not quite down to their usual standard, is it?" she said. "Bar the colour."

It was strident, but that's my style.

"They go in for dribbling cocks usually, not dribbling hearts."

Some of the hearers drew in their breaths hard, and she snapped: "Don't be silly, this isn't the Hive."

"You think it's a Sister?" asked the Watch Chief, catching on at last.

Zoska nodded her coif of plaits and I cursed silently: if she got much warmer things would be hot for me.

"Our vandal," said Zoska, "loves Honeycomb."

"There aren't any Sisters of that name," said the Ladderclimber. "Unless you mean Marthe's daughter Honey . . ."

Their heads followed one direction and I thought I saw my sweeting, so I waved my floppy hat at her. But it was only her grim mamma and I knew I was for it.

"I own up! I did it, I did it!" I shouted, jumping up and down.

"Thought so," said Zoska.

Marthe was looking black and I was beginning to realise why.

"Sister Raffy," said the Chief, "Womyn Only supports artistic expression but isn't this over the top?"

"Shucks Officer, I'm in LOVE."

"Honeycomb," said Marthe as though that sweet name was wormwood in her mouth. "Is that your name for her?"

I nodded, thinking oh-oh! My darling's name was Honey Marthe, the mother's name affixed to the daughter's, as is ghetto custom. Me, I'm Raphael Grania, but I only answer to Raffy. Coombe had been Honey's father, a sperm donor anonymous except in the genetic profile of his daughter. Hardcore dykes like Marthe (who never ventured from the ghetto nor indeed much from the Hive, our inner sanctum) detested the profiles—but kept them in case of genetic disorders. Honey had found the document, and discovered her humourless mother had made an accidental pun. I had laughed at that, at Marthe, but now I had made a laughing stock of her, and worse. It was bad taste to remind Womyn Only that its girl-children were not spontaneously generated.

Me and my big paintbrush. There was a long really nasty silence during which I mentally gave myself a hundred lashes, and crossed miles of paving on my kneebones.

"You'll never call her that again," said Marthe and strode off followed by a curious knot of Elders. The crowd was staring and Zoska had piggybacked her child and was pushing towards me. I didn't need comfort now, just action! So I pretended not to see her and nipped around the corner and over a couple of back gardens, short-cutting to Honey's home. It was empty; and I stood outside and thought of the hydroponic flowers I had thrown through her window. Then I embarked on a long and increasingly desperate tour of our trysting places. I found nobody waiting alas! and at the last the Watch Chief found me. She was embarrassed but stern.

"Marthe and Honey are in the Hive, from which the Elders have banned you until further notice."

I lay down by *our* fountain and imitated it for a while. Then I recovered and went to see Zoska.

"Ninny," she said.

We sat in the sunny brick courtyard behind her little house, she at her embroidery frame and Basienka, who had accompanied her to the meeting, wandering around the confined space in her enigmatic two-year-old's way.

"Oh I agree absolutely. Now what do I do?"

"Go to Bozena at Haven, until the fuss dies down."

Haven was the refuge we dykes were building in the country. I had scouted the site and normally would go there gladly.

"Can't leave Honey."

Puck puck puck went the needle into the stiff linen cloth.

"I get soppy just thinking about her."

"Creamy you mean," said Zoska. "I know you."

"No, this is the real thing. I'm so sentimental I could die."

Zoska sighed.

"You're old enough to be her mother."

"Not quite. Honey may be sixteen, but I—as you ought to remember—had a late menarche."

She did the sums with her lips.

"So you did. I was confusing you with Boz."

"Quite a party we had for it," I said, hopping over a wall in my mind into memory lane.

"Was it ever! You tore up the poem Grania had written for the occasion and when she created lit out with Boz. The pair of you didn't come back until six the next morning, when you burst into my bedroom shouting you were in love with each other. I haven't had intoxicants at a menarche party since. Won't have it at hers either."

She grinned at Basienka.

"Look at her. Aren't I clever? Forty-eight years and three months I was when I bore her. Broke the ghetto record."

I recollected that Zoska had begun the career of mothering with Bozena and had had thirty-two years at it since. Some daughters were hers; others came from Sisters who like Grania preferred not to have the rearing of their young.

She looked at me, reading my face.

"You and Boz may have had your adventures with Haven, but I've reared seven fine womyn. Mind you, it's early days with Basienka and with Urszula I'm not sure."

I stirred, perceiving how my least favourite sister might help my purpose.

"You could use Urszula as an example to Marthe. She's not much older than Honey, she's taken up with Bea, who's my age . . ."

"I've got enough chickens to take chances with them. Marthe's only got one."

"Let me finish. And Urszula's leaving the ghetto!"

"Oh Ishtar don't even think of saying that to Marthe!"

"Why not? Honey wants to."

"After she's been reared hardcore? To go among *men*? Raffy, she really must love you."

"I want to swear committal."

She reached into the basket between us for a new skein of wool, the colours jewel bright against her fingers.

"Wow, Raffy settling down at last. Okay, I'll talk to Marthe."

She snipped off a length of wool viciously.

"It won't be easy."

Her gaze was like a mirror, in which my scarecrow image—in old camouflage duds from Haven (worn to annoy the hardcores, who never went Outside), lurid pink shirt, embroidered scarf and old hat—was reflected with censure.

"Raffy, you're disreputable. You'll have to smarten up if I'm to get anywhere with Marthe and while I'm at it also stop teasing the Elders and getting into fights with the Watch. You're the last match Marthe wants for Honey."

"I'm the daughter of a famous poet."

"Yes, and Grania denounces you in verse for being undutiful."

"We never ever got on."

"So I got the rearing of you, half my luck. Raffy, I can't win Marthe without Grania"s help. You'll have to make up with her."

"I'll put a girdle round about the earth in forty minutes!"

"What's that? What do you mean?"

"It's poetry. Shakespeare, a man. I mean, I'll do it."

She was looking puzzled and I got up to stretch my skinny legs in the courtyard, puzzled myself. I keep my Shakespeare well-hid in Womyn Only, because of what it means to me: lost time with Benedict, a man. Swashbuckling Raffy might have had a child, a son even, and not by donor but by the old way, which Shakespeare writes about a lot.

There was no telling what a hardcore dyke would do if she knew her daughter was marrying tainted flesh. But Marthe would never hear of it, would she?

In my perambulations I nearly tripped over Basienka, who looked up from trying to unpick a wool flower on the skirt of the little peasant dress all Zoska's daughters, even tatty Raffy, wore. On her face was the same knowing smile as the Cumean Sibyl, whose painting adorns a wall in the Hive, and I was suddenly afraid. Marthe could discover Raffy's little secret, from Grania, who might tell her if we two were unreconciled.

I looked away from Basienka, to Zoska.

"Can you talk to Marthe? I'll do Grania."

She nodded her silver-brown head, and I took leave of her.

Grania lived outside Womyn Only, in a small brick house with a studied bohemian air. There was a hammock on the front verandah with a huge hole in it; the garden was a careful mixture of weeds and colour-clashing flowers; the brass nameplate said "Poet's Corner". Before I could knock the door was opened by Bea, lover of my foster-sister Urszula. She carried a carton of books for her shop, my mother's literary children, new branded with her squiggly signature.

"Hi Raffy, surprise to see you . . ."

"Here?" I asked dangerously.

She looked embarrassed.

"I'll get out of your way. Raffy . . . do you really want Marthe for a mum-in-law?"

"Anything for Honey."

She walked down the pathway with my brothers and sisters. I waved, then went noisily inside. Grania was in her visitor's chair, a monster of carved mahogany chosen to diminish the bulk of the womyn within it. From my mother I had my height, but I blessed her donor for a lithe figure, for his genes dominating over those which would have made me resemble a hippo. She batted not an eyelid as I sauntered in.

"Come to your mummikins, lambie-pie," she said icily. It was the standard greeting and as usual I kept my distance, leaning against a wall of this book-lined grotto, with its troll-queen enthroned.

"What, no fond greeting?"

Go cautiously, I thought.

"Did you ask Bea about me?"

"Of course. She said you were in trouble, big trouble if you come and visit me. There was mention of a sweet young thing locked away from your wickedness. Then she spied your approach and bolted, leaving me in a state of gossipus interruptus."

"I shall bring you to climax."

"This sounds like the tale of your lost month. The one time you confided in me."

I stared at her.

"Mother, we are of one mind. I want you to recall the incident."

She grinned evilly.

"How could I forget Raphael's *True Confessions*?"

My lost time had been thirteen years back, before Haven even, but it was vivid to me. When I dipped into the past with Zoska I had half seen the brickwork and moss beneath my feet strewn with coloured streamers and crushed paper cups. Now, instead of books I could see pollution-bleached grass, weird trees and eroded hills with knob rocks sticking out. She's very visual, Honey's Raffy.

I had been Outside both ghetto and City, sussing out a site for Haven in the countryside. When I remember, the mind's eye comes through first, then later the body with what my past-self was feeling. I had been happy, despite the desolation, which was coldly beautiful, and the dangers. The country had unmarked pollution dumps, which had already claimed one scout, wild dogs, and of course the bogey of man.

Ah, who cared! I was wearing camouflage clothes that were weatherproof; I had survival rations, weapons, mini-communicator, compass, heat detector, Auntie Cobley and all. The paraphernalia fitted neatly into a five-kilo pack on my shoulders that left me unencumbered, feeling free. There was a wild wind blowing, early spring sunlight and Raffy who had lived behind walls was madly in love with wide open spaces.

This was my first solo voyage. Previously I had gone with senior members of the Watch, who were supposed to restrain young hotheads like Boz and me, and then with Boz. That trip had been a mistake, for in the excitement we had revived our first love, only to quarrel so bitterly we resolved: never again. We were too alike, and I crave opposites, Honey.

I was walking through a narrow valley peaceful even though bisected by a service road, when I heard a droning roar, steadily increasing in volume. Diving into the nearest cover, a ditch curtained with green weed, I checked the heat sensor, which registered zero. My fears of a behemoth mutant vanished and I peered through the green to see a robotruck on the road, making its slow thunder from a macrofarm somewhere. False alarm; but nonetheless I left the road and went cross-country, moving swiftly until I came to a patch of burnt-out ground.

I started to weep then, and my future self, standing in Grania's study, sought for a reason. There was a memory within the memory and it was red, the colour of the fire that had engulfed a house on the edge of the ghetto. Five womyn had been inside and there were more dead, Watch members who had surprised the arsonists. "Men did it," Zoska had explained to little Urszula, who had only stared at her uncomprehendingly.

After the fire had been doused there had been more red, with a torchlit meeting in the main square I was later to defile with my "HONEYCOMB". The Elders had argued and argued what to do and slowly a consensus was reached. We were easily attacked within our enclosure, we needed to go beyond the city, found a city of our own. And so the Haven movement began, and changed the lives of Boz and me. We had been feckless ghetto girls, too wild for the Watch and too hardcore to find work in the straight world. Now we had a goal in life.

Standing amongst charcoal and singed trees, I wept for the dead, until it occurred to me that were it not for them I would still be cooped up in Zoska's living room. There was a site for me to look at; I went on.

Our Haven was defined by a list of desiderata, a majority of which had to be ticked before the Elders would approve the site. My destination had already accrued some ticks, if we were to believe the intermediary feminists who had investigated the site in the guise of a macrofarm consortium. They had liked it. Yet the site needed to be seen with a dyke's eyes, and secretly. The memory of the incinerated house still burnt.

I spent a day at the prospective site, being thorough. Womyn Only looked at many locations, finding some too marshy, too polluted, too grim et cetera. I was writing the report in my head as I trudged: "eminently suitable for our *queendom*, our *newfoundland*"— words Grania had used when she heard of my vocation, laughing all the while—"except . . ." It was insufficiently secluded, being too close to the farm I had seen the truck trundling towards earlier. And this farm, as the intermediaries had discovered, was not staffed entirely by robots.

I inked in the last mental full stop of my report and turned to go, when the late afternoon light caught a spot of colour on a distant hillside. When I pulled out my viewfinder I saw a scrawny blossom tree in its spring best. The flowers were chalky-pink, beautiful.

I glanced at the sun and again at the tree, estimating it was a kilometre away. Why not? I could take a pressed flower home for Zoska to copy and maybe another for a young lady of the Watch I had my eye on. What I had not expected, though, was the macrofarm's fence between me and tree, impenetrable even for a Scout equipped to the eyeballs. I followed it hopefully and came at last to a spot where an animal had burrowed beneath it. There was just room for Raffy, but not if she were hump-backed: I had to discard the pack in order to squeeze through.

The detour had eaten at the daylight and the hill was dusked over by the time I arrived at the tree. Feeling uneasy, I decided not to stay long and reached for a blossom. There was a growl and automatically I jumped into the branches as a low shaggy shape came up the slope towards me. It was a feral dog and it was followed by its brethren.

They clustered snarling around the base of the tree and I climbed higher. Hormones from the macrofarm had affected this tree's growth: it was some seven metres high, with sturdy branches. I sat in the highest of these, watching the dogs leap upward, snapping teeth on air and scrabbling their paws on the bark before falling to earth again. I was well out of reach, but I cursed, the dogs replying in their language. Any idiot would have checked the heat sensor for these pests, or considered that they might have dug under the fence. Any idiot, but not Raffy.

Packless I was not quite defenceless, wearing under my camo shirt a weapon as unphallic as a dyke could make it. I took out the gun and shot experimentally at the dog chieftain, remembering my target practice with the Scouts. It was close: there was a smell of singed hair and the pack ran off a little, yelping. I gloated until I registered another smell, that of singed tree. The shot had nicked a lower bough, had almost cut it through.

Rather than whittle my sanctuary away I stopped, and the dogs settled under the tree for a long wait. I considered my options: the gun had a limited number of charges and the waning light would not improve my aim. Better to wait until the morning. I ate a couple of blossoms and found them tasteless, then had joy of a half-eaten lolly Urszula had dropped in my pocket during the farewell. Lest I fall in sleep, I buckled my belt around flesh and tree trunks. The sun set and like the dogs I waited.

In the darkness maybe I slept, for when I awoke suddenly it was moonrise and all the landscape silvery. There was a pawing and moaning at the foot of the tree, as the dogs milled around something strange—a metal canister. As I watched it emitted white mist; the dogs sniffed at it and whined. I could smell chemicals now, stupefying, and below the dogs were staggering like drunks. I pulled my scarf over my face for a filter, feeling weak and glad of the belt that bound me.

Walking among the fallen, twitching forms was a figure oddly distorted around the face. It stopped and stared upwards at my form outlined against branches and sky.

"Here, catch!" and it threw a package to me expertly. The gift was a mask, like the mask, I saw now, of the giver. I pulled it over my head and breathed freely again.

"You can come down now.'

For the first time I noticed the lower timbre: a man's voice. Was I going from frying pan to firing squad? I began to pick at my self-made bonds watching *him* all the while. The canister had disgorged its drug and he was walking from dog to dog, pressing a rod against each head. There was a faint click, then death.

A deep-voiced thank-you, I decided, then scram! I rebuckled my belt and clambered down, too fast, for in the haste I put foot to the half-severed branch. It cracked beneath me and I fell in a shower of pink flowers made silver. With a splintering crash bough Raffy and all hit earth, just missing the hillock of a dead dog.

"Are you all right?"

He was bending over me now, and I heard him draw his breath in deep. I looked and noticed my leg caught between wood and ground. Funny, it never used to bend that way.

"If you don't mind me saying so, that's a godawful break. I'll have to take you back to the farm."

He was fumbling in a pocket of his coat.

"Can't have you screaming blue murder all the way there . . . sorry about this, mate."

His hand emerged from the pocket with another canister, and simultaneously he reached forward and snapped my mask off.

"Sorry," he repeated and cracked the canister under my nose.

Much later I awoke in yellow artificial light and found myself lying on a table, head propped up on foam. There was a machine covering one leg.

"Robo doctor," he said, from where he sat watching. "They gave me one 'cos I'm all alone here."

I stared at him; a smallish man with a lined, weary face, not young, not particularly muscled, and not threatening at the moment, although you never could trust them.

"Well, say something! Think you'll give yourself away? I can tell you're a woman."

"Womyn."

"And that you're one of those."

"I'm Raph-ael."

"That's a man's name, an archangel's."

"My mother says angels don't have gender, so there."

"Your mum knows her theology, Raphael. I'm Benedict. That means blessings, and I don't mean you harm. I even left your toy with you."

Sure enough, my right hand had been folded around the gun. I lifted both cautiously.

"Don't burn me," he said, and I lowered my hand.

"We aren't all beasts," he said seriously, and at that moment the machine on my leg thrummed. He got up to inspect it, and satisfied, lifted it off. Revealed were my camo pants cut off at mid-thigh and the rest encased in pale, stiff plastic.

"Like I said, bad break, and you'll find bruises and cuts too. To get you down to my transport I had to hook your belt onto the branch and drag it behind me like a peacock's tail."

Our gaze met.

"You're bigger than me, in case you hadn't noticed."

Perhaps he expected me to smirk. I merely changed the subject: "Can I have some water? That mist dehydrates."

"I'll make some coffee, grow it myself. Ambrosia!'

I looked puzzled, and he added: "Food of the gods."

"Goddesses."

He disappeared from my view, and I got up on one elbow to see where I was. From the curving plastic walls I guessed I was inside a housing module, but the high-tech was offset by an incredible mess. There was furniture, mainly in disrepair, plants in pots, odd bits of machinery, some half dismantled, tools, rusty wire, music tapes, collections of coloured stones—clutter everywhere. Vaguely I wondered how Benedict had managed to bring me in here, then realised with a grimace that he must have carried me.

When he returned from the small cook-unit set against one wall he handed me a cup, taking care our flesh never touched in the transaction.

"How did you find me?"

"I'm the caretaker, I know what goes on down the farm. The dogs showed up on the heat sensor when they broke in and so did you. When all the blips were grouped round the old cherry I could kill two jobs at once: get the pack and see who you were. From the wavelength I knew it was a human."

"Homo sapiens."

He put his cup down on the table hard. "Raphael, I've been talking to you fifteen minutes and this is the third time you've corrected me!"

"It offends my sensibilities."

"And being corrected offends mine!"

We glared at each other and he sighed.

"Sorry, I'm not used to *people* much. Maybe I'll leave you and your leg alone for now."

He went over to a packing case and dragged out a blanket, which he draped carefully on the table beside me.

"I sleep in the next module. If you want something, scream."

He shuffled away, following some invisible path that led him to the door without falling over anything. Pausing at the threshold, he put his hand to a knob in the plastic and the yellow glare dimmed down to nightlight.

"Thanks for the rescue," I said, and threw the blanket over my head before he could respond.

Daylight shining through the translucent plastic woke me, that and a pain in my groin.

"Benedict!"

He appeared in the doorway, in a change of clothes, but unshaven.

"I wanna piss!"

"Oh gawd," he said, looking from door to table and at the mess in between. I flung off the blanket and slid to a one-legged stop on the floor, forcing the issue.

He bent down and rose with a large broom, which he used to clear a haphazard path from me to the exit. Experimentally I hopped, and nearly went face first into a robot of some kind, its sharp guts exposed for maintenance. As I wobbled, he restored my balance with a hand to my sleeve.

"Can you lean on me, perhaps?"

Once Boz and I had gone out of the ghetto to visit Bea, now Urszula's Bea, and a man had grabbed at me. After we had rubbed his face in a mud puddle it had vaguely registered that his flesh felt no different from a womyn's. Then, as now.

Benedict lived in three small modules, living, sleeping and bathroom, all detached from each other and set in a circle. Although the day was overcast and chill it felt good to be outside, so afterwards I let go of him and sat on the little grass courtyard between the ovals of plastic. He brought coffee and insta-bread from the module and we breakfasted.

"Raphael . . ."

Only Grania called me that, and now Benedict. After his outburst I did not want to correct him again, to say: *Just Raffy.*

"What's to be done with you?"

"I'll contact the Sisters. There's a communicator in my pack."

"Pack, where?" and I said: "By the hole under the fence."

He groaned.

"Knew I'd have to fix it sometime. Okay, I'll kill two jobs again: get your handbag and seal the fence."

It was starting to drizzle, so he helped me inside again, then left. I very soon got bored silly in the crowded room and gazing around spotted a fat old book. After one glance I dropped it—full of strange words. Then I thought to clean my gun and found that Benedict had removed the charges when I was unconscious.

When he came back I threw it at him, shouting: "Pig!"

The impact left a white mark on his face, but he stood still as the gun clattered to the floor.

"How was I to know you wouldn't fry me for laying hands on you?"

"I don't care! Pig!"

His gaze flitted about the room.

"You've been at my Shakespeare."

I recalled the name on the old book.

"I'd have ripped it to shreds if I'd known you valued it."

He lunged forward and grabbed the volume. "For that I'd have killed you."

I had never cared for poetry, thanks to Grania, and so was struck mum by his feeling.

"You've never heard of Bill," he said sadly and opened the book. Seeing him distracted, I snatched at the pack, but he deftly kicked my good leg from under me. I fell heavily, breath and pride knocked out of me. While I lay, he began quietly to read:

"O! She doth teach the torches to burn bright.
It seems she hangs upon the cheek of night
Like a rich jewel in an Ethiop's ear;
Beauty too rich for use, for earth too dear!
So shows a snowy dove trooping with crows,
As yonder lady o'er her fellows shows.
The measure done, I'll watch her place of stand,
And, touching hers, make blessed my rude hand.
Did my heart love till now? forswear it, sight!
For I ne'er saw true beauty till this night."

I was a captive audience, but it was words rather than a shackle of plastic that held me. Words that summoned memories: in front of me was the beautiful face of a dark girl who had come just once into the ghetto. I had made enquiries about her and found her irrevocably straight, so I kicked a wall and went on living.

(Never would a face have the same effect on me until, years later, I came back from Haven to find little Honey had grown up. But by then I knew Romeo's speech by rote.)

Benedict stopped, and spoke his own words:

"See, it's not all rapes."

I was sitting up by then; he dropped the pack into my lap and went out. I opened it, found the communicator and began to cry.

"What is it?" he asked from the doorway.

"I—can't. I've blown it, I'm better off dead."

He sat down on the arm of a laden armchair.

"Have you noticed, Raphael, that I've never asked you what you're doing out here? You lot haven't been careful enough. For months now there's been rumours on the computer of walkers in the waste, consortiums nobody's heard of waving big money, a girl dressed like you found dead in a dioxin dump . . ."

I scowled, remembering how the Scouts had ascribed the death to inexperience: "Poor thing, let her go alone too soon." Now they would say the same about Raffy.

"Stop crying. I don't care what you're up to so long I'm left alone. And I never dob in anyone. Call the ladies!"

Maybe I trusted him, but the Sisters never would. Besides:

"I'd be a laughing stock, skiving off after flowers and having to be rescued—by an andro! They'd never let me scout again."

"So," he said. "I'm not going to tell my bosses and you're not going to tell your bossesses. What then?"

"How long before I walk?"

"Coupla months. The robo gave you a calcium accelerator, but you can't hurry *Mother* Nature."

He was looking glum and the emotion was infectious; the consequences of our silence were an unwanted guest for him and dependence on a man for me.

"I can modify a robo into transport for you," he said. "But it'll take time."

"Gimme materials and I'll make crutches."

He fished in the litter behind the chair, emerging with an all-purpose kit, its plastic grimy and dented.

"You can make one crutch from the broom—never use it anyway. I'll see what's handy for the other."

He was half out the door when I yelled at him:

"Benedict! I want something else."

He turned and I tapped the gun meaningfully.

"Promise you won't burn me?"

"I promise only if you promise not to—"

I stopped, for an extraordinary expression of grief had taken hold of his face.

"Lord, what we've done to deserve this, and rightly too!"

He took the charges from his coat pocket and rolled them across the floor to me, where they were stopped by my leg in its plastic chitin. I picked them up, counted them, slotted them into their pods—and looked up to see that Benedict had gone.

Good, because I needed to consider the strange situation we had fallen into. An analogy came to mind: Edge City, when two wildly differing ghetto factions united against the middle ground. Just because their interests coincided did not mean opportunities were lost for mischief to each other; I should remember that. He had several Edges on me: mobility and his computer, wherever it was, with which he could summon his bosses if the guest proved irksome. On the other hand I had the Edges of a gun and my communicator, for a last resort SOS.

Thinking of a Mayday caused me to remember that I had not given my daily position report to the ghetto. I glanced at my watch, noting I was several hours late. If I didn't send the Scouts off on a wild goose chase they would go straight to my last location, just south of the site, and from there track me to the macrofarm. Loss of face for me: but of life for Benedict, who despite his hospitality would be killed out of hand.

I unfolded my map, looking for a labyrinth or tanglewood, and found a marsh, probably once a sewage farm. It was off-course, perfect. I fed its co-ordinates into the flute, a coding device that unravelled information into its component yarns and sent it across space, to be knit up only at the other end. "Chased by wild dogs," I added for explanation, and flicked the communicator to receiving mode.

A jumble of symbols appeared on the little screen, resolving first into letters, then words. "OK. Come on home." Whoever was on the other end was in a laconic mood. I had a moment of conscience, as I remembered Zoska, Boz and my other foster-sisters, even despised Grania—then I turned the communicator off.

"The rest is silence," I said, as I returned the communicator to my pack.

Benedict spoke from the doorway, and I jumped:

"Do you know where that comes from?"

"How long have you been there?"

"Only long enough to hear you quote Bill."

He came in lugging a collection of staves.

"Any of these do?"

"Yeah, the longest," and we set to woodwork. Our hands dipped in and out of the kitbox, never coinciding.

After a while he returned to the quotation:

"Where'd you hear that?"

"Probably my mother."

"The authority on angels?"

"Yeah, I've got two mothers." He blinked. "One gave birth to me, the other reared me."

"So which knows Bill?"

"My blood mother, Grania Erato."

"Poetry woman, eh?"

Now I blinked, then I remembered that he read.

"You know her?"

He shook his head.

"I only read one book. See Raphael, I decided long ago that a man, begging your pardon, didn't have time to read everything. There's too many people writing and nearly all of them are mediocre. There ought to be a pogrom—they hide the really good writers with their verbiage. So I just stuck with the very best."

He gestured at the book.

"Before you flare up at me again, I'm not saying your mum's no good. I never read her . . . I'm restricted in my reading."

"But how do you know she writes verse?"

"Erato's the muse of love poetry."

"How pretentious," I said without thinking, and bit my lip, too late.

He looked at me, reading more than I wished him to, so I bent over the crutch and worked like a machine. After a pause, he followed suit. Even when we broke briefly for more bread and coffee, we did not speak—until the crutches were finished.

"Yeay!"

I pulled myself up to standing and fitted the pads under my arms. Suddenly Raffy metamorphosed from crawling caterpillar to a Mummy-Long-Legs, with limbs of wood, plastic and flesh. It was fleet, in a lurching fashion, for with three long steps I was down Benedict's pathway and outside, being buffeted by the late afternoon wind.

"Whee!"

He had followed me outside protectively.

"Don't overdo it. Years ago I was on those things and took days getting used to them. Don't think because you're muscled like a racehorse that you won't be sore."

Just for that, I left the courtyard, hopping through the gaps between the modules to the farm proper. It consisted of: more modules, but giant, in row after row with tidy concrete paths in between. I lolloped to the nearest and stared through the plastic opaqued by my breath, like a child at a shop window. There were many green plants, and the glint of steel as a robot gardener rolled up and down.

I glanced behind me and saw Benedict watching like a guardian angel. Irritated by his solicitude I swung away from the wall and went for a long walk along concrete, walled in always by plastic. He did not follow, perhaps expecting a clout over the head with a crutch.

When I returned, doused in sweat and radiating heat like a boiler, I found the courtyard littered with Benedict's junk. Dust blew like a mist from the door of the living module.

I sat down with a thump on the packing case and at the noise he came out, wearing a faded red scarf over his grizzled hair.

"You want your broom back for the spring-cleaning?"

He scowled. "I'm making space. If you're living here you'll need territory of your own. For *my* sanity I'm making a moiety of the living room."

"Need help?"

He stared at me. "Move furniture when you've buggered yourself with the most strenuous walk you could manage? Braggadacian!"

He disappeared inside again and I, feeling parched, went to the bathroom to get a drink without disturbing him. There was a mirror there, overlooked previously, and it reflected the new face like a stranger. I saw a girl weary and strained, with twigs in her brown hair and smears from bark on her face. The man's glass told me what I had not noticed in his gaze: this girl was attractive.

The water plashed into my hands and I longed for a bath, but only cleaned my face. To strip, and to have him sneak up behind me . . .

When I went out it was sunset and I shivered at the memory of dogs and flowers. I sat on the crate again and watched lights come on inside the living module. It resembled a giant phosphorescent slug.

"You can come in now, Raphael."

Within a low wall had been built of odds and ends; on one side was Benedict's clutter, on the other was an area cleared of all save a mattress with my pack and blanket set neatly upon it.

"I'll make the wall higher, give you privacy, promise. I'm just out of energy now."

"It's not urgent," I lied politely.

He grunted and dodged effortlessly to the cook-unit, where a saucepan bubbled. I looked for the table and found it pushed against the wall, at the end of the path. There were two chairs by it; I sat down and noticed the Shakespeare on the table, like a second guest for dinner.

Benedict brought stewpot, cutlery and crockery to the table.

"Let good digestion wait on appetite!"

"I suppose that's in your book too," I said.

"Bill says something about everything."

Chit-chat was forgotten then, as we ate like a pair of wild beasts. When the meal was over I reached for the book.

"What are you doing?" he asked suspiciously.

"Seeing what he says about the likes of me . . . *them*, as you put it. What's this, *The Taming of the* . . ."

"I doubt you'll find it there," he said and pulled the book from me.

"How 'bout this: "Would it not grieve a woman to be overmastered with a piece of valiant dust? To make account of her life to a clod of wayward marl?" That's feminist at least."

"Nice. Who is she?"

"Lass called Beatrice. A bit like you: fierce."

I twitched the book into my grasp again, accidentally losing the place. In front of me was a list of names followed by their speeches and I looked for Beatrice.

"Phooey. Here she's saying: "I love you with so much of my heart that none is left to protest" to a clod named—"

"—Benedick," he finished. Picking up the book he walked to the door.

"Goodnight," he said without turning.

"Goodnight."

I fidgeted for a while then shoved the robot against the door and went to sleep. In the morning I was awakened by the sound of an electric motor. Moving, I found my muscles sore (prophetic Benedict!), but pushed the robot aside and swung out. The courtyard was empty but through the gap I could see Benedict atop a squat vehicle with fat rubber wheels. He zoomed it down a pathway and out of sight.

Tied to the largest bit of the courtyard junk was a note:

"Off to check fences. Back late today. Place yours."

I stood there like a tripod, listening to the motor fade out of earshot. How lovely to be alone again! Then my solitude was interrupted by the tock of rain—within moments my hair was soaked and drops trickled down my neck. I laughed, throwing my head back to drink rain, and went to the bathroom module to finish what the cloudburst had begun. Only the mirror marred my mood; its big round eye seemed prurient so I made it stare at the wall.

Showered, I went searching for Benedict's computer and found the console behind a filing cabinet that looked as if the robot had kicked it in a pet. Raffy was never a hacker, except for a romantic summer with the ghetto's computer whiz, yet the sight revived memories. Benedict was no hacker either, for log-on instructions were taped to the keyboard. There was no password, but I guessed "Shakespeare" and guessed right.

The screen lit up with a list of options and I chose "Security" and after that "Heat Sensor". An infra-red picture of the farm covered the screen, with the small blips of wildlife and one big blip moving slowly around the perimeter. It would appear Benedict was truthful. I returned to the original list and took the option "Maintenance". This killed the curious kitten for diagram after confusing diagram of the giant modules appeared. The care involved indicated that the green crop I had glimpsed so briefly was highly lucrative. What was it? Best not ask. The seclusion of the farm and the fact that the intermediaries had not been able to discover the names of its owners argued a need for secrecy.

Benedict returned after dark, to the lukewarm half of a meal I had concocted from various odd edibles found around the cook-unit. He devoured it, then looked closely at me.

"Good, you had a bath. Thought if I went away you would— you were starting to pong."

I was silent, and he gazed around the module. After my hacking I had got sick of having to weave through his mess like a drunkard, so had added the more maneuverable furniture to the wall.

"And you made space! I can work in here."

"What on?"

"Robo-digger. To modify for *your* transport."

"I've got the wood legs."

He shook his head.

"Very soon you'll find them restricting."

He spread a plastic groundsheet on the floor and wheeled in the digger, which— shovel apart— was the baby of his transport. I opened my mouth and he said, raising his voice an octave:

"Need help?" Then, in his normal pitch: "No thanks Raphael, unless you're an expert on robotics."

I shook my head, reluctantly. He grinned, then saw my expression and pulled the corners of his mouth down.

"Why don't you talk to me while I work?"

"About what?"

"The ghetto. See, I'm curious—it's natural with something that excludes you. Years ago, before your wall went up, I walked through the ghetto fringes. Dirty looks galore, but nobody beat me up. I suppose being a little tich saved me."

I agreed silently.

"What did you see, Benedict?"

"Nothing much, just no men."

I snorted and he blushed rosy pink.

"I was only there five minutes, girl."

I gazed at him, gauging what information to give and what to withold. At Bea's house I had met straight women who would politely, deviously, direct the conversation to my lifestyle. All I need do was think of the most unsound of them, add a dash of caution, and I would have a recipe for Benedict.

"Why are you staring at me?" he asked.

Just for a moment, the image of a woman had flickered on his face.

"It's just a place where womyn live. We have the wall, and beyond that are "suburbs" where feminists and dykes who don't mind mixing"—like Bea and Grania—"live. The Watch, that's our Police, call them the first line of defence. Softcores live just inside the wall, hardcores further in."

"What's them?"

"Degrees of ideological rigidity."

"And what are you?"

"Guess," I said coldly.

"In between, I'd say."

Correct, but he needn't know that. He waited, then ventured: "And what do you lot do for a crust? You can't live off ideology and air."

"The suburbans pay tithes from their work in the andro's world." Grania had been bankrolling the ghetto for decades, to name one prominent instance.

"There's also workshops, factories, where goods are made to sell Outside."

"Like what?"

"I'm not going to tell you."

"Knitting," he fished, half-seriously. I smiled at his little joke and also at the thought of the systems that my old hacker love marketed to a lot of blissful ignoramuses.

"The ideal is self-sufficiency," I said, imagining the walled Haven in the country, our City of Womyn.

"In more ways than one," he muttered. "I've heard talk of a Hive."

Loose lips! I thought, but continued, trying not to let the exchange become an Edge Game.

"It's the centre, for us. To stay there long is to forget that your kind exist. Call it an editing device."

Any mention of andros was forbidden in our temple to the Gyn principle, which caused some bizarre conversations. Once Urszula, being a brat, had asked Zoska in front of hardcores where babies came from. ("Yes Mama, but what makes the baby grow in your belly? Why aren't I growing one now?"). She had got a flustered answer about cabbages and my accompanying raucous laughter got me thrown out of the Hive for the very first time. It had been "unseemly", in this quiet place decorated with murals of Ishtar, Athena and Joan of Arc sans Ur-Nammu, Zeus and the English clerics. I could feel uplifted, even refreshed in the Hive but ultimately it was claustrophobic. All restrictions annoy Raffy.

Benedict should not hear criticisms, but neither could I voice vague platitudes. I clammed up. The cessation obviously irritated him, for he began to quote his Bill, half to himself, a quarter to the digger and a quarter to me. I listened until we parted for the night.

In the morning it rained again, and Benedict's robotics were interrupted by the visit of a truck. He dealt with it, returned, and worked with a mixture of care and haste. By a happy coincidence the sun poked out moments after the contraption was finished. He pushed it out into the courtyard and through a gap to the start of a sloping path.

"Hop on."

He took the crutches, slotting them into a niche at the back of the transport.

"Oh, so that's what it's for."

"That, by your hand, is direction and this is speed. This starts the motor."

I forestalled him and switched it on myself. As the machine purred he grinned at his handiwork. Seeing him off guard I put my hand hard on the speed button.

"Hey, wait! Whoa!"

"Wowee!"

The machine shot down the path straight for one of the giant modules, and I grabbed the steering just in time to execute a two-wheeled turn. To show Benedict I had mistressed the vehicle I did a circuit of the module and risked glancing behind for his reaction. He was open mouthed like a yokel, so with a wave I disappeared around the module again.

When I had explored on crutches I had found the farm monotonous; riding, it was the same, although I passed a processing plant and the road for the trucks, which relieved the uniformity. There was more fun in being Raffy the speed maniac, careering around like a pinball. Pride cometh before a crash, of course, and I was sobered by a near collision with a robot gardener.

"Roadhog!" I shouted at its featureless metal carapace, largely to cover the pain from my leg, which had been jarred. Then I continued down the path and found I was free of modules, in open, tussocked country. Still adventurous, I rode to the fence and back, but at an invalid's pace.

It was late when I puttered nervously up to Benedict's home, and to my relief he was not waiting outside. I parked the transport and became a stick insect again.

He was sitting at the console.

"Have a nice time?"

"Yes, thank you."

"I watched your blip until it slowed down. Then I did some hacking."

I poled to where I could see the screen, which resembled the old samplers displayed in the Hive: across the screen was verse, Grania's verse:

Battersea blues couldn't keep me apart
I go to play songs in a grimy gutter
With you along—your clutter.

There's leaves in your hair, have you
been dancing with your old man again?
Walk on the wind of September evening
Don't come down until I've finished playing.

Lend me a mood, oh no
I'm not wistful, not jealous.
I have the music and you have the heart
Battersea blues couldn't keep me apart.

"She was very young when she wrote that," I said. "She still had her father's name."

"So I saw."

"You didn't get far with her verse."

"On the contrary. I accessed the biography first, which was mainly a list of prizes, then the contents page of the Collected Works. There were lots of poems about R. and Raphael, but I thought you'd thump me if I read them. So I accessed the cheapest poem about anything else."

"Thanks."

"Amazing! She's said 'thank-you' to me twice in one conversation."

There was a round scrap of plastic temptingly near; I leaned on one crutch and savagely batted it across the module with the other. It hit the wall with a satisfying clunk.

"I live in glass. Anything she hears about me goes into her verse! Vampire!"

"The parent feeds the child and then feeds off him . . . her."

I stared at him.

"You're not unique," he said. "With me it was my father."

"My father was 10CC of sticky fluid,' I said viciously. He ignored the goad.

"Lucky you."

He switched off the console.

"Dad was a drunk. Only good thing he did was desert the family. Trouble was he kept coming back."

I too had been incompletely deserted.

"Mum was all right," he said. "Earth mother type."

"Like my foster mother."

94

"That's right,' he recalled. "You said you had two."

"She says the world's oldest profession isn't whoring, it's motherhood. That's what she does."

"She good at it?"

I laughed: "You think so, on the evidence of me?"

"I meant, is she respected for it?"

"It's high status in the ghetto."

Zoska had been nominated as an Elder, but had dodged the election by beginning Basienka.

"That's how it should be," he said.

Both of us had become embarrassed by the confessions, and so gravitated to the table, where there was a bowl of fresh greens.

"Grow it myself," he said proudly. "One of the perks of the job."

"That and being alone," I said, and he nodded, a little too emphatically. We sat and ate, crushing crisp leaves between our teeth. The crunching made me aggressive, revived my daredevil high with the transport. Foolhardy as ever, I decided on an Edge Game. If Benedict was in a confessing mood, he might give information valuable to the ghetto and my curiosity.

I waved a strip of bok choi: "You grow other greens in the modules."

"You noticed?"

This was not a good sign, but I persisted: "I don't know botany, but they're like no plants I've seen."

"They're intoxicants. The only other perk of the job."

I had not expected him to fold so easily. Careful, a biochemical sensor warned.

"They come from what used to be the Amazon rainforest. Got saved from extinction when a scientist et one and had a nice time. They're still only quasi-legal, like the other substances that relax society's rules a little. That's why this farm is far from awkward questions."

He paused.

"Except when asked by Raphaels. You want to try some?"

We were both on the razor's edge now. His suggestion had caught me off-guard, but to signal that might be dangerous. I had to answer quickly.

"Sure."

He went out and I grinned like a wedge of cheese. Free intoxicant!

Benedict was gone a long time and returned, not with the expected green sheaf, but carrying a small box.

"Could have got raw stuff, just pull it off the vine, but it's rough. This is processed, ready for the truck."

He opened the box, to reveal grey crystals, more intoxicant than I had ever seen before. I nodded warily, thinking about dosages—in the ghetto only Boz had had a stronger head than Raffy for the drug. He set the box on the table and to my surprise ignited the crystals. A soft grey smoke, reminiscent of Zoska's old homespun shawl, drifted upwards.

"This is freebasing. Extravagant, but the best."

I attempted the worldly-wise expression of a drug savant, and obviously failed, for he continued:

"This extract's euphoric. Other types make people concentrate, make 'em sexy, send 'em to sleep . . . the many words that describe emotions, they're all covered by the drug. It's a universal, like Bill."

The smoke swirled round me, like the three witches on a panel in the Hive.

"Weird sisters," he said, and I goggled: did the drug cause telepathy?

"From the book," he explained. "Want to hear it?"

"Yes."

He read from his memory, speech after fantastical speech, and I savoured them. All, except for the initial extract from *Macbeth*, were descants on the theme of heterosexual love, which might have been oppressive had not the language transcended gender. I heard the love-talk of men and women, and interpreted it as that of womyn.

He stopped, dried out, and an eerie silence descended. The room was a ball of smoke and we were silhouettes to each other. Feeling nervous, I moved closer to him, and he turned his head.

"Did that upset you?"

"No."

"Very sexist. I'm sorry. I forgot with you it was girl and girl."

"It's much like the other," I said, recalling the language.

"Really? You've tried?"

I was feeling pleasantly confused.

"No, although Grania said I'd try anything except incest and folk-dancing."

He had never seemed threatening; that was his advantage, or Edge. Perhaps to convince myself he was still there, in this witches' brew, or perhaps for Raffy's damned curiosity, I reached out and touched him. His chest was as hard as that of a pre-pubescent girl.

"Is this an advance?" he said, cautiously flattered.

It was now. Raffy is also tactile.

He put his hand reverently over mine—they were almost the same size.

"Who'd have thought it? An old man like me."

Actually he was younger than Grania. Our other hands were grappled now.

"I'm out of practice," he said, and glanced around. The smoke had cleared a little.

"Not on that hard little mattress," I said.

We stood up, and I teetered as I tried to fit the crutches.

"Are we ever stoned!" he said. "You'll never make it out the door."

He tried to lift me but got hopelessly tangled with a crutch, and nearly fell over himself.

"Any suggestions?"

"Pig-back," I said muzzily.

He laughed: "Yeah, appropriate for a pig."

He knelt in front of me and I stood on my good leg, tucking the crutches under one arm.

"Hupsy-dairy," he said, and I rode him out the door to the sleeping module.

I awoke, again to daylight diffused through module plastic, and looked into the face of Benedict. Asleep, he looked like something the cat had dragged in: a little beat-up mouse.

As if on cue he opened his eyes.

"Raphael, that was sweet."

I rolled over on my back, to get the weight off my cast and also to escape his sooky expression. There, above me, was flesh, holos of naked women, all breasts, buttocks, thighs, taped to the module ceiling. They had a look of vacuous unreality suggesting the counterfeit; if not, they were like no womyn I had ever seen.

It had been dark in here last night. Intentionally? He saw my expression and groaned like a creaky door. I shot up and began to extract my clothes from the mess around his bed, swearing under my breath. Pulling on a garment I overbalanced and fell on top of him; he lay still beneath me. I scrambled up again and finished dressing. Then I found my crutches at the foor of the bed and poled furiously for the living module. There was a box of grey ash on the table and I knocked it to the floor, before grabbing my pack and heading for my transport.

He was standing in the courtyard, wrapped in a blanket.

"Raphael!" he shouted, "I'm only human and I mean a man!"

"That's no excuse!"

I started the motor and sped away, making a grand exit. Moments later I remembered my gun: should I return and use it? No. I never wanted to see him again.

My intent had been to follow the roboroad to the gate, the weak spot in most defences. However in my haste I had made a wrong turning and was as lost among identical paths and modules as an ant on a draughtsboard. The sun was out; I estimated east and headed that way. The maze of modules ended and I continued towards the fence, thinking to circumnavigate to the farm entrance. Idly I noticed the tracks of a larger transport on the grass before me. Then there was a cherry-bough, its flowers withered and dry, and beyond it, up a steep slope, the Rock-a-bye-Raffy tree.

I pulled out the communicator and held it in my hand like a shell. It was no use, for the same restrictions still applied. If I returned to the ghetto on a stolen transport questions would still be asked about my leg. For expediency's sake I would have to return and make peace with Benedict.

I drove along the fence to the gate, as planned, and found it open. Was this an invitation to leave? If so, I refused it and took the road back to Benedict.

He was waiting outside this time, looking worried.

"Why didn't you go?"

Dismounting, I tapped the cast with a crutch, in answer: it made a dull sound, like a prison door slamming.

"Yes, but after what we did? I did?"

His tone was guilty and something occurred to me: he had mentioned that the drug could make people "sexy".

"Benedict, was there aphrodisiac in that blend?"

"A little," he said sheepishly, a repentant ram. "Didn't think it'd work."

I struck him with a crutch, not hard, but sufficient to send him reeling back against the nearest piece of junk. He hit it at an angle, gashing his scalp. Blood dribbled down like water into his eyes.

"I can't see! Raphael, help!"

He was crouched on the ground, both hands over the wound. There was no way I could lift him.

"Stand up!" I said like the Watch Chief and he obeyed.

"Easy. I'm here."

He reached one blood-sticky hand out to the voice. I anchored the crutches and took hold of it.

"Inside," he said. "Doctor!"

Now I had the problem of getting him to the living module, for while he clasped me as though drowning I could not use the crutches. They required both hands. A sudden gust of wind flapped my scarf, left untied in the hasty dressing, and I had an idea.

"Benedict, let go!"

Very slowly, he complied.

"Now take this," I said, and brushed one fringed end of the scarf against his fingers. He took it, and I wrapped the other end around one crutch handgrip. Carefully I swung into the module, leading him by an embroidered tether.

"The lame leading the blind," he said.

Inside I sat him down at the table and found the doctor unit. When I activated it, the optical sensors swivelled and it made a clicking noise, tsk, tsk, tsk. Metal hands shot out of the body and began to minister. Within minutes the blood had been cleaned from him and the hair shaved from around the gash, which was staunched with a dab of sealant. The robot went into inert mode and I switched it off.

He opened his eyes and stared down at an anthill of spilt ash. Absently he smoothed it with the side of his hand.

"Raphael . . ."

"Yes?"

He doodled in the ash with a forefinger, then erased the design.

"Don't hit me again, but I'm not protected against fertility. Are you?"

I sat down too, feeling sick to my boots.

"Of course not. And I'm at full moon."

99

He sighed, and as if his head was suddenly too heavy, rested his cheek on the ashy hand. Realising too late, he withdrew the hand and stared at it glumly.

"Next it'll be sackcloth."

I made no reply.

"Say something. Laugh at slapstick old me."

"The doctor," I said incoherently.

"They programmed it for a man on his own, no gynie-cology. I've heard that jumping with your legs in splints . . ."

"Very funny."

"Well, surely the ghetto has herbal remedies."

"No need."

"No, I suppose not."

"I'm NOT speaking to you," and with that I retired behind the wall of China, or rather of junk, and huddled under the blanket. After a pause he went out, and I heard the noise of his transport, moving away.

He did not come into the living module the rest of that day, nor did I go out—thus we avoided each other. The following day the pattern was reversed: I took the little transport out around the farm while he was a stay-at-home. In this way we had the necessary illusion of being alone. If our paths crossed the junctions were marked by a chilling silence.

The routine was finally aborted one rainy morning, as we breakfasted—he on fresh-brewed coffee and I on food-concentrate from the pack. An electronic whine crossed the wall.

"The heat sensor!" he said, and dashed to the console. I followed in seven-league strides.

"What is it?"

He jabbed a stubby finger at the screen.

"Figures, just north. Your mates?"

I leaned closer to stare at the sexless blobs. The marsh had been north of the farm.

"Relax, this isn't the dyke cavalry. They're just being curious." (Taking a look at the farm and also the site, but I couldn't say that.)

He frowned.

"Don't think much of their tracking. You and the tree were on the other side."

"I gave them a position reading for the marsh centre."

"Gulper? They could have been killed looking for you there."

After all that had happened since I had crawled under the fence, I should have been immune to shock. Yet that jarred me. With my luck it would probably be Boz.

"Well, I didn't know it was dangerous. If I hadn't, they'd have burst in here thinking I'd been kidnapped for a sex slave—which is partly true."

He winced.

"Take the cart and catch up with them."

They would come back and kill you, I thought, but only said:

"I'd be pitied for the rest of my life."

"A fate worse than death," he said drily.

"And what if I were carrying?"

We had agonised silently about that question for three days now, but to voice it hurt not at all. He took the cue quickly.

"Any reason you might not?"

"I never tried. And you?"

"The ladies all took precautions. I never got close to one so she'd stop using them and have my baby . . . have a child with me."

I rocked on the crutches and considered.

"What are our options?"

"One—nothing's cooking. Two, there is, but you want to stop it."

That option was tricky: the knowledge lay outside the ghetto.

"Three, you don't."

"It might be a boy!" I cried. How unpleasant, to have the enemy growing inside me.

"Can't see him being reared by manhaters," he said.

"I suppose you'd want to keep him."

"I just remember," he said reasonably, "the one nice thing my dad did with me, which was fishing. Sitting by a stream, if I can find one unpolluted, teaching a small me . . ."

"Small you!"

He looked at me.

"He might take after his tearaway mum."

There was a pause while I tried to imagine a male Raffy.

"You'd not let me keep a girl?" he said.

I shrugged, recalling Grania's poems about father-daughter incest. On the other hand, the idea of returning to the ghetto with a female infant, claiming to have found her in bullrushes—the idea was preposterous.

"Look Benedict, aren't we counting chickens before they're hatched? There might be nothing in the eggshell."

"True," he said dubiously, and we left it at that. At least we were talking again, but the cautious cameraderie was gone. In the days that followed we ate together, did odd jobs around the farm together, but were emotionally apart. The book remained a common ground but we read it to ourselves separately.

Time passed in this waiting game. One day he put in hours at the terminal, while I hogged the book, enjoying the Three Witches and disagreeing with their images in the Hive (not evil enough). Sensing from his absorbtion that this was no farm matter, I sneaked up behind him, as quietly as a Woodeny could.

He was searching scientific literature, combining the terms "calcium accelerator" and "embryology".

"Raphael, quit reading over my shoulder," he said mildly.

"Tell me what you found first."

"See for yourself," and he dodged past me. I sat down at the terminal and saw that he had accessed several articles, full-text.

One dealt with white mice, the other with monotremes.

"What about people?"

"I tried that," he said from the other side of the room. "No research reports."

The door of the module slammed and I began to read the articles. The monotreme one was inconclusive and the white mice had eaten their young—not an encouraging prognosis.

I glanced back and saw that Benedict had snaffled the Shakespeare. Ah, well, it was his turn for it. To complete the reversal I began hacking myself, first checking the account to which the searches were credited. It worried me that Benedict's bosses might smell a lady rat if their employee ticked up searches unconnected with their product. However, the account was private, its searches—until recently—solely of the database Shaklit.

I returned to the original enquiry and discarded "embryology" to concentrate on the drug that was healing my leg. After an hour I knew that in the young and healthy the period of accelerated cure could be as short as one month. I patted the cast thoughtfully; it would be rushing things, but if Option One occurred I could be away much sooner that Benedict expected. A quick getaway was desirable—he was starting to look sooky again.

He made one more attempt to discuss our possible parenthood:

"Have you decided yet?"

"On what?"

"Options Two or Three?"

"Oh Ishtar it might well be neither!"

I stormed off, more bluster, for I was late and I think he knew it. Of course, the upsets I had experienced this month would have disturbed the cycle of a she-elephant . . .

One pale spring dawn I woke up very early and found it was Remembrance day, as in Grania's famous poem. Her words had never bobbed up in my mind much before, but now I was thinking in a mixture of Grania and Bill. I activated the Doctor and addressed it to my leg. It whirred, clicked again, shone lights, prodded me here and there—and then it extruded a nozzle which sprayed the cast with pink mist. The plastic melted away as I watched, leaving not even a discarded cocoon to mark my change. The leg underneath was scaly and looked strange; I cautiously tried exercises then shuffled up and down. It was whole.

Much of my silence had been put to the devising of contingency plans, and I knew what to do. I laid the crutches aside and *walked* to the console, where I instructed the gates to open. Then I shouldered my pack and left, pausing only to streak blood on the door of the sleeping module: my explanation.

He must have slept late that morning, for I had escaped the farm and was following the road through thickets of yellow gorse before he came after me. Hearing the motor, I moved to the roadside. Prickly leaves brushed my bare new leg—if I hid there I would be scratched raw. Instead I pulled out the gun, hating to use it.

Benedict was astride the little transport and for the first time I noticed, as he must have before, that riders of the converted digger looked absurd. He brought it to a stop on the other side of the road, several metres from me. Now I was in sight he seemed unable to speak.

"You got the message," I finally said.

He nodded. "Raphael! Not a word goodbye."

A buzzing insect shot past my head, going from gorse bush to gorse bush and incidentally from Raffy to Benedict. He continued:

"Oh I know that you couldn't predict what I'd do. Suspicious minds! I'm not here to compel you."

"What then?"

"I'm worried. What if you meet another pack of dogs? I know you accessed CA data, and that you think the leg's sound. But you could refracture if you run on it, and this time nobody might help you."

He was right: although I had paced myself carefully over the distance, I had developed a limp.

"Do you want to guard me back to the ghetto?"

"And ruin your reputation? No girl, just take the transport."

I started to demur, but he kept speaking:

"You can ditch it near the city. There's a homing circuit and it'll make its way back down the road."

"I can't."

He looked astounded.

"How do I repay you? I've taken and given nothing in return."

"But you have."

He clambered off the transport.

"Raphael, you've not been easy to live with. I cannot endure my Lady Tongue, not lately. But I've fallen in love with her."

He stopped.

"My first love! A lesbian who won't be tamed, won't play Beatrice with Benedict."

Slowly he moved away from the vehicle.

"It's a gift to me if you take it, stops me imagining you et by dogs."

There was no real answer to this speech, not one which would satisfy him. I took one step, then two, towards the transport.

"Thank you," he said, when I got onto it.

"Thank you! Goodbye."

"Goodbye," he replied, his expression bleak. I started the motor and coasted away, glancing back now and then to see him standing there against the yellow like a spoon in mustard. A bend of the road hid him, and I never saw him again.

Now I knew how he had felt. Oh Honey! The emotional ache had become physical—I stared at Grania, and suffered.

"How could I forget?" she said. "You limped in here like a wounded bellatrice, expecting me to shred the—quite good—elegy I'd written for you. When I didn't, you told me what you thought of me. It was a strange speech, first ghetto-gutter, then becoming arcane and archaic. 'Cacodemon' was one word used—I had not heard it outside *Richard III*. How strange to hear it from my Raphael's foul mouth. When you finished, your womynly chest panting up and down like a bellows, I remarked, quoting as is my way . . ."

"'She was wont to speak plain and to the purpose . . . and now is she turned orthography, her words are a very fantastical banquet—just so many strange dishes.'"

"And you turned to the bookshelf, and following the alpha-beta round, you discovered Shakes-rags and opened it."

"I said: '*Much Ado About Nothing* Act 2 Scene 3 nyaagh!'"

"Whereupon I remarked that while missing, presumed dead, you had attended classes on Shakespeare."

"And I told you the whole story."

"Which made me wonder why you, so secretive—"

"Because you write about me!"

"—should spiel the most profound experience of your life. Raphael, I know a dare when I see one. You were daring me to write that Raphael Grania had fornicated with an andro. Being contrary, a trait you have inherited, I didn't."

"Would you, now?"

"It's stale bread news. Haven's half-completed and I doubt anyone would murder that poor man for slipping you a mickey thirteen years ago. The hardcores wouldn't like it, but you dis-like them."

"I intend to marry into them."

This time she did blink.

"Oh, the sweet young thing. What's her name?"

"Honey Marthe."

"Is she pretty?"

"Very. And with a mother like a meat-axe."

She put her pink hands to her mouth.

"So that's why you want my silence!"

"I want a vow of it."

"On one condition."

"What?"

"Raphael, on that night you witheld information from your dear mamma. You never said what you thought of the heterosexual act."

I considered.

"Very well, but you must swear first."

"On something sacred. I know, you."

Feeling foolish, as she no doubt intended, I knelt down by the chair and she put her heavy hand on my head. An opportunity for caress, I realised.

"I swear, on Raphael, not to tattle."

I stood up.

"That promise covers what I shall tell you."

She nodded.

"Spit it out, this byte, this titbit."

I was silent, thinking of words.

"Mumchance! I see I must interrogate you. Was it pleasurable?"

"Of course. But not the real thing. Hence Honey."

She stored the information away.

"Well, my heretic, we both lose by this transaction, you some privacy, I for not being able to put this grain through the art mill."

"Crushing me," I said, continuing the conceit.

"You exaggerate, nothing could do that. I know being muse-food, museli, was irksome, but it cracked your indifference wonderfully. Naughty of me, but fun—you always bit."

"No more."

"No, if we are to be at peace. Allow me at least an Epithalamium."

"You do that. Make it good."

Interview concluded, I strolled down the hall and out. The garden summoned memories of other flowers, but I brushed them away. Benedict, my apologies . . .

I returned to the ghetto, encountering the on-duty Watch at the gate. Considering my scuffles with that body, they were friendly, which made me suspect some support. This inkling and the news of Grania I wanted to share with Zoska, but when I returned to her little house, she was out. From Basienka's room came a voice singing lullabies, probably Urszula bullied into babysitting. Not wanting questions, I raided the larder, mouse-quiet, and went to bed. Sated physically but not emotionally, I slept.

In the morning Basienka awakened me by crawling into my bed with a huge rag doll.

"You want breakfast, kid?"

She considered it like a duchess.

"Yes."

"Well, we'll make some for everyone."

We brewed coffee, chopped fruit and toasted bread rolls, then I carried the tray into the bedroom. Zoska was weeping.

"What is it? Row with your lover again?"

In answer she waved her hand at the little radio beside the bed, which received only the ghetto's weak FM signal. I listened, to an Elder talking excitedly about—

"Parthenogenesis! They've done it at last!"

Zoska blew her nose loudly.

"And it's too late for me. Curse the biological clock!"

With exquisite timing, Basienka plonked herself in her mother's lap. Zoska hugged her.

"Still, you two will benefit. No more seed and egg, just egg and egg."

"Omelette."

"Don't be facetious, you dreadful child. Other dreadful child, don't spill my coffee!"

Complete independance, I thought, as she fussed over Basienka. It had been the inevitable consequence of the Sisters' path, an ideal from the beginnings of the ghetto. Just because I had once been friendly with a man did not mean I regretted this innovation, that cast my kind adrift from his. Benedict, I was a Sister first, and there was no changing it.

"How did it go last night?" asked Zoska, munching fruit.

"All fixed."

"Good girl."

"How about you?"

"I talked my head off, first to Marthe, then I had tea with the Scouts and dropped in on the softcore leaders. On the way home I was met by the faction of hardcores at odds with Marthe. We're getting an Edge City."

"There's still the Elders."

"A Scout talked on the flute with Boz, and she sent the Elders a rocket, saying Marthe was behaving like a heavy father. I thought that too, but it takes the Head of Haven to say it and remained unscathed."

She gestured at the radio.

"But this news has done it."

I finished my coffee and lounged back.

"Sure it's wonderful, but how does it affect Raffy 'n' Honey?"

"Well it's like I'm fighting with the baby and the sky rains honey-apples. Instant end to hostilities as we gorge."

"Honey-apple," said Basienka.

"Silly," I said. "Now you'll have to get her one."

"Honey-apple."

"Later, sweet-tooth," said Marzie. "Talking of H-O-N-E-Y, I saw her."

I sat up straight, rocking the bed.

"What she say what she say?"

"She loves you."

I jumped off the bed and capered around it, followed by the imitative Basienka.

"She got Marthe out of the room to tell me that. Not as submissive as I thought."

"My bad influence."

"No doubt. But I still think you'll be doing the fighting when that girl leaves the ghetto."

"What if I take her to Haven?"

"A good compromise."

She paused.

"Is it as utopic as Boz claims?"

"We're working on it," I said.

"You do that. I'll stay at home, old imperfect ghetto, in case Haven goes . . ."

"Dystopic?"

"Dystopic. Forget I said that. I just realised I'm being thrown out with the bathwater. Still, it's the best way to get Marthe out of your hair, which now I think of it—"

She put her head on one side.

"—needs a cut."

She hopped out of bed.

"Let me bully you for the last time."

First she made me wash in the little bathroom cluttered with water-toys, then combed down my damp mop and trimmed it. With an air of relish, she next produced respectable clothes, bought in between the visits of the day before. There were grey pants, grey shirt, smart black boots and a stiff, sobersides hat. As I admired my well-behaved self in the bedroom mirror, I noticed her sidling out the door with my old gaudy rags.

"What are you doing?"

"Throwing these out."

"Including the scarf, your handiwork?"

She pulled it out and inspected it.

"No! But it's filthy, I'll get you another."

She rummaged in her work basket and withdrew a strip of linen embroidered with pink cherry blossoms. I wondered vaguely if there was a cosmic conspiracy to remind me of Benedict—Zoska had never seen the flowers, the dogs had prevented me plucking one for her. Smiling wryly, I put the scarf on.

"You look very eligible," she said and kissed me.

"Honey-apple," said the repeating machine.

"Come on," I said. "Let's buy one for her."

Outside the little street was bustling with womyn, some carrying flowers and all smiling.

"What's this?" I said to nobody in particular and a passing softcore replied:

"Party in the main square. To celebrate!"

We strolled towards square and Hive, infected by the festive mood. A junior Scout dashed by, came to a dead stop, twirled round and gaped at me. Recovering, she ran off in the opposite direction and returned with two giggling girlfriends, and the Watch Chief.

"Lay off," I said, embarrassed.

"Well," said the Chief, "you are nicely turned out."

"For the books," I muttered.

"Doesn't she look fine?" said Zoska.

"My word yes. Almost unrecognizeable."

I clenched my fists behind my back, momentarily regretting that all my rowdiness must be past. To my annoyance, the Watch Chief fell into step with us, chatting to Zoska about weddings:

"I cried and cried when my eldest . . ."

"Honey-apple," said the tireless Basienka.

"Soon, when we reach the square," I said. The Watch Chief bent close to me:

"We whitewashed your graffiti."

"Censorship."

"It benefits you. Marthe was turning cartwheels every time she passed it."

"What a sight. Well, thank-you."

But she was not finished yet:

"One of my lasses let in Bea this morning with a message for Marthe. From Grania."

She eyed me, awaiting the reaction.

"How nice," I said blithely. Maybe it was the festival ambience, but I felt as if I was riding the crest of a wave, which would not suddenly dump me in a welter of foam and sand. We were nearly at the square now, its proximity marked by music, the whiff of intoxicant, and thankfully for the little girl clasping my hand, a sticky-sweet smell.

"There you are, persistent child," said Zoska. "Raffy, do you want one?"

"Not in these clothes."

The Watch Chief had already, incongruously, been tempted by the confection.

In a procession of four, and attracting more womyn in our wake, hardcores, softcores, stray lovers, friends and the curious, we crossed the square to the Hive, our sunken fortress. The girl on guard was unexpectedly confronted by her superior, sticky.

"Tell Marthe she has visitors," said the Chief.

We waited, the crowd jostling and muttering around us. After a suitable delay, the door at the foot of the ramp opened and Marthe, flanked by the two hardcore Elders, ascended.

"Greetings, Raphael Grania," she said formally.

"Greetings, Marthe Maria," I replied, tit for tat.

I saw her gaze roll down my attire, but being as good an actor as Grania, she made no verbal nor physical comment.

"I have received a verse letter from Grania Erato. It commends our alliance."

Behind me, I heard Zoska intake breath in gleeful surprise and then let it out slowly, as if she would have liked to whoop. Several of the rowdier Scouts actually cheered, and this was picked up by the young, the noisy and the disaffected. It was in the end an impressive sound, threatening even. Marthe suddenly looked and I think felt, vulnerable.

"I am, of course, honoured to communicate with the great poet."

And mediocre parent, I thought.

"Having long admired her verse, I am pleased—my words can't express how much—to be given a holograph sample of it."

And to be the subject of it, I thought. Vanity! I could tell her it was no pleasure.

"For some reason," she added, her tone changing, "it's called *To a Fellow Widow Twankey*."

She looked flustered, and the crowd, equally puzzled, was silent.

"I never understand all her allusions," I said quickly, well-knowing Grania's dangerous humour. "Marthe Maria! Has my mother's intervention changed your mind?"

She regained a little of her dark composure.

"The Elders have informed me that in a day of such celebration, Hive cannot be off-limits. In view of that, the letter, and other factors . . ."

She looked pointedly at someone behind me, from the opposite faction of hardcores, I presumed.

"I have no choice but to withdraw the prohibition."

Zoska hugged me, releasing Basienka, who for some time had been tugging at her mother's hand. Seizing the opportunity, she ran down the ramp and through the slit of door held open by the Watchgirl. There were stairs behind that door—Zoska looked over my shoulder and screamed. The guard started and let the door clang shut.

There was a moment of agony and then the door opened slowly again. My Honey came out cradling my foster-sister.

Beautiful Honeycomb! I wanted to shout it, but that would have ruined everything. Instead I stood silent as a doll, watching Basienka offer Honey some of her apple. Honey, smiling, took a bite and the crowd went:

"Ooh!"

"Little scene-stealer," muttered Zoska. She walked halfway down the ramp and collected the baby. Marthe took *her* baby by the hand for a moment: goodbye. Then we faced each other, with no womyn between us.

"Get a move on," yelled somebody.

So, shyly, we met at the top of the ramp and kissed. The ghetto cheered and we parted, half-embarrassed by the noise. Her lips had tasted sweet from the candied fruit.

"Honeymouth," I said.

"Yes, that is her name,' said her mother. "Honey Marthe."

And I laughed, and Honey laughed, and it was all right.

THE LOTTERY

Imagine a small boat on a prehistoric sea. Imagine also, within it: a complex sculpture, part metal, part translucent scoops and tubing, occupying the prow; amidships, equipment and supplies, including a diving suit of a size to fit a small adult of the species *Homo sapiens*; and finally in the stern the time-traveller herself. She leans back idly, one hand on the tiller, as the boat moves through the shallow waters off the ancient continent Laurentia.

The motor of the craft is shockingly loud. There are few of the habitual seasounds here—no gull cries, for the evolution of birds, let alone their ancestors the dinosaurs, and before them the reptiles, is millions of years in the future. The coastline behind the traveller is bare rock, in a state of volcanic flux. The only life on earth is below the water; and it is mute.

The traveller considers names. Here she is, over five hundred million years in her planet's past, and the geological term for this era is the Upper Cambrian, literally Upper Welsh, from the location of the first rocks from this time to be scientifically described by her species. Thus an age predating humans, predating language, predating nationalism, received the latinized name of ancient Wales.

Sweating in the hot sun, she checks her location. Currently she is travelling above what will be called the Rocky Mountains, but which now are submerged in a tropical sea, close to the equator of Cambrian earth. She glances around, looking for a line of breaking waves, and finds it—a reef, at the dividing point between the wide lagoon and the open sea.

She approaches the whitecaps, and at a break in the reef edges her craft through. Puttering cautiously along parallel to the waveline, she scans the dark, distant shore, then consults her maps and instruments again. Here is the spot marked X, her goal. She stops the motor, and heaves the anchor overboard.

The boat rests, rocking slightly, the only sound the soft wash of the waves. The traveller stretches, then moves towards the machine in the prow. As she does so, a splash, small, very close, makes her glance over the side of the craft.

What she sees is a small bug-eyed creature, the size and roughly the shape of a mouse, floating on its back just below the surface. "Sarotrocerus," she breathes, "brushtail"—for this life form was named for its long tail, which ends in a cluster of spines. As she watches, it flicks the tail, darting under the boat in pursuit of some smaller prey.

She glances longingly at her diving gear but returns to the scoops and tubing of the machine. Finally satisfied that all is in working order, she opens the drawstrings of a bag, to reveal a host of small red balls, lotto balls. They are not marked with numbers; rather, each bears a pictograph in black, a silhouette of a strange, tiny creature. She takes a handful, three balls full, which she inspects for a moment, rolling them around her palm. "Waptia," she says aloud. "Opabinia. Wiwaxia." All three are named in Amerindian, from the names of mountains near where their remains were excavated. She dribbles these balls into the machine, then lucky dips in the bag, her hand emerging with a ball showing a spiky monster. She grins. "Sanctacaris," she says. "Santa Claws." This animal was named by a paleontologist with a sense of humour.

When all the balls are in the machine, each a representation and thus representative of all the life forms known on Cambrian earth, she hunkers back for a moment. She is about to replicate an experiment that took place on this planet over millions of years, in which a cosmic lottery, involving movements of continents, glaciation, and meteorites, determined which species would be fruitful and multiply, and which would decline and ultimately become extinct.

Imagine the tree of life, although the evolution of a tree is millions of years in the future. No, imagine instead the sponges and algae growing on the ocean floor beneath the traveller. They branch upwards from a single stem, broad at the base, then tapering towards a single leaf at the apex. There is more genetic diversity, more branches on the evolutionary tree in the water beneath the boat, than there is on the whole of the traveller's earth, with its birds, fishes, insects, plants, fungi, Uncle Tom Cobley and all. But with time, branches die, the index of possibilities becomes increasingly more limited, trilobites vanish, so do dinosaurs, until, 530 million years later, the range of species on the planet represents only a bare handful of those living and breeding in the Paleozoic era, the age of the oldest life on earth.

Can the outcome of the cosmic lotto be predicted? The traveller intends to find out, by asking her assemblage of balls and scoops: which species will dominate the future Earth?

The first stage is to discover who will survive the Cambrian era. She moves levers, presses buttons, and the machine hums into action, rattling the balls through the tubes, sorting and selecting, by chance, naturally. Balls are spat out, to go into the draw for the next evolutionary round. She catches them in her hand before dropping them into the bag. Sanctacaris. Ottoia, a worm. But little Sarotrocerus, the aquatic mouse with the spiky tail, fails to emerge.

With a feeling of regret at the loss of that happy swimmer, she discards the other balls and moves onto the next round. 200 million years ago, and the Paleozoic era is ending, along with 95% of the species on earth. Only a handful of balls are still in the game. Triassic, Jurassic, Cretaceous eras pass, along with dinosaurs, the therapsids (ancestors of mammals), woolly mammoths and sabre-toothed tigers. She has, in her palm, all the Cambrian ancestors of the life existing on her version of earth, the homo sapien's earth.

"Who will inherit?" she asks, and puts the balls through again. Only one emerges, and she stares at the form depicted on it, before saying: "Pikaia."

Her ancestor, her humble ancestor. She did not really expect a bizarre Cambrian alternative, like Opabinia—five eyes, and a frontal nozzle like the hose of a vacuum cleaner, except with fangs—but to find Lady Luck repeating herself, replicating the cosmic lotto, slightly shocks her. But she soon recovers. Before travelling back in time to her own era she has other work to do.

It is pleasant work, she thinks, as she dons her diving gear. She sits on the side of the boat for a moment, watching the sunlight on the waves. Then she dives down, following the anchor chain to the ocean floor. The reef is atop a submarine escarpment, and its vertical walls, some 200 metres in height, are adorned with brightly coloured sponges and algae, an enchanted garden. Something seems missing and she realises it is the fishes, for vertebrates have yet to evolve. But there is plenty of movement, though tiny, for most life on this earth is no longer than a few inches.

Most life, but not all. Something nuzzles her leg, and she twists around, thinking of sharks, only to see staring at her malevolently the predator Anomalocaris, at a metre long the largest Cambrian life form. Imagine utter weirdness, odd elements of other creatures jumbled together in a surreal mix: a swimmer like a ray, but with compound, stalked eyes, armed with huge spiny claws, above a circular mouth lined with teeth.

It circles her, claws opening and closing, and worse, that mouth too contracting, as if it munches her already. She turns to face the menace, at the same time trying to gauge whether it is alone, or hunts in company. One claw grabs at her— she dodges behind the anchor chain, and Anomalocaris clasps metal for the first and last time. She remembers now a small speargun up in the boat, included for emergencies like this. Fool! she admonishes herself.

It lunges at her again, and she feints with one arm. The claws reach up to rend and tear her unprotected hand. *Now* she kicks out, her foot striking the monster in its abdomen. The force of the blow tumbles it head over tail almost down to the sea bed, mantle flapping wildly. Then, stabilising, Anomalocaris beats a hasty retreat—it is a coward.

Wary of another Anomalocaris, she gazes around. The water is very clear, visibility good even at this depth, and she sees that the ocean floor teems with life. She recognises Opabinia, like a minute nightmare, and others, their forms mostly suggesting ragged claws. She swims above them for a closer look, and abruptly encounters a troupe of Marella, creatures like a cross between a trilobite and a lace doily. They balance gracefully on thin, delicate legs, their feelers and long feathery gills moving slowly, possibly even rhythmically, as if they are dancing in the ocean current. As she approaches they flee.

She shakes her head, glances at her watch, then begins to search the ocean floor for a particular trail. The mud here is unstable, prone to slides, so she digs carefully. Even if her ball game replicated the Cosmic Lotto result—Vertebrates Rule, OK?—her instructions are to make *quite sure*. Thus she seeks her distant ancestors in the Cambrian mud. They are not numerous, but after an hour's work, her collecting jar is full.

Back in the boat, she sets her specimens carefully in the shade of the lotto machine and starts the motor again, travelling southwards along the coastline. The day is beginning to wane, and she steers tensely, checking her watch often. The nth time she does this, a faint disturbance passes through the water. The boat pitches, and an instrument by her foot beeps, displaying a tiny array of flashing lights.

She grimaces at these signs of a minor earthquake, recalling the sloping ocean floor back at her collecting site. A mudslide has caught the weird, elegant creatures, carrying them in a roiling cloud down to deeper, oxygen-poor water. There, by a million to one chance, the small, complex bodies, will be preserved, soft and hard parts almost intact, within the geologist's delight her species calls the Burgess Shale.

She relaxes a little as the boat travels further away, into a region of Laurentia more geologically sound. It is close to the end of the tropical day when she stops again, and taking the jar, dives down to the Cambrian sea floor for the last time. This habitat is less densely populated; there are no Anomalocaris, no Santa Claws; in fact, hardly any predators at all. An ideal location, then, to release an inoffensive herbivore.

She opens the jar, and shakes her specimens out. The meek will inherit the earth—and you could hardly get anything more meek than Pikaia. Two creatures like fat slugs fall to the ocean floor and immediately burrow into the mud. There is nothing distinguished or distinctive about them, except that down their backs runs the notochord, the forerunner of the spine. Pikaia are the ancestral vertebrates.

"So long Adam," she mouths. "So long Eve."

Above water again, she finds that she has missed the sunset, and tropical night is falling like a shutter. Swearing to herself—for once her task is done, her orders are not to linger like a tourist, but return to the machine that brought her here—she removes her diving suit. As she does the moon rises, and she sees that its face is almost smooth and youthful. That is one wonder, but another is that, as the sea darkens, phosphorescence appears, patterns of light dancing on the water. She could watch it all night, but reluctantly she scans the horizon for the yellow pulsing beacon of her time machine, safe where she left it on the prehistoric beach.

She sees a light—but the beam is paler, constant, and moves above the surface of the water. A Cambrian precursor of the flying fish, she wonders, not recorded in the Burgess Shale? Then she puts her hands to her mouth, realising that the light moves too fast to be organic, far less anything belonging to this prehistoric Earth.

It nears, and she turns, frantically searching among her pile of supplies. Weapons, she thinks wildly, I need weapons—but the outfitters of her boat have provided her with only the speargun, of limited range, for they anticipated nothing larger than Anomalocaris. Nonetheless she grasps it tightly, standing defiantly beside the lotto machine.

Now she can see below the light a craft bigger than hers, and stranger—like a vessel seen through a distorting mirror. Shipbuilding from hell, she thinks: from the hull up everything is alien. Where are the crew? And as she wonders this, a mass she had assumed to be part of the structure moves. It is white, bulky, topped with a featureless round head—a figure not in the least humanoid.

"Who?" she yells. "Who are you?" There is no reply. Water churns as the intruding ship alters course, silently circling her smaller craft, like Anomalocaris, she thinks. Infuriatingly, it never comes within range of her spear, but it still is close enough for her to see equipment piled in it, of a function she cannot begin to guess at, and at the back a tank, of some translucent material, through which can be glimpsed traces of motion. For a moment a large claw is visible, as if—bizarrely—waving at her.

The bulbous head regards her blankly, quite impenetrable. She thinks now that the uncanny visitor is wearing a protective suit, with helmet and visor, but cannot be sure. The circuit completed, the craft moves briefly away from her, then stops. The sea water settles, then the figure moves to the end of the craft, busying itself incomprehensibly—until the tank rolls over, tipping into her safe Pikaia habitat a full load of Sanctacaris and Anomalocaris.

Even before the predators hit water she responds, jerking the motor into action. With a great flurry and racket she speeds away, leaving a trail of choppy darkness in the phosphorescence. Her hair blows behind her, near standing on end. Not only humans can cheat, she thinks. Whoever they may be—descendents of Opabinia, Naraoia?—they're altering the probabilities, ensuring the succession of their own ancestral line once Pikaia is removed. I've got to get out of here, back to the time machine.

She glances back once, at the receding light, then forward, intently scanning the coastline. There, faintly at first, then shining more strongly, is the signal, *on, off, on, off*, of her machine.

"Here I come!" she yells.

As if in response, the light pulses brighter, then suddenly winks out. She stares, waiting, but the mass of land remains black. Aghast and disbelieving, she stops the craft and checks her instruments, drawing another blank. There is no sign, visually or electronically, of the machine that would have taken her home.

The boat rocks in the Cambrian sea, the motion increasingly gentle, as if lulling a cradled child to sleep. She sits numbly, then suddenly becomes aware of water at her feet. Glancing down, she finds light at the bottom of the craft, a shallow sealet of phosphorescence. Slowly it rises, covering her ankles. Simultaneously she notices the scoops and tubing of her lotto machine becoming hazy, indistinct. And now it seems that her hands are fading, too. She lifts one above her head, and the Cambrian moon shines through flesh and bone.

They've won, she thinks, whoever they are. Pikaia has gone, and without it I can't exist, not on Cambrian earth, nor in its future. She feels no anger at her disinheriting, only a brief curiosity at the form the alien earth will take. It soon passes, leaving her resigned and calm.

The boat is slowly filling with water, not so much sinking as dissolving into the sea. She thinks that of all extinctions, the Burgess Shale fauna buried in mud, the mass asphyxiation at the close of the Palaeozoic era, the meteoric deaths of the dinosaurs, this is the most peaceful end, probably better than her species deserves. Now the water is bath-high and she leans backwards, floating in light. From her extremities inwards, she feels sensation go.

A sudden plash sounds near her, and langorously she turns her head to see Sarotrocerus, surfing on the gleaming waves.

"What will they name you, little fossil?" she says, her voice no more than a thread of sound, "the inheritors of this Earth?"

It seems to be looking at her, although the real interest, she suspects, is the small fry darting around her diffuse, fading form.

"Perhaps they will name you *Ancestor*," she adds, and with that faint whisper, the last human speech on the planet, finally disappears, leaving only a patch of clear Cambrian sea, and beside it a creature never to be called Sarotrocerus.

A TOUR GUIDE IN UTOPIA

I often start my day in a fug of unreality, but this was ridiculous. One minute, I was market shopping, next I witnessed an apparition: the thin polluted air swirled, and out stepped a girl my age. She looked like a Pre-Raphaelite pin-up—impossibly pallid and ethereal, her hair like a halo in the early morning sun— but with *intelligence*. As I watched, she blinked, focussing; then joyous surprise filled her face.

I glanced around, but the shoppers had taken no notice of this visitor. Someone else had—but Weasel the beggar, who lived in her own peculiar reality, merely had noted an easy mark. Instantly she insinuated herself through the crowd and into the stranger's company.

"Spare you two dollars?" the girl exclaimed. "But that's American currency! Have we been invaded?"

Weasel was momentarily thrown by that rejoinder, just long enough for me to intervene. As I did, a heavy bag in the arms of a man coming out of the fishmongers' split, and we were suddenly ankle-deep in whitebait. The girl took a step in her buttoned boots, but skidded; as if I was a romance hero, I offered her my arm. She accepted it, and I led her out of the fishy crush.

"Thank you, Sir," she said, releasing me.

I nodded in reply, wondering how to say that despite my cropped hair, jeans and Docs, I was a Ms. Moreover, I was acutely aware that her touch had felt glassy, unreal. She was corporeal, but somehow not quite there. The situation seemed uncannily familiar, as if I had read it in one of the musty, foxed, incredible books, that were the subjects of my thesis. And then I knew that I had.

My life was currently dominated by Catherine Helen Spence, Henrietta Dugdale and many minor others, nineteenth-century women writers of a future perfect society, an Australian utopia. I had read, until anybody else would have revolted, of Victorian women transported by laudanum dreams, or on angel-back, or time machine, into their future, an idealised era bearing minimal resemblance to my own, imperfect twentieth-century. For me to encounter, as if sprung from the page, a fellow-traveller of theirs, seemed perfectly natural.

The visitor was watching Weasel milk the people exiting from the delicatessan. "I perceive that some things haven't changed," she commented sadly. "Yet I've never been asked for more than ha'pennies before. Sir, I must know—are we now part of an American Empire?"

I paused, eyeing the nearby MacDonald's. "Not *formally*. And I'm not a man either."

She regarded me admiringly. "How splendid that the teachings of the Rational Dress Association should prevail! There were so few at our picnics, where we felt very daring in knickerbockers."

Luckily she had her back to the girl in hotpants and platform boots.

I hesitated, then since it had to be asked, did so:

"Are you, like Henrietta Dugdale, spending *A Few Hours in a Far Off Age*?"

"A great work," she said, smiling. "I longed to do the same, but differently . . ."

"And you have," I said. "In reality. Shall we talk further, in a quieter place perhaps?"As we crossed the road a tram passed, and she stopped in not only her tracks, but those of the tram coming from the opposite direction, until I dragged her to safety. "Exquisite, your modern transport!" she enthused, as I led her into the cafe I thought least likely to give her future shock.

She declined refreshment, but I ordered strong coffee, feeling in need of it, for she was now in an alarming state of excitement, squirming as if she had ants under her long skirt. The businessman at the next table took one look, then hid behind his newspaper. I was suddenly transfixed by its date: December 4 1993.

"You're Futura," I said.

She looked at me evenly. "My name is Ida Pemberton. Futura is a pseudonym, used for my little poems in *The Worker*."

I knew I had to tread carefully here. "Futura" had written the minor but intriguing "A Century From To-Day", a short story published in the *Worker*. It had been several chapters back since I had discussed the tale, and it had receded in my memory. Yet I could remember the specific date of Futura's day in utopia.

As if she could read my mind, she also glanced at the paper.

"Fancy! Exactly 100 years since Mr Radvansky suggested an evening of mesmerism."

It was slowly coming back to me that the narrator of "A Century" had been hypnotized . . .

"After he had waved his pendulum at me, I felt a sleepiness, from which I opened my eyes to find myself coiled around the gasalier, looking down at my pale, still form. I had a great sense of freedom, that I could go wherever I wanted, unfettered by the constraints of an earthly, girlish body. So I decided to visit the future."

My coffee arrived and she eyed it disinterestedly. "If I ate," she remarked, "would I be a Persephone, unable to return?"

I was wishing I could recall more of "A Century", which I now knew to be not fiction, but reportage, so that I had some inkling of what this unpredictable prophetess would do next. "You do return to 1893, I assure you," I replied.

"And to renown, I assume," she said happily. "Else how would you know my pseudonym?"

I hesitated, not wanting to say that only a specialist would have read Futura's solitary story. But she had become distracted by the passing marketeers:

"Oh brave new world that has such people in it!" she said, tears in her eyes. "We hoped so much for a better world, my friends and I . . ."

A world, I thought, where women voted, where no child lived in poverty (hum!), where the rich did not oppress the poor (hum again!), where education was a right and not a privilege (triple hum). I knew the dreams of the utopianists all too well. But, before I could become emotional myself, she had taken hold of my hand, entreating: "Please show me your wonderful time."

Vaguely I remembered that Futura had in her story, like many writers of the future, a native guide. Yet never could I have imagined that this useful person was Muggins me.

"Delighted!" I lied. My quiet day of thesis-writing would just have to be postponed.

The short walk back to my car was murder, for everything was new to her and she dawdled like a two-year old. Her first ride in an "automobile" left her awestruck and silent all the way back to my flatlet. After I stowed my shopping, we did a guided tour, of which the highlight, unexpectedly, was the toilet. Once I demonstrated the flush, she had to do it herself, repeatedly. Giggles and rushing water resounded through the flat as I took the opportunity to dash into the study for my photocopy of "A Century". It eluded me and I was about to re-read my critique of it in the thesis, when she reappeared.

"A future treasure!" she said brightly. "Unlike your maid, who's scamped the bathtub."

I forbore to mention that the slattern in question was myself and switched off my "typewriter run by electrickery", as she called the computer. Without guidance from the story, I would have to create my own tour itinerary for Futura, traveller from that foreign country, the past. Without thinking, I turned on the radio for the weather report.

"Well I never!" she said. "A newspaper, read aloud by an invisible spirit."

Words failed me at the prospect of explaining telecommunications, but she did not question me, listening intently to the bulletin. "Such strange placenames!" she said. "I thought I knew my geography, being a postmistress, but I am an ignoramus here."

It was an oddly benign bulletin, no bad news, except near the end, when I switched off at the mention of Bosnia. There were no wars in utopia, I recalled. What there were though, invariably, were institutes of learning . . .

"Our next stop," I said, "will be the University!"

It had existed in Futura's time and as we parked in sight of the familiar Gothic towers she nodded in recognition, rather curtly. When we entered the grounds she began to laugh uncontrollably.

"Oh, how delightful! To turn it into a Ladies' Seminary."

The fashion of the male students around us tending towards faux hippie, the mistake was understandable; and she soon noticed enough conventional lads to correct it slightly. But her glee remained. "I never came here," she confided. "My dunce of a brother did, because he was the only son."

We toured the library and the computer centre, where the sight of a girl at an open access terminal, busy typing a creative writing exercise (Futura sneaked a peek) made my companion sigh. "I had to hide my poems from Mamma. She tore them up, lest brainwork rot my womb."

"A phallusy," I said. To prove it, I made our next stop a Feminist bookshop, filled wall to wall with women's brainwork. She stroked the spines with their myriad Ursulas, Germaines, and Susans, then shyly asked the saleswoman:

"Do you have any Futura?"

Oh no, I thought, but the bookseller, not wanting to admit ignorance, saved the day.

"Not at the moment," she boomed. "But any Wimmins' book you want, we can order in."

"Thank you," said Futura.

And so our day passed, Futura's visit entirely in keeping with the utopias we had both read, texts edifying rather than thrilling, for perfection precludes adventure. I drove out to the airport, where a 747's take-off made Futura dance on the spot with delight; transported her on trains and trams; narrowly prevented her walking, all unawares, into a Sex Shop; and even showed her the most up-to-date gadgets of her time displayed as museum pieces.

All my thesis texts were from the viewpoint of the visitant, never from that of the visited, so I had never known that it was bloody hard work being a tour guide in Utopia. Trying to stave off exhaustion, I overreached myself. "How about Parliament?" I said, as we left the Museum; she nodded, still enthusiastic. Short-cutting, I took her through Chinatown, where she goggled in dismay:

"The yellow peril!"

"Ssh!"

"There's so many of them," she said, bewildered. I speeded up, trying to get into a more Caucasian area of town before we got into trouble. She trotted behind me, protesting: "Australia doesn't need their disease and opium."

From the frying pan to the fire, I thought, as I espied, unmistakeable in their Mabo t-shirts and red-black-yellow headbands, a group of—

"Darkies!" she exclaimed. "They shouldn't be here. Inferior races can't face Progress, everyone knows that. All we can do is smooth the dying pillow . . ."

The nearest Koorie raised his eyes heavenward.

"Well, they are here, in your future, my present, so you can just put up with it!" In the general direction of these original inhabitants of Australia, I yelled: "I apologise for my friend." There was no response, and I continued on, too angry to speak, although I had read far worse examples of nineteenth-century racism.

Futura lagged behind me, still arguing: "You didn't need to say sorry, they don't have feelings like we do."

You and John Bloody Howard, I thought. "Another word and I won't take you to see female Parliamentarians!"

She shut up, looking annoyed, an expression slowly superseded by joyous anticipation. "To think of women here!" she said as we walked up the carpeted stairs to the Visitor's Gallery. At the sight of the House in Session, I suddenly realized my mistake: rows of sombre suits confronted us, relieved only intermittently by the brighter plumage of the female MPs.

"Why so few?" she said. I looked away, ashamed, then brightened as a figure in red took the Parliamentary floor.

"Look, a woman Minister!"

"Never!" Her voice rose in anger. She had, I could tell, addressed a few public meetings in her time. "No respectable woman dyes her hair!" It was rather a lurid gold. "And her face! She's a painted harlot!"

The Minister had been called many things, from fake man to Thatcher clone, but this remark, clearly audible across the chamber, made the Opposition males snigger, and her dulcet tones faltered. What happened next I don't know, for we were unceremoniously hustled out of Parliament by the Security staff.

On the Parliament steps we sat, Futura weeping softly into her skirt. I watched the day wane, and the stream of lights from the rush hour traffic, wondering when to interrupt her grief. But she did it herself, suddenly sitting up straight, one last tear falling onto the granite, where it slid away like mercury.

"They're beginning to revive me from the trance," she said. She stood, composing herself. "Forgive me. Your world is stranger than I can comprehend."

The air around her began to eddy.

"Goodbye," she said. "I thank you, gracious guide."

I felt embarrassed. "Aw, it was nothing." She smiled, her widest grin yet, and then—vanished.

I reached out, and touched only air. "Don't go," I murmured, too late. I had wanted to thank her too, for my edifying, tiring, marvellous day with a C19th feminist. I couldn't use a skerrick of it in my thesis, but now I knew exactly what my subjects had been like.

Back home I finally located my copy of "A Century," and read it ravenously. The narrative stopped after the Museum visit, with the coy phrase: "And there was much more, which I cannot tell, lest I fatigue the *Worker's* readers." Or shock them, I thought cynically, as Futura had been shocked by multiculturalism and painted lady MPs. Otherwise it was all there—Futura's ever-helpful guide, the university, the airport—but seen through a rosy distorting mirror. My present, as coloured by 1890s idealism, the limits of Futura's perceptions, and my inept explanations, was recognisable, but impossibly benevolent.

Yet she told her tale well, and I wondered, as I had on first reading the "story", why she hadn't published more. Now, though, I had more than a pseudonym, but the author's real name. A nasty suspicion nagged at me; I recalled how unhealthy the Pre-Raphaelite lasses had been. Might Futura's otherworldly appearance have been due to more than mesmeric projection? A trip to the genealogy archives confirmed it: looking at the Register of Deaths, 1894, under P for Pemberton, I found Ida May, dead of tuberculosis at 26.

Poor Futura, I thought on the way home, never to have a brilliant career, never to see women's suffrage. But then it occurred to me that she had not lived to have her optimism destroyed by Stalin, or

Hitler, or the A-bomb. I glanced up, startled at this thought, to see a news-stand, with its tidings of overpopulation, ozone depletion, ecological disaster, our future dystopia.

"Oh lucky Ida," I cried, "to have the dream of a hopeful future!"

ROBOTS & ZOMBIES, INC.

EDITOR'S NOTE. *The following was transcribed from a tape, clearly record of interview, mailed from a fictitious address in Uzbekistan (we checked) to the Oakland PO Box of ConspiracyTheory. com. The quality of the tape is poor, with obvious miking problems at the time of recording. The interviewee is audible, but his interviewers little more than mumble, even with digital enhancement. Such would suggest an amateur recording, rather than that of an experienced journalist or police professional. But we see no reason to doubt its authenticity.*

My name? Well, there's two of them. George Washington Reynolds, also Donald McIvor Smith, depending which passport I was using. Such happens when you get split.

Same birthdate for both: 11/01/51. Fake, of course.

Ditto the birthplaces. Reynolds was Nutley, NJ. Smith, some godforsaken Scottish New Town.

We had each other, a necessary narcissism. And for back story, Reynolds had a wife, 2 kids, and a rottweiler, somewhere out beyond Langley, VI. Smith was less complicated—or so I thought. Gay. Kept gerbils. That's unexceptional in the British Secret Service.

The cover was various Spooky actions. It got strange at times. Like when I was acting Liaison Officer between the US & UK secret services, which meant liaising with . . . myself. No, nobody ever noticed. But just to be on the safe side, after that Smith went bald.

The first time I came to Tashkent was in 1975. An urgent security meeting of Mammelia Corp. My real employers.

Yes, that was also my first murder.

Well, what would *you* do with jetlag, the latest in concealed weaponry, and a jetlagged hippie earbashing you in the transit lounge about Giant Extraterrestrial Lizards mindcontrolling the world's leaders?

I later found out it was a genuine cult. Shame it was a little too close to the truth.

I blamed the KGB and just forgot about the murder, until now. Look, I had other things to worry about. Like eliminating the Soviets.

They were nearly onto Mammelia, that's why. After Tashkent we knew we had to get the Subjects into place and pronto.

Subject A had actually been a sleeper for some time. A back-up model, just in case. For a model blown up by the IRA, half our luck.

Yes, Subject A was experimental, and given to transmogrification. I did know about the sudden change of sex. Apparently it happened spontaneously.

Mammelia's British Office had to go and completely rework the back story. Including the spouse, Denise. She took it rather well, except for the time Smith sang Blondie's 'Dénis, Denise' *sotto voce* to her during an NATO reception. Burst into tears, and said she'd preferred being a woman, unlike Mal, I mean Mags.

The Office gossip was their sex had gone pear-shaped.

Oh, that was nothing compared with Subject B, Ronald Reagan. He only went and died in the middle of the Presidential election campaign.

Of course Mammelia revived him, nobody had thought to split a copy. What a pro, what a ham, even when dead meat. Knew his lines, well, at first. Projected avuncular warmth whilst stony cold.

No, that was rouge. Without it he looked like death warmed up.

My role as Reynolds was spindoctoring, everything from Chile to Gorby. Then Ollie North showed up.

No, I still don't know who North was working for. The competion was kinda nebulous at that stage. But I knew big trouble when I saw it.

I requested an immediate transfer. Ended up in the Canada office. Boring as batshit. But safe.

No, Reynolds never was on the team running Reagan. Nobody with any sense did. Of smell—he whiffed of the mortuary.

Yes, that's why they kept him a safe distance from the White House Press Corps in his later years. He was visibly deteriorating, and not only in memory.

The finger in the soup incident is perfectly true. Luckily it happened in front of the Australian Prime Minister, who was too drunk to notice.

Yes, he actually ate it.

As Smith I was in and out of Downing Street. Hands on. Unlike Reagan, Mags couldn't act for toffee apples. Completely synthetic.

The word Simulcra was never used by Mammelia. Officially the term was Subject, unofficially, Robot. Only R&D were so crass as actually to say Meatbot.

I heard they spliced in some components from an earlier prototype, a 1950s British Nanny. Without it Mags didn't know if she was Arthur or Martha. After that she at least crossed her legs when wearing skirts.

Came to terms with it eventually. Said it helped being ex-male, she knew how their minds worked, and they didn't expect her to think the same way. That's devious . . .

The beauty was the Brits got so fazed by a woman in power they couldn't spot Mags' total unreality.

Yes, they had the Queen, but she couldn't act either. Completely robotic, even though natural. Indubitably.

I beg your pardon. Smith had *nothing* to do with the Diana model. Another experiment—Helen of Troy was the working title. Quite prophetic, as without someone riding shotgun 24/7 she was way-out wayward. I think the Brit. branch of Mammelia never quite got things right. They deserved to be liquidated.

No, actually turned into liquid and recycled in the vats. Smith was in Paris by then, cleaning up the Diana mistake. He had the wit to move sideways when Mags managed a second transmogrification. Into a good actor, convincing even, as she fought for her political life.

Didn't work. After politics Mags went onto the lecture circuit. I heard somebody high up in Mammelia finally got jack of her and pulled the plug. Head first into the lectern, time to retire, girl. At least Reagan had the grace to zombify in a rest home.

Late 1990s. The times were a-changing, I could smell it. Like Reagan's decomposition.

The order came from Mammelia Central: splice time! I think that's when things really started going downhill.

Reynolds and Smith met in the Canaries, spent a week in a very exclusive health farm, and I emerged, whole again.

No, it was horrid. Smith had developed a taste for exotic rough trade, and had decided on the ultimate deniability: memory wipe. The sorta thing you see all the time now in politics. He had his done on the cheap, and it showed. Every time I got anywhere near a dodgy memory, I got an instant migraine.

Mammelia put me on light duties. Bloody Canada again.

If I'd known about Smith's affair with the Jihad mole, I'd never have agreed to a Middle East transfer.

What can I say? I was sitting in a bar in Cairo, and the pest from Tashkent reappeared. Still rattling on about giant lizards thought-controlling the world.

Of course I thought he was a split. In the world I live in, the coincidence was too big to be believed.

So I killed him. How was I to know he was natural—my original victim's identical twin brother? And vice-prez of the conspiracy theory cult, which now had a worldwide membership. Even in Uzbekistan, I can see.

I blamed the KGB again. Bad idea.

Because things were different. The Soviets had gone, but the Russian Mafia were picking up where they'd left off. Strange alliances were being made, between bedfellows odder than Smith and his gerbils.

I found myself bound and gagged, on a cargo flight back to Tashkent.

Yes, I know it's called rendition. But if you tried to torture all my secrets out of me, I'd just disintegrate. I'm made that way.

Does it really satisfy your paranoid fantasies that the world isn't run by giant telepathic lizards, but much worse? Well?

Since you ask, Mammelia is finished. The competition's simply too strong. And it's not just the Bush family franchise. They're probably finished too.

I can point to anywhere in the world and show you little Mammelias. Outrageous copies, of course. But slowly perfecting the business of Robots & Zombies, Inc.

THE LIPTON VILLAGE SOCIETY

FOR RENT: flatlet in Gothic Horror folly. Suit tenant with taste for weird architecture and/or sense of humour. Must be quiet. Apply V. Hirst, Times Gone Books, Hirst Building.

"I'm sorry about it, but there it is," said V. (call me Vini) Hirst. "Great Uncle William went a bit funny in his old age. He'd been a builder all his life, and he just got sick of ordinary architecture."

"Yes. It's the first time I've seen minarets and battlements combined."

"What was your name again?" he asked.

"Susan Gifford. I'm a Research Officer for the Department of Education."

"Shouldn't be too noisy," he muttered. Vini was interviewing me in his antiquarian bookshop, which occupied the ground floor of Uncle William's aberration.

"The interior doesn't seem too bad," I hazarded.

"It's not. I live on the top floor, with Rover—that's the cat. Being inside Hirst Building means you don't have to look at it. I pity the neighbours—no I don't. They ostracised poor Uncle William."

He gestured out of the front window at the tidy Parkville terrace opposite, painted and renovated in tedious good taste. Then he shrugged, and turned back to me.

"I suppose you want to see the wee flat."

"Yes, if I'm going to live there."

He smiled, and I smiled back. Vini Hirst was an agreeable enough man, in his late forties I supposed, with freckles and shaggy grey hair. He was agile too, as he demonstrated with a quick scuttle up the steep stairs behind the shop.

A peculiarity of the flatlet was that it opened off a large room, which was unfurnished except for a cedar chest in one corner. Otherwise, the rooms-for-rent were conventional, if having one surprising omission.

"Where's the bathroom?" I asked.

"Downstairs, behind the bookshop. It comes in handy with dirty books, I mean dirt of ages, not pornography. You can't serve a customer when you've dirty paws."

"I imagine you can't. Nonetheless, an outside bathroom is inconvenient."

"I'll take ten bucks off the rent."

"Done."

Even without this deduction, the cost of inhabiting Hirst Building was very moderate.

"Great. You look a suitable tenant . . . are you well paid?"

"Reasonably."

"Then why live here?"

"It's unusual lodging for a public servant."

He laughed. "I know what you mean. I used to be in the Ed line myself, before I inherited Hirst Building."

We stepped into the empty room again, and I glanced around admiringly. Vini remarked:

"I let this room to a dancing class, but the noise—Madame taught tap—upset the customers."

"Nice chest."

"The Lipton Village Society found it at a rubbish dump. They use this room for meetings, but they're a quiet bunch, won't disturb you."

I shaped my lips for a question, but the bell jangled in the shop below, and Vini hurried downstairs.

I moved my worldly goods into Hirst Building, and found myself oddly happy, although with a nagging curiosity about the Lipton Village Society. Vini was evasive about the subject, and after a while I abandoned queries, preferring to experience the phenomenon first-hand. In bed early one night, nursing a nervous headache, I heard muffled laughter from the great room, and the sound of footsteps coming and going on the uncarpeted wooden floor. A few nights later, they arrived at sunset, just as I was preparing to take a bath. I hesitated, and then made a sortie outside my door, clad in a quilted dressing-gown and fluffy slippers. A group of nondescript young people were huddled around the chest in its lonely corner; they turned and stared at me.

"Hello," I said.

"Hello," said one small voice. They had not turned on the light, and were illuminated only by the dusk outside the lancet windows. It was impossible to tell who had spoken. I went downstairs and took a particularly long bath. On my return, they had gone.

My attempts at image-busting continued. I sent off a mail order to Altered States Incorporated (Eltham branch), and eventually received a flat box in a plain wrapper. It was filled with moist earth, from which a fine crop of magic mushrooms was guaranteed. I decided to use the bathroom as a fungarium; it was suitably warm and damp. Within a week, little white pustules broke through the brown mulch in the box. They were quite numerous, and I considered stocking the fridge and getting wrecked on hallucinogenic shores at my leisure. Then, before the first anticipated harvest, I was nearly sacked from the Department of Education. When I got home to Hirst Folly, I went straight to the bathroom, to the shower recess which Vini never entered, and gathered the entire crop.

Coming upstairs, with a briefcase in one hand and the other holding up a skirt filled with fungi, I received a visual shock. A huge sheet of coarse paper was spread on the floor of the empty room, and beside it were half a dozen pots of paint, placed neatly on a newspaper. They had been opened, and dripped livid colour. I dumped briefcase and mushrooms in my flat, and returned to investigate further. Someone had begun to paint a map, obviously a bad copy of the more garish Middle Earth posters.

I went calling for Vini and found him in his heaven. He was sitting behind the Times Gone counter, reading a rare old book, with Rover asleep in his lap.

"You let the room upstairs to a playschool or something?"

"Huh?" he said, with a little start. Rover opened her eyes and glared at him.

"There's a half-painted kiddie map in the big room."

"Ah yes," he said. "The Lipton Village Society." He added, half to himself, "I saw the pots of paint go up there, didn't think to ask what they were for."

"That's an adult's work?" I asked, with exaggerated incredulity.

Vini suddenly lost his temper.

"What's wrong with artistic expression, Miss, and particularly on the part of unemployed youth? I suppose you'd rather they vandalised trains!"

It was so unexpected, pacific Vini snapping at me, that I turned and went back to my flat, doubly depressed. I ate one raw mushroom then and there, but the taste was repulsive. So I consulted a recipe book and cooked French mushroom stew, with capsicums and white wine. I guzzled the lot, then lay down on my bed to await the coloured lights and music.

And that was all I could recollect when I awoke in discomfort, to find myself lying on wooden floorboards. My head was against a carved lump of wood; I recognised the cedar chest. My sensory input was disorganised and it was several moments before I became aware of three factors: it was early morning, there was a smell of vomit and a pair of heavy boots loomed large in my vision.

"Vini?"

"No," said a male voice. I rolled over, clutching my head, to see better the wearer of the boots. He was something of a surprise, for he wore jeans, a rusty black frock over the jeans, and a raincoat over the dress. Was he queer? Although I could not be sure, I reacted instinctively to the presence of a strange man, and glanced down to check that my neat office skirt decently covered my legs. It was then I discovered that some time in the night I had been sick down my blouse.

"D'you want a hand up?" he asked in a broad accent, northern suburbs I guessed.

I fingered the sticky frill on my collar, but let him take my free hand and pull me to my feet. My head whirled, and I closed my eyes. He walked me blind across the room, to the flat. In my stupor I had fortunately left the door open.

"Thank you. Let me go now."

I shut out the stranger and stripped, throwing my clothes into the wash basket. I noticed that my hands were smeared with paint—how very odd.

Mister Mysterioso (could it be that he had attended a fancy dress ball?) called through the door.

"It's pretty messy out here. You got cleanup things?"

"Yes," I said, and got dressed in an old sweater and pants I normally used for dirty housework. The floor-boards creaked; he appeared to be pacing up and down outside. I opened the door and handed him a bucket of hot water. He looked at me.

"You all right?"

"It's no worse than a hangover," I said, turning to pick up the rest of the cleaning agents. "Oh my god."

With my eyes closed, I had not seen that the great room had what used to be called a psychedelic decor. There were rivulets of garish pigment on the floor, spreading outwards from the map, which had a mountain of emptied paint tins dead centre. Streaks of colour leapt up the walls, apparently applied with the fingers, for there was a bright green palm print on one window. It looked like a kindergarten suddenly exposed to Jackson Pollock. I glanced at my fingers and was caught red- (plus green and blue and yellow) handed.

"I did that?"

"You did."

The map was obliterated now, the soggy paper even torn in places. For the first time, I looked properly at my companion and saw that he was very young, poverty-thin. Unemployed youth, Vini had said.

"Was this your painting? I'm so sorry."

The apology sounded banal, and he grimaced.

"No use crying over spilt paint. Let's clean this place up before Vini sees it and has a heart attack."

It took us an hour. At the end I made breakfast in my flat: coffee, cornflakes, toast and eggs. It was the sort of meal I might have served to an exceptionally good one night stand. I was too queasy myself to eat more than cornflakes with skim milk.

"Just what I needed," said the visitor. "I got a job interview in half an hour."

"Dressed like that?"

"I don't want it."

He was obviously enjoying the breakfast, and I felt a little of my guilt subside.

"What's your name?"

"Thursday October."

I was nonplussed but tried not to show it.

"I'm Susan Gifford."

"Yeah, Vini said he had a new tenant."

"You're a member of the Lipton Village Society?"

He nodded, mouth crammed.

"I'm sorry I defaced the map."

He swallowed. "You said that before. What were you on?"

"Mushies."

"Drugs ain't good for people. Are there any left?"

I nodded, puzzled, and led him out of the flat, down the stairs and into the bathroom. Altered States Incorporated certainly gave value for money—there was a fresh crop of baby hallucinogens. He trampled them under his big boots. Then he picked up the box and went upstairs again, this time trailing me like a string-pulled toy. However, he didn't stop at the empty room, with its damp floorboards, but continued ascending, to the second floor where Vini lived. I was still a little uncertain of my surroundings and lagged behind him, reaching the landing just as he knocked at the bookseller's door. It opened grudgingly, after a moment, to reveal V. Hirst unshaven, in deckchair pyjamas.

"Hi Thurs," Vini said weakly, and the Lipton Villager stepped inside, closing the door behind them. I sat on the top step and waited. A few minutes later Thursday October emerged, empty-handed.

"What did you do with it?" I asked, as we clattered down the stairs.

"Told Vini it was a cat-dunny for Rover. She's getting too old to climb out the window every time she wants a piss."

"Oh. There might still be germinating spores in that mulch."

"That's Rover's lookout."

We returned to the flat, where I made two more cups of coffee in a stunned fashion. He drank his down quickly and stood up.

"Well, I'll be off now. That was grouse."

I suddenly remembered I had to face work that morning and felt bitter.

"You getting rid of my mushrooms wasn't."

"I just think there's better things than drugs."

"Like what?"

He hesitated. "The Society."

"Very well, I'll join and see what it does for me."

He shook his head.

"Why not?"

He shrugged.

"We need artificial aids to stand up to reality." I said in what I hoped was a reasonable tone. "You might give me some inkling what yours is."

He glanced at his watch, at the door. "I'll be late."

"You could not arrive at all," I said, anxious to talk further with him, "which would have the desired effect."

"They cut off the dole if you don't interview," he said, very seriously. Then he appeared to make a decision.

"Look, give me the money for new paint and you can sit in at the meeting tonight. Here, 9 p.m. Then you'll understand."

"All right," I said, fumbling with my purse.

"See ya."

"See you."

The quorum of the Lipton Village Society was fairly low, for only five members were present that night. They were all as thin as Thursday October, who arrived minus the dress and quickly set about introductions.

"This is Strongarm." A puny boy.

"Jeri." He wore glasses and had a pale, intelligent face. I guessed he had some form of employment, for he was (literally) better heeled than the others.

"Linear." A girl, sporting the punk rocker's bleached blonde scalp.

"Goosegirl." He had a sullen expression.

"I'm Susan Gifford. That's not much of a name in comparison with yours."

They laughed uneasily. Thursday fished a key out of his jeans pocket and opened the padlock on the chest. I pointedly glanced away, lest I give the impression of being inquisitive. When I looked back he had closed the heavy wooden lid and sat with a square of paper in his lap. It was a sketch in crayon, a miniature template for the great map I had vandalised.

"Where's the painting?" asked Jeri.

I stared at the floor and noticed, with a feeling of mild horror, a lump of congealed blue paint in the crack between two floorboards. Thursday answered, to my relief, with a lie: "Me dole's late, and paint's bloody expensive."

"Did you complain?" asked Jeri.

"Burn down the dole office!" said Linear, in an unexpectedly little girl voice. I smiled at the contrast with her looks and received a glare from Goosegirl. He opened his mouth but Jeri spoke first: "I'll get the paint."

"Thanks but no thanks, mate," said Thursday. "I did a spot of work for Susan, and she paid me."

"Very nice," drawled Goosegirl, finally getting a word in, "but why bring her along to the meeting? What's she doing here?"

Thursday October told the truth this time.

"Seeing how people live without drugs."

He was still holding the sketch, and now he passed it to me, presumably as a cue for a change of subject.

"What is this map of?" I asked.

"Lipton Village," said Jeri.

"Where is it?"

"Not—here." That was Strongarm. "Not on the earth."

It was a strange story, told hugger-mugger, with one speaker interrupting another, so only in retrospect was I able to make it coherent.

"We were at school."

"Sunshine Tech."

". . . we hated it . . ."

". . . used to wag all the time . . ."

"Did you ever get threatened with a special purpose school?" I asked, interested.

"What's that?" said Strongarm.

"Somewhere to put dead-end kids and forget about them," said Thursday. "Yeah!"

"Oh, the truant school," said Jeri. "We got close. Then there was Lipton Village."

". . . we were in Geography class, almost rioting . . ."

". . . and the teacher didn't know what to do. So he gave us a special project."

". . . instead of boring Iran and Iraq, make a place of our own."

"We took the name off a teabag," said Linear, and giggled. The others remained sombre and I asked: "How many are in the Society?"

"Thirty."

"And when you began?"

"The same. Nobody dropped out," Goosegirl said aggressively.

"It's just," Thursday said, "a lot live on the other side of town, can't always afford the fare. Some of the girls don't make the night meetings, 'cos that's when they work."

(Several days later I understood what he meant.)

"Everyone's still interested," said Jeri. "Totally."

Looking around at the five of them, I realised that the imaginary land, so quaintly depicted on the scrap of paper I still held, was of vital importance to the Society.

The next day was Saturn's and the first of the month, the appointed date for paying rent. I took the money down to Vini in Times Gone, where he insisted on celebrating the occasion formally, with tea.

"I met the Lipton Village Society. To be exact, one sixth of it. Thursday October, Jeri, Linear, Strongarm and Goosegirl."

"Ah," Vini said dubiously. "More tea?"

"No thanks. Where do they get those names from?"

"Lipton Village."

"Silly question."

"Thursday is actually Brendan Mahaffy, I think . . . it's hard to remember."

"I think they're sweet, really. So serious, about a fantasy world."

"It's not a fantasy, it's real for them. They genuinely believe the place exists."

There was a jangly crash as the door was flung open to admit a short man in a high temper. He carried a parcel wrapped in the shop paper. As he opened his mouth to speak, the door opened again (tinkle) and he received its handle in the small of his back. Thursday October entered, clutching a carton of paint tins and a roll of paper. Squeezing past the infuriated obstruction, he gave a nod to Vini, a half-smile to me, and flitted up the stairs.

The customer rubbed his back and stared at us with distaste.

"Mr Thornton!" said Vini.

"Is this the mad hatter's tea party? Ought to be, in the house of the mad builder—now about that atlas you sold me . . ."

I got out of the way, pausing only to slip the rent under the sugar bowl, for safekeeping. The packet of tea was nearby and I noticed its brand: Lipton's.

Thursday had spread the fresh sheet of paper on the floor and was prising the lids off the paint tins. He glanced up as I entered. "Do us a favour. Can you fetch the map from the chest? I'm messy already."

He had opened the padlock and I found the map when I lifted the lid of the box. Underneath it was a sketch of a peculiar horned animal.

"What's this?"

"Oh—a reo." He chuckled. "Harmless little beastie . . . now. The original version was a nightmare. Strongarm was into horror movies at the time. Well, we left the drawings lying about and it gave the dancing class the willies . . . Madame complained to Vini, you bet she did."

"There are reos in Lipton Village?" I asked cautiously.

"Yeah, settling in nicely."

"You've been there?"

"Just for visits."

I picked up an unopened paint tin, and rocked it in my hand, feeling the viscous fluid swell and slurp inside.

"I can't decide if you're crazy or not."

Someone stumped up the stairs and Thursday called out, "That you, Jeri?"

"Yeah." The boy carried a canvas bag, from which he unloaded books, mostly with the distinctive sticker of my old university library. One was unadorned, in a thick leather binding.

"That's from Times Gone," I said.

"S'right. Picked it up as I went through."

"Put it back," said Thursday. "He'll skin ya."

"Will do, but take a look at this."

It was a book of maps, their folds neatly mended with strips of white paper. He opened one out, a hand-tinted panorama of the West Indies. In the empty sea between islands the cartographer had inserted out-of-proportion sailing ships, giant puffing cherubs, a whale large enough to swallow Antigua.

"Inspiration," said Jeri. "Now I'll take it back."

"Is that Thornton's atlas?" I asked.

"No. Times Gone is full of map books."

The argument in the shop was percolating upstairs. I could distinguish words and phrases: 'incipit missing," "later edition" and "cost." Evidently some bibliographical minutia was in dispute. The door jangled again, then slammed shut.

"Thorny walking out," commented Jeri. "He'll be back . . . next time he wants an argument."

He and Thursday exchanged glances, as though to say, 'All the world's mad, save thee and me.' Both of them looked not a little smug. After a moment Jeri wandered off with the book, leaving Thursday staring thoughtfully at the blank sheet of paper. He gave me no chance to establish eye contact, to resume our interrupted conversation; I had to wait until Jeri returned to continue my questioning.

"Are you a student? I recognise the library."

"I shelve books," he replied.

I inspected the titles: a textbook of animal physiology, Bakunin, atmospherical dynamics, the sociology of groups.

"Wide range." (Meaning, do you understand all of that?)

He picked up the zoology book. "This was useful with the—"

"Reos?"

"And the rest. It's difficult to make an animal up from scratch. We had a few abortions."

"Who was it," Thursday asked suddenly, "who forgot the oxygen?"

Jeri pointed to the book on atmosphere. "That was years ago." He flicked through the pages of the book he was still holding, then put it down. "We're finished now. These are just refreshers." The tone of his voice altered, as if to exclude me. "Eh, Thurs, they've been at me again."

"Huh?"

"To do the Library Technician course."

"Well," said Thursday, "you can't."

"Yeah, but try and think up a good excuse."

I butted in: " Why can't you do it?"

They ignored me. Thursday said: "Tell them you won't be living here anymore."

"Oh come on, Thursday, I know you got out of a job you didn't want, but you can't advise Jeri, to forgo a decent opportunity . . ."

"You sound like a social worker," said Jeri, and that shut me up. Thursday explained: "He can't do it, 'cause he'll be living in Lipton Village. We all will."

Vini, in accordance with the trading laws and his own sloth, had shut Times Gone for the weekend. The shop was empty except for Rover dozing in a pool of sunlight beside the elephant folios. I tried upstairs, avoiding the room where Thursday and Jeri, had begun to paint, working together. Vini was in his flat, eating a bachelor's lunch: toasted cheese.

"Come in and collect yourself," he said, after a glance. "Care to join me for lunch?"

Inside there were a number of framed maps on the walls, and my suspicions were confirmed.

"Can you make some Lipton's tea?"

He scratched his sandy-grey hair.

"Ah, you guessed. Yes, I'm responsible for the Lipton Village Society."

"Who else would let them use that splendid room, rent-free?"

"I had a guilty conscience," he said and went into the kitchen to grill more cheese. I sat down and picked up the nearest book— Wing's *Short-Title Catalogue*, hardly enthralling reading. Vini reappeared after some time, with a tray.

"It was a pretty clever ploy," I said. "I mean, I don't see teachers much in my line of work, but horror stories seep through the bureaucracy."

"All true, all true," he muttered. "I was a hopeless teacher, only interested in old books and geography. At least I was enthusiastic about the subject. Eight years ago I managed, for once, to communicate that enthusiasm."

I took a gulp of tea. He added: "How kind of Uncle William to make me his heir. It saved my life."

I nodded, swallowing the sweet tea.

"The education system succeeds only in blighting the lives of young people."

"You enriched the lives of thirty little delinquents."

"I'm not so sure. Lipton Village is their obsession—they neglect reality. I write them references, nag the Social Security people about jobs . . . and they lose them! Too wrapped up in a dream world."

"They fascinate me."

"They have that effect. Sometimes I think I should sool a sociologist onto them. It would make an interesting case study—Collective Hallucinations among Unemployed Youth—bah!"

"They just told me they intend to live in Lipton Village."

"That's been their aim from the start," he said. "It's taken them eight years to make the place viable: maps, crops, food animals, detailed preparations. When Jeri couldn't get hold of the information he wanted, he got himself a job in a university library."

"I know, I've seen the books."

The thread of his discourse had been broken. "Goosegirl and Strawberry were appalling pupils, in one earhole and out the other. Yet I've overheard the pair of them talking about chemistry!"

He reached for the teapot.

"There's nothing we can do. Have some more tea."

When I came downstairs again, feeling rather full, I found what must have been a majority of the Lipton Village Society gathered in the great room. Some were helping Thursday and Jeri with the painting, others chatting among themselves. I threaded my way through the young people and locked myself in my flat. The sound of their voices was like a swell at sea. To drown the noise I switched on my television. I watched a Hollywood extravaganza about Sinbad the Sailor; the news (with unemployment statistics); a po-faced BBC dramatisation of an escapist children's classic; a gaggle of cartoons; the news again (with update); and a silly American comedy about a 'slum' school. When I felt hungry, I cooked vegetarian stew, using the French mushroom recipe as a basis, and ate it during the third news bulletin. As I was cleaning up, somebody knocked at the door.

"Who's there?"

"Me, Thursday."

"And Jeri."

I switched off the television and, with its blare gone, realised there was silence in the outer room. When I opened the door I could see, past my visitors, that everyone else had left. Thursday and Jeri sidled in, looking like a pair of children sent to the headmaster's office.

"Did we upset you?" asked Thursday.

"A little. It's so strange."

They swapped glances, with an air of *déjà vu*.

"How can you live in an imaginary place?" I asked.

"It's *there*," said Thursday. "It exists for us."

"A play-Utopia," I sneered.

"It need not be for good," Jeri said defensively. "We'll be back for visits. The quality of life here could improve. Then we'd return."

He made that sound a most unlikely contingency. "Okay," I said. "Who's to be tribal elder?"

"Nobody. It's an anarchy."

"I see—hence the Bakunin."

They were both hungrily eyeing the pot of veggie stew, which I had left to cool on the stove. I poured the remains into two bowls and brought it over to them, with a pair of spoons.

"Ta," said Thursday, and they sat on the bed to eat (heartily).

I continued to argue. "Bet it soon degenerates into fascism."

Both had their mouths full, which put them at a disadvantage. Finally Jeri said, "We don't expect it to be perfect."

"But better than here," said Thursday.

That remark defeated me, in an odd way. After some time I asked, "When do you go?"

"Not long now."

Not long now. When I returned to work on Monday morning I found the office in what passes in the Public Service for turmoil. A senior researcher, collecting data on rural schooling had had a nervous breakdown. The fruit of his labours would have been a report, due shortly, and his assistant couldn't cope with the extra work. It was simple stuff really—driving around the country towns interviewing school principals. Who could they send? What about Susan Gifford? The Public Service cosh was in evidence, though unstated; a refusal would mean a quick trip to the unemployment office, the domain of Thursday October and his friends. I accepted with extreme reluctance, also unstated. They had given me only a week's notification.

Thus it happened, in the month I was away, that I missed the grand exit of the Lipton Village Society. I sent Vini a postcard with a map on it, but there was no way, in this itinerant work, that he could reply.

On my return I found the great room completely empty, even the cedar chest banished from its corner.

"They said I should have it, sort of a cumulative rent payment."

Vini had installed it in the living room of his flat where, amid the books and clutter, it still succeeded in looking lonely.

"How did they go?"

"I didn't see. One day they just weren't around anymore."

"Didn't they say goodbye?"

"Yes, well in advance. But I never took them seriously, didn't believe they could . . ."

"Maybe they're hiding somewhere."

"Why?" he asked, but I didn't answer the question.

"I can't accept this. I have to make further enquiries."

After some hours, and much nagging, Vini produced a complete list of the real names behind the monikers of the Lipton Village Society. He could not tell me where they had been living, but I, with access to Education Department records, was able to find about thirty addresses of the nearest and dearest of these dead-end kids, years out of date.

The following day I made a preliminary venture to the other side of the city, to interview Mr and Mrs Mahaffy, the parents of Thursday October. They refused to speak to me, for I wore working dress, and they rightly suspected a connection with officialdom. I returned to Hirst Folly, changed into casual cheaperie, and went slumming again.

This time I received cautious help and an occasional insight into various members of the Society. Strongarm had a brother in jail, and the family of Linear seemed a prize pack of villains. One of the night-working girls came from a household of Plymouth Brethren, who pretended she was dead. I called their bluff and forced an admission that they prayed for her daily.

After five such visits, I could perceive a pattern, which recurred with depressing inevitability. No, they hadn't seen the kid for a while, and they weren't particularly worried. "You grow up in this district and you grow up a survivor," said Linear's thuggish father.

Jeri alone had no accessible kin, and I finally phoned the university library. The Personnel Officer was perfectly willing to chat.

"He left a month ago. Bright lad, we miss him."

"Did he say where he was going?"

"To a good job with a tea company. Tetley's, I believe."

Having followed my line of inquiry to its dead end, I returned to Vini. We talked about the Lipton Village Society, and then we talked about ourselves. Several days later, I moved upstairs, into his flat.

"I have to be honest with you. I really am only interested in old books of geography."

"I'll be honest too. I need someone to lean on, if you'll pardon the cliché."

So we wait, in a quare house, with plural old books and singular old cat. For what? A visitor from Lipton Village, home of the truants from reality.

DUCHESS

I saw her first in the gloom of a Milan fashion show, moments before kick-off, or as us fashionistas say, frock-off. She was more than fashionably late, she was as rudely late as a celebrity, pushing her way through the assembled throng. That would have been permissible for a Face from the gossip glossies, but to judge from the outraged looks, she was an unknown. Moreover the seat she was headed to was middle-ranked: two down from me, in fact, in my capacity as fashion journalist for an antipodean newspaper, and a long, long way from the rarefied front row, with its Hollywood stars and the heavy armaments of Anna Wintour, from American *Vogue*, and Suzy Menkes of the *International Herald Tribune*.

Full marks for a meteoric entry, I thought. Unlike most fashion journos, I choose my words carefully. For her the crowd was merely a dark backdrop, a sky against which she left a trail of dazzle, head and toe. Her shoes were state of the art basketball-players', with cute little inserts in the heels that flashed lightning with each step. From her ears depended an equally cutting edge iPod, the new model for cyclists, which shone luminously pink and green. When she neared I further noticed the silhouette of her skirt, unmistakably vintage Miyake, with concertinaed, tiered pleats dangerously close to resembling a Chinese lantern. Finally, as she brushed past me,

I registered, with the split-second timing of the seasoned fashion watcher, the other elements of her ensemble: vintage lace camisole, classic English tweed waistcoat, a fur stole, and a toque. There was something avant-garde in the jewelry line too, but my concentration was broken by her looking me briefly in the eye and murmuring, a very carrying murmur, as only the English upperclass can do:

"Live like bats and owls indeed!"

Oh, it was apt, for all of us fashion workers huddled together in the dark, a parliament of night-creatures, waiting for the fashion spectacle to begin. As it did, fashionably late to the point of rudeness, with a blast of sound, a candy-pink spotlight, and this year's Miss Anorexia Supermodel, posed in Bride of Frankenstein wig and cape—

—which she threw off to reveal not very much at all, ribbons of artfully slashed chiffon, as she sashayed down the catwalk. I opened notepad (lo-tech, hardback, art paper) and started making descriptions, either drawings or shorthand. I was barely aware of a hi-tech, very slim and dainty Notebook being opened two seats down, and a flurry of typing. Then I forgot about everything except the show.

X number of outfits later Miss Anorexia made her last appearance, as a bride, still with overtones of Frankenstein, and on the designer's arm. Both sported cocaine-eating grins. I made my last notes: bias drapes, laser-cuts, Retro-meets-Space-Age. Then I felt someone brush past me again.

And my jaw dropped, as it hadn't throughout the entire show, as the latecomer made an early exit, and in the light I could register her colors: emerald in the skirt; heather/lichen tints in the waistcoat, of Donegal tweed, I guessed; yellowing ivory of the vintage lace; offset by peacock feathers covering the toque; red fox tails in the stole, and amethysts in the jewelry (along with silver, and what looked like well-nibbled bones).

It shouldn't have gone together. But it did. That's fashion genius.

I turned, and looked into the square-framed glasses of my neighbor, a demure little Chinese lady from some Hong Kong glossy. But she said it first:

"Who the fuck was that?"

I had no idea, but a notion I would need to find out.

When in doubt, ask a PR lady, even if she is pawpaw-colored, with platinum-blonde tresses and cerulean contact lenses. But Carla's English was dodgy, and the name she gave me sounded very much like a malentendu: Lady St Parry. Not in Debretts, nor on Google, either. Rather more promising was the affiliation: *Twenty-First Century*, a new webjournal with some serious money behind it. Yet upon investigation the issue up on the Net seemed serious, boyish, and technogeeky. It certainly lacked the witty eclectic femininity of the Lady, *if* she was a lady with a capital L.

I sighed, and got down to work. Writing my copy, to be filed across several time zones and half the world away, is a ritual demanding perfect quiet, all alone in my hotel room. But tonight I was having difficulty maintaining my concentration. When I tried to detail just *what* about the collection was Retro-meets-Space-Age (what did I mean, and more importantly, what did the designer mean, apart from business?), a concertinaed skirt, a flash of lightning, the kiss of fur would come to mind and stop me in mid-phrase. Drat the girl! I thought. (Yes, she had been little more than one, quite petite . . .)

I wasn't being paid to describe this interloper, however intriguing. Drastic measures were needed. I ordered an affogato from room service, double strength, and on an alcohol and caffeine-fuelled burst of energy, wrote my 800 words of fashion column and emailed it into the ether. It was right on deadline in Sydney; and 2 a.m. Italiano time.

Tomorrow would be Prada, Emporio Armani, and several very important parties. Thanks to the affogato, I would now have the greatest difficulty getting to sleep. Drat the girl, indeed.

Milan passed, as it always did, in a high-speed blur. Frocks, lights, blaring music, more frocks, shopping, long taxi rides, coffee, frantically typing my copy, air kisses, "*Ciao, Bella!*", alcohol, more coffee, guilty cigarettes, insincerity by the bucket. The only relief came from the few old fashion friends I trusted, and Lady Whatever. I used to think a sight for sore eyes was a cliché, but not with her. I was red-eyed from the insane hours, but she always was not only eye candy, but eye balm. For Prada she wore a titanium corselet, milkmaid frills, a fur muff and jackboots, with a diamante comet in her long and undyed brown ringlets. Miuccia sent a flunkey out after her with his cell phone camera, I heard, which had to be a sign of approval. For Emporio Armani, she wore a leather bustle under a sequined tartan jacket, the muff again, and a hat I can only describe as deconstructed (with nail clippers, by the look of it). Isabella Blow eat your cold little heart out, I thought.

Oh, she diverted me, into a persistent piquant curiosity as to just who she really was, and where she was coming from (a direction of the compass, I surmised, where there was fresh, rarefied air). She also unsettled me profoundly. Precisely what about her had such an effect was harder to identify. I began to get an inkling at one of the avant-garde shows, held in a converted abattoir. Much dry ice was used, and every model wore buckled leather, even the obligatory bride. At the finale the buckles and models were attached to a gun carriage, on which the designer (a Slovakian, I think) was drawn solemnly down the runway.

The Lady sat there open mouthed, then remarked, loudly: "Have you no pride? You women labor like beasts! Carthorses or oxen à la mode!"

A comparison no girl, let alone a vain model, would appreciate, but luckily none of those on the catwalk understood English.

I frowned, something rare in the fashion world, thanks to Botox, and wrote in my notebook: Déjà vu. Not that I had seen her before, because I've trained a good natural memory to fashion-police level. It was her words, and the coincidence of interests she represented: English aristo+fashion+technology+the old-fashioned+feminism=????? But something was missing, some vital component. I underlined déjà vu and snapped my notebook shut. Now I followed my quarry through the milling throng. She had worn her iPod throughout the show, sensible given the fad for pain-volume disco at this year's Milan. As I neared, close enough to kiss, I could hear a faint tinkle from the iPod . . . surely not harpsichord music?

We were blocked briefly by the slow passage of one of the US buyers, a massive man on crutches. As if sensing my presence, she turned:

"You even dress like bats or owls, all of you, or Puritans!"

Just to one side was Carine Roitfeld from French *Vogue*, who claims only to wear colors in the countryside, and her crew of rockstar-wannabe minions, all of them clad inky somber. I blushed, and looked down: at my classic Jasper Conran jacket, Collette Dinnigan dress, and Prada boots, a perfectly coordinated outfit in basic . . . now suddenly boring, conformist black. All I needed was a Bible, a big white collar, and a stovepipe hat.

In the moment I glanced down, the crowd cleared, and off she went, striding through at speed, unimpeded by stiletto heels or other fashion foot-binding arts. I gazed at her retreating shape, a riot of colors, with hardly an item of her outfit which could be visually sourced to a designer (op or vintage shop, dressmaker?) and saw, unlike anyone else at the show, an individual, a true original. I thought again, *déjà vu*. Something about her resonated from deep in my past, from long before I could have appreciated the art in her personal styling . . . but from where?

It took me less than eight hours, my mind chewing on the problem while I drank wine, partied, showered, filed my copy, and got ready for bed. At 3 A.M. I suddenly sat up from a troubled sleep. Snap! I had it, the *déjà vu* was identified, and from a most unlikely source: the Duchess.

Once upon a time, I was a grad student, thesis underway, sessional tutoring for the experience, conference papers and articles in preparation, my life shared equally between my computer screen, the coffee shop, and the rare books section of the university library. It was intensely intellectual, also lonely as hell, but not without its passions. When I encountered like minds, we would go into a huddle over Mary Wollstonecraft, Kristeva, Irigaray . . . and more rarely, the Duchess of Newcastle. You had to be into the seventeenth century for her, but she had a small select fandom, including, somewhat reluctantly and backhandedly, Virginia Woolf, who namechecked her in *A Room of One's Own*.

For those of you not familiar with the history of feminist thought, a brief life:

Newcastle, Duchess of (1623–73), Margaret Cavendish, née Lucas. Younger daughter of the minor English gentry. Lady in waiting at the Court of Charles I and Queen Henrietta Maria during the English Civil War. Fell in love with and married the Duke of Newcastle, when they were penniless exiles in France. Both were writers, she most unusually for the time, which liked its women fecund and unlearned. She wrote and published under her own name poems, plays, works of natural science, novels, utopias— all imbued with a formidable facility for words, a vindication of women's rights, and a fanciful imagination.

Not least, she was a fabulous and inventive dresser. As she herself wrote:

And if a Lady dress, or chance to wear,
A gown to please herself, or curl her hair,
If not according as the Fashion runs,
Lord, how it sets a-work their Eyes and Tongues!
Straight she's fantastical, they all do cry,
Yet they will imitate her presently,
And for what they did laugh at her in scorn,
With it think good themselves for to adorn.

Get the picture? None alas survives of her fantastic regalia, but we do have her words, in quotable quantity. It was she who said (and I who recognized) the words: "Women live like bats or owls, labor like beasts, and die like worms."

In a different world, like Afghanistan, or seventeenth-century England, or even academia under economic (ir)rationalism, I might have lived like that too. It was thanks to the Duchess and her many successors, from Wollstonecraft to the Pankhursts, that I didn't. Even after I had belatedly realized that a professional love of the Duchess would condemn me to short-term contracts and slave labor working hours, and that my increasing addiction to designer clothes meant I would have to get a real job . . . I still loved her, as an amateur.

And I had no problem with someone else loving her too in sincere imitation (the greatest flattery), even quoting her. Postmodern intertextuality they call it in the academy, a polite way of saying outright theft, in areas where true originality has vanished, such as architecture, and above all fashion. Even the name, Lady St Parry, I could now recognize as coming from the Duchess too: "Lady Sanspareille," without compare. It was a paradox of her personality that the Duchess could also use the personas of Lady and Mistress Bashful: shy, yet with a sense of her own worth.

I could read that fanciful display at Milan Fashion Week as both the calculating act of a sharp operator, out to create an effect, and as a (secondhand) visionary. Not many people would have spotted the referencing, not in the frivolous world of fashion, I could pride myself on that. But did it go even further? The Duchess was in her time popularly regarded as mad, and anyone who used her as a performative model could run the risk of getting too close for sanity. To quote from another era, the 1960s movie *Performance*: "the only performance that makes it, that really makes it all the way, is the one that achieves madness."

I checked the quote on Google, and also spent a happy half hour rediscovering the words of the Duchess online, no longer only available in dusty rare books and dustier rare book shops. Then I shut my laptop down. Light was dawning outside, and I had to catch a plane, not to the antipodes, but to London, for an all-too short respite before the Paris Fashion shows started. Would I see her again there? I wondered. I certainly hoped so.

My antidote to Milan was an old school-friend's cottage, an amiable timeshare arrangement, in the bucolic English countryside of Kent. I bought organic produce from the hippie neighbors, spent a lot of time in country walks, and on the internet. It should have been ideal chill-out time, but the Lady continued to unsettle me.

First I saw her report on Milan, as posted on *Twenty-First_ Century.com*. As I had suspected, her brief for the shows was fashion vs new technology; and she generally found them wanting in that area . . . and others. It was quite the most uninhibited fashion journalism I'd read in years, and thus hugely enjoyable, not least for the way in which she kept sneaking in quotes from the Duchess. "Debauched . . . and loves his luxuries" (on a San Francisco buyer who would, I knew, regard it as a compliment); "necessity is a great Commandress" (on fixing up a torn hem with a safety pin and having it taken for a fashion statement); "sweet marmalade of kisses" (on the orange lipstick used exclusively for the Fendi show).

And yet, as I read on, with side trips to online archives of seventeenth-century poetry, women's writing, and the like, I found myself frowning again. It was not just the quotations and the odd occasional archaisms of style and vocabulary. Nor the fact of the writer speaking her (erudite) mind, with considerable passion and no care for what anyone else might think. The problem was, to me, that it read precisely as if the Duchess of Newcastle had been transported into our era via time machine, locked into a room with an internet connection to bring her up to our 24/7 speed, given an expense account, then set free.

The Duchess had in fact died at the age of fifty, prisoner of the seventeenth century, and that more mundane time machine, the ageing meat of the human body. She most definitely had not done an *Orlando* (thanks Virginia). And yet the words in front of me suggested otherwise.

Uncanny, I thought. Then, some ghost from my litcrit days said: no, when Todorov used that word, it was in reference to Ann Radcliffe's Gothic (another interesting woman, but several centuries after the Duchess), in which there was a physical explanation for all the apparently supernatural events of the narrative. How about Todorov's fantastic? I thought . . . where the supernatural is problematic, and the reader keeps oscillating endlessly between belief and disbelief. That was more how I felt.

I could hardly hope for the marvelous, where the supernatural is simply accepted as a feature of the world, for Lady Sanspareille to be the Duchess in actuality.

When I got onto my fashion contacts again, as the Paris shows inexorably neared, I found I was not the only person intrigued by Lady Sanspareille. Her article had created a stir, especially the quip that Versace was suitable only for frowzy, tatterdemalion bawds— which must have had the PR flaks reaching for the dictionary. Someone had found a blog site: GloriousFame.com. I spent an instructive hour there reading more channeled Duchess: she was in favor of technology, foxhunting (natch!); monarchy, but found the Windsors dreadfully dull and unstylish (as you would, I thought, after the Stuarts); and despised the current Poet Laureate. Yet most valuable was the information that someone else had recognized the lady . . . as one Charlotte Lukes, formerly a high-flyer with a distinctly staid English advertising firm and responsible for a notorious television ad for condoms.

I begged, pleaded, threatened, and finally got a copy of the ad sent to me, quite illegally, over the web. And I burst out laughing. In a charming English country garden, nymphs frolicked around a trellis containing a manic cucumber vine, over whose fruit they innocently fitted . . . you-know-what.

Virginia Woolf had written: "What a vision of loneliness and riot the thought of Margaret Cavendish brings to mind! As if some giant cucumber had spread itself all over the roses and carnations in the garden and choked them to death. What could bind, tame, or civilize for human use that wild, generous, untutored intelligence?"

What indeed? Even death, it seemed, could not bind her . . . so that she could apparently arise from the grave and take an intertextual revenge on the divine Virginia.

That did it. Paris might be imminent, but I had to satisfy my curiosity.

I took the train up from Kent, my destination not Knightsbridge, but one of the few seventeenth-century residential buildings left in London. It was in a tiny, forgotten corner, listed but disheveled, and not yet totally yuppified. Nervously I pushed the buzzer beside the name "C. LUKES." It rang, rang again, and then I thrust my hand into the pocket of my black coat, bitterly disappointed. The address I had obtained via an outrageous act of bribery (a Prada personal-organizer case, the latest model) had been correct. But my bird of paradise had flown.

I dawdled back towards the tube station, just as all hell broke loose. A crowd of commuters boiled out of the escalators and onto the pavement. Police sirens wailed, and it seemed like the entire cast of *The Bill* miraculously converged on the scene. They must be shooting an episode of the new *Doctor Who*, I thought. Then my brain belatedly registered the absence of lights and cameras in this action.

"Damned heathens," said a voice behind me, an upper-class voice, impeccably politically incorrect. A girl's voice . . . and I turned, to see my quarry, on a new, state of the art pushbike. She had dressed down slightly for the London streets: tweed knickerbockers, a military dress jacket, purple boxers' boots, and a safety helmet. The latter normally was most unchic, but she managed with hers to look alluring, a very simple effect achieved by letting the stray ringlet flow free.

"Another bomb attack?" I said.

"Or just a very good scare," she replied. Now she was eyeing me, an unmistakable *déjà vu* look. I held out my hand, and after a suspicious pause, she shook it.

"We met in Milan . . . Duchess," I said.

Not a blink in that steady gaze, but I knew she had registered the words.

"Ah, Madame Puritan," she said. "Amongst all the other Puritans. Except for the silly shoes."

"They're Manolos," I said.

From her expression she clearly pronounced the designer's name *Blah*-nik. "Still silly. The tube's closed now, and so are the buses. You'll have to walk."

Ohshit, I thought. "I've got to get to Waterloo . . ."

She looked severe. "Heaven does not always protect the persons of virtuous women traveling without their parents, husbands or particular friend to guard them . . . But sometimes lends a human help."

"That's from *Assaulted and Pursued Chastity* . . . I think."

A nod. Writers are vain, and I had just gratified her vanity. She stepped forward and onto the pedals, leaving the seat free, and jerked her head at me: come hither! I cautiously mounted behind her, and we set forth, via alleyways and mews, through the streets of London town.

The real Duchess, a protected aristocrat, would have been lost on her era's roads: her modern incarnation seemed thankfully more streetwise, and very well-informed, thanks to the GPS receiver mounted on the handlebars. I sat back, and watched the ringlets blow free in the newly unpolluted London air.

"What are you?" I murmured, half to myself. "A reincarnation?"

She gave no sign of having heard, but nonetheless answered. "That's more heathenism."

"Also Pythagorean, whom you doubtless read."

Another nod. "But it's not true."

"You are a relation, I checked you out. Lukes, a variant spelling of Lucas, descended from one of Margaret Cavendish's brothers, a cadet branch. She was fond of her family, and it makes sense that she would follow the line."

She dodged a clump of grumpy commuters. "Peradventure. Or as Charlotte Lukes would have said, maybe. She's not herself anymore, not the Home Counties girl from the lesser gentry, who got herself to university, and a good job in the city. Someone else is wearing her, as if she were a dress tried on, and found a becoming fit."

"Is that how you refer to your . . . her breakdown?"

"Breakdown? Fie! You have advertising industry gossips?"

I said nothing. Our current climate of terrorism means governments collect information on even their most law-abiding citizens—and there are ways to access it, connections in the most unlikely places with a taste for fashion industry freebies.

"I wore grey suits," she suddenly said. "A parrot-hued pashmina, that was the first sign. And a sudden addiction to rare book shops, eBay auctions for the strangest of things suddenly become desirable. A carmine velvet pixie hat, 1950s. It was only after I had bought a subscription to the *New Scientist* and the collected works of the lady whom great-aunt Eliza used to refer to as Mad Madge that the penny started to drop. The office was selling tickets for a charity ball, and I dressed myself up in a paste pearl cap, with a half-moon of diamante brooch at the front; blue bugle bead and pearl coat, fringed with red; green glittery boots, the whole finished with a spear, also glittery, in the shape of a comet. I said I was an Empress, and won first prize."

"The Empress in *The New Blazing World* wore real diamonds and pearls," I said. "But near enough."

"As I found when I got home, my head swimming, and opened the book." She continued, on a roll like her bike, which was picking up speed down a slight incline. "I swear I'd never read the description before, but I'd aped it faithfully. I got dressed up the next day in my grey suit, last time I wore it, the pashmina, and the pixie hat, carrying the spear under one arm. I hung it on the wall of my cubicle, and wrote an ad that day which earned me a promotion."

She glanced over her shoulder briefly at me.

"Charlotte Lukes was hardly that silly slattern Bridget Jones. But she was unhappy, and rather uninteresting. Far better to surrender, and let myself be a far more interesting person."

If this was madness, it was perfectly methodical, I thought, as an awkward silence fell. I knew I had to keep the conversation going, even only with commonplaces.

"I'll owe you for this trip," I said—as if the Lady were a taxi service. "Shall I buy you dinner in Paris?"

She glanced back over her shoulder. "Milan was *quite* enough for me. I asked *Twenty-First Century* for the test-drive column."

"Test-drive?"

"New tech . . . like this bike. The editor said: 'provided you don't make the column too girly.'"

She chuckled. I had no idea if the Duchess had chuckled, maybe this sense of humor was Charlotte Lukes'. I foresaw an extremely girly column.

"Margaret Cavendish was constrained by the sex roles of her time, just like your feet, Madame. Here she, or her shadow, can do anything she likes. I might go back to university and study science. Join the Royal Society, which now admits women. Find a nice older man, like her husband, the Duke."

"I dare you," I said, "to find a real Duke."

"Via the internet?" She chuckled again. "But he'd better be fertile. She always wanted a baby, no woman in her era was complete without one. I'd like to give her that, at least."

"If you have given her something," I said, "then it is far more than her wildest dreams, even in *The New Blazing World*."

A ladylike grunt, as we hit a rut in the road. Next she negotiated a group of police, who clearly didn't regard two women on a bike as terrorists. She kept sneaking glances at the GPS screen, and muttering a mixture of mouth-filling oaths and admonitions at it:

"God's blood! We're not in Dulwich!"

I tried to speak, but she waved me silent. It dragged on as we passed more homeward-bound commuters, women carrying their office shoes in their hands, and walking stocking-foot, fat men sweating in their Saville Row suits, the fitness fanatics looking smug. Now we neared the Thames and the great station. She brought the bike to a neat halt outside the main entrance, set both booted feet on the ground, and waited, back turned to me.

I'd once interviewed a Japanese designer, a man forthcoming only for 30 minutes at a time. Then he abruptly retreated into himself, recharging his batteries for the next design, or encounter. I sensed something similar here: a shy person performing sociability, but only in bursts.

"Thanks," I said awkwardly, since she clearly did not want to prolong the goodbye.

There was a pause, in which she should have answered. Instead, she hit the pedals, accelerating almost from standstill, around a corner and out of sight, ringing her bell as she went.

I gasped. There is a verb of somewhat flexible meaning: to duchess. It can imply anything from condescension to co-option to doing someone over. Whatever, right now I felt as though I had been thoroughly duchessed. After a moment I added, or *she* has. What an egomaniac! The whole length of the trip she had not asked me who I was, nor where I came from. I'm Livia! I mentally shouted after her. I'm from Sydney! And I know where you live, both places: the second being a magnificent tomb in Westminster Abbey, erected by the loving, grieving Duke of Newcastle

I went into the station and checked the time for the Eurostar. Around me the tabloids shouted: TERROR ATTACK FOILED! something for which I could not have cared less. Paris beckoned, and it was the nature of my bread and butter for me to follow.

I still don't know how I got through the next week. It was Milan, but *en Française*, Chanel instead of Prada, but the same old faces, to my jaded eyes almost the same clothes. I air-kissed, I filed my copy, I partied, but never was I so thankful when I could finally settle into my Business Class seat in the metal tube taking me home, to my sunburnt, blazing New World.

And somewhere over Kamchatka, a plan hatched in my mind, a revenge, and also a means to satisfy my curiosity. Lady Sanspareille was new tech; and new tech could analyze words in a way which the Duchess of Newcastle, sitting in her study at Welbeck Abbey, could never, ever have dreamed.

Way back, in my grad student days, I had eked out my grant by doing typing for a Professor, rendering the greats and not so greats of English literature into machine readable form. Mary Perdita Robinson, Mary Shelley, the Brontë sisters. Professor Burrows, of the University of Newcastle (yes, carrying coals to, indeed!) had developed one of the first stylistic recognition programs, determining how the vocabulary, grammar, especially the commas, could reveal a writer's signature. Even in anonymous texts.

I would need a large quantity of the Duchess' works, for comparison and statistical analysis purposes. Easy-peasy! Had not Virginia Woolf noted Margaret Cavendish's "torrents of rhyme and prose, poetry and philosophy . . . congealed in quartos and folios"? For Lady Sanspareille I would have the articles from *Twenty-first_Century.com*, also the eighteen months' worth of blog entries since Charlotte Lukes had taken a lucrative package from the advertising world. That should suffice.

And now I sit in front of a computer screen, waiting as the silicone chips crunch through an author's words. There are no two identical writers, especially in style. The vocabulary would be a point of difference, as so much has changed since the seventeenth century. But underneath, as the Professor says, remains the punctuation, the distinctive grammar, and prosody of the writer.

I had thought Charlotte Lukes' imitation of the Duchess uncanny, but there was no physical explanation. It was fantastical for me to vacillate between belief and disbelief as to whether she had been possessed by the ghost of a poet or not.

Yet was it too much to hope for the marvelous, that they were one—the individual, inimitable, indivisible Duchess of Newcastle?

MONTAGE

Gabriel was close to a nervous breakdown. Long service leave from the Research Institute where he worked was hastily arranged; and he was politely pushed out the door.

"Look, Gabe," said the Institute Director, "take a seaside holiday, move house, go back to playing your guitar . . . anything."

Gabriel did all three. He loaded the cheaper of his cars with essentials, including a guitar in a dusty case, and drove away from his home. He was wearing old clothes, and as he left the fashionable area of the city, he had a sense of diving into invisibility. When he stopped at a milk bar off the coast road to buy a copy of the local paper, he was treated like a resident. The mad scientist was camouflaged.

He sat outside the corner shop, and scanned the room-for-rent ads. This outgrowth of the city was distinctly tacky, but its real estate agents pretended it was a chic bayside suburb. Only five minutes to the beach, read Gabriel; but he knew that at the end of the distance were thin strips of gravel and litter, or boulders covered with graffiti. There was only one sand beach in the area— and it was inaccessible, behind barbed wire.

He folded up the paper, and made a visit to Coastal Vistas, Real Estate Pty Ltd. None of their prospects was very appealing, but Gabriel settled for a flatlet in a brick veneer bungalow, built in haste and decaying at leisure.

There was a new lock on the old door. As he put key to it, a cacophony came from the next flat. Gabriel started, and dropped his guitar down the concrete steps. It thudded horizontally on to the meagre front lawn.

"What the—"

He refrained from swearing, for a middle-aged woman had come out of the next door. She was plump, and carried a net shopping bag.

"Don't mind Sid," she said. "He's crazy."

Gabriel bent to retrieve his guitar, but she continued:

"It's not proper work for a young man. He says it's creative, making films, but he's up all night . . . and sponging off his mum too. Today he's fixing the soundtrack, and I said, none of that computer music till I'm out of the home. Little bugger couldn't wait."

The noise was repeated, at lower volume, and the woman shook her fist mockingly at a front window, through which futuristic equipment was visible.

"I'm Althea Degraves," she added, almost shyly.

"Gabriel."

"New neighbour? Welcome to this dump." Her grey, faintly porcine eyes gazed at Gabriel shrewdly.

"Well, I've got to do the shopping. Nice meeting you, Mr Gabriel; pop around any time."

Althea glanced at the window again.

"Be pretty noisy until I get back . . . maybe you should nick off too."

She trotted away to the accompaniment of the white noise, first muted, then returning to the original volume. Gabriel unloaded his car hurriedly. As a lover of classical music, he could not bear the din. He stacked everything in the front room, the bedsit of the dingy flatlet, and took Althea's advice and fled.

It was years since Gabriel had visited this area, and in that time brick homes had erupted like buboes over the bleak farmland. Yet the road was familiar, and when he finally left the suburb, driving up the dirt track behind the GOVERNMENT PROPERTY: KEEP OUT sign, he felt as though he were in a time warp. But this sensation vanished when he came to the spiky wire fence, with its big gate: the mesh was rusty, and the lock thinly crusted with salt.

Gabriel reached in his pocket, and took out a key, big and unwieldy, with a plastic identity tag that read: Hunter's Beach. He had taken it from the Institute—on the day he left, the staff had been preoccupied with a visiting army general, and the quiet theft went unnoticed. He did not expect an alarm: Institute staff never went to Hunter's Beach and it seemed that only Gabriel remembered this desolate place.

He went in, and noticed another change: the old Marine Research Station had been demolished. He wandered among the tussocky rubble, and was nostalgically pleased to find the doorstep intact. Years ago he had sat there and played guitar—a Bach suite—staring down at the beach of fine grey sand. The sound of the sea had strangely complemented the music, making a whole that was wistful and stark. He wished that he had brought his guitar to Hunter's Beach today. Another time.

Later, he followed the track down the bluff to the beach itself. The death calm had left this place now; and walking along the sand he saw seagulls and crawling sand creatures. There was no evidence of the accident years before—only the locked gate, the fence, and the sign.

When Gabriel returned to his new home, he found a weedy young man prowling up and down the front garden. The stranger was smoking, and grinned widely when he saw Gabriel.

"Hi, I'm Sid, son of Alf. Mum won't let me smoke inside, says it'll stunt my growth. Too late."

"I'm Gabriel."

"I know. Mum told me all about you. Big event in her day."

Sid drew on his cigarette, eyeing Gabriel as Althea had done. Feeling uncomfortable, the scientist sat on his doorstep, and took off his shoes, shaking out the silvery sand. He glanced up and saw that Sid had stopped smoking, the neglected butt glowing in his hand.

"Where's the sand from? You weren't away long, not so you had time to drive to the rich peoples' beaches."

Gabriel grabbed the shoes and started for his door, at the same time reaching in his pocket for key. As he pulled it out he dislodged another, larger and heavier, which fell at Sid's feet. The young man pounced.

"Hunter's Beach," he read. "The hidden beach. I always wanted to go there—got as far as the fence, once."

He stared at Gabriel.

"Take me there."

"Not permitted," Gabriel said quickly.

"Oh yeah? You went there today. Look Mr Gabriel, I make videos, Super-8, and I like a bit of atmosphere. Sand and waves, the wind blowing, no people around—"

He raised his hands, as though aiming an invisible camera. The cigarette had petered out.

"—just great!" Then the joyous look faded from his face, and he clutched the key tightly.

"Maybe I'll go down to Hunter's Beach on my lonesome."

There was a long pause. Would it matter, thought Gabriel, if the kid made a home movie of Hunter's Beach? Nobody at the Institute would see it.

"Oh all right!"

"When?" Sid asked.

Gabriel recalled that Sid kept vampire hours. "Nine a.m.," he specified in revenge.

"Oh . . . thanks, mate."

"The key, please," said Gabriel. He went inside, shaking a little, and played guitar until he felt calm again.

At nine a.m., precisely, Sid, carrying a camera several sizes too big for him, knocked on the door. He was out of his time zone and looked ludicrous, his pale nocturnal face screwed up against the thin sunlight. Gabriel found himself grinning at the sight, something which Sid pointedly ignored.

They travelled to Hunter's Beach in complete silence, Gabriel driving, and Sid filming the suburbscape with his eyes.

At the gate, Gabriel said: "You keep out of my way, right?"

"Sure," Sid said absently, gazing at the scene through the mesh. Once inside, he hurried down the path to the beach, while Gabriel lingered by the ruins, cradling his guitar. There was a brief horrible screeching, as Sid disturbed some gulls on the way down; and then there was only the sound of the sea. Gabriel tuned the instrument, then began to pick out an intricate sequence of notes, the same Bach suite he had played years ago.

His music had fallen into desuetude shortly after the accident at Hunter's Beach; he had to stop and start many times. When he finally finished he looked up and found that hours had passed, and that Sid was sitting quietly nearby, listening.

Nothing was said, for the mood of Hunter's Beach pressed upon them. They drove back, again without speaking.

Several days passed before Gabriel saw Sid again, and on this occasion they met in Sid's time. Around two a.m., one night, Gabriel awoke from an evil dream, and turned on the light. Shortly afterwards there was a tapping at the bedsit door, and Gabriel peered nervously through his front window. Sid was outside, standing on the doorstep with the air of loitering with intent.

"You wanna see the film?" he asked, when Gabriel unlocked the door.

"Now?"

Sid nodded.

"I'll get dressed and come over."

At the entrance to the Degraves' flat, Sid pressed his forefinger to his mouth, and they tiptoed inside, mindful of a soft blubbery snore in the background. Once in his room, Sid relaxed, and proffered whisky, from the bottle. Gabriel hesitated.

"I don't have myxomatosis," said Sid.

Gabriel drank, observing the room, which was furnished largely with film and video equipment—the space machines he had seen through the window. Sid motioned him to sit in front of a screen; and then sat cross-legged alongside Gabriel, fingering a control panel. The film-maker was in his element here; but somehow he seemed not quite at ease.

"I was running through the film, seeing what I could do with it, really. Then I noticed things on the screen I couldn't remember filming on the beach."

"Things?" Gabriel interrupted.

"Figures . . . mostly. I didn't shoot anybody on the beach—there was no one else except you, and you didn't want to be disturbed. Twang, twang." He imitated the gesture of plucking at a guitar.

"Get on with it," said Gabriel.

"Anyway, there's these figures—strange people—superimposed on my beach footage, like someone had been making a montage. Not me."

He touched switches on the control board, and the screen lit up, at first blank—then tussocks, and irate seagulls fleeing skywards.

"Silly buggers—but pretty. This is where it begins."

In the next shots, Sid had been filming down the slope of the bluff, towards the beach. At the edge of the sand was a square object, and Gabriel leaned forward.

"That was never there."

Sid halted the film, and they stared at the still for a moment—but the square remained an enigma.

The next footage was of sky, tussocks and sea. Watching it, Gabriel fidgeted. Sid was taking a long time to descend the bluff, and he wanted the mystery cube to come into view again.

"There it is!"

Seen at close range, the square was unmistakably a hut, built of driftwood and what looked like bleached bones. In front of it was a grubby heap of furs. As they watched, the pile stretched, stood up, and was a hulk of a man dressed in skins. He yawned, revealing huge yellow teeth bled into points.

Gabriel shivered. "What a monster."

The nightmare moved towards the camera and out of focus. Now he was a hairy blur gobbling up more of the frame with each step. Then abruptly he turned, and disappeared from view.

"Almost on top of me," said Sid. "But that's not the last of the big bloke; he followed me down to the beach."

He glanced at Gabriel.

"You've gone white, mate. Have some more whisky."

Gabriel took a swig, and watched long vistas of Hunter's Beach, shot from near the high tide mark. In one, the composition was unbalanced by the big yeti, which sauntered across the background.

"Boss," said Sid. "Look at the way he walks."

Gabriel silently agreed, remembering an army general walking down that beach in the same manner: as if he commanded the very sand on which he trod.

There was an abrupt discontinuity, as Sid switched from views of the beach to studies of seagulls. One silver gull padded away from the camera, stopping at a safe distance to preen.

"Look at what's behind the birdie."

A small fire had been built; and crouched beside it was a boy, cooking small fry on a spit. He was runtish, scraggy and wearing dirty rags.

"Funny how the gull isn't scared," said Gabriel, "only a few feet from fire, and a human being."

"Not when I took the film."

Suddenly the hairy monster stepped into the frame. Gabriel jumped, and so did the boy cook. The latter recovered quickly, despitted the fish, and placed them in a square box. The boss grabbed his dinner, and strode off without a sign of thanks. The boy stared at the man, following him out of the frame and down the beach with his gaze—a visual pursuit. Sid snickered.

"If looks could kill. I know what that was about protection racket."

The gull unexpectedly lifted off, and the screen returned to long views of the beach. Sid was wandering back to Gabriel. Almost the last shot was a silhouette of the bluff, which, unexpectedly, was crowned with a line of squares and triangles.

"That's the old Marine Research Station . . . no it's not."

Sid obligingly stopped the film again.

"Could be a village, but it's too far to tell," he said.

"Go on," said Gabriel.

The next shot was of the approaching tide, and then the screen went blank.

"Show's over," said Sid, and switched off the machines.

They finished the whisky, and then Sid suggested, 'Ghosts?'"

"Those two were white people."

"So?"

"They were dressed all wrong. The only white ghosts you'd see on Hunter's Beach would be Victorian or later. They'd wear top hats or crinolines."

"And not be got up like cavemen."

"Yes," said Gabriel, thinking *not only the clothes*. Physically the figures had been disturbingly like reconstructions of primitive humanity built from bone jigsaws. He shook his head.

"Mystery," said Sid, and they parted.

Back in the flatlet, Gabriel lay on his bed, fully dressed, and pondered Sid's film. Something dug into him, disturbing his concentration. It was the Hunter's Beach key, protruding from his pocket. He threw it irritably, wildly, away from him, and it landed in the centre of the bedsit floor. The tag shone in the electric light. Pick it up tomorrow, he thought, and let sleep wash over him.

When he awoke, the light was still on. It was early morning, and something from the footage nagged his mind. He ran over to Althea's flat, and knocked loudly on the door.

"Hold on," someone said; and he heard a heavy tread, accompanied by the slip-slop, slip-slop of slippers. Althea was resplendent in an aqua dressing gown, and held a fork, to which scraps of scrambled egg adhered.

"Where's Sid?" he asked.

"Asleep, the lazy brat. Go and wake him up."

Gabriel turned into the front bedroom, and found the film-maker invisible beneath a tangled heap of bedding. He prodded the lump cautiously.

"Get up."

"Mmn."

"I want to see the fiim again."

"Piss off," said the heap. Gabriel despaired. Suddenly an appalling clank-clang resounded from the doorway, and Sid leapt out of bed, as naked as a fish.

"Get out, Mum!"

Althea beat a final crescendo on the greasy frying pan, and shut the door behind her, grinning. Sid wrapped a blanket around himself, and sat on the edge of the bed. He looked half dead, but was alertly awake.

"You had a thought, too? After you went I wondered if maybe there was a shipwreck off Hunter's Beach, before the city and all."

"Like several hundred years ago? No. Those aren't ghosts . . . well, not from the past. Run the film, and I'll show you."

They sat and watched as the scenes repeated: Sid in apparent calm, Gabriel impatiently.

"Stop!"

The film halted at a frame of the ragged boy, as he served the fish.

"See what he puts them in, before he feeds the general?"

"Plastic ice-cream container," said Sid. "It looks ancient." He stared at Gabriel, realising what the artefact meant.

"Future ghosts."

"*Homo devolutionus,*" said Gabriel. He had minimal Latin.

"What's that?" Sid asked crossly, then "Hey! Where are you going?"

Gabriel babbled something unclear, and dashed out of the flat. In the front garden, he suddenly remembered that he could not telephone from his flatlet, for no phone had been installed. There was no question of returning to Althea's and using her phone—he needed privacy for this call. He ran to his car, and drove off in search of an unvandalised, functioning phone booth.

There was only one Institute colleague with whom he could possibly discuss this matter: Herne, a scientist widely and weirdly read. But even with Herne he hesitated to blurt out the full story, so he decided on an indirect approach.

"Gabriel here. I want to search your mental database."

There was a pause.

"Go ahead, Gabe," Herne said cautiously. "What's the keyword?"

"Tachyons."

"Those postulated massless particles some ratbags thought would foretell the future? That's fringe science these days."

"What happened?"

"Theoretical dead end. Nobody could prove they existed."

Gabriel.

"Maybe they looked in the wrong places," said

"What do you mean?"

Gabriel did not want to mention Hunter's Beach.

"Have you ever wondered if our work might have temporal effects?"

Herne paused again.

"Interesting. Can I get back to you on this? I want to look at the tachyon literature."

"Is there a lot of it?"

"Not as much as there could have been. Maybe it was hard to fund."

"Not like military research?" Gabriel asked innocently.

"You shouldn't say things like that' said Herne, his tone halfway between chiding and sarcasm. "Look, I'll ring you later. Number?"

"Haven't got one. I'll call you."

Gabriel put down the receiver, and spoke to the cracked glass in the booth, the tattered phone book, and the graffiti on the walls.

"I've seen the future and it's a future I helped make."

Returning to the flatlet, he found the door open, and had wild thoughts of burglary, but nothing seemed to be missing. Clearly he had omitted to close the door when he rushed out early that morning. He had a late breakfast, and played guitar a little, since there was no computer music to disturb him.

Around midday, Gabriel felt tired, so he lay on the bed and dozed. He had a vile dream, the details of which vanished upon waking, leaving only the certainty that it had somehow involved Hunter's Beach. Involuntarily, he felt in his pocket for the big key. It was not there, and he recalled his previous night's fit of bad temper.

A cursory and then hands-and-knees search around the area where it had landed proved fruitless. The key had vanished. He went outside, and found Althea washing her front windows.

"Sid home?"

"No."

"Where is he then?"

"Dunno. He never tells me where he's going. Just took his camera and went."

Gabriel, growing increasingly suspicious, sat on his concrete step and waited. Althea wiped the foam from Sid's window, and went back inside, glancing warily at Gabriel. The shadows lengthened. Finally Sid arrived with his heavy camera, his winkle-picker shoes wet and sandy.

"My key, please," Gabriel said, and Sid handed it over. The film-maker said, defensively:

"You get me all fired up to go to the beach again, and then you just disappear. Your door was open, and I had a look inside—saw the big key. I can't resist temptation."

He shifted the camera from one hand to the other, and Gabriel noticed for the first time that he was paler than usual; he looked exhausted. Gabriel felt an odd sympathy.

"Did you walk all the way?"

"No. I, er, borrowed a friend's car."

"Sit down for a moment."

Sid sat beside Gabriel and lit a cigarette.

"I figured if anyone was down there I could say you wanted a film of the beach made."

"Thanks," Gabriel said bitterly.

"Smoke?" asked Sid.

"No. I should never have taken you there."

"Why? Who owns that beach?"

"The army."

Sid drew luxuriously. "You don't look like a soldier."

"I'm a scientist."

"Oh, Doctor Frankenstein."

"More or less," Gabriel said. "I work on an alternative to nuclear war. It's regarded as humane—not everyone is killed. Although the first time we tested it—by accident, the experiment went wrong—we wiped out the entire littoral zone of Hunter's Beach. Every living thing."

"I never heard that."

"It was classified."

"Then why tell me?" Sid asked sharply.

"The figures on the film."

"I don't see the connection," Sid said. "Okay, so they're future ghosts—are you saying something you did makes them show up on Hunter's Beach, *and* looking like that? When you called them *homo devolutionus, you* meant they were devolved—didn't you? If you did that, then I don't want to know."

He stood up and stubbed out the cigarette, grinding it into the sandy grass.

"Where are you going? Gabriel asked.

"Home. I'm whacked."

"I want to see the new film."

"But I don't. I don't even want to think about it—or you."

He walked away in the dusk, leaving Gabriel alone, and thinking furiously.

The next day, Gabriel rang Herne, and arranged to meet him outside the coast road milk bar. It was a mutually unsatisfactory rendezvous: Herne had not wanted to leave the Institute, and Gabriel refused to go near the place.

"Here's the video camera," said Herne. "Now can I ask why you wanted me to raid the audiovisual lab?"

"Making a film."

"That is obvious. Gabe, stop stonewalling. This road leads to Hunter's Beach—I checked, and the key's missing."

Gabriel, suddenly tired, pulled the key from his pocket, and displayed the tag.

"I want to make a film of Hunter's Beach."

"Is this anything to do with your nervous break-down?" Herne asked.

Gabriel ignored the query, and told Herne the story of his trips to the barbed wire beach, and Sid's film. Herne listened without interrupting, stowing away the information. At the end, he asked:

"Any possibility the film was tampered with? Super-imposed images?"

"I don't know. That's why I want to film the beach myself."

"Duplicating the experiment," Herne mused. "You need a control film shot by an impartial observer."

"Well, Sid was when he took the film. I didn't tell him about the accident until later."

Herne took a pad and pen, both Institute official issue, from his battered rucksack.

"How do I reach you?"

Gabriel gave his address.

"And Sid Degraves lives next door?" asked Herne casually.

"Next flat," said Gabriel. "Hey, what about your search of the tachyon literature?"

Herne closed his rucksack.

"I'll have to look at it again, in the light of your revelations. In fact, I'll go back to the Institute now."

He drove off with unusual speed, Gabriel noted, recalling a police car he had seen on the coast road earlier, and hoping that Herne would not get booked. He regretted now he had not voiced a request in a corner of his mind: would Herne accompany him to Hunter's Beach? Now he thought about it, he did not much care to go there alone.

By the time Gabriel arrived at Hunter's Beach, it was a grey, high tide afternoon, with a brisk wind scudding the waves. He lugged the Institute camera out of his car, and realised that conditions for film-making were less than ideal—and he a novice, too. Nonetheless, he checked the light meter, and panned across the ruins of the Research Station, feeling slightly ridiculous. In the future, people would live here, perhaps that ragged boy; but all he was filming now were broken bricks and weeds.

He started down the track to the beach, but stopped after a few steps, with a surge of panic, remembering the photos of the hairy bully. After several minutes he was able to continue, shaking a little, but he passed at a run the spot where the hut had been filmed. When he was well beyond, he turned and shot a few frames, aiming at a clump of tussocks that seemed to mark the spot, like an X on a treasure map.

He wandered down the beach, the wind blowing salt and grit into his face. At one point he nearly trod on a crustacean, and at another his shoes were drenched by the tide as he tried to film the silhouette of the bluff. He looked for the place where the boy had fed the 'protection man', but there was no helpful gull to guide him. Finally he abandoned the search, took some long vistas of the beach, and then began to walk back.

He was halfway up the bluff when there was a scream from the beach *(the boy, warning)* and he felt a mass come up behind him *(the monster, poised to strike)*. He dodged, lost his footing, and fell heavily, dropping t he camera upon impact. The surprised seagull—it had only been riding an updraft to the top of the cliff—screamed at him again. Gabriel lay with his hands in tussocks and his cheek on dirt, staring dully as the camera rolled down the bluff. Slope and gravity gave it speed—it hit a protruding rock, and ricocheted into the sea.

He stayed there a very long time, his mind empty, until he noticed that the sea was receding, and the light failing. The realisation that he could not climb the bluff in darkness forced him to his feet, and back to the car. When he reached the flatlet, it was dusk, and Althea's lights shone across the front garden. But the front window of Sid's room was black, opaque.

"Oh, it's you again," said the fat woman. "Sid's gone."

Gabriel reached automatically in his pocket for the Hunter's Beach key, and looked up to find Althea gazing at him bewilderedly. There was salt on both their faces, but hers had come from weeping.

"Car theft," she said. "They came and arrested him this afternoon. Said he went joyriding down to a beach somewhere."

Gabriel took a step back into the dark, lest she should notice the sand on his damp shoes.

"It's funny. I thought the films were keeping him out of trouble, but even that turned out to be shady.

"What do you mean?"

"After they took him away, another lot turned up for the videos and stuff, said they were stolen property. Fair cleaned the place out—didn't leave a film canister. Odd bunch they were . . . I know the local cops, but these were strangers . . . like you."

Her tone was flat, expressionless. Gabriel turned, and ran for the shelter of his flat. After he had slammed the door shut, there was a silence, then he heard Althea close her door softly.

He knew he had to leave before someone came for him too. First he picked up a pile of clothes, then stood hesitating, wondering where he could go. His home, the Institute, the beach—all were unsafe. He strewed the clothes around his feet and picked up the guitar. I can't go anywhere, he thought, and hugged the instrument tightly.

As he stood, he was disturbed by an insistent percussion. Somebody was knocking at the door. He considered the possibilities, not lifting his head: Althea; Sid, out on bail; the police; Herne; the Director of the Institute; or his bosses from the military. Maybe the pair from the montage, the boy and the bully, stood on his doorstep.

The noise seemed to go on and on. It filled his head. Somehow he had crumpled up, sitting on the floor, his guitar wedged uncomfortably between chest and knees. He straightened out his knees—it required a real effort of will—and started to play.

ALBERT & VICTORIA
/SLOW DREAMS

I'm not telling you my name, because I don't have one. Never had the need—it's you blinks of the eye that have to label everything. And it's not like the parrots, careering around the sky shouting Kee-ah, who became Keas. They had some say in it! Some of us were trundling along happily and anonymously for millennia, until all of a sudden you blinks slapped a label on. And with the name came an explanation of how we came to be, imaginative mostly. Then, next thing another lot of blinks come up with different names: Albert and Victoria, a new explanation. Then it changes yet again—sure as rain turning into snow. But if anything changes with me, well drastically, then the world is coming to an end. Your world, blinks. Remember that.

Ngaire, Glacier Cop

The working week begins at dawn in her kitchenette, with coffee and the contemplation of her schedule. With any luck, it will be typical, she hopes, her usual Monday morning ho-hum. Happy tourist capitalism, business as usual in Franz Josef township,

Westland, the West Coast of the South Island, New Zealand. Supply: one glacier. Demand: huge. At the height of the season the percentage can be ten to one, one Coaster or South American visa worker to ten tourists. Wicked Camper vans of greens with dreadlocks. Busloads of grey nomads, backpackers, *Lord of the Rings* fans, extreme sport enthusiasts, bright young partythings. Loopies, the Coasters called them. Get them in, relieve them of their dollars, get them out.

"Or think of it this way," she says to the coffeepot. "Snow in at the top of the mountain, water flowing into the Waiho river out. Just much slower."

Light breaks, as a strand of sun finds a gap in the clouds, shooting downwards to hit the top of the mountain and refract onto a long trail of white, a momentary gleam-gilding. Twelve kilometres of ice, the source high in the summit, its long gravity fall leading down to the green of the temperate West Coast rainforest, and the grey of the Waiho.

"Kia ora Ka Roimata a Hinehukatere," she says. Greetings, glacier! in Maori, her grandmother's language. Literally, Kia ora means, be well. Of all the glaciers in the world, most are in hasty retreat from the increasing human warmth. Only Franz Josef and its near neighbour, Fox are healthy and advancing, thanks to the wet weather of the West.

Outside is a fine drizzle, and she pulls the hood of her parka over her head. She prizes the walk to the Tour Guide offices, a little spot of peace before the village rises and shines its hiking boots. But as she skirts the puddles, a motorbike comes up behind her, potato-potato, the only Harley in the village. Sergeant Maw Purdy, the official glacier cop, slows beside her.

"Mornin', Ny."

"Kia ora," she responds, still in Maori mode.

"Well as I can be, Ny. How's business?"

"History and Culture vultures today. And your business?"

"Goin' well. Speeding fines, two Canadians. Three missing passports—bloody Mossad! Drunk and disorderly, five Aussies and a Finn. Someone's selling dodgy E's again. Two sweet Yank older ladies, reporting their tent's been slashed. 'Yes, ma'am, I know the perp. He's one foot tall, covered in green feathers and answers to Kea. No, I'm not yanking your chain, they do that.

And they're now a protected species, even if pesky.' Oh and Den the Denier cautioned for winding up greenies again, dunno why I bother."

"He's your cousin by marriage, even if he is totally contrary."

A shrug. "And Ny, it's none of my business . . ."

But, she thinks, you know my business is being the alternate glacier cop.

"It's your Reinhold."

"Surprise me."

"He's been in the danger zone again. At the glacial snout, near the portal."

She sighs. "I'll have a word."

"You're staunch. Wouldn't want anyone hurt. Like Reinhold, or the DOC rangers who don't need the Loopies seeing and imitating."

He potatoes away, considerately avoiding the puddle in front of her.

She sighs again.

The day doesn't improve when she collects her charges in the tour van, from the various hostels and motels around the village. She gauges them, remembering the elderly guide from her OE (Overseas Experience) year in Germany, who had begun by asking: "Do we have any Israelis in this group?"—as though working out how much to apologise during his tour. There are Germans in this group, a mixture of nations. Mostly—apart from three muscular young women—they are middle aged, with an aura of formidable education. A side trip from a University conference, she decides.

First stop is St James Anglican Church.

"Does anyone notice anything different about this church?" she begins.

Long pause. They gaze down the nave, at the window behind the altar, with its view up the river valley of the Waiho, and distantly the wall of ice. A man with a grey goatee grins.

"Behind the altar usually is a crucifix"—in a Germanic accent.

"Correct. Instead, St James has a panoramic view of the glacier."

A soft aside, in German, but she hears, and translates.

"You said: 'Almost as if they worship the glacier', correct?"

Grey goatee blushes like a stormy dawn.

"Perhaps, but always in a Christian context. I was christened here, married here, I sing in the choir."

But Goatee is right: what happens in the village, every day, amounts to glacier worship. In leaving the glass of the church window unstained, with a clear view of the glacier, even the most devout Christian acknowleged who, around here, ruled.

She herds them into the van again, and they cross the bridge across the wide Waiho, its braids of gravel, its rushing blue-grey, near-opaque waters.

"The colour's not pollution, folks," she says into the microphone. "Just snowmelt, mixed with pulverized rock dust. Glacier milk, some call it, or glacier flour. Any rock that meets a glacier gets ground and crushed as if passing through a flour mill."

A small boy seated at the front says, loudly, in a polite English accent: "I'll grind your bones to make my bread. That's the giant in Jack and the Beanstalk. Fee fi fo fum, I smell the flesh of an Englishman."

What a helpful little prompt. "Well done. Rock bones ground into flour."

Downstream from the glacier, at the drop-off point, she begins the culture part of her spiel, first opening a button on her shirt to reveal the greenstone hanging on its thong. Several of the tourists already sport miniature tikis, or meres, of the stone. Didn't they tell you, she thinks, that pounamu should not be bought, only given, because otherwise it brings bad luck? Oh well, it's not their culture, and only partly hers, by the strict separatist reckoning.

"The name of the glacier is now Franz Josef, after the Austro-Hungarian emperor." Germanic grins. "As bestowed by explorer Julius Haast, in 1865. Franz Josef and Fox glaciers were also called Albert and Victoria, after the English queen and her consort. Strange for ardent lovers, parents of nine, hey? But there was a precedent. The Maori name is Ka Roimata a Hinehukatere, the tears of the avalanche girl. Two ancestor beings, tupana, lovers, went climbing on the mountainside. The woman, the wahine, was an adept mountain climber—"

The trio of young women are paying intense attention.

"—her lover Tawe a novice. He got buried in an avalanche and killed. His grave is Fox glacier, 20 miles away, Te Moeka a Tuawe, Moeka meaning final resting place. Franz Josef was formed from the tears of Hine Hukatere."

"Cry me an avalanche," says an American. They all gaze at the glacier, the bridal veil of ice, with at the bottom, where crevassed ice meets the Waiho, a dark hole, the glacial portal, an ice cave.

"Ahem!" Back to business. "Now until 1 am is your free, unstructured time, to explore. Don't go beyond the warning signs, we had two Indian brothers do that at Te Moeka a Tuawe. They got buried too—under 100 tonnes of ice. Keep alert: if you see a big chunk of ice fall off the glacier, get out of the riverbed fast! The water level can rise up to a metre, and I wouldn't like you to drown."

That gives her a window of time to herself. She reverses the van, narrowly missing a tour bus, and speeds back alongside the Waiho. A turnoff takes her down a dirt track towards what was once a caravan park, abandoned after a year of flooding excessive even for the West. A few abandoned caravans, too decrepit to move, remained, among them one with a trail bike parked in front of it, with an Austrian flag sticker.

The spare door key is in the usual place, underneath a scrawny potted geranium. She enters, to find the tattered curtains drawn, and fetid male dark. She pulls the curtains back to reveal a view of treed green hillside fit for a tourism poster. Then she plumps down beside the shrouded shape on the bed. It groans, faintly.

"Wakey wakey, Reinhold. Shall I be wifely and bring you coffee? Or just kick your arse, also a wifely act."

A head slowly emerges from the sleeping bag, grizzled, thinning chestnut curls, then a stubbly face, and hangover breath. She kicks an empty bottle by the bedside, which rolls, stopping at a logjam of assorted camping and climbing equipment, from a chilly-bin to a camp stove.

"If you must drink moonshine, stick to Old Hokonui, they claim quality control."

She sniffs, noting a meaty smell from a saucepan atop the camp stove. "Possum stew? You really have taken to our local ways."

A mumble.

"Coffee? Aren't you lucky, I keep a thermos in the van."

On the way out and in again, she clocks the overhanging cloud, the tingle in the air that means building thunder. Reinhold at least is sitting and has his eyes open now. Still a good-looker, godammit.

His lips move, he concentrates on forming the words. "The Rangers?"

"No, Maw sent me." She nods at the chilly-bin. "What were you up to? That old party trick, Ice Sizzle?"

Glacial ice often contains air, imprisoned under pressure. When dropped in Scotch, or if pushed, moonshine, it crackles as it melts, cheap entertainment, a way to impress some gullible girl into bed. It had worked with her, in a Tyrolean ski lodge, on her OE . . .

He drinks, goes into a coughing fit, and wordlessly touches the pounamu.

Why do you have to push my buttons? she thinks. The greenstone she had found during the heady days of their Kiwi courtship, washed up on a gravel bank of the Waiho. It had a hole at one end, as if bored, a fragment of an artifact, smoothed by the passage of water laden with rock flour. The nearest greenstone deposits were distant: somebody had surely dropped it. Reinhold had got a spare shoelace from his pack, threaded the pounamu on it, and tied it around her neck. Where it had stayed ever since, despite rows, drinking, and the trial separation.

For a moment they just stare at each other in the darkening space. Then comes a sudden flash of lightning, followed by a thunderclap, closely. The lightning has struck nearby, on or around the glacier.

"I must get back, my charges could be struck by lighting."

"So I am spared the lecture," he says, enunciating properly at last.

"Consider yourself warned, then," she says, near snatching her cup back.

"I know, I know. But wait—"

"I can't!"

"What was it you said, when you found the pounamu?"

The recollection halts her. "We were talking about Ötzi."

"And how there were no legends about him in the Tyrol, he was covered by the Ötzal glacier 4000 years ago."

"And I said, 'the tupana, they had only a quarter of that time here. But they are remembered.'"

And at that moment, that was when she had seen the vivid green . . .

"Then, Ngaire, you said something about a gift. Chosen as if your mind had been read. Fanciful, I thought, but didn't say. New lover's tact. But in fancies are sometimes truth. I . . ."

Another lightning flash, this time the thunder simultaneous, rocking the caravan, followed by rattling rain.

"Reinhold, I can't reminisce right now!"

"Then what do you make of this?" He reaches under the bed, emerging with what looks like a bullet case, flattened and twisted. "I found it, below the glacial snout."

"Guns, bullets, we're the wild West here."

"And next, not so easily explained . . ."

His hand unclasps on an iron cross, so battered a truck could have run over it, almost unrecognizable.

"Where d'you find that?"

"At the bottom of my glass! I've got witnesses, too. In ice I'd collected at the portal. As if it was meant for me, my great-grandfather's medal, from WWI . . ."

"Some Goth tourist dropped it down a crevasse," she says quickly. "And now I gotta go."

Leaving him open-mouthed, she dodges the raindrops to the van, and heads back to the glacier as fast as the ruts will permit. Her tour group she finds huddled under scrub bush, damp as water rats, but as a quick head count establishes, all present, not one drowned or struck by lightning. And grinning all over their faces.

Kee-ah!

The kea was simply unlucky. Foraging, it flew too close to a human, armed and dangerous. The bullet struck its breast, drew blood. It fled up the mountainside, but began to weaken, drifting downwards to meet the crevassed wall of ice. The powerful clawed feet skidded onto the névé, and trying to flap upwards, it fell back in a heap. This time it did not get up, and the snow beneath it tinged red as its underwing feathers.

Snow began to fall. Hypothermia is not a bad way to die, even for a bird, the cold entering the body giving the illusion of basking sunwarmth. Soon the kea was but a heap under the snow. And, as it stilled, began to freeze, it became one with the ice of the glacier. Its walnut-size brain is among the most highly intelligent, for birds, and as its memories went, of hunting, tormenting tourists, other memories sneaked in. Slow dreams . . .

The earth remembered from 600 million years ago, one great ball of ice, the greatest ice age, all life almost wiped out. Millions of years blink by, and a warmer era begins. On a steamy sub-polar day, the keas' ancestors, tupana who were small feathered dinosaurs, wheeled and howled in the sky above Gondwanaland.

Twenty thousand years ago, the mega-saurians had gone, and one third of the earth was covered in ice sheets. The kea dreamed slowly now, in glacier time, riding the mass of ice, over 60 metres thick, as it swept down to the sea, clutching boulders in its icy grip, scouring them along valley walls, a juggernaut of destruction. A moa, the extinct giant bird of Aotearoa, bobbed its head in the scrub, a pair of keas screeched at the advancing ice.

The mound of feathers under snow twitched in response, then went completely still. The memories of the bird mingled with ice, adding its flash and swagger to the slow dreams. A year later, the kea was encased in firn, the intermediate stage between snow and the blue glacial ice. Slowly, centimeter by centimeter, it travelled down the valley towards the sea.

Decades later, from out of the glacial portal, a battered red feather floated into the Waiho.

It looked as if it had been through a mill.

Ngaire

That evening, she is frankly exhausted. One of the three beefy young women had a limp, which as she disembarked from the van crumpled her in pain. A slip on the glacial pebbles, a fracture of a footbone, turning Ngaire into nurse, then ambulance. Still she did the right thing, earning a farewell hug:

"We loved the story about the Avalanche Girl."

In the pub, the rougher, less touristy and the more favoured by locals, she orders an Emerson's, the Taieri George, with a flavour of Christmas pudding, an ideal comforter. Several bottles later, she is replete, and only picks at her hamburger and chips, her body language saying: leave me alone. Then a familiar voice, loud and grating, catches her unwilling attention:

"An' this man, US military scientist he was, sez as he got off the bus, thanks for the talk, you're a straight shooter, all this global warming is a load of bullshit . . ."

Den Bamber, alias Den the Denier, the local contrarian. When the place was crawling with hippies, he went even too right-wing for the National Party. Then, after some fool of an uncle died and left him a property up Hokitika way, he became the only anarchist dairy farmer in probably the whole of Aotearoa. Pity it didn't extend to the cows. The farm predictably going belly-up, he drifted around, relief tour bus driver, but only in emergencies, thanks to his habit of regaling the Loopies on his latest contrary craze: what was wrong with the greenies, the Maori, the global warming conspiracy.

She glances around, spots his audience: by the look of it adventure tourism Yanks, and their paunchy, Republican parents. And also the involuntary listeners, getting wound up. She would have to stop the fight before it started . . .

She sidles behind him, puts a hand on his shoulder. He smirks at the contact, then registers her voice, inches from his ear.

"Maw's sick of cautioning you, he says. So put a sock in it."

"Shan't. What's wrong with free speech?"

"The defence some of these good folk here will be using, of provocation."

He pushes her hand aside. "Now, as I was saying . . ."

"You heard her, didn't you?"

She jumps, as Reinhold comes barreling in, cleaned-up and sober, separating them, and at the same time getting between Den and a couple of dreadlocked, big guys, who have stood, their fists clenched. Deflected, Den turns on Reinhold . . .

"Kraut, you got something of mine!"

Oh gawd, she thought, not that again. We were only fifteen, there weren't many sexual partners at high school that I wasn't related to in some way . . .

Then a girl seated at a windowseat at the other end of the bar screams, and falls to the floor as if lightning-struck.

"OD!" somebody yells. Ngaire goes into automatic, first-aid mode. She pushes her way through the onlookers, a female battering ram, to find the girl conscious, but freaking out, thrashing around in a puddle of spilt beer. She grabs the girl, pulls her upright to a sitting position, registering the bulging eyes, the racing pulse, the snow-sunburn from one of the Adventure tours. So you thought you'd get even more adventurous, sample the local drugs . . .

"Whatcher take? There's some dodgy E's around."

The girl nods, gulps, speaks in broad Mancunian: "That glacier, it fookin' opened an eye in the ice and blinked at me."

The muffin top is cold beneath her hands, the heavy cleavage goose-pimpled.

"Winked more like," says an onlooker.

"Shut up, you callous shit!" Big Rewi the bouncer shoulders his way into her vision. She yells at him: "Get Maw, and the paramedic! And if Den and Reinhold are still at it, throw them out!"

She cradles/restrains the girl, speaks gently. "Calm down now, hush. Take slow breaths. We've seen it all before, we can deal with it."

She lifts her head, stares out the window at the fall of white, now silvered by moonlight. You don't need drugs to see strange things around glaciers, she thinks.

Harry Bamber

Harry Bamber, in his leftover army greens like an ambulant kea, hadn't meant to chase the deer onto the glacier. But his nong of a dog had, and he had followed, only to crash through a carpeting of snow into a crevasse. Halfway down the blue glassy chimney, a shard of ice pierced his ear and into his head. He died instantly, upright, rifle clenched in his hands like an Empire recruiting poster.

As his blood froze, as he became ice, the glacier tasted a different kind of dream, a whimsical plan. Of Harry carting a canoe up the Waiho, with the Missus and her Chinese parasol, and young Whippersnapper, Harry Jr, all off to have a Sunday afternoon paddle on the lake that had formed below the glacier. They said such lakes didn't last long, those smart-aleck geologists. Make the most of them while you can. Well, he'd do that, do Whippersnapper some Kodak shots, to show to his whippersnappers, by and by.

The impossible dream faded out of his mind, absorbed into the glacier. A week or so later, a famished, desolated dog found its way out of the forest and into the village. Even later, the lake breached its frozen dam, draining torrentially into the Waiho.

Ngaire

She should sleep well that night, after the long, tiring day, but she bobs between waking and dozing like a swimmer in surf. She gets up, brews coffee, tries to extract what is lurking in her mind.

Why should Reinhold find an Iron Cross in his moonshine on the rocks? Certainly his Austro-Germanic family had included Imperial officers in WW1, keen Nazis in WW2. Could he carry such baggage to the far antipodes? Was it really like when she found the pounamu, at a time when, returned from the OE, she was feeling her homecoming and her hybridity acutely? A gift from Ka Roimata a Hinehukatere?

She looks up at the moonlit fall. "You aren't so simple," she said. "Nor so simple as to wink or blink at a silly young girl, like a Coaster male."

Like Den, and suddenly she knows she is on the right track. What was it he had said to Reinhold? *Something of his* . . . but Den had been long past, a lot of water and lovers had flowed under their respective bridges. He'd never shown any jealously to Reinhold before.

Suddenly the memory comes, sharp and clear. Den and she, two randy teens, sneaking one night into Granny Bamber's house, the old, sad woman deaf to any lovemaking in her spare room, however noisy. The framed photos along the stairwall, the man formal in army uniform, the bride wearing what looked like a cut-up lace tablecloth; the wedding party posing awkwardly outside St James Church; the service revolver and medals in a glass case . . .

And Den, dragging at her hand, skiting: "The best one, the Kraut one, went missing with the old feller. Kill for it, I would."

She pulls on her toughest boots, roused into urgency. In local lore the disappearance of Harry Bamber had been a genuine sensation, bets being equal on him doing a runner or having a hunting accident. Neither were unusual with Westland males—even the only Bamber in living memory who wasn't ratty. The villagers had been kind to the unwidow, with Harry Jr and another baby on the way. Gradually the story had faded, with Granny Bamber in the graveyard now, her little house demolished for a backpacker's hostel. Few would remember that Harry Sr had been a war hero, European theatre, except Den, who had gone through a neo-Nazi phase. So when the inevitable gossip had circulated, of how Ny's Kraut hubby found a surprise in his iced moonshine, what a hoot . . . Den would have seen no prank at all. "You've got something of mine"—to Reinhold. To the teenage Ngaire: "I'd kill for it."

"Spare me men with obsessions," she mutters, zipping her parka.

She takes her trailbike, riding in the dawn grey across the bridge and to Reinhold's lair. The trailer door flaps open, Reinhold's bike, the twin of hers and a wedding present, gone. Swearing, she hits the dirt tracks again, shortcutting to the river. She skids to a halt on the Waiho bank, gazing through the mist towards the grizzled bulk of the glacier. And as she does, a light winks in the portal, winks out again.

DOC will kill me, she thinks, but bounces her bike along the gravel, throwing up stones and puddlewater. As she nears, the rising sun develops the scene before her like a photo, first the darkness of the portal, Hell's icy mouth, some called it, then the forest greening around her, and finally the juggernaut of ice. An awe-full sight, as she passes the sign marking the danger zone, splashes into the Waiho, freezing water, freed from ice, rising in a plume around her.

Reinhold's bike is drawn up under an overhanging bush. All around are stunted trees, water, the great wall of ice, but no figure in sight. He must be inside the portal. She parks the bike beside his, a marital statement of a sort, and wades into the Waiho, her toes starting to freeze inside her boots.

Water under her, ice above, the darkness of the portal in front. "Reinhold!" she calls. No reply, but she enters, clenching her teeth against chattering.

The light here is a grey-blue, refracted from the meltwater, and what has found its way through layers of ice mixed with ground rock. She breathes ice-cold air, laden with a faint, unpleasant odour. Like Den, she thought, on the dairy farm and covered in cowpats. Glacial air should be clean, unless . . .

A memory stirs. Way back in the Tyrol, she and Reinhold had been manning a hiker's hut, in between lovemaking, and an Italian tourist had burst in screaming that there was a body in the ice, another Ötzi: "*Spicciatevi!*"

A splash in front of her, further into the darkness. She wades towards it, urgently whispering: "Reinhold, Reinhold, it's not worth the danger, you remember the body in the Tyrol, what it looked like . . ."

The smell is stronger now, surely adipocere, a waxy styrofoam that the human body decomposes into without oxygen, with one of the worst stenches on earth.

Reinhold answers, in a similar carrying whisper, tinged with exasperation and fear. "Tell Den that . . ."

"Den?" Oh no . . .

"He made me take him to where I found the iron cross ice. And then we had to go inside . . ."

"Ny, you skedaddle!" Den's voice, his usual volume. "I'm not having Grandad Harry's grave profiled."

Profaned, she thinks, but I'm not correcting you here. "Den, listen," she says. "You don't want to see Harry, really you don't." How to get her point across quickly? At the Tyrol they quickly discovered that the body wasn't another Ötzi, thanks to its yellow beanie, but a missing climber from a few decades back—something not uncommon in the Alps, that home of ice tourism. Ötzi had been a freak of preservation, a mummy with artifacts, thanks to an accident of locale. Not this Tyrol body, which had been mashed, elongated, ten feet of grisly ribbon, barely recognizable as human.

"See this, Ny!" A torch switches on and she sees the two men, Den with his grandfather's old service revolver held to Reinhold's ear.

"Den, do you really want to see your granddad and vomit? Because that's what glacier bodies do to people." The Italian tourist had brought up her breakfast, tinned spaghetti con carne, which had then set Reinhold and her off, dry-retching . . .

"Ny, I toldya, piss off!"

She only takes a step further inwards.

Den swings the gun towards her, and as he does, Reinhold jumps him. They wrestle, she splashing in the icy water towards them.

A thunderous crash, the gun going off. And immediately the sound of cracking, the tinkling of small fragments of ice, then louder cracks and splashes, as big chunks of ice hit the water. It rises, so that she is instantly swimming, being swept backwards towards the light. Just as she reaches it, the portal collapses, throwing her into icy, drowning dark.

Slow Dreams

Ngaire, caught between life and death, watches a procession along the Waiho riverside, the dreams her kind have projected like a magic lantern onto the glacier. Leading it, muffled in mist, is one, possibly more figures, their silhouettes suggesting Maori feather and flax cloaks. In their wake trot a matched pair of dappled horses drawing an open landau, inside a couple and their young children waving at an invisible crowd, their older offspring riding shaggy Shetland ponies and following like a triumphal guard. Mother and children all have the same face, pale, pouchy, faintly pop-eyed. The stately visit of Albert and Queen Victoria, with their brood, come to see their namesakes.

Following trot a troop of horsemen in full military uniform, the helmets and decorations of the first World War. Leading them, on a majestic black steed, is an old man, his moustache as proud and snowy a fall as the glacier. The Austro-Hungarian Emperor, Franz Josef himself. Beside him, on a lesser but still magnificent horse, rides his heir, Franz Ferdinand, assassinated at Sarajevo.

"Wasn't the story that your great-grandfather was an imperial aide-de-camp?" she says, turning to Reinhold at her side. But her husband has become an aged, bent man, leaning on a stick; and the hair that blows into her eyes is similarly grey. A red sun sinks over the sea, tinting the glacier blood red. As she watches the ice fall diminishes before her eyes, retreating up the mountainside, the forest withering, the river shrinking in this nightmare to a sad trickle.

Someone is shouting at her, coldly angry, speaking Kiwi as if through a layer of ice, of which most distinct are the last words: "Just you wait!" Then she breaks into consciousness, finding herself lying on a stretcher, gazing upwards through slits at the cool blue sky. Her head feels bandaged, immobilized.

"Reinhold!"

Maw answers. "He got first go at the helicopter, he needed a blood transfusion. Head wound."

Distantly she can hear the throbbing of the rotors, heading up the valley.

"And he's broken a rib or three. Count him lucky. And you, too. Broken leg, maybe your jaw, nose as well, shiners to both eyes I've not seen outside an All Black scrum."

"Den?"

"With old Harry, caught on a dead tree, upriver. Not a pretty sight, either of them. When Reinhold's fit for interview, I'll ask how Den got a bullet in the face. I know *why*, I helped Rewi throw those two out of the pub, Den broadcastin' loud and clear. Might have been just his talk, but still I told me spies to keep a lookout. First I heard was two guys on a trailbike, heading up the glacier road. Then you sped off an hour later, as if you're psychic. Or just with good wifely antenna. I roused the rangers, we followed in time to see the portal collapse. Everyone thought you were dead."

She reaches out, a wordless thanks. For a moment his big rough hand enfolds hers.

"Ny, you look totally munted, but when the rangers found you and Reinhold, they thought they'd arrived at a reconcilation. Passionate kisses on the riverbank, until they saw he was pouring blood from the head, yet giving the kiss of life. DOC Tim took cellphone footage, as proof. And when you can see properly again, I'm gonna make you and Reinhold watch it. Because I'm hoping that if the glacier hasn't knocked sense into the pair of you, the footage will. Sure he threw a tantie when you proved to be the better climber, sure you retaliated with bells on. But he just found out, and you did too, that he cares."

A roaring in her ears, wind in her face, the helicopter landing. Like Hinehuketere, she weeps, warm tears, never to turn into ice.

Last words

I'm not telling you my name, because I don't have one. Never had the need—it's you blinks of the eye that have to label everything! And it's not like the parrots, careering around the sky shouting Kee-ah, who became Keas. They had some say in it! Some of us were trundling along happily and anonymously for millennia, and all of a sudden you blinks slap a label on. And with the name comes an explanation of how we came to be, harebrained mostly. Next thing another lot of blinks come up with different names: Albert and Victoria, a new explanation. Then it changes yet again—sure as rain turning into snow. But if anything changes with me, well drastically, then your world is coming to an end. But remember you blinks, fire follows snow follows fire. Sure you've made the earth too hot for you, but you won't stop the cycle. I'll be back, bigger and badder than ever. Just you wait.

ARDENT CLOUDS

Call me suicidal (many do). Call me a paparazzo, specializing in subjects blowing their top. Call me a groupie for danger. I just love the spell of sulphur in the morning . . . or any other time. Someone from film school said it best: "You, Bet, are a powder monkey."

Yeah, powder monkey, those boys employed by the British navy to feed gunpowder to the cannons, darting through the noise and smoke of battle. I can just see myself in navy breeches and pea-jacket, my A-size breasts concealed beneath a bandage, wrapped tight. Way back then, if a girl wanted a career that didn't involve babies, wanted adventure, she disguised herself and went to sea. I'd have loved it!

But in terms of fire, noise and explosion, a cannon just doesn't cut it for me. Give me a volcano anytime. That's how I make my living, travelling from eruption to eruption, filming the biggest, most explosive, most uncontrollable things on earth.

It started with an SMS from Spider, as I call him. To others, he's Herr Professor Doctor Sigurrson, theorist of volcanology. Spider makes his lair at a University in a cold and geologically stable part of Europe. There he sits, at the centre of a web of information stretching all over the planet, like lines of longitude and latitude, provided by seismological sensors. If there's a twitch from a volcano anywhere, Spider knows about it.

But he can't go and investigate, because he's in a wheelchair, some sort of fragile bone syndrome. He doesn't travel, and we met only once, at a conference on his home turf. When we met, he couldn't even risk shaking my hand, in case I squeezed *his* too tight and broke a finger. That's how some tell if others are OK, by the handshake. Spider does it at one remove, visually. The clear blue Viking eyes behind those bottle glasses, they looked me up and down.

It wasn't with desire either: I tend to the stocky, and have no-nonsense hair. I also dress super-sensibly—that's not a gun in my bulging pocket, but a spare lens. Volcanologists do fall in love and get married, even Spider, who has Magga, a devoted nurse-wife, always one pace away from his wheelchair. But their real passions are elsewhere. You could see lust in the eyes watching my film, of an undersea volcano hitting the ocean surface in a maelstrom of steam, stinkgas and lava.

In my accompanying presentation, I threw in a few specialist volcanological terms, to show I was smarter than the average nature documentary maker. And, to show I meant business, told how I'd bribed the coastguards to take me into the danger zone. The boat had been bucking underneath me, I had to keep wiping pulverized pumice off the lens, I was drenched in sulphur-tinged spume—and none of that mattered, because I got great footage.

I also gained something else: a boss. Every grouping has its moieties, opposing parties. I privately grouped volcanologists into Spiders and Powdermonkeys. My family, who are old airforce stock, distinguished between Shiny Ass flyers and Aces. The former flew desks, the latter Spitfires. If I'd had the math to be a volcanologist in actuality, instead of just a hanger-on papparazzo, I'd have been an Ace, yes siree! If Spider hadn't been doomed by nature to a life lived apart from his precipitous, dangerous objects of research, he might have been the same. Instead, he was king of the (computer) desk flyers, and as such, needed a proxy.

Spider and I have a deal: he tells me where the volcanological action is, I go there and film it. I also report back: I've been his ears and eyes all over the world. In the process, though I've never seen him again, we've developed a rapport. He gets oddly solicitous: if I'm going to Alaska, he tells me to wrap up warm; or in the Philippines, he'll recommend insect repellant. All this for someone at a far remove, going places he can never physically visit.

"Do you envy me?" I emailed him late one night.

The reply came at the end of a long list of technical data, stuff I really had to know for the latest hotspot in volcanology. Then he got, briefly, personal.

"No. Sometimes when I see your footage, almost. Then I remember that I'm better in my office, away from the explosions. Magga says she doesn't know why anyone would marry a volcanologist otherwise. Someone like you gets up close, but I get the big picture. I don't envy Bet the ant, walking on a ticking bomb."

Which was to me, and to many of the people I met in the field, or at conferences, precisely the fun of it. The Powdermonkeys, we got dirty and dangerous, taking photos or collecting gas from steaming fumaroles; the Spiders kept their distance, analysing the figures, building mathematical models.

I guessed that more likely Spider-proxies, grad students or colleagues, were ruled out for reasons of possible professional jealousy. And in choosing me, I don't flatter myself falsely that he'd been very astute. Not even top volcanologists can go where I've gone. Money is tight in Universities these days, business schools are more important than science. What with teaching, grant applications and admin, few volcanologists can drop everything and dash off to an incipient eruption. But I have connections to tv networks, specialist heat and chemical-resistant cameras, and an ever-increasing reputation for spectacular images.

"I don't know how you do it," said Cody Veitch from CNN. "Always the money shot."

I bit my lower lip. Network execs tend to the crass, but it was true—although my money shot was largescale, rather than in the intimate, bedroom realm.

"It's like you go there, the volcano blows. I remember being an anchorman way back with Mount St Helens, waiting god knows how long for the fucker to shoot its load. And thinking: hurry up, it's a real slow news day! With you, it's like you're in and out of the hotspot within 24 hours, with your footage. So what's the secret?"

"Connections. The best."

Silken ones, I thought, leading to my master, sitting in his wheelchair in front of a computer screen.

But latterly I had began to wonder: how come Spider gets it so right? Sometimes a volcano can get active, but just sits and grumbles, letting off gas or steam, without doing anything newsworthy, let alone cataclysmic. The locals would get evacuated, a costly exercise, and nothing would happen. Spider might have the best information, but clearly he had something else. Scientists don't sacrifice goats and consult their entrails, even for something as unpredictable, even godlike, as a volcano. Spider was a theoretician, and I figured he was perfecting a theory, perhaps a formula: if $x = y$ to the power of z, then the volcano will blow. Being able to predict eruptions would have huge prestige—it would pay to get it absolutely right.

Someday, I thought, I'll be at the Nobels, filming Spider as he wheels himself up for his glittering prize. In the meantime, though, I was having the greatest of times. I went everywhere from Iceland to Antarctica, following volcanic action. I've even been undersea in the *Mir* submersible, filming the weird and wonderful fauna that hang around hydrothermal vents, and their warm, mineral-rich emissions. After that anything seemed possible, like a trip to Jupiter, and its volcanic moon Io. A girl can dream . . .

And then I awoke to the sound of my mobile, 5am in my Miami hotel room at a documentary film fest. Spider was calling.

It was a SMS message, one word:

CHILLIPEPPER.

That was the nickname of a volcano in South America. The real name signified some unpronounceable pre-Columbian fire god, Chillipepper was the easy alternative. Obvious, since it was dead centre of an area famous for its chilli production. The soil around volcanoes is typically fertile, it's one reason why people don't keep the hell away from them. Chillipepper's pickles had a cult following, almost an Appellation Contrôlée, as the hottest and tastiest peppers around. The jar labels even featured an erupting volcano, a bit of a fiction, as Chillipepper had rumbled into life a few times last century, causing a stir, but nothing really dramatic.

The name rang a recent bell, but I couldn't recall anything more. Early in the morning is not a good time for my synapses. I ordered coffee, double strength, from the dozy room service and got onto the net, googling for more information. A name instantly familiar hit the screen: JOE BOY BARRETT. I groaned. Spider might rule the desk flyers, but Joe Boy, Emeritus Professor Barrett, was King Ace and thus eternally at war with Spider & Co. He proclaimed no theorist could predict an eruption, you had to get up there, smell the sulphur. Like some of the flying aces I'd met as a kid (okay, the family were ground crew) Joe Boy had elephantiasis of the ego. He was big, boomed a lot, and shook hands like it was a strength contest. He had a cowboy image too: boots, Texas buckle on his jeans, and once he'd hosted a formal conference dinner in a genuine Nudie suit, complete with sequinned volcanoes.

When I started out, I might have idolized him like the postgrads he trailed in his wake, as the man who would stick sensors into smoking fumaroles, while the mountain shook beneath him and lightning danced in the air. After working for Spider, I saw things differently, that in his quiet abstracted way my master was getting things right, while others strode around, trailing sulphuric glory and yelling: Look at me, Look at me!

Now I avoided Joe Boy, especially since he'd started putting the hard word on me, not sexually (he had another of these devoted faculty wives) but to make a documentary about him. He even had a title for it, *The Danger Man*.

I shuddered, sipped more coffee, intent on my laptop screen. This long weekend Joe Boy would be keynote speaker at a Chillipepper conference, to be held in a city literally underneath the volcano. I scanned the list of speakers: mostly Joe Boy's pals, or if not, considered to be no threat, or easily putdownable. Not like Spider, the ultimate physical weakling, but who on an intellectual level fought like Shelob. Relations were so poisonous between the two they wouldn't even email.

I sent an SMS back to Spider:

JOEBOY! MUST I?

(Spider's response to the idea of *The Danger Man* had been in Icelandic, and, he assured me, obscene).

A few moments later, he replied.

YOU HAFTA

ITS WORTH IT

GETTAMOVEON

I glanced at my multi-timezone watch: networks would not welcome a call now, nor would my travel agent. And I was feeling a little unwelcoming myself. Over the past year there had been—for lack of a better term—a husbandly tone to Spider's missives, as if he'd got used to having me at his beck and call. I was starting to bridle at it. OK, so he thought Chillipepper was worth it. But *I* needed something else.

I got onto VOLCANO-LOVERS. In Internet-land, there's discussion groups for everything, from morris dancing, to (coded) incest, and several on volcanology, varying from the highly technical to the fannish. Deep down, those who love volcanoes are simply groupies, for the baddest, deadliest, most temperamental things on the planet. They just talk in different languages. I could understand scientific papers, though Spider's recent publications were eye-watering. But for simple gossip, easy info, and yes, like souls, I turned to VOLCANO-LOVERS.

Alluringly, there was a thread for Chillipepper. I read through it, stopping at a message sent from a Russian server:

Larissa: My allowance came through! So Chillipepper here I come!

That settled it. Chillipepper here I come too!

I first met Larissa on a grubby little ferry crossing the Bay of Naples. She walked up to where I leant on the railing, gazing at the waves.

"This should be Roman galley," she said.

I looked up, registering the small figure, the raven-wing of hair and her Arctic eyes. Identifying the accent took slightly longer. Unlike some Russians I'd met, including a volcanologist I termed Ivan the Incomprehensible, she spoke clear, if slightly MTV English. But I blinked: how could she know what I was thinking?

As if registering that thought too, she said: "If Bet Murray, famous volcano photographer, is crossing Bay of Naples from Cape Miseno to Vesuvius, then she's being pilgrim, on trail of first volcano-lover."

Russian has no articles, so those learning English as their second language have problems with 'a' or 'the'.

"You're right, I am following the seatrail of Pliny the elder," I said.

Pliny, Commander of the Roman Navy, had on a fine August day in AD 79 seen what would later be called a Plinian eruptian column arising from Vesuvius. And set off across twenty sea-miles for a closer look.

She had a book under her arm, and though I couldn't read the cyrillic on its cover, I could guess it was a translation from the Latin of Pliny the Younger, the Commander's nephew. He provided the eye-witness account, since Uncle Pliny did not survive his powdermonkey curiosity.

"You know who I am, but you are . . ."

"Larissa."

"You're from VOLCANO-LOVERS."

"Also PhD student. My diss is on Bezymianny."

Larissa might look childlike, but she had picked a volcano that even the most macho of volcanologists found scary. In 1956 Bezymianny blew its top off, creating a crater over a mile wide, with a Plinean eruption column reaching 21 miles skyward. It would have been lethal but for Bezymianny being in relatively uninhabited Kamchatka.

"Bezymianny? Bozhe moy! [My god]" I said, in my minimal Russian.

She smiled, a faux-pas smile, but not unkind.

"My pronunciation?"

"No. But Russians say 'Bozhe moy' for ordinary things like cabbages and people. Not volcano."

"I'm sorry."

"Nichevo. That means, no matter."

We fell silent, watching the expanse of water, the cone of sleeping, silent Vesuvius, as if seeing 2000 years ago. I thought of how Pliny the younger had stayed behind, but nearly got killed anyway. He saw a terrifying black cloud, torn as if by giant lightning, with at its centre massing flames. It sank down from the volcano, onto the sea, and rolled the twenty miles across the bay. Darkness came with it, like a light going out in a closed room. Ash began to fall on young Pliny, a teenager, and his mother. They thought the world was ending.

Yet Pliny had survived to provide the first existing account of pyroclastic flows—from the Greek, 'cracked fire', the lethal, fast-moving clouds of gas and ash that are the real volcanic killers. You can outrun a lava flow, but not something moving at 300 miles an hour, at its worse hot enough to bbq you, or suffocate you with hot ash.

"Larissa, what do Russians call pyroclastic flows?"

She looked wry. "Loan word. Piroklasticheskie potoki. Why not borrow 'nuées ardentes'?"

It was French, glowing clouds, ardent clouds too, if we were punning.

"It sounds better, yes."

"I want to see one!" From her face, an ardent wish.

"I might have wanted to be the first to film them, but Maurice and Katia Krafft" (alias the volcanic Cousteaus) "got there first."

"And died for it."

"At 840 degrees fahrenheit, their clothes and hair alight, instant human carbon."

Even for a pair of powdermonkeys, it was sobering. I looked over the sea, at modern Naples, the sprawling houses, and thought of teenage Pliny, watching the nuée ardente rushing towards him like a hellish bat, fire on its wings. He was lucky: in the twenty miles across the bay much of its force, heat, and hydrogen sulphide were dissipated. Otherwise he would not have survived to tell his tale.

Still in Vesuvius mode, we visited Pompeii the next day. I'd been before, but Larissa never had, and she was duly professional when regarding the famous casts of the volcano's victims, the father and son holding hands, or the leashed dog, twisted in agony. We heartlessly speculated about temperature, velocity, and ash distribution. Only the sight of a doll's head, found with the bones of an eight-year-old girl, clutched for comfort in a horrific death, gave Larissa teary pause. "So sad!"

Then we separated. I had a meeting with an Italian production company keen to use my footage in a projected remake of *The Last Days of Pompeii*. They were paying, so I wasn't going to tell them what the *Lord of the Rings* special effects guys had done to simulate a lava flow from Mount Doom: CGI graphics on top of KY jelly.

Larissa had to go to a wedding: "My cousin. They hired Versailles for reception. Why didn't they hire somewhere with volcano!"

In the new Russia, nobody asks where people get their money. At the least, Larissa's family were oligarchs, at the worst, mafia. I got the impression they were so relieved at an heiress not behaving like Paris Hilton, that they would subsidize an expensive volcanological habit. It was probably cheaper than cocaine, anyway.

I continued to the next port of call, some serious talks with *National Geographic*. Life continued as usual: dangerous, solitary, and rather too weird for friends, unless they happened to be fellow-obsessives. Now Larissa was a frequent guest in my in-tray: a photo here (the Versailles wedding looked like Fellini gone Slavic), a comment or professional query there. I figured at first she was networking, then that life had so blessed her that she simply gambolled through it like a friendly puppy. Finally I realised that I liked her, and that unless she was a really good actress, it was reciprocated.

I could put up with Joe Boy Barrett for Larissa's sake.

But what was it about Chillipepper? Spider and his department had compiled a huge form guide to the world's and even some extra-terrestrial volcanoes. I would be sent an extract, everything I needed to know this time. But on my preliminary e-research, it wouldn't seem that Chillipepper rated significantly in the volcano stakes. It wasn't snow-peaked, nor did it have glaciers draping from its slopes like bridal trains (and if melted by eruptions, causing torrential, lethal floods). It didn't have the stately cone of Fuji, nor fountains of picturesque, fiery lava. Sure it was an active stratovolcano, which means explosive, but not very, on the available evidence. It didn't have a bodycount, not like Vesuvius nor Krakatau (36,000 in 1883).

That was offputting, as was the fact that the Chillipepper region was currently in a state of—if not active—then grumbling civil war. For twenty years government forces and rebels had been at odds: holdups, murders, even massacres. The US State Department did not recommend the area for tourists, to put it mildly. There were only two entry points, a minor airport, with an indifferent safety record, and a highway frequented both by guerillas and the local bandidos. My travel agent would freak, and I didn't know how I was going to pitch such a relatively boring volcano at the powers-that-pay. I could always write the conference off as a business expense . . .

But, but, I thought, I'm the Powdermonkey who brings home the footage. I could just simply trade on my reputation. I reached for my address book. Then my in-tray beeped, as it received a huge infodump from Spider. The accompanying message read: What are you waiting for?

What indeed? What do you know, my master?

It took some time to get down to Chillipepper. I only got the fare together after promising Cody Veitch some footage of the chillis, for use in a lifestyle gourmet program. As it was, I missed most of the first day of the conference, after further delays caused by fog in transit. It was dark by the time the elderly prop plane passed the volcano, and I only perceived Chillipepper as blackness between the lights of the city and the stars. And when I got to the site of the conference, I found a major traffic headache.

"Festival time," said the taxi driver. His day job was teaching English, he said, which spared him my dog-Spanish.

Outside a gaggle of girls, wearing scanty frills in various shades of red, yellow and orange, and a lot of glitter, banged on the rear window.

"It's OK," said the driver. "They don't mean robbery, they just want to give the gringa a present."

I wound down the window and received a necklace of fresh chillis, pointed as shark teeth. Dependant from it was a doll, made of one large chilli, wearing a peasant scarf, shawl and frilly skirts roughly fashioned from corn husks.

"Chilli harvest festival?"

"And Don Nestor's day. Our Saint Nestor, if he makes it past the gringos in the Vatican."

He sounded doubtful.

I was intrigued. "Isn't Sainthood automatic since the Pope abolished the Devil's advocate? All you need is a miracle."

Outside, a conga line of costumed animals, pumas, parrots, jaguars, passed gyrating wildly to the amplified beat of drums, electric guitar and some screeching local variant on the fife.

"We've had our miracle: no eruptions since 1872."

I'd read Spider's form guide to Chillipepper, so I knew the driver was slightly exaggerating. There'd been no major eruptions, but plenty of tremors, rockfalls and clouds of ash.

"And how did Don Nestor achieve that?" Volcanology wasn't a science in the 1870s; otherwise some rival researcher would probably have killed Don Nestor, for getting there first.

"He sprinkled holy water on the volcano."

Remind me to suggest that to the Shinto priests near Unzen, I thought, the Japanese volcano where the Kraffts and forty others died. But the driver continued:

"That's what they say in the church. But outside the church, they say different. You see, Don Nestor wasn't *just* a Catholic priest. That's Rome's problem."

A gap in the traffic appeared, and as the driver accelerated to fill it before someone else did, I glimpsed a procession, priests in robes, banners, huge crosses. The Catholic church might be the religious supremo in South America, but underneath the veneer of Christianity are all sorts of wild and woolly variants, with pre-Columbian elements, or incorporating deities brought from Africa, given a quick scrub and a namechange, just like their worshippers, the slaves. Santeria, Candomble, Vodoun; it was interfaith in practical, colourful action.

"What's the story they tell *outside* the church?"

"Don Nestor, he hiked up his skirts and climbed the volcano. And when he got to the top and looked into the crater he saw fire: a god, woken from a long sleep, hundreds of years, and mad as hell to find that in the meantime all his temples had been razed. Now Don Nestor, he grew up here, he knew how things worked. He sat on the crater rim, his feet dangling, and explained. Like how people might go to church on Sunday, but they'd hedge their bets, show respects to what was here first. When they planted crops, they'd turn towards the mountain, and say please silently, and when they harvested, they'd show thanks. But to the gringo priests they'd pretend that the dollies made outa chillis and corn husks were kidstuff. Nobody would say why the dolls get thrown into the harvest bonfire."

"Displaced sacrifice," I said.

"Whatever you call it. Don Nestor, he cut a deal. You're feeling a bit neglected, hey? How about we throw a volcano party each year when the chillis get harvested? I'll host it, to keep the Monsignor happy, but everyone will know who's really being honoured."

Outside firecrackers popped, the partygoers broke into raucous song.

"And in return you lay off the fire from above, for your people, who show you the proper respect."

"And what about other people?"

He grunted, gunned the motor, which backfired in response.

"You'll have to cut your own deals."

I hedge my bets too. Once I'd dumped my baggage at the hotel, I took an everyday, non-volcanological camera, and went out to the street party again. If nothing happened with the volcano, I had just the footage to chilli-spice up Veitch's cooking program, or even a travel show. It was 2 am by the time I hit my pillow, totally wrecked. I made a very late entry to breakfast, when most of the conference attendees were heading to the day's papers. Still I managed a few greetings and had pressed into my hand the latest issue of a volcanological journal. I flicked through it, while breakfasting, then became riveted by the lead article.

"It's Professor Barrett's keynote address from yesterday, mostly," said a lugubrious voice.

I looked up to behold Zapata, to a T, complete with drooping moustaches. The nametag said: Gonzales. He was director of the Observatorio Volcanológico, a local boy who had been studying the volcano most of his life. The conference had been his idea, he headed the organising committee. Then Joe Boy had decided to take it over. Which meant Joe Boy got the glory, Gonzales got a heap of extra work.

We swapped pleasantries, how nice the conference could accommodate me at such short notice, even without space on the program to show my films, yes, such a pity, some other time, maybe. But his mind was not on chat, from the way his gaze kept returning to the article, which was practically burning a hole in the tablecloth beside my orange juice.

"It's fighting words," I said. The usual stuff, but positively incendiary, this time.

He frowned. "He and Professor Sigurrson, pistols at dawn . . ."

"On top of some volcano."

An almost-smile, interrupted by several flunkeys dashing in, with a computer printout. Whatever it was, they didn't want me to know, for they hurriedly withdrew. I finished my breakfast, studied the conference program. Tomorrow was excursion day, including a field trip to the volcano, today was speakers and the conference dinner. Currently Ivan the Incomprehensible was speaking on the chemistry of cooling magma. About as interesting as watching . . . magma cool, I decided. I went back to my room, checked Spider's Chillipepper file against last night's information. Yes, there had been an eruption in 1872, smallish in volcanological terms, but which had nonetheless sent a nuée ardente shooting down the mountainside for several kilometres. No casualties, but clearly enough for Don Nestor to gird his loins and ascend the volcano.

My SMS chimed, again Spider:

LPE.

Oh! I thought, suddenly realising what the huddle had been over the printout. Had I looked over Gonzales' shoulder, I would have seen an image like a fringed caterpillar, a seismic signal. They were called Long Period Events, and measured the vibrations caused by superheated steam, within an otherwise peaceful volcano. Spider had published about them lately, articles studded with ornate equations. If he was right, then Chillipepper was suddenly going to get much more interesting.

I eyed the doll, now hanging from my mirror, then threw the window curtains open. Revealed was my quarry, a brooding bulk, dominating the landscape as volcanoes inimitably do. I sat back on the bed, gazing at it. A familiar adrenaline surge began to build in me, which if I intellectualise it, is the closest I get to sex.

Chillipepper here I come!

Downstairs, it was morning tea time. I went looking for Larissa, but found her conversing with Joe Boy.

"Bet! Goodtaseeya!" He was a man who went in for bear hugs, unfortunately. As I disengaged, I noticed that his beard had whitened and his big mitts were liver-spotted. "Bet, loved your work on Redoubt"—an Alaskan volcano overlooking a major oilfield, which had meant lots of lovely oil money. "Any more on *Danger Man*?"

Larissa was standing to one side, just looking at me and smiling. Somehow I had to get Joe Boy to piss off. So I opened my mouth and said the very thing to piss him completely.

"Well no, I got an approach from an European network for a documentary on Professor Sigurrson. The Stephen Hawking factor, you know."

For a moment I thought he was going to explode.

"Sigurrson! When he's trying his best to ruin this conference!"

He stormed off towards a group of what, to judge from the concerned, adoring glances, were his grad students.

"Ruin?" I said to Larissa.

"Professor Sigurrson sent out—what do Americans call it on police shows? APB. Watch out for perp, one stratovolcano, 10,000 feet tall, armed with explosives and dangerous."

I glanced around, looking for Gonzales, who was bailed up in a corner, pulling at his moustaches and talking glumly into his mobile.

"I was behind him in coffee queue, US Geological Survey rang. Next City Council."

An LPE, if I'd followed Spider's math correctly, was no joke. Neither was the possibility of having to evacuate a city. In the process a major volcanological conference would be disrupted, in which, I would bet, knowing how Joe Boy operated, substantial US funds had been sunk, with the lure of more in the future. If Gonzales wanted up-to-date instruments for his Observatorio Volcanológico, something no Third World government could easily afford, he couldn't annoy Joe Boy. And Joe Boy, I thought, recalling the article, had no time for LPEs, preferring magmatic quakes, vibrations you could feel underneath your boots, godammit, a real man's seismic shock.

"Field trip's off?" she queried.

"Over Joe Boy's dead body." What, miss an opportunity to show off?

"But Gonzales has say, surely?"

"Not a very loud say. He'll mumble something like: on your own head be it."

She shrugged. "We had paper on Chillipepper yesterday, it's not Bezymianny. I'm going on field trip."

"And I am too, Larissa."

In the morning, at 6am, packing for the mountain, I sent an SMS to Spider, to say what I was doing. It was a message that brooked no opposition, he'd know that.

A reply came: REMEMBER WHEN I ASKED YOU WHAT YOU WANTED?

I remembered, from last year, in that curious remote intimacy we'd reached, when I'd asked him if he envied me. What I wanted . . . I'd thought of the Kraffts, then of volcanologists David Johnston and Harry Glicken riding a helicopter to Mount St Helens the day before it erupted. They were all dead now, from nuée ardentes: Johnston the day afterwards, at St Helens, Glicken at Unzen with the Kraffts.

I had told Spider then: I want to take the ultimate volcano photographs, no matter what. I repeated that now, signed off. Dawn was rising over Chillipepper, the mountain—and the field trip—awaited me.

Downstairs, in the lobby, I found a milling crowd of scientists, and Gonzales, shouting to be heard:

"I said, we have a new field trip option, courtesy of the Provincial Agricultural Co-operative: tasting tour of chilli farms and wineries."

Clever, I thought. If there was one thing to compete in the macho stakes with volcanoes, it was chillies. I wandered out of the hotel, to find a waiting line of jeeps, and warmed up with a brief recap of my nicotine habit. As I blew smoke rings—top that, volcanoes!—I watched Joe Boy commandeer the newest and biggest jeep. A group formed around him: the co- and junior authors of his incendiary paper, his grad students, Ivan the Incomprehensible and Boris, his twin and much more understandable brother, me and Larissa.

"Don't we get a guide?" I said.

"I've been up the mountain before," Joe Boy almost snarled, plainly not forgiving me from yesterday.

Russians sit down quietly just before a journey, I knew that from *Mir*. I check my backpack.

"What's that?" Larissa asked. We'd been drinking chilli-flavoured vodka last night, which had left her apparently untouched, and lurid in magenta–green Gore-Tex.

"The corn dolly? Local colour, for my film."

She shook her head, pointed at the air canisters. "You're not diving."

"If I'm caught in a nuée ardente, then I don't want to die with a lungful of scalding ash. That is, if I'm not totally crisped first."

She stared at me, the steel-capped boots, the photographer's multi-pocketed vest and my backpack over thermo-safety overalls, with a hard-hat dangling on its string from my neck, like an old-fashioned bonnet. Nobody else on the field trip was dressed so protectively.

From the other side of the jeep, Joe Boy distinctly said: "Old woman."

Without looking at him, I replied: "The networks won't insure me otherwise."

Our driver arrived, we piled in, and set out, through the sprawling city, passing through slums, then outlying farms, and as we ascended the foothills, thick fog.

Chillipepper consists of two parts, like a layered pudding. One, the bulk of the volcano, is an ancient caldera, broken in parts like battlements, the second is within it, a much smaller and recent cone. We drove up pitted and winding roads, stopping at a small building just below the rim of the caldera, no more than a hut for mobile phone transmitters and geological instruments.

The driver had got out a comic, and a packed lunch, settling in for a long stay. There was no way to go but down, into the crater via a guide line of posts, connected with rope. Nothing could be seen except mist. I gazed into it, trying to locate the cone, and its own personal fog. The caldera looked like San Francisco on a bad day, hardly something to get the adrenaline flowing. While I brooded, Larissa bummed a cigarette from me. And as I watched her head in its beanie bend over the flame, something really strange happened: I felt the chemical surge I should have got from Chillipepper. When I stared into the volcano again, it dissipated. Shit! What was wrong?

Barely able to see beyond an arm's length, we formed a descending crocodile down into the crater. At the bottom, the combination of the rising sun and a stiff breeze wrought a miracle: the fog cleared, blown through the battlements, and we could see. The caldera looked, as usual this close to a volcano, like the surface of the moon, but smelly. The cone rose in the centre, the colour of an ash heap, and to my jaded eyes not much bigger. An unimpressive dribble of steam rose from it.

That mattered not, we had work to do. I got out my best camera, now I had something to film. All around the scientists scattered, the equipment of their various arcane specialities in hand: geochemistry, seismology, petrology. But for the babble in various languages, the soft phonemes of Russian, Joe Boy's Texan drawl, it was completely silent. My boots crunched new-laid-down rock, kicked up soft ash. I still hadn't got the expected surge, well, not from the volcano, and that bothered me. It was messing with my head, as was the remnants of the vodka, and I knew my personal edge was missing. I was like a lens which couldn't focus: nothing seemed clear, or right.

Shots of the caldera soon palled, and that left only the cone. It got bigger as I neared, and started to climb, not as steep as the ancient walls around us, but still not for the unfit. Halfway up I passed a grad student, examining rocks through a lens, and a little later the co-authors, collecting gas from a steaming fissure. One yelled as I passed: "195 degrees C!" At the top I paused, not at the view from the summit, of the surrounding landscape, Chillipepper's domain, but the sight within the crater. It was slightly domed in the centre, a clot of cooled, sealed lava, with who knew what beneath. But nonetheless Joe Boy and Larissa were racing across its surface, like a pair of science-crazed kids.

My mobile beeped. "Oh shut up, Spider!" I muttered. On the other side of the crater, the twins glared at me. I reached into the pack, switched the mobile off, and as I did touched vegetable matter: the doll. Without thinking consciously, I pulled it out and tossed it into the crater. The doll came to rest against a rock, bizarrely upright in its skirts, as if stopped for a rest. Larissa looked up, laughed, then went back to what she was doing. *Now* I felt the surge, and I filmed the doll, filmed her and Joe Boy's antics.

What happened next? There are gaps in my mental records, where the film is my only witness. The earth shook, I knew that, and I froze, as beneath me, with a deafening roar, the floor of the crater split open in a cascade of fire. The view skews up, catching a glimpse of the twins, now cowering. Then a handheld blur, of rocks beneath my running feet, some grey, some eggs newlaid, red-hot and shot from the volcano. The angle careers, as I dodge more rocks, boulder-size and spat out with incredible force. I must be off the cone now, and running across the caldera floor, the most dangerous place to meet a nuée ardente. Then I fall, and the camera view tilts upwards wildly, recording Chillipepper's latest Plinean column, as it reaches for the skies. The film goes blank.

I woke up, in an air ambulance chartered by CNN, that was flying me to the best medical treatment network money could buy. I had a broken ankle, burns from sulphuric acid and red-hot rock, also a compound fracture of the skull, from a projectile that would have mashed me without the hard-hat. As I lay, looking up at the nurse, a seasoned emergency evacuations professional, she cooed: "Your camera's okay, you were protecting it beneath your body."

And thus the footage was saved, much more valuable than any photographer.

I opened my mouth, found it dry and cracked. "And everybody else?"

"They're all fine."

"Liar," I said, a good line on which to pass out. I knew nobody could have escaped from the crater, and the rock barrage would have felled an army. Later I learnt the rescue workers found most of the others in pieces, burnt and bloodied traces. Joe Boy's Texas belt buckle somehow got spat out recognizable, if twisted and half-melted. Of Larissa there was no sign, as if she had been vapourized.

When I next woke, I wept: survivor guilt, the worst loneliness.

I spent a long time in hospital, which I largely remember in short filmclips. Cody Veitch, walking in with a big grin and a humungous basket of hothouse orchids. Cut to a trayful of blackened objects in front of me, all of which I had carried up the mountain. The backpack and vest had smouldered, only the thermal overalls stayed largely intact. I picked up my mobile, its case singed, but miraculously still working. Then I turned it so that the network team, the bland interviewer and her cameras, could read a SMS on the screen, from Spider: GET OFF CHILLIPEPPER! NOW! The date was two minutes before the eruption, when nobody standing on the cone had any indication, from gas emissions, or perceptible tremors, of the fiery force about to surface. But Spider knew, the formula or whatever it was deadly accurate. His Nobel was assured.

Cut again, to an Orthodox priest, bearded, yet with a strong resemblance to Larissa. I asked him for a prayer, in Russian, for his sake as much as mine. He obliged, the unknown words flowing over me like an aural balm.

Cut, to more family, this time my parents, prepared to take me home and nurse me. As they said: "We've been expecting far worse . . ."

Cut one last time, to the network team again, filming me as I watched my Chillipepper footage on a widescreen console. This was their climax, a pound of flesh, or vicarious emotion. The only way I could view it was at a technical remove, ignoring the hype: "the ultimate volcano footage, from someone totally on the spot!". Thus detached, I watched, thinking I'd filmed bigger and better volcanic explosions, though at a greater distance. The eruption of Chillipepper wouldn't have killed anyone, if people hadn't been fool enough to be actually standing on the damn thing as it blew.

I dabbed my eyes discreetly for the team, the expected network emoticon. When they were safely gone, I cried rivulets, for the deaths I had just seen, even Joe Boy's. I'd wished him harm, but not that much—he was simply an ageing insecure man, protecting his scientific glory. At least he went the way he wanted to, pure powdermonkey. I guessed all of them had. But *I* didn't want to, not anymore. My powdermonkey days were gone, the surge, the thrill lost with Larissa on the volcano. So was my career, I guessed.

Could I ever look through a lens again, after filming the fiery death of someone I had only just begun to realise I loved?

The only thing to do was . . . do things. First was an email to Spider. I sent him two words, terse as our relationship had always been: "I resign". No reply was needed, but I got it anyway: "I understand".

Next I summoned Cody Veitch and resigned in person.

"Call me when you need a book agent," he said.

Cody might be a network asshole, but he read people well. Words weren't entirely a new tool for me: I'd always written to the family, even if it was all about volcanoes. I'd also loved posting to VOLCANO-LOVERS. Could I make something of a new medium, get it to say what I wanted?

One day, months later, I was sitting in the family backyard, the new spring filling the trees with blossom. I had the laptop on my knee, playing scrabble, that's how boring and invalid I'd become. Suddenly I closed the game and started typing frantically.

There are ways to tell a story. Something had happened on Chillipepper to make me the only survivor, but there was no easy way to express it.

A dream? Too pat.

Magical realism? Don Nestor and the volcano god arguing my fate? Too arty.

Crime? There was more to it than that. Horror? Beyond the wildest imaginings. A ghost story? Maybe.

What was the best form for my truth?

I let my fingers do the typing or talking, and left it at that. If my film and my writing are at variance, then consider Don Nestor and the volcano, the tales told inside and outside the church. Both have equal validity.

I'm back at the volcano, amid the roar and the fury, running down the slope for my life, and I hear someone coming behind me, a girl's voice, swearing in Russian, of which I understand two vital words:

"Piroklasticheskiy potok!"

I know the recommended procedure, find a hollow, don gas-mask and cover myself. A hideous wait would follow, as the nuée ardente passed over me on its fiery journey down the mountain. Should I be really lucky, it *might* not be hot enough to char the flesh off my bones. I eyeball the craterscape frantically, seeking sanctuary. Next moment I trip, go sprawling into . . . just the ticket. I place the camera underneath me, heap ash over my steel-capped but possibly not fireproof boots, lie down with the backpack over my head.

"Larissa! I've only got the one gas mask, you'd better have it."

"Nichevo. I'll lie on top, protect you."

And although she is so small, she stretches my body-length and more over me, her skirts and shawl like a thick, rustling blanket. She wraps both arms around me, clasping them beneath my chest. The lappets of her long headscarf trail down into the ash, sealing me off from what is coming.

"Here it is!" she says. Hot darkness flows over us, and all I can hear is the crackle of the corn husks all around, as they burst into flame.

LA SENTINELLE

. . . beautiful, deep, azure, enamelled eyes of dolls, with flesh modelled of roseate porcelain . . . that marvellous and oh so adorably pretty little automaton which the good Lord gave you to amuse yourself with. Play with your doll; have some fun and attribute to her sentiments she could not possibly entertain; breathe life into her with your imaginations . . .
                    —Albert Arsène, *Mercure de France*, August 1891.

A psychiatrist's office in Paris, early 1930s. The middle-aged, couturier-clad woman sat herself down on the red velvet couch, crossing her legs, glossy in their silk stockings. The psychiatrist, a young woman with horn-rimmed glasses and an earnest air, stared at her patient expectantly. Something was different: this patient had *la neuralgie*, was a veritable compendium of nervous disorders. She had been quite profitable to the psychiatrist, who was only just starting her career, and had already been sketching a scientific paper, à la Docteur Freud, her chèr maître, about this subject. But today La Veuve Chaussivert looked different, vigorous, perhaps healthy even. Surely not . . .

"I want to show you something," Madame Chaussivert said. She pointed and the psychiatrist eyed the large wooden box, resting neatly beside Madame's feet, in their chic shoes. Shopping, she had concluded, but from the tone in Madame's voice it had more importance.

"Mademoiselle Lazarus, do you know what this is?"

The psychiatrist didn't know what to say. The box looked increasingly like the coffin of a small child.

"It is my cure!" Madame Chaussivert said.

Cure, thought the psychiatrist, in panic. Yes, she definitely saw roses, not rouge, in Madame's cheeks, not to mention this new-found assertiveness . . .

"Perhaps you can show me, then," she said, fighting to regain control of the doctor-patient situation.

Madame Chaussivert's hands, in their kid gloves, rested upon the box. They drew back the lid . . .

Annis stares at the expanse of varnished wood in front of her, and mentally puts herself into the shoes of the person on the other side of the door. It's difficult being an ambitious assistant art curator when you happen to look twelve years old. She can't help being under five feet tall, and being so slender as to be hardly womanly; her round unlined face, she knows well, is childish, as is the fine dark hair that will never stay tidy. She has camouflage, high heels and a smartly cut miniskirted suit in a mature shade of black, moreover a chic hat over her pesky hair, but still when the door opens, the first thing the—extremely Gothic—old woman says is:

"SFBJ!"

These antique dealers! thinks Annis. *Société pour Fabriquer les Bébés Jumeau*, indeed!

"I am not," she says between clenched teeth. "A French antique china doll."

A modern girl couldn't be more insulted, unless termed a Barbie, which Annis knows isn't accurate. The bitch has everything, including capacious tits . . .

The old woman grins like an imp.

"Not really. But I had a Jumeau pass through my hands many years ago, wearing a very similar hat."

Annis resists the temptation to grind the hat underfoot, aware that this perverse crone would only cackle at the sight. She knows now that the impression created by her appearance will now stick like glue. Dollybird. Dollface. If only I looked like Action Man, she thinks. Then people might take me seriously.

"In any case," continues her interlocutor, "I'd rather have a dolly on the doorstep than a vulture."

"Vulture?"

"Dear old George's relatives or old loves. The ones who want to lay hands on all his goodies."

"If you recall our phone conversation, then I'm afraid I am a vulture rather than a dolly. I'm Annis Graham."

The old woman lazily blinks her kohl-rimmed eyes, an unnerving gesture. Annis continues regardless: "Assistant curator, Temporary Exhibitions, City Art Museum. My card . . ."

Fingers heavy with rings and magenta nail-polish take the little rectangle from her.

"What a lot of contact numbers you have. Makes me glad I retired before the communications revolution."

"It's only work, fax, mobile and email." Annis has a strong suspicion that an attempt is being made to sidetrack her. "As I mentioned on the phone, the Museum is holding an exhibition devoted to the Naughty Nineties, six months from now. George Quaine was a notable collector in that area. So we want to get our hands on, temporarily, the goodies of his personal collection."

Again that blink, and this time Annis falters: "You *are* Eliza Kirk, his executor, aren't you?"

"Come on in," says Eliza, with the air of being the keeper of an enchanted kingdom, to which Annis has somehow passed the entrance examination.

Ten minutes later, Annis is goggling. She knew George Quaine was a dealer with infallible acumen for what was about to become collectable and expensive. She hadn't realised that he was such a hoarder. The house is a mansion, yet every inch is stuffed with objets d'art: from umbrella holders to fossils, a suit of Japanese armour on a stand, armadas of china, pewter, crystal, a statue of Lenin, life-size, New Guinea fertility emblems, Chinese scrolls, a Hansom Cab, framed oleographs, a meteorite the size of the stone of Scone, architects' models, a stuffed crocodile, maps, coalscuttles, flotsam and jetsam (certified as being from the *Lusitania*), omnium and gatherum. One almighty mess.

"How could he live in such chaos?" Annis says.

"When last I visited, two years ago, this place was orderly. That was before George went funny. A succession of teeny tiny strokes, the doctor said, affecting the balance of the brain. And then one massive one, which he had, most theatrically, in the middle of the local shopping centre." Eliza shrugs, but the gesture is heartful, rather than heartless. "Coffee?"

There is one space in the house, the small glassed-in upstairs verandah, which does not partake of the general museum ambience. It is set up as a bedsit, with a kitchenette, a sleeping bag laid out neatly on the floor, two chairs and a coffee table— ordinary things, not antiques. Eliza fusses around the tiny gas stove, bringing Annis a polythene cup. "Saves washing up," she says, sitting down opposite. "Always have hated that. That's why I never have anything to do with china, nor crystal."

"There's plenty of china and crystal here."

"Yes, George knew a bit of everything about everything. Antique, that is. Not like me. I was just a dabbler, and then I retired to my beach house and forgot all I knew about the business. Until George's lawyer called me up with the glad news."

She sighed. "The real problem is the provs."

"Provs?"

"George-speak. Provenances. Records of where, when, how much, and what these goodies would be worth if Sothebys got hold of em. George always kept meticulous records. If only he hadn't taken them out of his file drawers and scattered them throughout the house. Just like everything else, in fact."

She sighs again.

"There's logic in this mad mess, though I can't fathom it yet. See here!" She reaches into a pocket of her black velvet skirt and removes a wedge of index cards. "Meerschaum model tram, c. 1890, Portobello Road, 6 shillings, 1969. Yes, George, but where is it? Whatnot, possibly Duncan Phyfe. Is that the one in the attic or the one in the hallway? Stuffed chudditch, 1950. I haven't the least idea what a chudditch is."

"A marsupial."

Eliza replaces the cards, and sits, chin in hand, despondent.

"He rearranged this house with a purpose, but what it was quite eludes me. The place is a gigantic puzzle. I realised the other day that everything he'd heaped in the upstairs bath began with z: zebra tail fly whisk, zither, zoetrope."

"Bizarre."

"Like anything Christian being in the pantry. Now something, somewhere, some connection in his sick brain, told him to do that. He filed their respective provs in a first edition of Mrs Beeton."

"Food for the soul," Annis suggests diffidently. Eliza makes no response, still musing.

"But the oddest one of all . . ."

She gets up, takes Annis's wrist. "Come and see what you make of this."

They stumble up a stairway lined with assorted sculpted busts to find a tiny back room, perhaps intended originally for a servant. The window is shrouded with ivy but in the dim green light Annis can discern that the furnishings consist of: a mummy case, gaping and empty; a small marble weeping angel; a neon sign, unlit, advertising a funeral parlour; a box lying on the floor, possibly a small coffin, given the rest of the furnishings; what looks like horse trappings, heavy and black, mounted on a wire frame; and a line of toys sitting stiffly on the mantlepiece.

"Now, tell me something about the horse clothes."

Annis obediently edges closer, circling the frame. "To be honest, it looks like something from an old fashioned funeral procession."

Eliza raises one pencilled eyebrow. "You're right. And the dolls?"

Passed that test, thinks Annis. She turns, eyeing the row of dolls. "The Woodeny, wearing the black veil—it looks like someone dressed her in mourning. But next to it, the chinese dolls in white—well that's mourning too, Chinese style."

"You know your dollies. I think George arranged this room as a *memento mori*. But there's one thing I don"t understand . . ."

She bends over the box on the floor. Annis crowds nearer.

The psychiatrist saw . . .

Annis sees . . .

A round china face, with the colouring of peaches and buttery cream. The bisque is smooth and matte, a simulation of very young, flawless, flesh, modelled into the form of an adorable girl-child. The imitation even extends to rings moulded into the china ears. Impossibly round brown eyes stare at Annis from between painted eyelashes and the mouth is a pouting rosebud, lined with little white buds of milk-teeth. What a doll, thinks Annis, noting that it is dressed in the height of fashion c. 1890—a little girl's party dress of cerise brocade trimmed with lace and pleated satin, with a matching velvet reticule, attached to one china wrist by a silky ribbon.

Eliza lifts the doll out of the box, turning her slightly to reveal a fringed sash tied in an ornate bow. "And look at her little underthings!" She flips the skirt upwards to reveal petticoats and lacy long drawers. Annis admires the sight, covetously noting the attention to dressy detail that had placed, at the end of those well-rounded calves in their black stockings, leather slippers trimmed with cherry-coloured rosettes.

"Now what," says Eliza, "is a 19th century bisque doll in its original box, mint condition, doing here, in George's morbid room? Well?"

"She might have came from a graveyard or mausoleum," Annis proffers.

"Ah, the curious French practice of incorporating a child's favourite toy into its gravesite, as part of the memorial."

"Under glass, often," adds Annis. "Like Snow White."

"And that is why greedy antique dealers have taken to, not bodysnatching, but dollysnatching. It's a possibility, yes, if only I could find the prov."

They both stare at the doll, who stares blindly yet knowingly back.

"Chèr Maître," wrote the psychiatrist. "I regret to inform you that I have failed utterly with Mme C. She persists in her delusion, that when she was a child she caused the death of a family servant, a coachman I think, who was found in her room one night. I had so nearly convinced her the incident was merely an infantile sexual fantasy! Moreover, she declares I am quite wrong, the doll proves it, she even offered a demonstration here, in my office . . . but I naturally refused."

Annis sits in the Temporary Exhibitions office in the City Art Museum, on one side of an antique rosewood desk, one of the perks of the job, as Cristofer likes to say. He sits on the other side, playing boss as usual. Cristofer has his formalities, such as his immaculate suits, and his informalities, notably a disarming honesty in front of Annis. He's good, even fun to work with . . . provided his orders are obeyed.

"So old Eliza let you inside. I rather thought she would."

"We did have an appointment," says Annis.

"She slammed the door in the face of a Sothebys rep only last week."

"She did mention vultures . . ."

"Which was why I sent the most harmless-looking and personable girl-vulture at my disposal."

"Gee, thanks."

"Be complimented. It worked, didn't it? Now what has she got that would suit our Naughty Nineties exhibition?"

"Lots. But then I think you knew that already . . ." Seeing as you sent me down there in the first place, she silently adds.

"I've known George since I was a schoolkid, he'd pay me to go round garage sales for him, looking for collectables. I got my first practical training in aesthetics that way. So yes, I had a fair idea of the sort of gold you were likely to strike."

Annis opens her electronic notebook. She hadn't dared bring it out under the kohl-lined, disconcerting gaze of Eliza, but had driven around the block after leaving the house, to make frantic notes from memory, watched curiously by some deros sitting drinking in a vacant lot. The screen scrolls, and she recites, a catalogue of treasures . . .

"Is that all?" says Cristofer.

Annis jumps. She had been mentally back in the house, with the treasures, as if just reciting the list had summoned her, in spirit, to their valuable presence.

"No, of course not. The house was packed, as I said. And I hardly saw a tenth of what might have been relevant to the exhibition."

Cristofer pauses, thinking. "Try and get the doll," he says. "At least temporarily, if not permanently."

"I thought you might say that."

He shrugged. "The public adores such cutesy Victoriana. As long as they don't think too hard about it."

"You mean?"

He leans back, puts his feet on the desk. "I've never had the slightest interest in little girls."

Well no, that's obvious, thinks Annis. And thank god for that!

"But every time I see a Jumeau, or one of those insanely valuable Brus—see, I do know a bit about the subject, though not exhaustively, not like the maniacs of china doll fandom—I get reminded of certain things. Pretty Baby. Lewis Carroll taking photos of little naked Alice. The Victorian trade in young girl whores. They're alarmingly alluring, those French bisque bébés. Fetishistic, even. I'm too sexy, they seem to be saying out of those innocent little rosy mouths. For what?"

Silence falls in the office. Annis never disagrees with Cristofer if she can help it, so no way is she going to blurt out that she collects dolls, in a minor, inexpensive fashion, and a Jumeau to her is delicious for reasons that are purely aesthetic. And yet, she acknowledges, there is something in what he says. She remembers a Czech film of *Alice in Wonderland* from her unit of media studies, a surreal, dark, and imaginative interpretation, involving live action, claymation and puppetry. Alice had been represented by a spirited child actress; and also, when miniaturized by the EAT ME pills, a Jumeau Alice, essence of girl-power in concentrate, far more cute and charismatic than the living child. The juxtaposition had been disturbing, making Annis recall the more unsavory aspects of Carroll—but she had no intention of admitting that to Cristofer.

"What is it, by the way?" he says, after a moment. "I mean, the make of the doll."

"I don't know. But I'm working on it," she replies.

Working on it, because in the brief time she had spent with the doll, she had inspected it for a maker's mark, as best as she could *unobstrusively*. Eliza, she had decided, knew as much about dolls as did Cristofer—she knew the names and what commanded a price, but lacked the knowledge of a connisseur. As she cradled the doll, she felt sure that here was something French, but not one of the easily recognizable brands. Short of undressing the doll, it was hard to be certain. Dim as the room was, she had noticed a crest impressed on the wooden lid of the box, and had silently filed it away in her mind. She had a good visual memory, and this device seemed vaguely familiar to her.

"It's not a SFBJ," she says finally. "But certainly its equal, in terms of quality."

The conversation ends and Annis leaves the office, wandering out into the museum via the staff security door. Closing her eyes momentarily, she summons the image of the crest on the box, then takes the lift, two floors up, to Fine Arts and the ceramics section. No dolls are displayed here, despite the common clay matter; but nonetheless she crouches down beside the display stands devoted to French china of the nineteenth century, inspecting the contents minutely. The crest associates itself in her mind with a dinner service, rather than anything she could recall from the arcane reaches of Victorian doll manufacture. But as she stares into the glass, the image of the crest wavers and fades, leaving her frustrated. I'll have to go back, she thinks, to see Eliza . . . in fact I'm obliged to, as she didn't say one way or the other whether she'd loan anything to the exhibition.

Doctor Freud, in his Vienna office, wrote: "My dear pupil, what a fascinating pathology! Of course you must persist with the patient, of whom I have taken the liberty to term the doll-lady. Do go and visit Mme C. & impress on her the terrible consequences of discontinuing a course of psychoanalysis. The case study will make your name . . ."

This next appointment, Annis leaves her hat back at the Museum, but nonetheless, as Eliza lets her in, she still feels very much an SFBJ. She clutches at her bulky shoulder bag, recalling Cristofer's instructions, which among other things include softening up Eliza. Yet Eliza seems evasive, preoccupied even, as she shepherds Annis down the hallway, only showing interest when Annis mentions the doll.

"No, I still haven't found anything about her. Though I had one success: just when you knocked I found a prov for something dead obvious. That couch upstairs, on the back landing."

"I don't recall."

"The red velvet, Napoleonic one, with the gold fringing. I always did think it looked like a psychiatrist's couch, and now I know for sure . . ."

She leaps up, eager to show Annis her cleverness. At least we're going in the right direction, thinks Annis, puffing a little in Eliza's wake, along the cluttered hallway and up the back stairs again. The old woman is surprisingly fit. Yet at the landing she abruptly stops, exclaiming under her breath.

"You all right?"

"Mmn? Of course I am. Just got a little surprise, that's all."

Annis follows her gaze, to see through the open door of the morbid room, the doll, as starry-eyed as a child watching television, sitting on the closed lid of its box.

"You were playing dolls and sat her up so cutely?"

No, thinks Annis, I wasn't. She eyes Eliza covertly. Is this eccentric woman going unbalanced, like George, with a teeny stroke or two?

Eliza saunters into the room, and returns with the doll, whom she lays down on the couch. "Go on dolly, tell me your secrets." She grins at Annis's bemusement. "This couch belonged to a genuine Freudian, the prov says. There's even an authenticating letter stapled to the prov. Gift from Sigmund himself, it says. I'll have to get onto the Freud archives."

Annis sits down at the end of the couch, thinking that its red velvet and fraying gold fringe is more suggestive of a prostitute than a psychiatrist. "I want to authenticate the doll. Or at least find her maker's mark."

"Well, go ahead, don't mind me, I'll go and boil the kettle, since I've got company . . . again."

Left alone with the doll, Annis then inspects the sole of the shoe and the nape of the neck, the obvious places for maker's marks. Then, very carefully, she undresses the doll, until the kid leather body with its china limbs sprawls naked in her lap. The innocence of dolls, she thinks, their asexuality, and yet at the same time there is something quite provocative about the French bébés . . . Feeling guilty at the thought, she dresses the doll again. It had been as free of brand names as a new born infant.

Perplexed, she opens the reticule, more from curiosity than anything else. She expects to find a doll-sized handkerchief, at least, but the bag is empty. To make sure she sticks her forefinger into the reticule and her nail catches on some stitching, half-unravelled. She feels around, sliding a fingertip into the lining fabric, and touches something stiff as cardboard, but smooth. Tearing the stitching but not the fabric, she extracts a small photograph, no two, and greedily inspects them.

The first is from the thirties, a head shot of a young woman with bobbed dark hair, glasses and a serious expression. The second is older, from the late nineteenth century, a family grouping of four generations. Around a child, perched on a pedestal, are father, mother, grandfather, and even great-grandfather. The men are dark, aquiline, bearded and patriarchally proud, all from one family; unlike the mother, standing to one side, a lighter brunette, to judge from the tone, her face intelligent but sad. Yet it is the child, a darkly pretty little girl, dressed to the nines circa 1890, who holds Annis's attention.

"Clever you," says Eliza.

Annis jumps.

"No, don't look guilty, I always move around silently, that was how I used to surprise shoplifters in my olde curiosity shop. You're a sharp one, to think of looking in dolly's little bag."

"The doll is the child," Annis says. "The dress looks an exact copy. And the face, that's from the child, just idealized a bit."

Eliza looks from Annis to the photo to the doll.

"She's a bit like you."

"Gee, thanks."

"I know I said when we first met that you looked like an SFBJ. But there's a resemblance to the child as well."

"In as much as we both have dark hair and round faces!" Annis replies, annoyed.

Eliza ignores the tart response: "Is this woman with the glasses the child grown up? No, too young. The next generation along?"

They compare the photos. "No," Eliza concludes. "No resemblance. Apart from being dark and clever-looking. And what my mother used to call 'furren'."

Annis turns the photos over, to see nothing on the back of the thirties snapshot. However, the other, of the family group, gives the photographer's name: J. Chevalier, Vessy. I know where that is, she thinks, and a small lightbulb gleams in her mind.

"They are 'furren'—French, like the doll," she says.

"No, I mean more than just French. That young mother, she's got a very gallic face, but not the others. Russian, maybe. Can't put my finger on it, though."

Annis slips the photos back into the reticule, knowing now she has at least one clue to the doll's 'prov'.

"Shall I put her back in her box, safe and snug?"

"Do so."

Annis takes the doll and goes into the morbid room, finding the box by feel rather than sight. She turns, listening to the sound of Eliza on the stairs, going down. She'll check, she thought, to see if I snaffled the photos . . . which I will, of course, but not the way she thinks. She reaches into her shoulder bag and removes Cristofer's polaroid camera.

"Say cheese, dollie," she says.

"Soften up Eliza," Cristofer had said. "Make a record of the doll, and also anything else suitable for the exhibition. And . . ."

"And what?"

"I think that can wait until after your next visit."

Madame Chaussivert put the letter aside and sighed. That poor girl, so persistent, so convinced she had the right answers, even getting Docteur Freud to write on her behalf . . .

She glanced at the doll in its box. "We will show her, some time," she said, aloud. "But not now."

She closed the lid on the staring glass eyes.

Annis's mobile phone rings as she skips down the steps of the Quaine mansion, and she rummages for it in her bag.

"Where have you been?"

"Cristofer! Doing what you wanted, of course."

A passing youth is staring at Annis. Now he stops, nears her ingratiatingly.

"Have you forgotten?"

She smells from the stranger the fumes of tobacco, alcohol, something else rank . . . oh one of those deros, she thought, like the guys watching me the other day. Feeling a sudden surge of pity, she fumbles in the bag with her free hand.

"Forgotten what?"

"You Annis?" says the youth. He is sandy-haired, spotty, muscular, and she knows she has never seen him before, not so he would know her name.

"The dinner, with the new Minister for the Arts! Tonight!"

"Yes I did forget," she says, staring at the youth, the two-dollar coin also forgotten in her hand.

"Lucky you live in the CBD then. You'll just have time to dash to your flat and get changed. Something demure, I suggest. Then pick me up at the Museum, back door, and we'll fly."

"You Annis?" The boy repeats. He gestures with his head at the house. From behind her she hears a window open, Eliza peeking out. For a brief moment she is poised in perfect indecision.

"Yes, of course I'm Annis!" Some rough pub, she thinks, back in the days when I was a student, though he really isn't my type. "Take this!" and she hands him the coin.

"What's going on?" Cristofer interjects as she breaks free, running to her car.

"Some beggar. But hey, Cristofer, I've got a lead on the doll, it could be very important. She's from Vessy, in France. Does that name ring a bell for you?"

"Later, later. And don't forget, the demure look."

Yet, fifteen minutes later, as Annis drives up to the back entrance of the Museum, to find Cristofer waiting in his best suit, she is still in her work clothes.

"Didn't I tell you?" He hops into the passenger seat, then half rises, nearly cracking his head on the roof. "What are all these books doing here?"

"I did a detour to the Art School library. My student card's still current. That's everything the catalogue threw up under Plantin. The china manufacturers, from the otherwise unremarkable town of Vessy."

Cristofer lifts the books from beneath him, and transfers them to his lap.

"Oh, I've heard of them. But look, Annis, I really think you should get changed."

"Take a look at these!" She fishes in her bag, brings out polaroids, of the doll, the mark on the box, the family photograph and its verso. She hands them to Cristofer, who gives them a cursory glance, then sticks them in his jacket pocket.

"You live in one of those riverside flats, you said . . ."

"That's the doll, and the family photo was in its reticule. From Vessy it says—and I'll bet you anything the people in the photo are the Plantins. Who else could have made such a beautiful piece of bisque, in a town with a fine china factory? And why otherwise dress doll and child alike?"

"So we'll just detour chez Annis on the way to the dinner," he said.

"Cristofer!" she says, indignant yet obeying. "I don't want my boss in my apartment. And I want to tell you about the doll!"

"Tell me while you change."

In her flat the first thing Cristofer says is:

"Ah!"

"OK, I admit it. I collect dolls, but 20th century only—it's all I can afford."

He eyes her display cabinet, grinning wickedly.

"I think you should dress like—that one there."

"That's Skipper, Barbie's kid bridesmaid. Are you serious? To meet the minister?"

"I've been researching him: middle of the road and brow, but knows what he likes in architecture—yet again. Favourite film:

Picnic at Hanging Rock. Favourite photographer: whatsit who does misty teenage girls in ballet gear or on push bikes. Favourite holiday: going on church youth camps, usually involving teenage girls, surprise. So, if you own any dresses girlish and floaty and romantic, in pastel or white . . ."

"Yes, but it was from a uni production of *The Three Sisters*, and I'd have to iron it."

"Do so." He sits down on the nearest easy chair, stretching like a cat. "This should be a fun evening. If you see quite a few arts apparatchiks showing off their cleavage or their muscles at the new man, don't be surprised—I've been spreading misinformation like jam. Half the guests think he's into iron men and the rest that he's a Dolly Parton fan."

"I'm supposed to be nice to this creep?" she yells, from deep inside her wardrobe.

"Not *that* nice."

She ducks round her bedroom door, displaying the *Three Sisters* dress on its hanger. He nods, then returns his attention to the book in his hand, and she suddenly realises that he has brought the pile of library books up from the car with him, without being asked. So he *was* interested, she thinks, and moments later observes him pull the photographs out of his pocket, then consult an index.

"What do they say about Plantin?" she says, wrestling the ironing board into submission.

"Firm started seventeenth-century, well-regarded, though not something people went gaga over. Nearly went broke during the various French upsets and revolutions." He turned a page. "Benjamin Plantin, who guided the firm into its greatest prosperity—blah, blah, blah. One of those French public intellectuals, did a bit of artcrit. His son Jacques-Simon actually studied sculpture." He whistles under his breath. "Now that's something I'd love for the exhibition."

The iron is still warming up, and she ventures into the sitting room to inspect, curious.

"It's quite well-known, that figurine of the sad shepherdess," she says. 'I've seen it before . . ."

"If you've been to the Louvre."

He picks up the photo of the doll. "Compare the modelling of the hands."

"Oh!" she says. "Like, very like."

"You were supposed to be ironing your dress," he said.

She flounces back to the bedroom. "Keep up the commentary! Ironing really bores me!"

"OK, here's a precis. Jacques-Simon Plantin studied under Rodin and met Claudette Charpentier, another student, daughter of academician, Alphose C., qv. Oh yes, I remember him. Incredibly huge history paintings in the conventional manner. Claudette was more up-to-date, hence becoming Rodin's pupil. Cupid shot at her and Jacques-Simon and Rodin got the pip. Said they would waste their talents painting porcelain forever. Tang of sour grapes in that comment, I think—he probably had ideas about Claudette."

"Like he did about Camille Claudet?"

"Indeed, what a lucky escape."

"Go on."

"Well, art-wise Charpentier-Plantin was a fruitful union. They started designing for the firm, figurines mostly, to judge from the illustrations here. Jacques-Simon had a tendency to grotesquerie, Claudette to the pretty . . . So I'd say the shepherdess was hers."

"Any illustrations of the family?"

"I'm getting to that."

She pulls the door partly to, in modesty, though with Cristofer she wonders why, and struggles out of her suit. Have I got a clean white bra and knickers? she worries, ferreting through her underwear drawer.

"Not in this book. Ah, French women artists, a thin volume. Morisot, Bonheur, Charpentier-Plantin. Bit of a gynaecological disaster area, it says. One child survived infancy. Died at the age of 32."

"Ta-da!" she says, throwing open the bedroom door.

"Oh, very nice. One detail—have you any pale rosy pink lipstick? For that certain je ne sais quoi."

"Yes! Here, in my bag. Now give me those books!"

"No dear, no time for you to sit and read—except for the while it takes me to use your bathroom." He hands her the topmost book. "It's her, by the way. Claudette Charpentier-Plantin. Very bad, grainy photo, but that's unmistakably the same woman here, in the book, and in the family portrait. I don't know who the old fellow is, but the other two men are Benjamin and Jacques-Simon Plantin."

"Yes, but did she ever make dolls?"

The bathroom door closes behind him. Next moment she hears the ring of a mobile phone and makes a dive for her bag, before realising the sound comes from the bathroom.

"Oh hallo, mother," says Cristofer.

Annis glances up, her eyes narrowing. If there is one thing she has observed while working for Cristofer, it is that his mother is very hard to get off the phone. A delay of around ten minutes can be expected, time enough for her to read the artbooks properly . . . or to boot up her computer, get onto the internet and post a query to the newsgroup REC.DOC.ARTS.DOLLCOLLECTING about whether Plantin & Co ever made dolls.

The psychiatrist wrote: "Mon chèr Maître, since you persist in enquiring about the obdurate Mme C. I must tell you about a strange encounter. I had an invitation to stay with friends at Vessy, where Mme, as you recall, has a chateau. I would have not been surprised to encounter her, and in fact while walking in the woods I met Mme mushrooming. She invited me to tea at her home, which was nearby, on condition I said nothing about psychiatry. She said it so charmingly I had no choice but to accept. But as we walked in through the garden I noticed statues, immense clay grotesques of warriors. "My father made these," Mme told me. "Why?" I asked, for they were most horrible creations, with gaping mouths, even (I think) fangs. "For the same reason my mother made dolls, I suppose." Then she laughed. "Who can understand the artistic temperament? I never did, for I inherited my grandfather's good business sense, though not his fondness for pamphleteering." I thought both her parents sounded like ideal subjects for you, chèr maître. We had a charming tea, and I am thankful to say the doll was not in evidence."

As an exercise in chatting up the Minister, Annis decides, the evening has been a success. She sits, digesting gourmet food and good wine (though not too much, to keep her wits about her) aware of Cristofer still talking, the Minister all drunken ears. Then, from the bag at her feet, she hears her mobile phone.

"Scusie!" She squeezes past the tables of arts workers until she can find a spot to chat relatively unheard, in the atrium of the hotel, all marble, glass and potted palms. She leans against a pillar, staring at her reflection in the nearest window. Yes, I really do look like a girly bridesmaid, she thinks. Cristofer, you'll pay for this someday.

"Hallo?" she says into the receiver.

"Annis?"

The voice is female, querulous, and Annis can't recognise it.

"Yes."

"Eliza here. I got your mobile number off the business card. You're not far away, are you? I mean, you suddenly haven't decided to go skiiing in the mountains, have you?"

"No, I'm at the Hilton."

"I'd like you to drop by. Now. I'll even say please."

"Eliza, it's nearly midnight . . ."

"Tell that conniving old Cristofer he can have his doll for the exhibition, maybe even have it permanently . . ."

An offer we can't refuse, thinks Annis. She glances through the glass doors into the dining room proper, seeing Cristofer still in colloquy with the minister. Well, that's our funding for next year wrapped up, she thinks. Cristofer's got what he wanted, for I charmed the vile minister . . . and he can get himself a taxi home, rather than having me play chauffeur as well as simpering dollybird.

"OK, but just for a few minutes." She hangs up, and as she drops her mobile into her bag, a penny drops with it.

Eliza had sounded different, because her voice had fear in it.

Madame Chaussivert rubbed her eyes. She was getting a headache, but this little job of transcription, typing up grandpère's notes, could only be done by her, and behind locked doors too. She glanced at the notebook, reflecting that grandpère's handwriting had degenerated in the final year of his life to the point of illegibility. Not for the first time, she wondered about his sanity. For a man so rational, with his calm logical writings on economics, art, and anything else that took his fancy, the contrast with the last notebook is almost shocking. Yet, though she was only a child of six, she recalled him quite well, and he was certainly sensible enough, though very upset about poor Captain Dreyfus . . .

On her way across the city Annis hits a clump of road accident traffic, and while being slowly diverted around the site where a truck has hit a power pole, for the first time properly observes the neighborhood of the Quaine house. It looks good to the casual observer—trendy shopping centre, nighclubs at one end of the street, parkland at the other—but the gentility has a seedy edge, girls (and boys) wait meaningfully on corners and syringes gleam in the gutters. Once a suitable place for a mansion, she thinks, but no more. She speeds and slows towards the house, dodging road humps, suddenly very worried, because all the streetlights are out. The truck has caused a power blackout and it has made the street very dark indeed. She feels a twinge as she waits on the doorstep after ringing the bell, the sense of being watched. Glancing around she notices, a little way down the street, a figure leaning against the trunk of a palm tree, almost invisible except for one spot of red, a cigarette end. Eliza, where are you? She almost screams in gratitude at the sound of footsteps in the hallway, and the sounds of an aged hand grappling with a stubborn lock.

"Eliza!"

The old woman makes no response, only takes Annis by the arm. She pulls her bodily across the threshold, then slams the door shut. There is light inside the house, yellow and flickering; Annis sees on the hallstand a large candleabrum, its seven branches decked with mismatched candles. The light it casts into the hallway makes dancing shadows, puts a gleam of malevolent life into the glass eyes of the tigerskin rug, causes the oil portraits on the walls to grimace and grin. Eliza opens her mouth.

"What happened?"

No sound emerges, and the old face dampens with tears, mixed with kohl.

"I won't say 'Are you all right?', because I can see you aren't. But I need to know: are we alone in this house?"

The answer is a hesitant nod, yes.

"It's secure? Nobody trying to break in?"

This time Eliza shakes her head. Annis lets her breath out—she hadn't been sure what to expect, prowler or burglar or god knows what. "Then we're safe," she says, thinking: from anything real, at least. She had always prided herself on being a material girl, untouched by metaphysical speculation; but this house, by candlelight, would probably unnerve the most devout atheist.

"Well perhaps I should make you a coffee and you can tell me all about it." Whistling in the half-dark, she knows, but coffee is a great cure-all, and a means of getting people talking.

Up on the balcony Annis prepares coffee by candleabra light, bringing polythene cups to the table where Eliza sits, still dabbing her eyes a little. The coffee is a cheap instant mix, foul compared to what she has been drinking at the Ministerial dinner, but no matter. She is starting to shiver under the muslin of the Three Sisters dress, and needs the warmth.

"Was it the lights going out?" No answer, but she keeps talking. "It would scare me, being in the dark here." By candlelight, the place is very Addams family. "That morbid room is creepy enough, even by daylight."

"There's worse than that." Eliza's voice is moist, little more than a whimper. 'I found a cupboard full of magic stuff, Haitian dollies, African fetish idols, what I think must be a churinga."

"Well, that would scare me."

"It didn't! I'm made of stronger stuff than that!" This time her voice is stronger, clearer. "But it's cumulative, this house, and the history of these objects, day after day thinking about George, the responsibility he left me. You know I feel I can't even leave the place? Not with the vultures." She sighs. "Somewhere around here I had a bottle of brandy, I think quarter full. I'd have emptied it and given myself some drunken courage, but it's gone missing. Things do around here . . . I swear it's not my imagination, but you put something down for a moment and it vanishes. Things move, when you aren't looking at them, I swear. Like that damn doll. I know you can't be moving her around all the time, unless you've got a secret key. Or perhaps somebody else has . . ."

Her voice breaks, quavers again.

"I wake up in the night, and I think I hear footsteps. I go

looking around, and there's nobody there. But I know, I've heard a little pad-pad, like a cat, or someone in runners or slippers. I heard it again, when the lights went out. That's why I rang you."

"Why not the cops?"

"Never trusted the bastards, not after the way they used to rough up me and my girlfriends, just for running a little bar where we could meet and chat and flirt."

Annis puts her head in her hands. "You said before there was nobody here except you and me."

"Intellectually, I know it. Nobody could break in here without me hearing. I may be old but no way am I deaf. But on an emotional level I know I heard something." Her face crumples like a tissue. "And I don't like the idea that my mind is playing nasty goosebumps games with me."

Annis puts her arm around Eliza, and is very grateful for the warmth of a human body.

"Perhaps we should take that candleabrum and go through the house."

"It's a menorah, actually, from a synagogue. Didn't you know that?"

"Not in my background, that I know of." She picks it up. "Now let's start, room by room, and chase out the bogey." She avoids the suffix 'man'. "With a weapon that we can brandish at the rat or whatever it is."

Eliza smiles for the first time. "No such luck. George was a card-carrying pacifist. But I keep a poker beside the sleeping bag, just in case, and any one of those small marble busts would make a useful cosh."

It was late at Vessy, past midnight, but Madame Chaussivert did not care for witnesses of her little experiment. She shivered in her satin dressing gown, watching the statue like a hawk, and then, after counting to twenty, gave it a good firm kick with her slippered foot. *Rien.* She put her hand between the boar-like tusks, into the gaping mouth itself, then withdrew it. For a moment she stood in indecision, staring across the rose garden to the next statue. What, test the entire corpus of dear papa's statuary? And if one of the bonnes should chance to gaze out the window, would they send post haste for Mlle Lazarus and Docteur Freud, to say their mistress had lost her mind for certain?

No, she thought. She had typed the word often enough in grandpère's notes: prototype. That was *La Sentinelle*. There had been nothing to indicate that the later models had ever got to testing stage, despite the hope in all those scribbled words. The answer perhaps lay in all those manuscripts in Hebrew, in the old man's hand, her great-grandpère, or by even more distant ancestors. When she thought of the old man, she recalled the smell of mothballs, and something she had later come to identify as old age. He had been a kind man, she recalled, for he had comforted her mother, his gentile grand-daughter-in-law, as she cried over the latest empty cradle. The last she had seen of him, he had been weeping in his turn, as Maman was being carried to her grave, the first Plantin to die in the influenza epidemic.

Moving slowly, she crept back into the house, locking the door softly behind her. Once, as a child, she was afraid of the dark; but now, with the touch of age upon her, she feared little . . . unless it is this Herr Hitler, young but like any infant snake, so poisonous.

Annis lies wrapped in layers of patchwork quilts, on, for lack of any other option, the Freudian couch. From her position she has a good view of Eliza on the verandah, coiled up like a coccoon in her sleeping bag, and also down the stairs, both scenes tinged with red, from the tinted shade of a little oil lamp, which burns beside her, a night light. They had found it shortly before opening the black magic cupboard, a blessed bit of serendipity. Eliza had relaxed considerably at the extra light, even showed off the contents of the cupboard like a tour guide.

"No sign of provs, but it's not hard to recognize a Haitian pin-dolly."

"Well, no. And what's this?" Annis had said, bending down to examine the bottom shelf of the cupboard. A heap of fusty, dusty papers, vellum, even scrolls . . . she unfurled one and saw Hebrew writing. Then she noticed a thick manila envelope at the back, with a familiar name on it: Plantin. I need to investigate that, she thought, but not while Eliza's watching.

"Maybe I should stay here until the power comes on again. Just for your peace of mind."

Amazingly, Eliza had bought the story; perhaps because it was more than half true. She had then made up her makeshift bed on the couch, waiting for Eliza to doze off—but the old woman was restive, and Annis, worn out from the long evening, found herself nodding.

Now she twitches, rising from sleep, eyelids barely opening . . . to see through that chink a moonface, round and white, bent over her. Suddenly awakened into instant alertness, she opens her eyes wide, but the face is gone. A dream? From the balcony comes a tremendous snore, from Eliza, but beyond that, is there another, softer, sound? She sits up, gazing 180 degrees around her. Nothing to see, untoward that is, but does she hear, very faintly, the tap of footsteps?

She gets up, throwing off the quilts in a musty heap, and reaches for the night light. Eliza stirs, mumbles, pulls the sleeping bag's hood over her lank grey hair. Annis gazes down the stairs. Was that a moving shadow she saw in the hallway? She grabs the bust of Beethoven she carried around the house earlier with Eliza, and slithers down the banister.

There is nothing in the hallway, despite its clutter, so she tries the main front room, in which everything is, for George's own perverse reasons, blue: sapphire-coloured glassware, including lustres on the mantlepiece and the chandelier; a stuffed peacock; a oriental rug the colour of the sky; furniture upholstered with tapestry and beadwork in various shades of cobalt and navy. As she pauses in indecision, she hears a phone ring, but not from the mobile in her bag upstairs. She follows the sound, finding a bakelite phone under an eggshell blue dish cover, a fanciful furniture rearrangement, but not one likely to feature in *Home Decorating* magazine.

"For pity's sake it's two o'clock in the morning!"

There is a gasp and the line goes dead. She stands still, listening— did Eliza wake? At the same time she hears, from the yard behind the house, a leafy crash. She grabs cosh and light again and runs towards the back of the house. As she does, the power suddenly goes on again, the mansion lighting up like a Christmas tree.

"Hurrah!" calls Eliza, from upstairs.

Annis, still determined to investigate the noise, puts down the lamp on the kitchen table, and, Beethoven in hand, nears the back door warily. It is locked—and the view through the bars shielding the kitchen window, of the little paved courtyard, illuminated by an outside light, shows nothing but ivy and the dustbin. Probably a stray cat, she decides, but I should really take a look at what's behind that wall. Laneway? Despite the light, she feels disinclined to investigate.

She turns, suddenly noticing, now the threat is gone, that her throat is dry, from all the alcohol of the evening. The kitchen sink is full of assorted fossils but the tap looks usable, and she could do with a drink of water. She pulls open the cupboard above the sink, looking for a cup or glass, and lets out a shriek, as out comes a cascade of cards, more provs.

"Annis? You okay?" calls Eliza, fear in her voice again.

"I'm fine," she shouts, though internally she feels furious. Having suddenly had enough she blows out the night light and stalks towards the stairs. She pauses, though, in the hallway, staring at the doll, who is seated neatly on an antique high chair. It had been like that when she arrived that evening at Eliza's, but—and this was the puzzling part—she could not remember seeing the doll during her reconnoitre. She reaches out, touching the cold bisque of the brow. A scrap of gold thread has stuck to the doll's dark hair, and she automatically moves to pick it off, then is distracted by the touch of the soft curls. Of human hair? she wonders.

"Annis!"

"Coming!"

Upstairs Eliza has divested herself of the sleeping bag, and is looking very relieved.

"You off, then?" she asks.

"Yep."

"Thanks, dear." She reaches out as if to hug Annis, but settles finally for an awkward handshake.

As Eliza lets her out Annis sees her reflection in one of the house's many mirrors. She no longer looks like a bridesmaid, more like Miss Havisham, the white frock being creased, filthy from dust, with even the odd spiderweb attached. Out in the Brotherhood bin you go, asap, she decides. In her car, she turns the heater on full blast, the fan lifting the muslin skirt like a playful breeze. A few doors down is the entry to a laneway, big enough to admit her car, and on impulse, she drives down at snail's pace, bouncing over cobbles. At the cross-lane she takes the fork running behind the block, counting the houses as she goes. The Quaine mansion she recognizes, by the back wall being covered in ivy—except for one gap, clearly visible thanks to a nearby streetlight. Ivy leaves are scattered in the car's path, and it looks very much as if something large had gone over the wall, in a tearing, clutching, hurry.

She flicks her headlights onto high beam and stares down the lane, but nothing and nobody is in sight. Sighing, she returns the lights to normal and takes the next entrance out into the street again, finding herself at the little local shopping centre. It being so late, there is minimal traffic, and she is soon back at her flat. One Berocca later, she crashes, to wake seconds after, it seems, to bright morning light, and her alarm.

Slowly getting into the swing of her everyday life again, she showers, breakfasts and makes herself presentable for another day at the Museum. At the end she still has fifteen minutes or so to spare, so she switches on her computer, to see if rec.doc.arts. dollcollecting has any answers for her.

She scrolls across the screen and sees her original query: *Did Plantin & Co ever make china dolls?*

There are thirty-seven replies.

My dear Mlle Lazarus . . .

Madame Chaussivert stopped writing and closed her eyes for a moment. So difficult, to think of the phrasing to use with this young woman, so sure in her adherence to Dr Freud's science. Jewish science, that was what the new curé had called it. She had felt a certain chill, yet determined to challenge him. "Monsieur, you are of one mind with Herr Hitler? Do you know what he proposes to do with France? You have read *Mein Kampf*, maybe. From that it is perfectly clear what Herr Hitler wants." That had shut him up completely, but she imagined by now someone in Vessy would have had words with the curé, explained the reason behind Madame Chaussivert's harsh words. People remembered, after all these years, the grave in the town's Jewish cemetery, paid for with Plantin money, though the rest of the family were buried safely with all the other good Catholics. Such a pity too that the police chief was a Bataille, very self-important for all that his grandfather, the filthy pervert, had been the Plantin's coachman. The family had been pensioned well, for the unexpected loss of their breadwinner, but they had never taken the money with anything else but bad grace.

N'Importe—she knew the warning signs of heart disease, from her father's last illness. Even before she consulted the doctor she knew what the diagnosis would be. She would not live to see what Herr Hitler would do with France, not live beyond this winter, in all likelyhood. How to find the words, knowing that you would die soon, yet needing to address your legatee?

"Mlle Lazarus, it may surprise you to know that I have certain things in common with you and Docteur Freud, for my great-grandfather was a rabbi in Prague . . ."

Cristofer that morning is hungover and pallid, but nonetheless Annis throws the pile of computer printouts onto his rosewood desk.

"Read these."

"Must I?"

"Yes!"

"On one condition—tell me who you sloped off with last night."

"Eliza."

"May and December," he says instantly.

"Not what you think . . ." and Annis tells him the whole story.

"Eliza always had a rather nervous temperament," he says. "Her nickname, in collecting circles, was—"

"Spare me the antique gossip. This is much more important." She pats the printouts. "The doll's a Plantin."

"I thought we established that."

"Not conclusively, it was just a surmise. But I know a little about bisque dolls, and I'd never heard before of Plantin making them. I bet Eliza doesn't either."

He gazes down the sheet of printouts. "Look, summarize these. I'm seeing spots."

"OK. Remember Claudette Charpentier-Plantin? One daughter, and a lot of stillbirths. Several people on rec.doc.arts.dollcollecting sugggested she had an RH negative problem. She started making sculptures of her dead infants, we'd call it art therapy these days. Bébés. She smashed them in the end, because —says Moira Rosen of Chicago, here—her wish had been to resurrect her dead children, and a clay effigy was no substitite. But it did get her interested in making dolls, and she later made a sculpted doll of her living child, Marie-Simone, then the children of various Plantin workers. Because she died young, there's very few of these dolls surviving. About 11, half in collections, the rest privately owned. The Getty museum got hold of one a few years back, and paid a record price. I remember hearing about that on the Net, but I didn't pay much attention—in fact I thought they'd bought a Bru."

"So, he said, "rarity value, coupled with the inflated value of French bisque dolls and the cachet attached to Plantin work while Claudette and Jacques-Simon were designing for it."

She nods. "We're beginning to talk serious money. And there's more: I think it's the original Marie-Simone doll, because it's so like the little girl in the family photo. Now that doll has always been thought to have been lost. As a result it's assumed almost mythical, holy grail status in certain dollmaking circles."

"Eliza knows nothing of this?"

"She herself admitted she was weak on chinaware."

"And she said we could have it? Delightful!" He steeples his hands, deep in thought. "Did you know our esteemed Director has a grudge against the Getty museum?"

"No, but you know everything."

"They've pipped him at the post in auctions throughout his career. As a result he has one almighty chip on his shoulder. To better them, in the collection area, and cheaply, would make him one happy little Vegemite."

He grinned like a dog and picked up his phone.

"In fact I'm going to spread it on his breakfast toast right now."

"My grandfather Benjamin," Madame Chaussivert wrote, "he saw but one way to succeed in the gentile world. So he left

Prague and travelled to France. There he lied about who and what he was and established himself as a journalist under a new name. His reputation became such he gained entree to the salons of the great, where he caught the eye of the heiress of a chinaware firm, a young widow who liked clever men and was about to be married again to a dull, but titled one. So he and my grandmère Marie-Dominique eloped and got married. The Plantin family, making the best of the situation, took the new husband into their arms, little knowing what they had there. They thought he was an arriviste and dilletante, who would be too indolent to involve himself with business. But he had an eye for the arts, and what people like to have around them, he had written on economics, he even had some understanding of the nascent art of advertising. He took the name of Plantin, as the family insisted, and doubled the firm's profits within 10 years . . ."

The conversation with Eliza, Annis ringing from the director's office, does not go well, perhaps because both Cristofer and the director are practically sitting on Annis' lap to listen in.

"Eliza, I was just ringing—" She pauses, distracted by the director taking a pinch of snuff, a hitherto unknown quirk to her, though Cristofer no doubt knew all along.

"Ringing about what?" The voice on the other end sounds impatient.

"Are you all right?"

"*Now.* When the lights went out I gave myself a scare, that's all."

"When you talked about footsteps I was worried . . ."

"Don't you take the mitherings of an old lady too seriously. In the cold light of day I can see I didn't really mean it. Or anything else I happened to say that night."

"You promised us something," Annis blurts.

"Us?"

"The Museum."

"Oh, you mean about the doll. Sure I made promises. But not in writing," Eliza fires back. "That was just to get you over."

"Thanks."

"Well, you admitted you were a vulture, the first time you came to visit. And a prettier one I never saw in my life."

"Eliza, I don't need compliments, I need to keep my job."

"Cristofer's been at you, has he? Little twerp." This is said loudly enough to carry beyond the receiver, and to Cristofer's ears. He affects not to notice, and Annis tries not to giggle.

"As regards your little exhibition, I'm thinking about it. So far I haven't come to a definite conclusion. But come and see me anyway. Saturday. I need to do some shopping."

"That's tomorrow."

"Tomorrow pm, about three, suits me fine. And now, if you don't mind, I'm expecting a call from the Freud archives."

Annis puts down the phone, thinking: shopping?

"Eliza always was fey," Cristofer says to the Director. "Famous for it, in the antique trade. But luckily she fancies my assistant."

Annis glares at him. If a glance could kill, Cristofer, you'd be dead meat.

"I think we have the lady hooked, and expect to land her and doll high and dry real soon now."

"Benjamin was widowed after twenty years of marriage, leaving him with one son, Jacques-Simon, a talented artist. Like will to like, and Jacques-Simon married another artist, Claudette Charpentier. They were my father and mother. Then came the Dreyfus case, a young army officer victimised, sent to Devil's island, simply because he was Juif. My grandfather, who had pamphleteered all his life, would have added his weight to the voices of protest—M. Emile Zola asked him specially. But he feared exposure, as a fellow-Juif. So he was silent. Yet he sent messages to Prague, to ask if his father, the rabbi, was still alive, and recalling a conversation of forty years back, when the rabbi had spoken of anti-semitism, and a means of magical defense, which he had called not fantasy, but a possibility . . ."

It was, Annis had to admit, very neatly done. Upon her arrival at the Quaine mansion she had noticed several empty carrybags by the front door, and also that Eliza seemed to be in a high old state of excitement about something.

"You know those provs you discovered by accident? When you opened the cupboard over the sink?"

"Umn Eliza, I know I left them all over the floor, but I simply wasn't in a mood to tidy up . . ."

"I don't mind, because you solved one of the mysteries of the Quaine house for me. Go and have a look at them—they're on the kitchen table."

Curious, yet aware something is not quite right, Annis wanders into the kitchen and picks up the topmost card.

"Haitian wax doll, 20th century, New Orleans . . ."

The next card is for an African fetish figurine, and she knows then that this is where George had filed the provs for the magic cupboard. "Hey, Eliza," she calls, "well spotted". The response is the sound of the front door slamming shut.

"Eliza?"

She gets up, prov in hand and runs into the hallway. Eliza is nowhere to be seen—and neither are the carrybags.

"Eliza!"

The slit cut into the front door for letters slaps, and she catches a glimpse of Eliza's black clothing. "I said I had to do some shopping, didn't I? But what with the vultures and everything, I feel I'm deserting my duty every time I leave the house. So I'm leaving you as my sentry. All the outside doors are deadlocked, by the way, and the windows are barred. Much as I like you, I know Cristofer is dying to get his mitts on certain things in this house, and I'm not about to gratify him."

"Eliza, you're locking me in?" She pounds her fists against the door.

"Only for the time it takes to do my shopping. It's daylight, there's no fear of power cuts. I know I'm being silly, but peace of mind is beyond price. Bye for now."

The old, hesitant footsteps sound on the stone steps, then on the brick paving to the front gate.

"Oh, and if you're stuck for something to do, try and work out the reason why that doll's prov is with the magic stuff. Not with the contents of the morbid room, whose provs I found, by the way—in the dog kennel. I begin to understand George's mad mind a little now, and that's scary. But, oh yes, dolly! Plantin, she is . . . know the name, but never that they did dolls before."

Before Annis can think of something to say, Eliza is gone. She grabs the door by the handle, rattles it ferociously . . . but the lock is secure. The back door, too, is locked, and Annis runs from room to room on the ground floor. Every window is indeed barred and she goes upstairs, to find only one attic window not completely secure, and that with a sheer drop to the street.

Cristofer, I'm not breaking a leg on your behalf, she thinks, and goes downstairs again. As she passes the magic cupboard, she recollects the envelope marked Plantin, and retrieves it. She has nothing else to do, so she might as well make use of the time to investigate the Plantin connection further—even if Eliza is beginning to get an inkling of the doll's worth.

She starts in the kitchen, shuffling through the magic provs. About five in she finds: Plantin family papers, holograph mss and typescripts, in Fr. and Hebrew, property of Berthe Lazarus, therapist, acquired from her niece, St Kilda, 1977. See also red velvet couch.

At the very bottom of the card George had written: See also doll, the last word being underlined three times.

She lays the card aside, keeps searching, until she has the prov she wants. It is all too clear:

Doll, china bisque, 36" high, Plantin, c. 1890. Left to Berthe Lazarus in will of Madame Marie-Simone Chaussivert, nee Plantin. Probably elusive Marie-Simone doll. See Plantin family papers.

Underneath in a handwriting just recognisable as that of George Quaine, though it sprawls and shakes:

La Sentinelle?

The phone rings. She stares at the manila envelope longingly, but takes it to the phone, which is still under the dish cover.

"Hallo?"

The line goes dead.

"You rude shit!" she says, slamming down the receiver. She sits down on a beaded chair, starts to open the manila folder, then finds it already unsealed. She is just about to empty the contents into her lap, when the phone rings again. She lifts the receiver, ready to unleash the dogs of invective, when a woman's voice says, quite sweetly:

"Miss Kirk? This is Dallas in New York."

"I thought Dallas was in Texas," Annis says, surprised into politeness.

"No, no, I'm Dallas Pruitt, PhD. PhD student, I mean. I rang yesterday, I was so excited at the news that I forgot about the time difference. So I'm sorry I woke you up."

Excited about what? thinks Annis, but Dallas supplies the answer: "The Freud archives faxed me about the couch and I just waltzed around my office! I'm working on Freud's women disciples, and I knew Berthe Lazarus got out of France, fleeing the Nazis just before WW2, and went to Australia. I just didn't know where Downunder, exactly."

Annis thinks fast, recalling the words on the provs: Berthe Lazarus, therapist . . . see also couch.

"Ah yes, the couch," she says. "With the red velvet and gold fringes." She is still of the opinion it looks more suitable for a brothel than a psychiatrist's office.

"I know my grant doesn't extend to buying the couch and having it shipped from Australia, but oh wow! Was there anything else, by any chance? Any papers?"

The tone of the distant, American voice has changed, to one Annis knows well: trying to disguise acute covetousness. A dead giveaway, when collectors start acting unconcerned . . .

"Well, this place is a shambles, but . . ."

"I suppose I shouldn't hope for too much, and I have got all the letters she wrote Freud. About the doll-lady, Mme C."

"I know nothing about Freudian psychiatry," Annis says truthfully, trying to disguise *her* acute covetousness—for further information.

"It's quite a famous case, if you're into the Freudian disciples. Madame C—she's not identified beyond the initial but I have my suspicions—was one of Berthe Lazarus' early patients. She was hung up about a childhood experience: the family coachman died in her room one night. Heart attack, apparently, but Mme C. fantasized the incident, quite bizarrely. Nowadays we'd ask what the servant was doing there in the first place, read him as a child molester, but Freud had discarded the seduction theory, the idea that his patients were describing actual childhood traumas, long ago. To him it was just an infantile sexual fantasy. He was sketching out a paper in collaboration with Berthe, on the doll-lady, as he called her. But hey, I'm getting offtrack. *Have* you found any papers?"

"I found a photo," Annis admits.

"Of Berthe Lazarus?"

"I don't know. It was loose, not with the couch." And I'm not going to tell you where, she thinks. A doll's reticule, put there by a doll-lady? It sounded deranged. "What did Berthe Lazarus look like?"

"Dark hair and eyes, round face, horn-rimmed glasses—went for the studious look, though she was quite attractive. There ain't no PC way of saying this, but without the glasses and severe bob she might have been one red-hot Jewish momma."

Lazarus, thinks Annis, suddenly intent on the name. She mentally compares the photo she is now sure depicts Berthe with the three men and the child in the Plantin family group. She sees now a resemblance, non-familial, but possibly racial.

There is an awkward silence, Annis thinking, Dallas impatiently awaiting an answer, finally butting in with:

"Well, does that sound like your photo?"

"Yes," Annis is surprised into admitting.

"Well, if you could send me a photocopy, I'll be your slave for life. And if you find me some papers . . ."

"You'd go beyond slavery?" says Annis, thinking that the conversation is on the brink of getting kinky.

"Maybe."

This is mad, thinks Annis. But then here I am sitting in the house of a man who went seriously bizarre shortly before his death, surrounded by a giant collecting puzzle, rooms of antiques arranged in subject categories, or colour, or in alphabetical order. I've been locked in by a woman who is starting to be more than eccentric, and I'm now conversing with a stranger on the other side of the world, about psychiatry. She laughs.

"Huh?" says Dallas. 'What'd I say?"

"Nothing, I was thinking how strange this conversation would sound to anyone eavesdropping."

"Hey, I live with the Freud disciples, I'm used to it, but I see your point. The doll-lady's pretty weird stuff."

"Weird in what way?" Now Annis is sounding far too unconcerned, but she can't help it.

"Well, Madame C had this big china doll. She told Berthe Lazarus the doll had caused the servant guy's death, by attacking him, she thought. Berthe had just about talked Madame out of the delusion when she discontinued the treatment. Freud was practically distraught."

"Um, er yes," says Annis, suddenly desperate to get off the phone, but Dallas burbles on for some five minutes more, about Berthe Lazarus getting some sort of tropical infection on the boat to Australia, which left her stone deaf, worst possible thing for a psychiatrist, and she never worked again, just lived off a niece, such a sad letter she wrote to Anna Freud . . . Only a pointed remark about the cost of international phone calls gets Annis free. Immediately she runs to the kitchen, and picks up the prov for the doll. The names leap out at her: Berthe Lazarus, Madame Marie-Simone Chaussivert, nee Plantin.

Very thoughtful, she wanders out to the hall again, coming to a full stop in front of the doll, still in its high chair.

"And you have a connection with Freud as well. What a singularly valuable doll you are!"

She doesn't mean to speak aloud, addressing a toy like a small girl, and in the quiet of the house the sound grates. She reaches out, touches the hair again, then suddenly withdraws as if she had been bitten.

The doll hadn't stirred, but she had suddenly noticed again the scrap of gold thread caught in its hair. She picks it off, this time identifying it as coming from the fringing on the couch. With a sudden chill, she recalls the white moonface of her dream, gazing at her. She narrows her eyes, gazing at the doll between her lashes. It is possible she might have seen the doll's face, but surely it couldn't have got up the stairs, unless it was an autoperikatetikos, a clockwork walking doll, and she knew very well it wasn't.

Of course, she thinks, the gold might have got there before, when the doll was lying on the couch. But then she recalls Eliza's ramblings about the doll being moved from place to place in the house, or simply moving, by itself . . .

I really am going mad, she thinks. She pauses in indecision, then lifts doll and chair bodily and takes them into the blue room, where the Plantin papers still await her. She sits the doll opposite the beaded chair. Being dressed in cherry-red, on a chair painted green, it of course ruins George's colour scheme, but no matter.

"I want to keep an eye on you," she says sternly.

Silence.

"Mademoiselle, I have all their papers, the scrolls the old rabbi brought from Prague, the notes made by my grandfather Benjamin, and his son Jacques-Simon, my father, who became drawn into the project, at first against his will, then increasingly avidly. Claudette, my Maman, she had been brought up a good Catholic, and what they were doing had the smell of sulphur and brimstone about it. But it was hard for her to live in the same house and not have some involvement. She did not consent to help these men, with their heads full of ancient mystical or magical writings. Yet still she let them use a prized sculpture of hers, the doll made in the image of Marie-Simone, in an experiment, never thinking that they would succeed . . ."

Annis stops reading, glances at the nearest clock, a wag on the wall, and realises an hour has passed. Surely Eliza can't be much longer! She shrugs, then seizing the moment, phones Cristofer on his mobile.

He answers, panting.

"You haven't by any chance, got a French dictionary handy?" she says, without preamble.

"Annis, I'm at the gym!"

"Gotta date tonight?"

"No just going down the clubs, and I like to look trim. But why can't you just go off to your local library or find an Internet dictionary, surely there must be one."

She explains why not, tersely.

He gasps again, not from exhaustion, she realises, but happy surprise.

"What a wonderful opportunity!"

"Cristofer, like I said, I'm locked in, so I can't very well steal anything for the exhibition."

"Ah yes, but you can find something of mine, maybe."

Mr Ulterior Motive! she thinks. "What, of yours?"

"Letters."

Oho! she thinks. "You knew George Quaine *that* well?"

He clears his throat, non-committally. "When I was in Paris on my first art history scholarship I wrote him some indiscreet letters, which he kept. Nothing compromising, but the embarrassment value was considerable. It taught me a useful lesson: if you've been naughty, never put it in writing. Now and then, if George wanted something—confidential info, a grant for his latest sweetie, or for me to work harder on getting the Museum to buy various items in his stock—he'd gently remind me that he never threw anything away."

"I thought you were too smart for blackmailers."

"After that experience, yes."

"Cristofer, this place is an utter mess, there's papers everywhere, and I don't know when Eliza'll be back . . ."

"She might never be back. Her nickname in antique circles was The Bolter. Things got tough for her, she'd disappear, go on an overseas holiday or a beach trip."

"Oh great!"

"Please try to find the letters," he says.

How odd to have her boss almost plead with her. "OK, but you can help me with a bit of translation, as your French is better than mine. I've been going through Plantin family papers, and while I think I've got the gist, they're puzzling. The family seem to have gotten heavily into some form of mystical alchemy . . ."

"Annis, my French is good, but not with regard to mysticism. Or alchemical terms."

"Well, what's La Sentinelle?"

His voice, when he answers, is disconcerted. "What it sounds like. Sentry, grammatical gender feminine in French. 'Etant père, elle-même, votre excellence comprendra notre joie.' I really heard someone say that at a diplomatic reception in Paris, and got the giggles, excellence being excellency, as in your excellency, which is gendered female though the ambassador in question was male. All I can say is thank god English got rid of its grammatical gendering."

She ignores the digression. "La Sentinelle reappears in the typescripts. Half the time I think they're talking about a new line of figurines, maybe with a militaristic theme, but then all this mystical gobbledygook surfaces again."

"Sounds fascinating," he says drily. "Look, Annis, be a pet, put the Plantin lunacy down and try and find my letters. Promise you, there's a pay rise in it for you. That enough incentive?"

"Oh, all right!"

"Now I must hop into the spa," he says, and rings off.

"Who knows what they might have done, given the first attempt had been so successful. But it so happened that an epidemic of influenza hit Vessy soon afterwards, and when it had passed, Claudette, Benjamin and the old rabbi were all dead. I was six and the only family I had left was Jacques-Simon. My father, he was an artist, but not disciplined like my grandpère, nor greatly knowledgeable, like the old rabbi, my great-grandpère, nor with the special spark that made the designs and figurines of my mother Claudette the most popular in the Plantin range. In any case, he had to take over the firm, which meant he had little time for experiments. Oh, he kept making his statues, peopling the grounds at Vessy with monsters, but not one of them was like La Sentinelle, not one of them would move."

Annis sits on the stairs, dejected. After Cristofer had rung, she had dutifully started a search of the house for naughty papers and had managed, after two hours work, to establish only that the attic and top storey did not appear to have anything of her boss's, naughty or otherwise. Now it is beginning to get dark, her hands are filthy with dust, she is hungry—and most worrying of all, where is Eliza?

She fingers the mobile again, about to ring Cristofer and suggest he find some after hours locksmith, or preferably a battering ram, when she hears footsteps coming up the front path.

"Eliza!" she calls, in her haste near skidding on the hallway tiles.

"No, alas, from your point of view, but from mine . . ."

She stops in front of the door, numb from disappointment at the sound of Cristofer's voice. The letter-slit opens, closes again. "Ah, thought I remembered the dimensions," Cristofer says. "Annis, take this!"

She looks down, sees the edge of a plastic container protruding through the slit.

"Sushi!"

"Thought you might be getting peckish, and they do have those nice slimline takeaway boxes. Got it? Because there's more to come."

The next item through the letterslit is a hipflask. "To keep your spirits up," Cristofer says. "But not all at once, mind you. I'd also post you a French dictionary, but my *Petit Larousse* is on the bulky side."

"That's all right. You're an angel!" she says.

"I'm not going to tell you who, or under what circumstances, last said that to me. Look, I've got to go, got a date, but I'll come back tonight."

"You really think Eliza's done a bolt?"

"If she was scared, or feeling unable to cope, yes. On the other hand she might just have decided to make the most of a free housesitter. I'll give her the benefit of the doubt for the moment. If you're still here when I get back, then I'll get the police operations group to rescue you."

"Promise?"

"Promise!" and with that he is gone.

"I excerpt here a letter from my beloved maman, her last message to me. She wrote that she had not approved of the experiments the men of the family had been doing, but she was glad that there was a Sentinelle to watch over me, small thing though it was. It had my photo in its little bag, with the rest of the family, so that, unthinking clay though it was, it knew who was friend, who was foe. I have put your photo into that safe guardianship, Mademoiselle. But as a Sentinelle is perhaps not enough against *Mein Kampf*, I have also left you money, the means of escaping France, should that be necessary."

Perhaps it is the promise of a police rescue, perhaps the food and alcohol, or even Cristofer showing unusual consideration, that sends Annis into a mood of temporary frivolity. She does not continue her search for the letters, nor researching the Plantins, but rather acts like a child in a sweetshop, with the goodies of the Quaine mansion there before her, for the sampling. She wanders from room to room, opening drawers and burrowing into hatboxes and wardrobes. In no time she has the ingredients for a game of dress-ups: costume jewellery, a feather boa and finally an antique tutu, rather too large, but covered with spangles. Decked out like a bizarre ballerina, she goes in search of accompaniment, and finds it downstairs in the blue room: a musical box, lacquered in a screaming shade of cerulean. She twirls to its tinkly tune, 'The Dance of the Sugar Plum Fairy', but after attempting a pirouette on tip-toe point, she collapses onto the beaded chair. The sushi had not been substantial enough to prevent the spirits going to her head. She closes her eyes, imagining the scene that would ensue should Eliza arrive back now, though she wonders if the quirky old woman had also been unable to resist playing dress-ups with George's treasures, albeit in a more lady-like, staid fashion. Suddenly she feels very tired . . .

She awakes again, to a room completely dark, except for the reflected light of the streetlamps through the uncurtained bay window. Her mouth feels like the inside of a vacuumn cleaner, and she badly needs to pee. Then the bodily sensations of discomfort are completely forgotten, in a white rush of adrenaline, fear chemicals coursing through her blood. She hears a barely perceptible soft pad pad, then a susurration that might be breath, might be the sound of clothing brushing against furniture. Behind her the floorboard creaks and she hears a faint glassy tinkle, not the chandelier, for no window in the house is open. She stands up, tries a scream that comes out of her mouth a squeak—

And the sound breaks off into a moan, as something hard smashes into the back of her head, disintegrating on impact. She falls to her knees, limp with pain, nothing in the world mattering except for the aftershocks of the blow, still reverberating inside her skull. Something grabs hold of her; she hears words she can barely comprehend.

"Where is it? Where is it?"

She might answer, were it not that her mouth is full of blood and her tongue scrapes raw and painful against her teeth. The blow had made her bite her tongue, she realises. At the thought she could just curl into a ball and die, but hands are now pulling her upright, the voice is insistent. Lost within a private world of hurt and shock, she barely pays attention to anything exterior. It is only when she bumps, or is bumped against the highchair, knocking it over, that she realises that the doll is not in it, for only wood, not china, crashes against the flooring.

"You been searching around, you and the old witch, you musta found it by now."

A face bends over her, and she registers that it is not a moonface, but thinner, young, masculine, with the adolescent acne still on it, like an algal bloom.

"He said he had a present for me, that'd set me up good and proper, for being a nice boy. He said he'd put my name on it, but the witch, she wouldn't let me in, said I was a vulture."

A car making a u-turn outside shines headlights through the bars on the bay window, and in the striped light she sees the stranger briefly and brightly illuminated. He seems vaguely familiar, but she cannot place him. At the light, he ducks, sending them both sprawling on the floor.

"Not here," he says, so close she can feel his breath on her face. It smells dank, of tobacco, alcohol and some other unidentified chemical. "Someone might see . . ."

He drops her, and she hears his footsteps on the ground floor, going from hallway to kitchen, pantry, and the other rooms. Not a pad pad, she thinks. A footballers' walk, even when he's trying to be stealthy.

He returns, and roughly drags her upright in a fireman's lift. Upside down, she dimly sees the blue carpets, then the stairs and its lining of busts, Chopin, Mozart, unidentified, receding beneath her. She tries to spit, to clear her mouth for yelling, but can only manage a thread of dark dribble.

At the landing he stops, her mount, and sets her down, not on the floor, but some other surface. The back of her head presses against upholstery and she nearly faints with pain, as something sharp caught in her hair digs deep into her scalp. She writhes, turning her head to one side, feeling against her cheek the pile of velvet: the Freudian couch. Now the moment of acute hurt is gone she is weak as a kitten, but nonetheless intent on the intruder. He leans over her, nearly sitting on her bare legs.

"You musta seen it," he says. "He said it'd be signposted loud and clear, my legacy. You're the niece—"

She thinks: it's that tramp or whatever, who stopped me outside. He said: You a niece, and I heard: Annis, and said yes, like the fool I am.

"You're inheriting all this lot, can't you spare one little thing?"

She tries to nod, or shake her head, anything to get across the mistaken identity and that she hasn't the least idea what he's talking about. But the motion nearly makes her vomit.

"Could make you tell me . . ."

Doesn't he see, she thinks from an increasing distance, that I'm concussed or worse, with a chewed up tongue, in no state for anything, let alone confessions? He moves closer and again she smells his breath—no, of course he doesn't, she realises, because he's tanked up to the gills on whatever gives him courage.

"All right then," he says. He pauses, as if deciding what to do next, and in the silence Annis hears—do her ears play tricks?—the pad pad again. Then she puts it out of mind, as another sound makes her suddenly understand just how he means to make her talk. I wanted to pee earlier, she recalls, surely that should be an anaphrodisiac? But it is harder to wet herself in public than she expects. She feels his hands now, tugging at the tutu, but ballet clothes are not made for easy egress, not made for sex. He turns her on her side, clearly puzzled at the array of hooks and eyes on the tutu's back, and her head lolls over the edge of the couch.

Coming up the stairs, she sees a white shape like a balloon floating several feet above the ground, that as it nears becomes eerily familiar, but is utterly impossible. The doll pauses at the top of the landing, glass eyes and array of tiny white teeth shining in the dim light. The head turns as it surveys the scene, expressionless but nonetheless *sentient*. Then it moves towards her, the gait having something of the crab and also the clumsy care of the automaton, setting its feet, in their broad soft shoes, one after another as if tightrope walking. She feels rather than sees it clamber onto the low end of the couch, as the boy lets go of her, also sensing the new arrival.

"Bloody cat," he says and turns to eject the unwanted feline. From where she lies, she can't see much beyond his face, the tulle wheel of the tutu's skirt blocking her view. She can't imagine what might be going to happen . . .

He screams, a sound she never heard a man make before, low and agonized. Next moment the hands gripping her abruptly let go, and she rolls over the edge of the couch. As she tumbles she sees the doll go flying upwards, in a swirl of white petticoats. If it falls she doesn't notice, for at that moment she hits the floor, receiving another jolt of pain. He jumps up, moaning and swearing, almost treading on her in his rush for the stairs. She hears his feet, descending in a hobbling hurry, then the sound of the front door banging wide open. Next she hears a car nearing, then the scream of brakes, the boy or somebody else yelling.

She is sick then, vomiting raw fish, rice, and alcohol down the front of the tutu—but it makes her feel much better. Slowly she pulls herself to her knees, using the couch for support. "Dolly," she whispers, "Dolly?" No sound . . . and she begins to wonder whether, for one horrible second, she had taken leave of her senses completely. Half crawling, half walking, using the wall for support, she moves towards the stairs. At the sight of the descent her nerve deserts her, and she makes her way downwards on her tulle-covered bottom, bumping from stair to stair. It seems to take years. In the hallway cool night air comes through the open front door, clearing her head. She is able to stand now, make her way outside, to enter into a street scene, passers-by grouped around a car, others staring from the pavement, an ambulance nearing, siren at full wail.

"It's her," a voice says. "She must have done it."

Annis turns her head, aware of the spectacle she must present, tutu, diamente, boa, blood and vomit, and sees a police officer. He stares at her as if she is the creature from the black lagoon. I hope, she thinks, he isn't wondering whether this is part of some weird S&M ritual, and as if the very idea gives her the vapours, passes out.

"Mademoiselle, you recall that when I first came to see you, I was newly widowed, a childless woman and unhappy. I was trying to make sense of my life, but some things in it, that I could remember acutely, made no sense at all. You said the doll story was my imagination, and I accepted the judgement. But then, while searching through some of the firm's records at Vessy I came across the doll herself, and the notebooks of the experimenters, including the letter from my mother. If this was imagination, crazed fantasy, then others had believed it too. So I resolved to test the story the one way I knew, and that was to take the *shem* from the doll's bag, where it was kept when not in use. 72 characters, the secret name of God, written small on a scrap of parchment and put between those pearly white teeth.

I did this, and saw the doll clumsily kneel to me, recognising its maîtresse. Then I cried, the doll watching me uncomprehendingly, for I knew that I had never been sick at all."

Annis wakes, rising from unconsciousness as if out of murky water, to see faces, vaguely medical, gazing at her in wonderment. She submerges again, and the next time surfaces to find a policewoman, asking questions. When she starts to cry a nurse hustles the questioner away. The third time, she opens her eyes to see a familiar face, dressed most unfamiliarly: Cristofer, suited as usual, but in leather, topped with a military-style cap.

"So this is what you do in your spare time," she tries to say, but her tongue is still swollen, and all she manages is a croak.

"I said I'd come back, didn't I? But when I did, it was to see you being carried into an ambulance. "That's my assistant!" I said to the nearest and prettiest cop, and got a free ride in a police car to hospital. You were a fair mess when they brought you here, they spent ages picking bits of glass and china out of your scalp. He hit you with one of George's lustres, did you know that? I'd have recognised that shade of blue anywhere. The philistine—they were a matched pair, family heirlooms . . ."

She can't speak, but her mouth twists downwards.

"Hey," he said. "Looky here!"—and produces from under his leather jacket a child's toy, a toy writing machine, with stylus and cellophane screen. "Snaffled it from the child care centre downstairs."

She is surprised he was allowed in there, given the way he is dressed, but takes the toy eagerly, resting it against the folds of her white hospital smock.

DOLL, she writes, then erases it quickly, before Cristofer can see. To convey such a dream sequence in this childish medium is too surreal, too hard.

AM I ALRIGHT?

"You bit your tongue, but you probably know that already. Concussion, they suspect, also shock. You had multiple lacerations in your scalp, so they shaved and stitched, and now the back of your head reminds me of Frankenstein's monster. But you looked a damn sight worse all bloodstained, and in that tutu . . ."

He pauses delicately, questioningly.

I WAS PLAYING DRESS-UPS, she confesses reluctant.

"Not the first time that would have happened in the Qaine mansion," he says.

OHO!

"Not telling . . ."

She tries another tack. WHAT HAPPENED TO HIM?

"You mean the philistine? Someone I knew by sight, oddly enough, not that I'd ever sampled his rentboy wares. I was able to tell the pretty policeman that I'd seen him and George together, when George was going gaga and had lost his usual good taste. I mean, a petty thief and druggie . . . He's in a secure ward, with a guard, don't worry about him, he's in trouble enough as it is. They found Eliza in the alley that's a shortcut to the shopping centre, she'd been mugged. Same MO, but with a broken bottle. No, she isn't all right, she's got a skull fracture. In post-op now, definitely no visitors. It could have been worse—luckily he was disturbed, only got away with her handbag and keys. That's how he got into the house, the pretty policeman reckons, and he still had the keys when they picked him off the road."

HE WANTED SOMETHING GEORGE HAD PROMISED HIM

"The moon, I suppose. George did that to quite a few people in his last weeks."

HE THOUGHT I KNEW ABOUT IT, AND SO HE TRIED TO

She lifts her hands, unable to complete the sentence.

"My dear, you don't have to spell it out. A girl that's been hit over the head and a man caught with his trousers down . . .give the police credit for some intelligence."

He flashes a sideways, furtive glance at her, and she thinks: why is everyone, including Cristofer, looking at me as if I've grown horns?

"In any case, he broke a leg, so he's not ambulant."

WHAT HAPPENED TO HIM? This time she underlines the message.

"I just told you . . . or is it . . . ?" He starts to laugh. "You don't remember?"

I REMEMBER EVERYTHING, BUT I CAN'T MAKE SENSE OF IT. LIKE HIM SUDDENLY YELLING AND RUNNING AWAY. WHY DID HE DO THAT?

"You really don't know, do you?" Now he leans forward, conspiratorially. "He came screaming out of the house, the witnesses said, hobbling and holding his pants up with one hand. That's why he didn't notice the Merc until it literally ran into him. He's been babbling to anyone who'll listen that the doll tried to bite his balls off. You were dribbling blood from the mouth, and they naturally think it's you. So the women in this place want to give you a medal, and the men think you're the original castrating bitch."

Berthe Lazarus put down the letter from Madame and sighed. She remembered so well the letters she had written to Freud about this case. How excited she had been, she had thought she had a Wolf-man or a Dora on her hands. It had seemed so perfect, the delusion that Madame, as a small child, had woken to a scene out of fairytale in her bedroom, the family coachman in his nightshirt, being menaced by her china doll. However, the patient had proved resistant, withdrawn from treatment, withdrawn even from discussing the subject with Berthe, and gone on with her life. They had kept meeting each other, thanks to the happy chance of Berthe's friends and their house in Vessy, even over the years established something of a friendship. It was kind of Madame to remember Berthe in her will, though the gift . . .

She looked at the wooden box, and shivered. Not for a moment would she indulge Madame's fantasy, and actually put the tiny scrap of parchment in the doll's reticule, this *shem*, between the gateway of those tiny white teeth. What, was the poor sick woman hoping, even beyond the grave, to pervert Berthe from the beliefs of the great Docteur Freud?

Annis lies back in her hospital bed, thinking hard. The more she thinks of the Plantin family papers she read, the more her schoolgirl french starts to come back to her. "Rabbi . . . Prague . . . Dreyfus." Connections appear between the islands of disconnected information, like bridges, and it all begins to make sense.

She opens her mouth, carefully tests her wounded tongue, then speaks a word aloud: "Golem".

That had been the title of a German expressionist film she remembered from media studies. It had been effectively menacing, yet in the details somewhat ridiculous: the actors had worn medieval dress, but their heavily painted eyes and gestures had been most un-medieval, the rabbi who moulded a giant statue in clay for the defence of the Prague ghetto being particularly unlikely. The statue had looked daft too, a ceramic clodhopper with a pageboy haircut.

She couldn't recall if the word "golem" actually appeared in the Plantin papers, but the careful fashioning of a graven image in clay, that could be activated by mystic lore into a bodyguard, a Sentinelle—it might have been expressed on a small scale, and in the incongrous form of a doll, but she had seen for herself how this ghetto power fantasy could have an effective reality. She remembers that the golem had ended up smashed in the film, and in all versions of the legend she knew. Was that what had happened to this golem? She had a memory of the doll flying through the air, but not the smash of breaking china. It was still in the Quaine house, she supposed, but in what state?

She thinks: it protected me, although my photo wasn't in the reticule. Was it because I look doll-like, like itself, or like the child Marie-Simone?

The question had preoccupied her, all through the police interview, which involved two cops, the male obviously Cristofer's pretty policeman and the woman who had tried to question her earlier. He looked nervous; she had a slight but unmistakable smirk. Annis had made her statement via the medium of a laptop computer. She had found, unexpectedly, that it was easier to lie in print than in speech, to say she remembered nothing beyond the blow on her head. To confess anything else was to venture into the realms of fantasy. She knew she had not bitten the intruder; but she had not seen who had, and to accept that it was the doll was to believe in a very strange universe indeed.

At the end of the interview she had typed:

I LEFT MY SHOULDER BAG AND OTHER THINGS IN THE QUAINE HOUSE

"We can let you in," said the policewoman. "In that mess I doubt we could find a thing. Easy enough to arrange, once you get discharged."

Easy enough, thinks Annis. Almost as easy as, when the swelling in her tongue had subsided, and she could make herself heard, to persuade a hospital orderly (female) to wheel her up to the ward where Eliza lay. Without her black clothes, and the kohl rings around her eyes, the old woman looks shockingly wan and frail. Only the chipped magenta nails and the rakish grin as Annis approaches, show a vestige of the triumphant goth eccentric, growing old disgracefully.

She waits till the orderly has retreated, then bends over the bed. They clasp hands, united survivors.

"Eliza, there is something I have to tell you, something very strange, but I think you will believe me. You were right to feel scared in the house, the night of the blackout. I woke up thinking I saw a face looking at me. It was a warning, because there *was* a prowler outside, the boy you called a vulture. I went downstairs to investigate, but the phone rang, and then the lights came on, and he panicked and jumped over the fence.

I heard your pad-pad, did you know that? Just before I got hit with George's lustre. But it wasn't the sound of the vulture, but something else, what in the Plantin papers was called La Sentinelle. Remember how you thought I or someone else was moving the doll around the house? Well, you were right about that, too . . ."

George Quaine, busy in the arrangement of his funeral parlour, as he privately termed the little back room, heard a pad pad slithery sound, and saw the doll enter bow first, dragging its box behind it.

"Oh, decided you don't want to stay in the cupboard," he said. "Not that I blame you, but you'll spoil the arrangement. Confuse old Eliza utterly." He chuckled at the thought.

The doll, having found a spot for its box, exited, and he listened to the receding sound of its soft footsteps. He had noted its perambulations around the house, and come to the conclusion it had a purpose. Probably looking for its former owner, a harmless enough pursuit, he supposed. He rather liked the company; all the diversion of a cat or dog, but without having to open cans or clean hair off the furniture. In the twilight world he increasingly inhabited nothing seemed to shock him anymore, even the uncouthness of that young boy last night, Danny or Damian or whatever, though seeing the toy actually move *had* been a surprise. He had thought of taking out its *shem*, but the doll had simply clashed its teeth at him when he tried.

Oh well, somebody else's problem, he decided. Like this house. He grinned, wishing he could be there to see nosy old Eliza discover the complete lack of rhyme or reason in his arrangments, other than giving her an extremely complicated job of sorting out his effects.

The real joy, he thought, will be finding a hiding place for Cristofer's letters—silly boy, fancying ekeing out his scholarship money by doing piecework for art forgers, and then writing home about it. He could have completely ruined his reputation in the art history stakes, which was why George had taken care that nobody else had ever seen the letters. But where to put them, he thought. It needs to be somewhere that only Cristofer would think to look, but let's not make it obvious, the boy isn't getting back the fruits of his folly that easily.

Annis not only has to get her bag and clothes from the Quaine house, but also she has a mandate to fetch and carry for Eliza. After a conversation with George's lawyer, she gets the keys for an afternoon. She takes Cristofer with her, since he has come to collect her from the hospital.

"I want company," she says. "And I know you want those letters."

The mansion in the early morning light is cold and still. Annis still feels a little wobbly, a useful reminder, she thinks, that though the house seems as unchanged as when she first saw it, momentous events have happened here, hard though they are to credit. She puts her hand to her head, feeling the soft angora cap, a gift from Cristofer. "You'll need an avante-garde haircut, at the least," he had said. "But this'll conceal things for the moment." It is, she must admit, becoming. He had also brought her the tracksuit and runners she had never quite gotten round to taking home from the office, after her membership at a nearby gym had lapsed. It is adequate dress, and for that she is thankful.

On the ground floor she gives Cristofer the obligatory tour of George's rearrangements, ending at the blue room, where they find Annis's shoulder bag, underneath the beaded chair. Nearby is the envelope of Plantin letters, which Annis quietly tucks under her arm, to pass to Eliza, as requested. Upstairs is next—and Annis, staring at the busts as she ascends, sees a trickling line between them, a dark stain on the carpet. She shudders, and tries to put it out of mind. On the balcony, she quietly sorts through Eliza's things, a small and pitiful, camping-in-someone-else's-house collection, and puts them into one of the old woman's many carrybags. Cristofer has gone exploring, or letter-seeking, and she hears a faint whistle from the back of the house. Investigating, she finds him, as she half expected, in the morbid room.

"I'm just getting an idea for an exhibition. Funerals through the ages."

"I'm sure," Annis says, and hustles him out, thinking of the next floor, where she is sure she left her street clothes. She doesn't really want to stop and contemplate the couch, to recall what nearly happened there, but Cristofer drags his feet.

"Is that . . . the scene of the crime?"

"Attempted crime," she says curtly.

"I mean, what an appropriate site," he says, touching the velvet and gold fringe. Then he bends down, inspecting the space behind the couch.

"What's that?"

She glances over his suited shoulder and sees, sticking out of the heaps of quilt she had discarded on the night of the blackout, and Eliza had just left lying there, an expanse of white petticoat, with in its centre two chubby legs in black stockings, wearing shoes with cherry-coloured rosettes.

"Oh!" she says, and dives to extract the doll.

"Is that what I think it is?" says Cristofer. Annis nods, busy inspecting the doll for damage. It is dishevilled, but as far as she can see, unbroken. She sits it down on the couch, pulling down its skirts, tidying the wild dark hair.

"It's got blood on its face," says Cristofer.

Indeed—the teeth are stained red and a vampirish trickle decorates the mouth and chin. Cristofer has gone very pale.

"He said the doll bit him . . . oh my god! It's an automaton?"

"In a manner of speaking."

"I don't see any clockwork."

"There isn't any." It's not the same, she thinks, something's happened. The face looks slightly different—still exquisitely lovely, but stiffer, a less realistic and vivid simulcra of a child, more doll-like, lifeless. Well, only one way to test that . . .

"Annis, what are you doing, don't stick your finger in its mouth!"

She feels cold china, the shapes of the teeth, a moulded little tongue, all sticky with dried blood . . . but nothing else. The animator, or *shem*, is missing. She withdraws her finger and stares frantically at the floor surrounding the couch.

"What are you looking for?" he asks.

She opens the pack of Plantin letters, finding on the top the letter from Marie-Simone to Berthe Lazarus. "Read that, it saves explaining. I'm going downstairs for a moment."

What does a *shem* look like? she thinks, as she makes an intent reconnoitre of the landing floor, then step by step, the stairs. A bit of parchment, if she read the French aright, with Hebrew writing or cabbalistic signs, all 72 of them, written small enough to fit into a doll's mouth. She thinks that during the scuffle on the couch, the *shem* might have been jerked out, might have adhered to the vulture, with his blood perhaps. Nothing else can explain the new blank look of inanimation on the doll's face.

She opens the front door, inspects the little front garden minutely, even venturing onto the street, where she picks up dead leaves from the macadam, in the hope of seeing lettering on their dry, brown versos. A motorist hoots at her, and she reluctantly withdraws into the house. When she returns to the landing, she finds Cristofer, sitting on the couch, the letter folded neatly in his lap. He is, she notes, a safe distance from the doll and his expression can only be described as gobsmacked.

"All clear now?" she asks.

He nods, beyond speech.

"Relax. Little Miss Golem won't bite you, not anymore. She's lost her *shem* and I can't find it. For all I know it got discarded with the hospital rubbish."

She wanders over to the balcony's kitchenette, collects a box of tissues and fills a polythene cup with water. Then, she sits on the couch beside Cristofer, resting the doll in her lap.

"Hold this." She hands him the cup, and he clutches it obediently as she dampens a tissue, and starts dabbing the blood off the china face.

"You're destroying forensic evidence," he says.

"I had a chat with Eliza. 'If the doll got broken,' she said, 'then leave it that way. If it's still roaming around the house, then lock it in George's safe until I get out of this dump and can think clearly what to do.' We couldn't think of a third possibility, but just in case she gave me carte blanche as regards the doll. 'You're a sensible girl', she said."

He stares at her.

"Carte blanche," she repeats.

She takes a clean tissue and wipes the doll dry. Now she lifts it, dandling it like a child.

"So, I've made a decision. Without the *shem*, and without the blood I'm a castrating bitch—which I quite like, it'll make people take me seriously. And all the Plantin notes and papers are just ravings, interesting ravings, to be sure, but nothing to show that the fruit of their labours was the world's only genuine surviving golem, albeit not in perfect working order. That way madness lies, Cristofer, though I see from your face you've been doing mental sums, trying to commodify La Golem Sentinelle. Far simpler if she is only a china doll, with whom I have been playing, in an idle moment." She laughs then, and taking one chubby bisque leg in her hand, jerks it up and down in a cancan motion, in the general direction of Cristofer. And after a moment he laughs too.

FROZEN CHARLOTTES

We have long forgotten the ritual by which the house of our life was erected. But . . . when enemy bombs are taking their toll, what enervated, perverse antiquities do they not lay bare in their foundations? What things were interred and sacrificed amid magic incantations, what horrible cabinet of curiosities lies there below?
—Walter Benjamin

That night, she thinks: never again. The woman to the left of her, a mere girl, has wept on and off, all afternoon; on the other side are a pair already into baby talk, and not even pregnant yet. She knows what the nurses say privately, to each other: raving bloody loonies, all of them, it's nature's way of preventing hereditary insanity. Sometimes she wonders if she is going mad herself, as the drug-induced depressions hit. No more, she thinks, this is it, now or never, even if that does mean *never* . . . And as the black tide of misery rises within her, squeezing out through her eyelids, she too weeps, but with an edge of relief.

Next day he visits. He takes her hand, doesn't squeeze it, just holds it, in silence, waiting for her to speak. In the end she whispers: "Get me out of here!"

Getting out of the hospital is easy. What is harder, though, is coming home to the big white outer suburban house, and looking out the window at the rows and rows of houses undulating away, their hills hoists blossoming with little white squares, little blue or pink clothes. Nappie Valley, the real estate agents call it. And the glances of fake sympathy hurt as much as the real sympathy, from relatives, and so-called friends. She can't bear, either, anyone so forward as to commiserate with her: leave me alone! In the end she doesn't go out much, creating a comfort zone around her: junk food, daytime tv. Until one day Jerry Springer's topic is *her* topic, too close to home, this home no longer, not to a nuclear family, two parents, one cat, one dog, a little boy and little girl. Not even one child lives here, despite the sunny room upstairs, all filled with nursery things, in their cardboard boxes, never unpacked. A monument to the what-might-have-beens . . .

He comes home to find her flipping through the real estate sections of the Internet. "I'm getting us out of here," she says.

He sits down, ready to listen. She moves from site to site, clicking on buttons.

"Remember when we were the renovators from hell?"

He chuckles, and she knows she is on the right track.

"And we'd talk about *Projects*, Wrecker's delights really, but we'd find 'em, buy 'em, do them up, sell 'em . . ."

He says: "I remember: how we never wanted anything beyond six square metres of recycled Baltic Pine floorboards, or a match for the odd antique doorknob. Achievable things . . ."

Before, she thinks, before we decided we had to get real jobs, and with that everything that came with them: the suburban dream home, the pension plans, the desire to perpetuate ourselves . . .

She clicks again.

"So you're looking for a Project," he says.

She nods. "Just getting a feel for it. And then we can call up the old contacts, find which suburbs are about to boom, where you get good tools, or where the wrecking yards are these days."

"We can't go back in time, love," he says after a while.

"I know. But we have to move, move on, and this is one way. And it was fun, remember that? Despite the hammered fingers, the dust and dirt. You felt you were doing something creative, something positive."

He thinks. "I'm sick of driving a desk," he says finally. "You win. We'll give it a go."

Selling the big white house is easy. Selling his business, resigning from what she knows might be the last good job she'll ever have, is harder. But hardest of all is finding the Project, after they have narrowed down their hunt to a suburb where nobody knows them, a forgotten knot of old working-class inner city, stuck between industrial areas, and a rubbish dump about to be reclaimed.

It turns out to be one hell of a Project: a little two-room cottage of stone, with behind it shoddy addition after shoddy addition, on a block of land half solid concrete paving and half weed wilderness.

He says: "It's classified—oldest surviving building in the area. Which saved it from being flattened, at least."

She says nothing.

"I know it doesn't look like much, but you wanted a Project, love . . ."

She takes a deep breath: "It'll do . . ."

They buy a second-hand caravan, to live in during the worst of the renovations, and park it behind the house. The first night, they sit outside in the dark, balmy night, eating pizza and drinking beer. Around them is the concreted back yard, with fruit trees sticking out, above them the expanse of stars, dimmed by city lights.

"Tomorrow we start," he says, looking at the stars.

"Tomorrow," she says, and slips her arm around him. Later, they make love in the caravan, with no consideration for days of the month, charts and temperatures—just because they want to.

The old bluestone is sound on its stone foundations; the rest of the house is another matter, the stumps decaying, the floors pitched every which way. In the lean-to kitchen, water in the sink tilts at an uneasy angle. Each decade or so, something has been added to the house: an 1890s annexe, a 1920s kitchen, 1950s bedroom, 1960s bathroom, 1970s brick patio.

"We'll have to demolish and start again," he says. "All except the bluestone."

"History," she says, stroking the blocks of stone. "I should go to the library, the local historical society, see what they know about it."

But in the morning, waking bright and early with the thumps as the skip is delivered, she forgets about research in the fun of getting dirty and sweaty again. In the garden they play tiger in the weed jungle, hunting rubbish for the skip: old tyres, half a bicycle, broken bricks, a rusted old barbeque. In one corner, under the weeds, is buried treasure, an old claw-footed bath, which they manhandle out into the centre of the back yard, for somewhere to put it. She is tipping a laden wheelbarrow into the skip when an old woman comes past, pushing a shopping trolley. She looks and bursts out laughing, a thin cackle, with little of fun about it.

"You won't catch me, you won't catch me . . . doin' that!"

Crash! The contents of the wheelbarrow hit the bottom of the skip, the noise relieving her feelings at the interjection. When she looks up, the old woman has gone.

The rest of the day passes in a blur of work. When they stop for coffee and sweet biscuits, their hands are so filthy they leave grimy marks on the mugs. Otherwise, though, they are happy as a sand boy and girl. Late in the day, they are ripping up onion skins of mouldy carpet, then the lino beneath them, then old urine-yellow newspaper, so brittle with age it flakes in the fingers.

She stops, bending over the exposed floorboards.

"I can hear something. Hush!"

"What?" he says. "I don't hear anything."

"It's like a scratching, as if something's trying to get out." Cocking her head to one side she follows the thread of sound, her Blundstone boots echoing on the newly exposed boards. She tries to tiptoe, to minimise the sound, something hard to do in the boots.

"Watch that floor," he says, as she disappears through the doorway into the 1890s addition. "It's borer central in there."

A creak, a loud crunch, and then a shriek. He rushes in, to find her waist deep in rotten timber.

"Jeeze! You all right?"

"Better than the floor," she says. She wrinkles her nose. "It smells like a stray cat lives down here. A tom, too. Maybe that was the sound I heard."

"Room enough for a wine cellar," he says, gauging the space between what is left of the flooring and the cracked, dry clay beneath. It forms a subterranean cave, littered with broken bricks, bottles and rusted cans. He tests a joist, finds it sound. "Here, I'll give you a hand up."

But she is looking at something small but shining whitely in the gloom. She crouches, brushing off a layer of powdered timber from it. Next moment she screams again, not the little bat-squeak of surprise, but the stuff of nightmare, and keeps on screaming.

He's run to the nearest off-licence and bought a bottle of cheap brandy. Now he hands her an inch of the liquid in a hastily-rinsed coffee mug. She drinks, chokes, drinks again.

"I'm sorry," she finally says. "Did you see it? A little white hand, it looked like, reaching up at me. The size of a fetus in a bottle."

She drains the rest of the cup, stands. "Well, they say you should face your fears." She is, though, none too steady on her feet, as they near the gaping hole in the floor.

"Let me do it!" he says, and lowers himself to the ground. He bends down then lifts his head, eyebrows raised.

"It's just a doll, love. See?"

"Leave it," she says. "Let's call it a day and go get a video."

But in the morning, though she is almost too stiff to move with the unaccustomed exertion, she pulls herself painfully through the house in her pajamas, and into the 1890s section again. Wincing, she lowers herself into the pit

She hears his footsteps in the next room along.

"Hey! D'you think you could get me something to dig with? Please . . ."

The doll is china, and it has, quite definitely, been buried. The clay is hard as concrete, but she hesitates to use more than a trowel, lest she shatter the china. At the end, she has a blistered palm, but holds a baby doll, moulded all in one piece: head, legs, arms and torso. In the bathroom, with its peeling op art wallpaper, she washes off dirt from the doll in the basin.

"History," she murmurs. "Or herstory, given that a little girl must have played with this. I wonder how old it is."

That wonder sees her dry her hands, get dressed properly, and head off to the big city library. She comes back hours later with a sheaf of photocopies, so eager she starts talking the moment she sees him. Which is on the front doorstep, where he stands broom in hand, sweeping several years of accumulated leaf mould off the verandah.

"It's a type of doll made from 1850–1914—so it's the same era as the front sections of the house. They're called Frozen Charlottes, or Frozen Charlies. There was this popular song, called 'Fair Charlotte', about a girl who went for a sleigh ride in the snow. She had a party dress she wanted to show off, so she refused to wear a blanket to keep herself warm. Nineteen verses later, she comes to a bad end:

'He took her hand into his own,
Oh God! It was cold as stone
He tore her mantle from her brow
On her face the cold stars shone

Then quickly to the lighted hall
Her lifeless form he bore,
Fair Charlotte was a frozen corpse
And her lips spake nevermore.'"

"Is that it?" he says.

"Yes."

"Charming," he says. "I'm not sure I could have sat still and listened to twenty-one verses of that."

From the street behind she hears the rattle of trolley wheels on pavement, a thin, cold laugh.

"You won't catch me, you won't catch me . . . doing that."

She turns, resolving to be neighborly.

"Surely *you* must sweep your verandah?"

The old woman continues on, not stopping. Over her shoulder she speaks, a parting shot, but a passing truck nearly obliterates the sound. Then she is past.

"Did you catch that?" he says.

"I'm not sure. Did she really say: 'catch me sweeping the house of horrors'?"

274

"House of mumble was what I heard. Clearly the local weirdo. Ok, so you've been researching. I've been checking out the floors, and I think they'll all have to go. But that's not all: there's another of these freezing charlies. I just found it, under the floor."

She kneels in front of the bathroom basin, a nail brush in hand, scrubbing dirt off the new doll.

"They're identical," she says.

"Like outa the same mould," he says, glancing over her shoulders.

"They *were* a popular, mass-produced doll. But why bury them?"

"Some little girl had a sadist for a brother, I'd guess."

She lies the dolls on the bath mat to dry.

"Oh, there's a foot missing. I'll see if I can find it."

He leaves her to it, starts taking a sledgehammer to the concrete footpath in the front yard. In the crunching of the hammer, his huffing and puffing, he forgets her, forgets the time. When he looks up it is sunset, and she is standing in the doorway. Even in the dim evening light he can see she is covered in dirt, and deathly white in the face.

"I found more than the missing foot. I found a whole army of dolls, all much the same, all buried. There's more to this than some poor little girl with a nasty older brother. It's like the day of judgement or something, the last trump, and up comes the dead . . ."

"Maybe the house was a doll factory once," he says. "And they had a lot of rejects."

Behind them, from the street, comes a now too-familiar sound, the sound of a shopping trolley. She crunches over the lumps of broken concrete, vaults the gate in her hurry.

"Hey you with the trolley! You know all about this house, you keep laughing at us! So tell us what the joke is, with all the dolls."

The old woman gapes and ducks past, breaking into a shaky run up the street. Her shoes flap, her knee stockings, neatly darned, slip down her skinny shanks. She thinks of tackling, if she knew how to do it, but instead uses her relative youth (elderly primagravida indeed!) to outpace, then confront the fugitive. It isn't hard—the old woman's trolley is laden, and she is panting hard enough to give herself a coronary.

"What is it about all the dolls buried under our house? You know, don't you?"

The old woman halts, slumps over the handles of the trolley and gasps for breath. Finally she speaks.

"I don't know 'bout any dolls. But I do know they dug up every inch of the land there was, and they found nuffin'. Like she said: 'you won't catch me'. And they didn't."

"Who said: 'you won't catch me'?" Apart from *you*, she thinks.

"Old Ma Wynne. Most famous person we ever had from round here. No footie player, no crook ever got her headlines. One of those series killers, they call 'em now. But they never found the bodies, and there must have been dozens of 'em."

Widow Wynne locked her front door and strode down the street, carpet bag in her hand, the cherries in her bonnet nodding with her passage, her long coat flapping in the cool breeze. The coat was black for widowhood, the cherries red, for merriment. Little enough of that around here, though. Three doors down, bailiffs at the door, loading furniture into the van. Empty house beside that, the tenants did a scarper, the rent well in arrears. Three children, their clothes clean even if they were coming out of their boots, dogged her footsteps, keeping a safe distance. They're getting thinner, she thought, their eyes hollow, their fingers like chicken bones in the old German story, Hansel and Gretel. Weren't those children abandoned in the forest by parents who couldn't feed them? Must have been a depression, whenever it was, just like now.

"Witch, witch," she heard behind her, a child's jeering whisper. She whirled round, clawing her hands and they took to their heels. When she turned, back was the respectable widow and small businesswoman. Things get much worse around here, she thought, your mama and dadda, they'll abandon you . . .

At the train station she bought a return fare to the city, third class, and also a copy of the evening paper. In the classifieds there were her advertisments, each with a post office box number. Business was booming, about the only business that is, it seemed. She glanced through the rest of the news. LEGISLATURE DEBATES FOUNDLING HOSPITAL BILL is the headline. She skims the article quickly, pursing her lips at its conclusion: the bill was defeated 'lest it encourage immorality'. And whose immorality might that be, honourable sirs? Yours and the housemaid? You're not the one who'll be sacked without references when you start to show. On the same page was the result of an inquest into a case of overlaying—a mother rolling on her baby when asleep, and smothering it. Third case this week. Drunk, was she? Husband out of work? How many children did she have? Not guilty . . . just like Hansel and Gretel's parents. At least they only abandoned their babes in the wood.

She folded the paper and devoted the rest of the ride to eyeing the scenery. The train passed through rows of mean little suburbs, their back lanes full of washing and brats. The pleasures of the poor, she thought. Not a penny in the house but rich in children. We got steam trains, we got telegraph, but you'd think some know-it-all would come up with some way of giving the womenfolk a rest . . . And put me out of business, she thought.

Several stops before the city, she alighted, checking the address on an envelope before striding through sidestreets. She moved quickly, for this was slumland, dangerous for anyone who had the faintest whiff of prosperity. The single-fronted little terrace might have housed a small family once, but now it had been let, and sub-let, to boarders. At the end of the passage was a room, and her client. Irish-accent, hurt, bewildered eyes, pretty enough, if you liked carrot-tops.

She wasted no time. "You've got the money?"

The girl laboriously counted it out, as if expressing drops of her own blood, or milk.

"All ready, then?"

The girl nodded, her eyes filling. All in one movement she turned and bent, lifting from the mean little iron bed a limp bundle, in baby clothes. Mrs Wynne bent over it, seeing the infant is clean, wrapped in a shawl, and on its lips the unmistakable smell, opiates and alcohol, laudanum, the mother's friend.

"Dear little thing," she said.

In a moment the transaction was over. Mrs Wynne walked out the front door, leaving behind her weeping client, in her carpet bag the sleeping, drugged, baby.

She didn't look like a monster . . .

"She doesn't look like a monster," he says. They have spent all morning in the archival section of the library, reels of microfilm beside them, ancient newspaper history scrolling before their eyes. Now they sit at a communal table, in front of them a microfilm photocopy. It shows an evening paper of a century ago, a line engraving of their house, c. 1890s, the front yard full of policeman, digging. On the same page is another engraving, a middle-aged woman, in her black bonnet a nodding spray of cherries.

"'A kind face, seemed very fond of children', that's what witness A said. After handing over her baby and paying money to Mrs Wynne's adoption agency. Which consisted of various PO boxes and one woman with a carpet bag."

"Who was a mass murderer. 'Massacre of the innocents' . . . 'Out heroding herod'," he says, reading from the screen in front of them. "And I thought media frenzy was a modern thing."

"If she was a mass murderer. Remember, she was acquitted for lack of evidence."

"Then what did she do with the babies?"

The question hangs in the air. In front of them is a line drawing, showing a witchlike crone, cherries in her hat, throwing an infant in the harbour, a cartoonist's response from a century ago.

"Look at these papers," she says. "Birth notices, welcoming fifth, sixth children. Overlaying, whatever that was. Babies found on church doorsteps. The past is a different country."

"I wouldn't like to have lived there," he says.

"Even though we could have adopted 12 kids or more if we wanted, nobody wanting illegitimate babies, especially with the over-supply?"

"Let's go," he said. "I'm not sure I can take much more of this."

Back at the house, she wanders through the 1890s rooms, trying to imagine a black coat, a hat with cherries. Finally she crawls under the house again, unearthing more dolls. He trundles in the wheelbarrow, and they fill it with the finds. When the barrow is laden, he takes it out to the yard. It seems a sacrilege, after what they know, to just dump the dolls on the brick or concrete, so he lines the claw-footed bath with an old blanket, and carefully lays the dolls on top. Then he returns to help her with the dig.

Hours later, utterly exhausted and filthy, they sit on the back doorstep, sharing sips from the bottle of brandy. Moonlight shines down on them, and on the bath, filled with little white forms, the heads turned towards them, the little dark painted eyes watchful. It is very still, hardly any traffic, but the empty air in front of them teems with movement, as if filled with moths glimpsed only from the corner of the eye, that slip out of sight if you try and look at them directly.

"Do you see?" she whispers.

"Not—see," he whispers back.

The contents of the bath seethe, sending dolls falling out onto the concrete. They break, a plaintive plink like drops of rain, then a shower, as they continue to tumble. The remaining dolls in the bath have transmogrified into chubby toddlers, who totter on the rim of the bath, fall to join their fellows. Child-dolls, taller and thinner, play in the bath, tussle, fight, and also topple. A group of boy dolls play soldiers, marching over their fellows, growing taller and thinner, into grown doll-men, short back and sides, painted moustaches. They form a battalion, then, as if to a 'Hup, one, two three!' march in formation over the side of the bath, crashing and breaking. A pause, then two doll nurses appear over the side of the bath, carrying a stretcher, with a sick doll, its arms flopping helplessly. They toss it over the side, return to the writhing pile for another patient, then a third. Other nurses appear to help in the grisly task, with their own stretchers and sick. They finish, then throw themselves after their patients. A pause, then a doll dressed flapper-style appears over the side of the bath, sexily posing as she walks. Another doll approaches, pushes her off . . .

She closes her eyes, hides her head in his shoulder, unable to watch anymore. She hears, though, the continual crash of breaking china.

Finally the noise painfully stops. Around them it is still now, utterly quiet, even in the centre of the city. She opens her eyes. Around the bath is a mass of broken china. They approach, stare into the depths, to see movement.

He gets the torch from the kitchen. They see one doll left, an old woman—except that nobody has ever made an old woman doll.

She claws at the side of the bath, the wool of the blanket, trying to get out. Finally she collapses in a heap, stills. Before their eyes the doll breaks into pieces as if ground under a heel.

He turns off the torch. She reaches out to the pile of broken dolls, feels the china faintly warm and gritty under her fingers. Some of the dolls have been reduced to powder, their constituting earth.

"'Dead and turned to clay'," he says. "That's a line from somewhere."

"And I also remember from somewhere about bone china. That's china with bone ash mixed in with it."

She shivers.

He says: "I think it was the lives they would have led. Infant mortality was high at the time—that was the first wave. Childhood diseases, diphtheria, whooping cough, typhoid did the rest. Then we got 1914, followed by the influenza epidemic . . . and so on and so on. One made it to old age, it looks like."

"If they'd lived they'd all be dead by now."

"To this end we must all come, love, though we try and hide from it, by perpetuating ourselves, busying ourselves with Projects."

"Hush," she says, and takes his hand. Hand in hand they stand before the mass of china and clay dust, pondering their lives and those of these poor broken others, pondering the what-might-have-beens.

MATRICIDE

There is an afterlife . . .

And it appears to be an international airport terminal. How strangely suitable, she thinks, given the time I spent in such places. Charles de Gaulle, Heathrow, LAX she knows, but this terminal is not so immediately familiar. It is typical, though: computer screens, garish carpet, travellers crowding the departure lounges. Departing for where? she wonders. Some other terminal, some afterlife Paris, Athens, Rome?

An announcement comes over the loudspeaker in a string of translated languages. She catches in each the word Changi. Singapore, she thinks. They named it after a prison . . . again appropriate. No heaven, she thinks, but hell—I've felt that often enough, stumbling jetlagged off a plane—or even purgatory? She stares at the fellow travellers, but they seem just like any tired passenger encountered in life. Young girls in high fashion, older women in tracksuits, parents pushing strollers, little children running across the carpet. Suddenly she glimpses a women oddly familiar, seen through the glass of a departure waiting room: middle-sized, between youth and middle age, thin, hair cut conveniently but modishly short, her clothes chic, but comfortable for travelling. Then she realises the woman is not seen through the glass, but darkly reflected *in* it.

How I used to be, she thinks, with a pang of pleased vanity. Well, better that than the wreck of what I am now. Or the vomitbucket of a few months ago. She moves on, becoming aware that she is not so much stepping as gliding across the concourse. Ghosts walk, she recalls, the thought summoning the memory of a television program, chilling when seen in childhood. Involuntarily she glances down to see her feet, clad in modish, all-purpose (from citywalking to boardroom) boots, which are firmly planted on the black plastic of a conveyer belt.

She relaxes and lets the belt transport her past the departure lounges, into the gift shop section. At the end of the belt she steps off, into walls of duty-free Hermes, cigars, Scotch whisky. Then she stops. Behind one glass shop window is a woman, familiar, older, also stylishly but comfortably dressed. And, she notices, just on the legal edge of air travel, to judge from the bulge beneath her Pregnancy Survival Kit black frock.

As it is the afterlife, she can do now what she wouldn't in real life, satisfy an inappropriate curiosity.

"Excuse me?"

The woman looks up from a display of little Chinese dolls.

"Excuse me, but you were the judge . . ."

She thinks: Judge Judy I called her at the time, it was Judge Judith something.

Judge Judy gazes at her, head slightly on one side, as if sorting through a mental card file.

"I was the defendant in a case you presided over. In New York. I was sued: Tenenbaum vs Lester. I'm Lester, Sylvie Lester."

"Oh yes," says the judge. "The case over that ridiculous doll. The hallucination in wax. It made me feel ill just to look at it." She frowns faintly, remembering. "I was only just pregnant at the time."

"You threw the case out. I was so glad, I wanted to thank you."

"No thanks necessary."

"And to say I'm sorry about you and the baby . . ."

"Sorry?"

That faint frown has returned to Judge Judy's face.

Now I've put my foot in it, Sylvie thinks, but nonetheless can't stop the words.

"Sorry, because you're both dead . . . like I am, otherwise we wouldn't be here."

"Don't be ridiculous," says the judge. She gestures at the passing passengers, singling out a group of depressed-looking Middle Eastern men. "Do you think that's Mohammed Atta, and his merry men? And, just disembarking, the planeloads of their victims?"

"No, it doesn't exactly look like him."

"Of course it isn't. *I'm* very much alive, and so is my child. So are you, Ms Lester, for the moment. What happens next is up to you, it always is. We can't pick our beginnings"—with a downward glance—"but we should try and control our endings. Life's that way. And now excuse me, I have to buy a present."

And with a wave of her hand Sylvie is dismissed, out of the judge's sight, out of the gift shop, out of the airport concourse. She curls up foetally, eyes closed in a personal darkness. We can't control our beginnings, she quotes to herself, but we can control our endings. Yet where in the Sylvie-story do I begin? It'd make a novel in full, and somehow I don't think I've got enough time. Choose scenes, fast backward. Pause.

Maybe it begins with Miles . . .

Immediately she has the sense of wind in her hair, the indefinable scent of imminent, looming snow, overlaid with coffee and Gauloises. She uncurls, into a Paris sidestreet, the outdoor settings of a café, coffee and frites on the table in front of them. She looks up, smiles despite her jetlag.

"At last!" he says, lifting his coffee cup. Miles, a big, amiable bear of a man she'd met on a language course. He was polishing his French, before his move to Paris: to my dream life, he had said. Why she was doing the course she couldn't recall. But they'd gotten on, found a common ground in the arts, their conversation, even in French, a pleasant exchange. They had parted with a kiss on both cheeks, French-style, an invitation: "If you're in Paris, get in touch."

With an implication, a possible double meaning, double entendre.

On the flight from Singapore she hasn't slept well, she could just fall into bed at this point. But whose? That point remains to be negotiated. Miles met her at Charles de Gaulle, took her into town, deposited her bags at the hotel. It's her first time in Paris and despite her tiredness, the boulevards, the rows of Baron Hauptmann's terraces, the style of the Ile de France fascinates. They've spent the morning wandering around, seeing sights, Miles' Paris.

"What is your dream life?"

He answers unhesitatingly. "A studio apartment in a building so full of history the similes fail me. Writing my books. Being a consultant on various art and museum projects, even a film. Just being here."

"I can see why."

He nods, staring back into her face. And so the day passes. Without a word being spoken, just the pressure of her gloved hand on the woollen sleeve of his greatcoat, after dinner they go back not to her hotel, but to his apartment. If a pass has been made, she has caught it. And so she falls into his bed, to sleep profoundly, the bulk of his body keeping a chaste distance, on that night at least.

As her head hits his feather pillow in its cool linen cover, the images of Paris slowly fade. They are replaced something closer in time, something painful: a doctor's surgery in Brooklyn. A vial of yellow liquid, as yellow as the good French wine she drank with Miles, sits on the table. Beside it, a sensor slowly turns a lurid pink.

"It was just a one night stand," she says.

Or rather a succession of one night stands, every time I flew into Paris . . . To the studio apartment, a small space, monastic in its simplicity, the furnishings of good quality, from china to towels, but austere and plain. Everything is functional, no thing extraneous or frivolous. And this from an expert on the beaux arts! She intuits it is a reaction to the collections and collectors he associates with on a daily basis, other people's frippery . . .

"Maybe. But my dream life is stripped down to essentials," was all he said. "Paris is an expensive place."

She compares her succession of rooms in share houses, her flats here and there, full of mess, valuable or otherwise. Working for Sothebys, then as a freelance, setting up her own business, meant she was forever discovering arty bits and pieces imminently about to appreciate in value or that she just had to have. Riots of fabrics, and rugs, paintings and photos, cushions and objets d'art, pouffes and feathers, bric-a-brac and unalloyed kitsch. Completely unlike the décor chez Miles. There is no place for her here, she thinks, except as a brief visitor, a one-night's guest.

"A one night stand," she repeats firmly.

The Brooklyn doctor very slightly purses her lips. In answer Sylvie feels first a twinge, then a rush of nausea. She turns away from that scene, into the blackness behind her eyelids again. No, she thinks, I'm going too fast, slow down.

She opens her eyes, to see the terminal again. A man clears his throat behind her. "You're Sylvie Lester?"

In answer she reaches for her card carrier, of antique jet, and withdraws the card. *Sylvie Lester, Dealer and Location Service, Antiques, Fine Arts and Collectables.*

"Then you're my date."

He looks—there is no other way of saying this—like some sort of Samoan Goth. Dark crinkly hair, a mid-Pacific face, offset by small round shades black as night, that resemble eyeholes in a skull. The clothes are very expensive, but worn like a Thunderbird puppet's. They don't fit, and neither does he, in this life or any other.

"Mr Ween," she recalls.

"Call me D.C. Remember I wanted to buy you a drink, as a grateful client?"

"You're trying to kill me," she says.

He stares at her, impassive. "Not just yet. This is the only time we met, remember, outside the Internet."

Behind him the terminal swirls in her vision, changes slightly, imperceptibly, the colourful plaques of tourist advertisments now showing images of Jazz Festivals, Mardi Gras, the voices around them suddenly dripping Southern US honey.

"This is Baton Rouge," she said. "Or New Orleans. And I'd been asked to give a speech at some Antique collector's fair."

"Of which I could only make one afternoon. So I said, let's meet at the airport."

He leads the way through the crowd, people eddying as if preferring not to touch or near him, to a lift doorway.

"The VIP lounge. I'm a member."

"Of course."

They disembark at the top floor of the terminal, a big, gilded room looking over the expanse of tarmac, the planes taxiing, circling, landing, regular as some clockwork toy. He chooses a window table, and they sit, against a backdrop of metallic, stormbringing sky. As a waitress takes drinks orders, flakes of snow blow past outside, some briefly attaching themselves to the glass before an ephemeral melting. This isn't Baton Rouge, she thinks. Not exactly. But what or where it is I don't know.

Two margaritas arrive, and as she sips he gestures sideways with his head.

"See the guy over there, the corner table?"

She follows his gaze, sees a mop of greying hair, thick glasses, a vaguely familiar face.

"That's Stephen King. My man, my kind of dude."

"He looks like a college professor," she says. A brutal one. Well, that's what they have to be these days to survive, that's what Miles said . . . At the thought the scene wavers and dims slightly, as if something is trying to return her to Paris, and Miles. No, not so fast, she tells herself. You want to be back there, that's obvious, but don't rush. Otherwise you'll miss something important.

"A great man," D.C. continues. "To reach into the world's psyche, and extract a can of worms, bring out what scares folks most and rub it in their faces."

He's a good client, she's not about to tell him he's mixing his metaphors.

"'I'm more intrigued by his sheer grip on narrative," she says. "To keep on reading, when it's four am on some red-eye shuttle and you're totally grossed out. That's ability."

"I still say it's the scary stuff that makes him powerful. Guess we'll have to agree to differ." He sips from the margarita glass, spraying salt. "Hey, what scares you?"

The way the question is asked, the sly sneaking out of left-field, does something to her it shouldn't, brings back a memory so compelling she can't confess it, especially to a stranger and client. She had been nine or ten, impressionable. Idly she had been watching a television program, a fifteen-minute filler before the news. The topic was famous ghosts, and this week's episode was a historic haunted hall in England. It had burnt down and witnesses saw two figures walking out of the flames. The commentator said: "one had the form of a young woman, the other was a shapeless thing."

The memory still made her want to shudder, at what the 'shapeless thing' might have been. It was suggestive of so much, once you let your imagination play with it, as children will: like pulling a scab off a wound, horrified, hurting, but unable to stop.

"You tell me what scares you first," she counters.

"I could . . . but I won't."

The creepiness she first perceived as an affectation in her client now seems genuine, in much the same way as does Stephen King. If it really *is* Stephen King, she thinks. Isn't he a reformed alcoholic, not seen in bars at all? As if reading her thoughts, Ween lifts his glass in the direction of the novelist—and for a moment it seems that King lifts his glass of Coke in response, a returned salute.

"A very powerful dude. You ever hear about the guy in the car who ran into King when he was jogging? Near killed him. And guess what, he's dead now. You can't tell me that's an accident, anything less than a revenge. There are dark forces out there, just ready for payback, for an injury to the guy who let them walk free among us."

His tone is admiring, and now she has had quite enough of this weird exchange. "You should be writing horror yourself." She drains the dregs of the margarita, stands. "And now I have a plane to catch."

Without looking up, he says: "You haven't, not here . . ."

And as she turns to go, he adds, a faint, parting shot: "Unless the plane catches you."

She steps out of the VIP lounge, aware as she does that there is some commotion behind her, people craning, staring out the windows. She walks on, not wanting to look back, not at Ween and his implied threat. Outside she looks for the lift. She finds it, but merely opens the door on a very plush Ladies, marble-topped tables, hibiscus in the vases, gilt-rimmed mirrors . . .

In which she sees herself, as she was a few months ago: hair lifeless, skin white and crepey, even green in tinge. At the sight the nausea rises again, and she rushes, for the nearest receptacle, luckily not the flower vase, but—unhygenically—the basin.

As she holds onto the taps, washing away the regurgitated margarita, somebody comes into the room behind her. She looks up into the mirror, and sees her Brooklyn doctor.

"I know they call it morning sickness, but this is morning, noon and night sickness!"

"It goes with the territory sometimes," the doctor says. "Pregnancy hormones, being overproduced. Unpleasant, but nothing to worry about, unless . . ."

She walks up behind Sylvie, takes the skirt of her pleated Miyake pullover dress (asymmetric, no crush, go anywhere) and pulls it tight. Revealed is a bulge, not the extent of Judge Judy's, but more than just stomach flab, girly jelly belly.

"Elsewhere I'm thin," Sylvie says helplessly. "And I used to be thin there too."

"When *did* you last have your period?"

"I told you, I don't notice such things, but I definitely last had intercourse two months ago. On the 14th of July, the French holiday."

"And before that?"

I will not say "I only have sex in Paris", she decides. "Um, March."

The doctor releases the skirt, runs her hand over the bulge clinically, a non-caress.

"You look more than two months. Either you're hopeless with dates, or it's a multiple birth . . ."

At that Sylvie dry-retches into the basin.

"Or . . ." the Doctor trails into silence, releasing her.

"Sorry," Sylvie mutters to the porcelain.

"It goes with the territory. But Ms Lester, I'm sending you off for a scan, an ultrasound. If it is more than one foetus, then you need to think hard about your options. You told me you hadn't decided what to do yet."

"I have now." Of all things, it was the memory of a Paris shop, the delectable, tiny bébé-things displayed in the window, suddenly now terribly covetable, in all their frills and lace, unexpectedly necessary. If that's a reason, she thinks, it's a bad one. But it is a deciding reason nonetheless.

"I'll take that as a yes?"

Sylvie nods, the motion setting off the nausea again.

"It's hard enough with one, on your own. Can't the father help?"

"Him?" She laughs, without humour. "He's got a perfect life."

"Wife?"

"No life, no room in it for a child."

Or me, being around all the time, she thinks. She starts to cry, and the bathroom blurs around her. In the time it takes to collect herself, wipe the tears away, she finds herself no longer in the bathroom, but the lift. The doors open at the ground floor, and she steps into . . . chaos. People are running down the concourse, their screaming near drowned out by the wails of fire-engines. Speeding towards the terminal is a taxiing plane, too fast to stop. She stares at the narrow window where a pilot should be, but sees nothing, a void. The plane screeches across tarmac, its nose cone hitting the glass of an observation window, shattering it.

And then, for that brief moment, time is slowed. She sees the glass shatter, and through the gap comes cold wind, and eddies of snowfall. I could run, she thinks, save myself . . . if I want to.

The plane slams into the terminal, in a shower of glass and snow, the wheels rucking up carpet and demolishing the departure lounge chairs. The wings strike the side of the terminal, concertina, break off in chunks.

It's like my body, she thinks, a plane wreck, hit by a plane, hit by Miles, even if unintentionally. Still her feet in their smart boots remain planted on the floor, as if she has no flight reflex, no sense of fear.

The plane bursts into flame. And in the centre of that fire, as she smells the acrid gasoline plastic smell, coughs at the billowing black smoke, she sees something she recognises: an ovoid shape, grotesque and pretty, like a hallucination in wax.

That is where it really begins, she thinks. It all started with that doll, when my life started to go pear-shaped. The day I went to Miles', as usual, after a flight from Bali. I unpacked my suitcases there and then on his polished wood floor, to show off the weird and wonderful things I had found for my clients. And, as I sat there, bubble wrap and dirty washing strewn around me, the thought struck me that every time I saw him I got more fond of him, his accepting my dropping in with minimal notice, uncomplaining as I temporarily took over his life. And I liked so much his laugh, his concocting divine meals from things he just happened to have in his fridge, like mini zucchini and goat cheese, his being the perfect gentleman, particularly in the bedroom . . .

But did he like me *because* I wasn't there all the time?

"I have something for you," he says. "Or for one of your clients. Though I can't imagine who would want it."

She pauses in her unpacking. "But Miles, you don't collect, you say you haven't the space."

"I don't. But as I was passing through a flea market, in a town where I'd stopped to buy Doyenne du Comice, the queen of pears, I saw this little doyenne, weird though she is."

He hands her a cardboard box, tied with string, which she unties like a child at a birthday party. Underneath is a layer of aromatic wood shavings, which she lifts to reveal a monstrosity. An egg made of papier-mache, with breaking through the shell the limbs and head of, not a chick, but a baby doll.

"I think it must have been some Easter gift," he says.

The cracks in the shell are realistically etched; the doll's chubby limbs are moulded in translucent, flesh-coloured wax. Impossibly blue china eyes stare up at her from a wax face surmounted by a tuft of curly blonde hair and a lacy bonnet.

"Originally confectionary inside," he says. "The head comes off"—and he demonstrates. Revealed is an empty void, with a fusty, vaguely sickly smell, as if of antique sweetmeats.

"I'm impressed," she says after a moment, "That is really, truly, deeply grotesque."

"I thought you'd say that."

"I had a doll collector on my books, but kewpie only. And I can't think of anyone else among the clients. Maybe I'll invite bids, like with ebay. I've got an intern back in New York, it'd give her something to do . . . just put it on the website."

She has a brand-new mobile phone, with digital software, in her luggage. She locates it, positions the doll on Miles' scrubbed wood table, takes a photo. Eat your heart out, Ann Geddes, she thinks, as the image wends its electronic way across the oceans.

Hours later, in bed, the mobile rings.

"Did you have to get Chinese Revolutionary Opera as your ringtone?" Miles murmurs into the pillow.

"The mobile's duty-free, I haven't had time to customise it."

She sits up in bed to talk, in the dark.

"Who was that?" he asks, as she ends the call.

"A Mrs Lotte Tenenbaum. I think she must have bribed the intern to give her my mobile number."

"The name is horribly familiar. And I mean horribly. Let me waken my brain cells." He switches on the light, slaps his broad brow theatrically. "Oh dear! Sylvie, what abstruse collecting universe have you been inhabiting? Mrs Tenenbaum's famous, indeed notorious in some circles."

"She wants the doll. She says her family used to own it."

"She says that about a lot of things. Her family lost everything in the Holocaust. Including her sanity. She's old, very rich, and trouble. I refuse to sell this doll to her."

"But . . ."

"I'm the vendor, and I insist on my right to refuse objectionable offers."

She stares at him. "But I practically said yes . . ."

"I overheard and you didn't. You had a tone in your voice: well, if she wants to make out on the first date, what will she do afterwards? Like the shrewd businesswoman you are. And if she wants it so badly, who else might?"

A silence, broken by the sound of a car in the street below, then the phone again.

"I'll kill that intern," she says. "Or sack her. Whatever comes first."

Again, after the conversation she reports to Miles, the prospective vendor of the merchandise, being businesslike even if stark naked. 'That was D.C. Ween.'

"What sort of a name is that? Deceased Ween! Like Halloween without the hallow?"

"'What abstruse collecting universe have you been inhabiting?'" she echoes. "It's a stage-name. You ever hear of D. C. Ween and the All-Hallows Band? You ever hear them? Particularly unlistenable death metal, but sold millions. He's retired now, but still reacting against what must have been the fundamentalist upbringing from hell. Very selective, will pay anything for the right stuff, if it's horrific: mortuary memorabilia, mojos, voodoo. He too wants the doll . . ."

"No doubt to stick pins in it."

"You may not be so wrong there." She thinks uncomfortably of D.C.'s most recent purpose: some hand-made voodoo dolls, in a crude wooden boat, found washed up on a Mexican beach.

"Well, he can't have it either. I refuse to let this doll, grotesque though it is, get into the wrong hands."

"You're making things very difficult for me," she sighs.

And what eventuates is their very first row. It arrives in stages, as does their cooling. Each time she'd arrive in Paris, she'd update Miles on the trouble he'd caused her. Never anger a client, that was one of her rules, and Miles had got two clients murderously mad with her, expressed in their own insane ways.

"What's this?" he said.

"Take it. Open it."

He cocks one eyebrow at her, but takes the heavy paper envelope, sealed with red wax. The seal is a grinning skull, and with an expression of distaste he slips a thumb under the flap, cracking the skull from crown to bony chin.

"It's a hatpin. Nineteenth-century, from the look of it. And dirty . . ."

"The tip is crusted with blood. I had the last one analysed."

"The last one?"

"It's the latest in a series, sent via Fed-Ex, security express, Gorecrow if he could."

He looks obtuse, and she nearly yells at him: "D.C.! It's from D.C. Ween!"

"How childish of him," Miles merely says.

Next time she comes armed with a tape from her answering machine. Not content with losing the law case, Lotte Tenenbaum kept calling, somehow locating the mobile numbers, even when changed, the silent New York number.

"It's Yiddish," she says. "And I've had it translated. Read it!"

He reads the transcript, hands it back to her. "'May an umbrella enter your belly and open up!' That's a classic Yiddish curse. She's said worse to several dealers or curators of my acquaintance."

"Do you have to be so calm and collected all the time?"

"I'm not getting myself flustered about it, if that's what you mean. If you are, then you should go and get an intervention order."

"It's your *fault*!"

"No it's theirs, for thinking the answer to their personal problems lies in possessions. Even if that is how you make your living."

That does it, her temper bolts away from her, as if running for freedom down the streets and alleys of inner-city Paris. She says things in the heat of the moment, to be remembered and regretted later, like a cold-collation revenge. He gets storm-sullen in response.

Slamming the door she goes out for a walk alone, amid the happy French families, celebrating the national holiday. She returns in the dark foot and heart -sore, with the stars out. The apartment is dark, and she can see his hulking silhouette by the open window. Inside, she nears him; pauses. In response he takes her by the hand.

Yet even sorting things out in bed resolves only the physical tension and not the emotional. She hasn't been back to Paris since, she doesn't know what Miles did with the doll, she didn't ask. Maybe he locked it up in some Parisian safe-deposit box.

But now here it is; in the centre of the flame, the exploding aircraft, beginning to burn, baby, burn. So this is all about you, she thinks. A doll that two rather strange people wanted desperately, but that everyone else thought weird. You made Judge Judy feel nauseous; but not me. When I was pregnant I didn't think of you once. Perhaps I should have, because what happened was even more grotesque than you, Easter dolly.

Snow is drifting still into the terminal, despite the fire. It settles on a green-tinged screen beside the table where she lies now, legs drawn up in a technological rape, the scanner coated with gel and inserted, revealing her most secret places.

Where's the baby? she thinks. Instead she says: "That looks like snow."

"It isn't," says the scanner technician, a statuesque black women. Then: "Honey . . . I'm really sorry."

"It's not a baby." It's a statement, no question in her voice.

"What you see as snow is called a mole."

"Mole?" A snow-mole?

"A hydatidiform mole. It's rare but it happens. A sperm cell hit an egg that was defective, without a nucleus. You've got the symptoms of pregnancy, but no foetus."

All she can think to say is: "Why me? Why me?"—as if it were something personal.

"There's risk factors, like being Asian, which you're not, age, nutrition . . ."

She thinks: I'm not young, I know I don't eat properly, except in Paris.

". . . but understand honey, it's not your fault. You gotta understand that, whatever happens. Because the snow on the scanner is placental cells, developing uncontrollably."

"It sounds like a tumour," she says dully.

"It can be. You need a D&C, dilation and curettage. ASAP."

In pre-op, she finds herself on a production line, women entering in day clothes, then being sent to cubicles, where they changed, to emerge identical in white hospital gowns, white bathrobes that are one size, oversize, paper mob caps on head, paper bootees on their feet. And suddenly she starts to cry, for something she has lost but never really had, no time even to buy pretty French babyclothes, no time to plan, no time to think of a potential, now lost. And the crying continues as they lift her onto the hospital trolley, wheel her into the operating theatre. She is nearly hysterical as the anaesthetist lifts her hand, strokes it clinically to reveal the vein, pricks her with the poisoned needle.

"Are you still there?" says a nurse.

She clenches her fists, answers through sobs: "Yes, unfortunately."

A nurse strokes her cheek, a professional sympathy. Then blackness. She wakes later in a room full of curtained beds, for a moment forgetful, then with consciousness coming the memory: of waking up the day after an exam failed; of a boyfriend dumping her; of her non-existent child. And she rips the drip from the back of her hand.

Nurses and later counsellors come and talk to her, the sounds of their voices like water over smooth riverstones. She coils around her internal void, slowly beginning to shift from depression into anger.

A counsellor: "Do you think of the baby as an angel?"

"I most certainly do not!"

She gets discharged, she heads back to her apartment and her lonely art deco bed. Next morning she gets up, goes to her computer terminal, then the office. The following day she is out of the city, heading across the airways to do what she does best, finding things (and in the process losing herself?). She is back briefly, then jets down to the Southern hemisphere, more searching. At some point an airline clerk offers her a flight through Paris, but she refuses. Would Miles really want me to land on him with the ultimate sob story? she wonders. When a man expresses his tenderness with sex, what happens when that is temporarily forbidden, by medical interdict? The nights and days blur across time zones, she knows she eventually stops bleeding, but can't pinpoint just when. She just keeps on working, travelling she realises increasingly frantically . . .

Until even she has to stop, to come back and find a series of phone messages, urgent demands, this time from her Brooklyn doctor.

"I told you that you were to come back for tests!"

Yes, she did, Sylvie thinks. "You also said complications were rare." But I couldn't stand the thought of coming here, to this surgery with all its implicit reminders. And so I left, not really caring about anything much.

"But not impossible. Well, since you're here, we'll check your beta-HCG."

"That's the pregnancy hormone," she recalls.

"And if it's still there, so is the mole."

"But how?" Hadn't it been removed?"

"Metastased—travelling though your system."

"That sounds like cancer," she says.

"It is."

After the test, the Doctor's face says it all.

"Do you have someone to care for you?"

Maybe, she thinks, then shakes her head. If I couldn't even tell Miles I was pregnant, how can I tell him what's happened now?

She closes her eyes again, in sudden fear. Darkness returns behind her eyelids, bringing with it the smell, not of a doctor's office, but an aviation disaster. And I'm a gynaecological disaster, she thinks. I thought I had a baby, but I never did, my egg was addled, empty in its core. My child transformed into a monster, and now it's trying to kill me. What's the word, the child killing the mother? Matricide.

She opens her eyes, to a stinging reminder: the acrid chemicals smoking out the terminal. Her feet move now, taking one step, then another, towards the burning plane. The doll is at the centre of the flame, as if on a stake. It started with you, she thinks. My clients cursing me, and as if they really had power, the worst thing in my life occurred. And I'm still paying for it now, with chemotherapy. My life—such as it is—is measured in hospitals and drugs, my business and my body have gone to hell. Which is where I could go too, just now.

The heat is intense, and the doll is succumbing to it, the lace cap flaming in little points, the mohair wig frizzing, the papier-maché smouldering, the chubby wax limbs deforming, the pretty face melting, with only the embedded glass eyes keeping their shape. One falls out, revealing darkness. The doll is becoming something shapeless . . . which seems to advance towards her.

"No!" She reaches through the flames, the pleated polyester of her Miyake smouldering in the heat, and takes hold of what remains of the doll. The hot wax burns but she doesn't let go. Her hands move, cupping, caressing the wax, which almost seems to squirm between her fingers. In her grip the wax loses its formlessness and takes shape, not the doll as was, the weird easter baby, but a ball. She moulds it slightly at both ends, and there she has it: an egg. She presses it to her, the fabrics of her ruined clothes falling away. The wax shape presses into the flesh of her belly. She pushes hard, and slowly it sinks in, the flesh closing and flattening over it. Now it is just an egg, an unfulfilled potential, hidden inside her.

Someone grabs her arm, yells at her. Now she is running, in the grasp of a fireman, as firetrucks converge, fill the terminal with white chemical foam.

He releases her, pointing to a line of waiting ambulances, shouting: "Lady, life's that way!"

She flees through the terminal, now empty except for disaster crews. Well, almost empty: slumped in a departure lounge she finds two figures, side by side: an old, withered woman with bitter, hawk-like features, and a man in black, his dark glasses askew, to reveal unexpectedly milquetoast eyes. Her former, vengeful clients, she realizes.

"I'm sorry," she says. "I'm sorry for what happened to you, Mrs Tenenbaum. And whatever it was that turned you into an aficionado of evil, D.C. But the universe is like that. Look what it did to me—not even in your most vindictive dreams could you have expected such a revenge. So, we're quits."

Neither move nor respond. Are they dead, overcome by fumes? She suddenly couldn't care in the least. All she sees is the word flashing on the departure screens: Paris. She could just go through those gates, step onto the waiting plane, and within hours be stepping into Miles' little apartment again. She can almost . . . no, she *can* see him now, televised on the screen. He sits at his table, a half bottle of wine and the remains of a baguette beside his piles of books and papers. For the first time she realises that his perfect life is actually rather lonely.

She reaches into the pocket of her ruined Miyake, brings out her mobile. As she activates it, the same image of Miles appears on its miniature screen. She presses buttons, summoning his oh-so-familiar Paris number. And as she does, the terminal fades. There is just a pool of light around her, night in her New York apartment, where she lies on her art deco bed, surrounded by medications and her once-prized collectables, a sickly stick of a woman suddenly at the point where she has to ask for help, or else.

She presses the final button, to dial a small apartment in the Rive-Gauche. And she waits for Miles to reply.

SOMETHING BETTER
THAN DEATH

For anything I know it was all due to jetlag, that curious fugue state in which the body has leapt over space and time as if in seven-league boots, with the protesting spirit, or soul, striving to catch up. Or due to the jetlag medication. Or else that I was betwixt and between stages of my life, or thought I was, and my subconscious was trying to tell me something. Whatever the cause, I walked between waking dreams, intermittent hallucinations, in which what was real and what wasn't mingled and merged madly. In the end it didn't seem to matter—I just went with the flow.

It all began in the International Departures check-in, where the teenage girl ahead of me exclaimed:

"Ohmygod! Tell me I'm hallucinating!"

Gladly, sweetie, I thought. I hadn't slept the previous night and was decidedly on edge, my body on automatic pilot, my mind darting every which way. Terminals always are artificial, in their air-conditioned saccharine blandness, and today this one seemed particularly unreal. That what *seemed* might actually *be* a genuine unreality was a notion I could welcome.

I followed the direction of her pointing, black-varnished finger, to see four figures and a trolley piled high with flight cases. And a part of me that I had resolved to leave behind pawed the ground and said: Aha! A band.

The trouble with music promotion, if you've done it too long, or long enough that it stops being fun, or fannish, is that you automatically categorize market niches. The girl was an obvious Goth. The band were a little more difficult: tatts, black clothes, long hair can indicate anything from stadium rockers to Norwegian Black Metal, who are more trouble than they're worth, as they have an annoying habit of burning down churches. Probably Speed Metal, I decided, as the girl started hyperventilating. Cult-level, if they're at the economy counter. I could guess at the festival they'd just attended and even take a punt at the promoter. My old life pawed at the ground again, raring to start a professional chat, about festival logistics, equipment, transport. Not the least of the fun would have been giving the Goth fangirl the vapours. To her, I was over forty, and thus nigh death—but I could still best her in the catty cunning stakes.

Instead I suppressed the urge, and stood meekly in queue. Was I not en route to a new life, leaving all frivolous, pop-culture things behind? The band passed through check-in, then security without incident. If the Gothgirl got autographs I didn't see, for I was deep in Duty-free. What can you get a serious-minded man, apart from seriously good drink? Then I stretched my legs for the last time until Changi, a long walk around the corridors with my headphones and German-language CD. The Gothgirl I spotted in the lounge for Vanuatu, which would surely ruin her graveyard pallor. My flight had been called, I was handing my boarding pass to the Stew, when a bloc of black joined the queue—the band again, clutching tacky outback souvenirs. Not as evil as you like to pretend, I thought. Like most metallists—who upon acquaintance tended to be polite and obliging, the reverse of the Christian rockers.

I have flown so much it has become routine, but even the tedium failed to deaden my jangling nerves. I watched a movie, *The Jane Austen Book Club*, and decided I didn't believe a word of it, apart from Jimmy Smits playing against type as a nice family man. I ate automatically, listened to my tapes again, dipped into my E-book, which was programmed with everything about Germany, from the *Rough Guide* to the Brothers Grimm. The Stews handed out cocoa, started dimming the lights. Outside it was dark, as if we were passing through an interminable tunnel. It was 2am my time, and there would be light, and an airport in a few hours. I took a pill, and, just to make sure, chased it with the last of my dinner red wine.

And awoke, with all around me sleeping passengers, and my nerves jangling again. My feet, in their airline socks, felt cramped, so I wandered down the aisles. As I neared the back row, the middle aisle, I had a sense of being watched, and traced it to a hulking dark shape, almost entirely muffled by an airline blanket worn like a hoodie. Eyes showed beneath it, large and lustrous. Beside my watcher were several other forms, similarly shrouded in blanket and curled up in the narrow seats like a pet in a basket. I caught only a glimpse of dyed Mohawk protruding. The band, I thought.

It was easy enough to catch my travel dress on a protruding, blanket-clad limb—elbow or knee I don't know, as he overflowed his seat in several directions. As I crouched down to extricate it, the "Sorry", "No I'm sorry" morphed into a whispered conversation. The accidental proximity of air travel can make for unlikely fellow travelers having even more unlikely conversations. But, as I crouched beside him, whispering into the space beneath his hood, and he whispered back in an accent I couldn't trace, it all seemed natural and easy—in retrospect too easy.

In dreams or drug trips, events occur without apparent connection, and very quickly. They cut to the chase, without small talk—and that's what happened here. Within a short time we were getting personal in a mixture of English and German, a language I was still learning.

"Warum?" Why? Why was I traveling?

"Ein mann,"—the truth, just to stave off any possible pass.

"And what sort of man, to take me half the length of the world?'

"Ein musik-mann."

He emitted a soft laugh, breathy, harsh and nasal, and with more wryness than mirth in it.

"Nobody you'd know. He plays Classical, and conducts a small avante-garde consort at the Music School in Bremen." I pronounced it the correct German way, Bray-men.

"Donkey," he said.

"I beg your pardon."

"Katz."

"Yes, I'm Jane Katz,' I said. Had he been ever a client, in some previous band incarnation?

That laugh again, but less wry than simply pleased. "Donkey, katz," he repeated. "And hund. And rooster."

"Oh," I said, catching on. "Well, Grimm to you too!" I had just read the story, on the E-book, and it was fresh in my mind. On the first day of Christmas my truelove had even sent to me a stuffed toy, the tourist symbol of the city, a donkey with a dog on its back, on the dog a cat, on the cat a rooster. The Four Musicians of Bremen, made in China.

"That's an interesting story, more than it seems. Like most of Grimm."

"It begins with a donkey," I said.

"Too old to work on the farm anymore."

"And rather than die for the only thing valuable left on him, his skin, he gallops away, down the road to Bremen."

"And there I think is an in-joke. Why does the donkey head for Bremen? To be town-musician. Which indicates the Bremen musicians had the reputation of being worse than donkeys."

"Interesting," I said. "He says he can play the lute."

"How can a donkey play the lute?"

I considered this. "With his teeth, like Hendrix. Or using one hoof on the fret, like a bottleneck or slide."

"Vir gut," he said. Very good.

"The hound says he can play kettledrum," I said, leaping ahead to the next character. "Maybe with the stick tied to his tail."

"To show you can teach an old dog new tricks."

"He too has run away, because he is too old to hunt, and his master has nearly beaten him to death."

"Then they meet a cat."

"Wet through and thoroughly pissed-off."

"Escaped from drowning."

"Because he is too old a hunter, even for mausen."

"What does the cat play?"

I thought again. "Probably some kind of string instrument. With those plucking claws."

"They've already got a guitarist."

"Bass, then." I had dabbed at bass, like various girls in '80s bands. When I got beside rather than on the stage I gave it up, but still harboured respect for the bassists I encountered. They were cool cats mostly, especially the jazzers.

"And the last one," he said. "The rooster."

"Crowing as loud as it can."

"The phrase is 'through marrow and bone.' Vir gut, very creepy."

As is your being word-perfect in a story I only just read, I nearly said. Odd little doubts stir below the surface of dreams, but are never expressed.

"His fate is to be made into soup."

"That's farm economics," I said. "Utterly unsentimental and practical. I grew up on a farm." And got as far away from it as I possibly could.

"And so the rooster completes the band," he said.

"As lead singer, with his penetrating voice."

"All of them seeking in Bremen 'something better than death', as the Esel, the donkey says."

Now that really was creepy. If there is something that everybody fears, and avoids as hard as they can, it is growing old, finding yourself beyond a useful date, and the end nearing. Old boiler, that's what they say of women, only suitable for soup, like Grimm's rooster.

I think at that point I returned to my seat, too unsettled to continue. Next thing I was waking from a totally unrestful doze, with the cabin lights on for the descent into Changi. There I used the free internet, to send a message to Bremen, and because the line about something better than death was really getting to me, some Duty-free but still expensive night cream. At the bar, I encountered the band again, looking thoroughly unslept—and noticed no Mohawks. Nor were any of them particularly big. And, I suddenly realised, whoever I was talking to, he was older, because he kept emphasizing the animals' age. A young man wouldn't do that, they believe they're immortal. Get off that fire escape now, drink this water, no, don't try and snort wasabi . . . all from days when my promo work shaded into nannying.

Who was my conversationalist of the night-flight? Someone out of the common, certainly unlike the fellow passengers lining up for airport security yet again, in their tracksuits and jeans, the children clutching *Harry Potter*. He must be on the German-bound flight, he spoke German to me. I scanned the line of passengers, but drew a blank.

No matter, I was really tired now. I wrapped myself in blanket, closed my eyes—and kept waking every fifteen minutes or so, all the way to Hamburg. Mein mann had told me of a spot, hidden but known by seasoned travelers, where you could sit in reclining chairs and watch the take-offs. I found it, but still couldn't relax before my connecting flight to Bremen.

The flight was full of German businessfolk, who disembarked with their briefcases, or waited somberly by the carousel for their suitcases. There the strangeness started again: I swear I saw a sniffer dog leap onto the carousel. Oho, a drug bust! I thought, glad this time I wouldn't be getting any client out of trouble. Instead the dog took hold of a suitcase handle in its mouth, and dragged it off the carousel, for the benefit of a man who merely picked it up, and walked away, the dog trotting briskly at his heels. The things they teach seeing-eye dogs these days! I thought.

I found that Germans took dogs everywhere, into department stores, museums, so a dog in an airport soon seemed not so strange. Not as strange as the new country, even with a native guide in the shape of the musik-mann. How to describe him, except in terms of the stereotypes of love, of race? He was tall, blonde, blue-eyed, handsome (natch!), earnest, methodical, serious. Reader, I fucked him—as soon as we got back to his tidy apartment. Then I slept, despite my resolve to stay up until I was in sync with the local time. Sex does that to me, even earnest, methodical, serious sex. I woke, to find him dressing for a class he had to teach. Why didn't I come and take a look around the wintermarket while he worked, see the Christmas schmuck (baubles), and drink Lumbaba (coffee with rum)?

So, not long afterwards, I was alone in Germany, in below zero cold, bundled up in woollens, in a Christmas funfair. Here were mistletoe branches, the first time I had seen them in their cold green actuality, there were merry go rounds, plywood silhouettes cut into Xmas scenes, gingerbread hearts. It was a festival that said: Be merry and keep the frost giants away!

"Ich möchte ein Kaffee," I said carefully to the man at the Schmaltzküchen. Then, "Danke Schon," when I got the coffee.

It raised my body temperature a notch. But still I felt the chill penetrate the sleeves of my coat, cutting through to the marrow and bone of my forearms. Looking around for something to do, preferably warm, I saw a tour for the historic Rathaus, that's Ratehouse (Townhall) auf Deutsch and in English.

I paid my euros, joined a queue again, of people in padded jackets, and woolly hats, usually with technicolour plaits attached, a fashion that was no doubt practical, but too hippie for my tastes. Inside was warmth again, and our guide.

"Do we have any Israelis in this tour?" he said.

Great, I thought, now we get anti-Semitic jokes, unless I tell him how great-grandma eschewed pork chops. But we got nothing of the sort, unless he told them in German. The bi-lingual tour was detailed, but told with a light, witty touch. I learnt about the Hanseatic league, Bremen as republic, Bishop Ansgar who evangelized Scandinavia from Bremen, about 1000 years ago. And Sydney town is only two hundred years old, I thought, unless you are Yothu Yindi.

Interesting though the tour was, odd details kept distracting me: the dog which padded along with the tour, as if it too had paid its Euros to attend, a gargoyle face squinting from a riot of wooden carving, the wry, nasal laugh of the guide . . .

"Someone has just asked me about the symbol of the city, the key. It was not like now, where keys of the city are given as honours. Not a symbol of opening, but closure. Medieval cities were walled, against what might attack them from outside the zone of tilled fields and pasture, from robbers to robber barons. The keys were closely guarded, for behind the walls were not tolerant places. They had to be that way, to survive."

I looked properly at the guide for the first time. He was large, male, graying, about my vintage, nondescript almost by intention, as if trying to fit in as precisely as a jigsaw piece.

"Since you're talking about symbols, what about the musicians of Bremen?" I asked.

It was as if the rest of the tour group had vanished, and we were just talking to each other one to one, as we had in the plane.

"They never got here," he said. "They got diverted."

"By the lights of a house in the forest," I breathed.

"And when they looked in the window . . ."

"They saw firelight and robbers, feasting around a table."

"Their mouths started watering, with the hunger."

"And they slunk back into the dark."

"Discussed what to do."

"And devised a plan."

"They watched and waited until the robbers were drunk, but not legless."

"Then the donkey sank down on his knees, and the dog scrabbled onto his back."

"The cat elegantly leapt onto the back of the dog from its vantage point on a water barrel."

"The rooster swallowed his nerves, and fluttered onto the back of the cat."

"The donkey stood carefully, lifting the pyramid of animals."

"And a monstrous silhouette appeared in the robbers' window, followed by an equally demonic sound, in concert. The donkey brayed."

That laugh again.

The dog, who had been sitting quietly by, ears pricked, emitted a small bark.

"The cat wailed," I said, groping in my linguistic memory for the word. "Das miaoen!"

From the tour group came the final sound in the quartet, a crowing ringtone from a mobile phone. It broke the spell, as the guide sighed, and wagged a finger at the perpetrator. Now he was just a tour guide again, and I was just another tourist, alone in an alien country.

Another day, another place, more disorientation. Mein mann had a free weekend and was taking me on a tour of his favourite Germany. This meant a 6am start, when I had woken at 2, and lay beside the sleeping six-foot of him, unable to doze, unable to find something to do in a strange flat full of books I couldn't read, appliances of which I was yet to learn the nuances. We caught the ICE, the inter-city express, at the Hauptbahnhof as the sun rose. Gradually the landscape emerged from the darkness: mostly windfarms, and winter-brown woods. We changed at Hanover, changed again at a station I only remember for a tree delineated in ice like a faery toy, a moment of sheer magic despite my fatigue. Then, hours later, we reached Arnstadt, famous for Bach. The tour had been organized methodically, chronologically, Arnstadt being where Bach had his first job, as organist at a Lutheran church.

We stood, boots on frost, and surveyed the memorial statue. "Seated one day at the organ," in the hoary old song. Mein mann was reverent, but I had to suppress a giggle. The young Bach was unmistakably phallic, suitable for a father of twenty. And hadn't he wielded a sword, too? He reminded me of the young Keith Emerson but I knew better than to share that thought, especially with the man I with whom I would be sharing my life. We entered the Neuekirche, and my irreverence continued, for the interior was like a white and gold wedding cake, even the organ. Can I have a cake like that? I very nearly said. We would have to get married, if I was to stay in Germany, rather than pursue a long-distance romance. He had the steadiest income—I was the alien immigrant, seeking the keys to the city, to let myself into the warmth and the firelight.

The walled cities were not tolerant places, I remembered, from the tour guide's talk. I shivered. He misunderstood, and put his wool-clad arm around me. A warm misunderstanding, in which I could luxuriate for the moment, as we stood like bride and groom in the middle of a white and gold church.

We had lunch in the Musician's Café (of course!): kaffee, Schwarzbrot, Tagessuppe (Day Soup, of the day, and vegetarian, for unlike my escort I didn't fancy the chicken broth). In the pearly-grey winter light I watched a stocky white cat skirt the Arnstadt Rathaus, appropriate given the bi-lingual pun.

"I have an appointment for the early afternoon. Musical."

Of course, I thought.

"While I'm away, would you like to see the Puppenstadt?"

"Dollhouse?" I said, after a moment's translating thought.

"Famous. From Bach's time."

Whatever you say, I thought. He could have suggested I go ice-skating on the nearest pond, such was my passive desire to please. But a dollhouse, when I was neither childish nor twee? What did he think of me?

Unexpectedly, it captivated—80 or so rooms in glass cases, a German principality in miniature, compiled by the childless and widowed Princess Auguste Dorothea, a plump and amiable lady from her portrait. Well, it beats music promotion as an achievement, I thought. I moved among the cases, nose almost touching glass, reading the details of a lost time, musicians, maids, weavers, bakers, dancing bears and all. Behind me came and went a tour group, German old age pensioners, and their guide. Someone lingered, I was aware of the presence, but was otherwise intent on a miniature replica of the Princess's Audience room. The detail extended to a pet monkey—and was that also a cat?—lurking by the folds of her brocade silk skirt.

"Would you like to go in?" said a voice behind me, one with which I was becoming very familiar. A hand moved briefly into my peripheral vision, holding between finger and thumb a tiny key.

"To the dollhouse world? Is it any different from the medieval walled cities?"

"The seventeenth century was more civilized," he said. "The Princess was fond of her court musicians and her pets. But observe the man selling rat traps, the dancing bear"—polar, made of real white fur—"and the old beggarwoman."

"We might come to that yet." Such a fear, to be alone, and old, poor and friendless. I shivered again.

"Imagine," he said, "if I stand at the window, the dog on my back, and you, Katzwoman, between dog and rooster, and we open our mouths and make the biggest cacophany we can—"

"To scare away the dollhouse folk, like we did the robbers," I breathed. "Miaoen!"

My mew was soft, but it seemed shockingly loud in the silence of the museum, somehow augmented, by the laugh behind me, the bark of a dog, even that ringtone cockcrow again: hee-haw-arf-meow-cock-a-doodle. As if the glass before me were water, a surface to shimmer with my breath, it shook. I suddenly found myself not outside, but *within* a 1700s provincial audience room, crouched at the foot of a throne upholstered in yellow silk, around me Chinoiserie wallpaper and marquetry furnishings.

The monkey and I were face to face. I bared my teeth at it, hissed, and it slunk away. Then I did what any cat would do, jumped up and settled myself in the best seat in the room, the princely throne with its soft yellow silk, underneath a matching Austrian blind of a canopy.

"And what is your decree, Princess Catwoman?" said the face in the glass, occupying one wall of the audience room.

I waved one paw airily.

"Release the monkey from its chains, also the bears, take the horses out of their harness, and ban all rat catchers, except me!'

"Vir gut," said the voice behind glass, laughing again. The glass quivered and the vision reversed, so that I stood once more gazing into the audience room, with its static doll-princess, monkey and cat.

"What are you?" I said. "Some kind of animal liberationist?"

"I can hardly be anything but," he said, his voice a trailing thread of sound, ending in silence. I turned and found myself alone. The mobile mein mann had given me rang in my pocket, a Bach fugue. It was time to go.

The next few days passed in snapshots, images of a fairytale tourist German Christmas. Dinner that night was at the Goldene Sonne, where generations of the Bach family had an annual musical meet, and we slept in the hotel above, all to ourself. Sex was 6/10, from my continuing tiredness perhaps, or else some unacknowledged sense of disapproving Bach family ghosts. To the Lutheran Church the next day, to hear Bach's organ being played, although I nearly nodded off during the sermon. Back to Bremen in the train, snow having fallen so that the countryside was almost over-the-top picture postcard, except for the windfarms. Left alone the next day, I watched German TV, and found it equally trash culture as elsewhere. Feeling very brave, I walked from the Neustadt (new town, typically a name hundreds of years old) along the riverside, all by myself.

I wanted to see the famous statue of the Musicians of Bremen, cast in bronze. It was polished keen by tourist hands, and I touched it too, first the katz, then the donkey, but felt not warm hide and hair, but cold metal. I waited, as tourist happysnappers came and went, as if listening for a distinctive breathy, braying laugh. Nothing happened; and I consoled myself with some glühwein, drunk in a booth while the Christmas revelers all around slapped backs, dispensed Christmas cheer—to everyone except me, it seemed.

Night, and I put on what I had of winter glam, and went out with mein mann, to see his consort perform. Avante garde meets with rock music at some junctures, especially at arts festivals— and thus ageing lady rock promoters meet serious classical music dudes. I knew my Steve Reich, my Phil Glass, even if I preferred my beloved Sonic Youth. Why did the performance then seem a cacophony dressed up as art, not even with the honest purpose of frightening some robbers away from their ill-gotten gains? Not to mention that I really did fall asleep during the "quiet movement". Result, in the freezing wind outside, a blazing row, luckily for any relationship grudge sheet largely conducted (by him, berating) in German. Under different circumstances I might have stomped off angrily, but in sub-zero temperatures, in a foreign country, I had no choice but to follow him meekly home, to his home.

By next morning we had sort of made it up. He ate salami for breakfast (German habit, bad as Vegemite) and we took another train, off to Lübeck, where Bach had walked all the way from Arnstadt to hear Buxtehude play. How young, how fannish, I thought, but did not say. The ICE was crammed, with Germans, their suitcases and Xmas parcels, all last-minute panic as they headed back home to the volks for Weihnachsfest. We changed trains, as we had on the way to Arnstadt, but this time in a major city. I had missed my essential morning coffee, to make the train, and was decidedly blurry, not-with-it. As we waited outside the coffee booth, I said:

"Where are we?"

His face said: she doesn't know? "Hamburg, of course."

"Oh," I said, suddenly locating a culture point I recognized. "Where the Beatles honed their art!"

And then stopped cold, as his expression changed from condescending amusement to naked disgust. So you think that of me, what I have done, what I adore! With a psychic jolt, as of a train coupling, my jetlagged spirit or soul caught up with me, and with it came my senses. I knew then, that I had made a huge mistake: had I really believed true love was possible with a stranger who was my musical opposite?

"Snob," I shouted, a word identical in English and German. From around us came answering shouts, an approaching roar of song, even what sounded like gunfire. Feet tramped, a whistle sounded, and police in uniforms, with batons and guns, surged into the station. On the next platform a train pulled in, full of football fans, singing lustily and setting off firecrackers. The police flowed to meet them, and within moments there was a riot going on, not only on the platform, but between us lovers-no-more, as last night's row flared again. This time I gave as good as I got, in words with Germanic roots, four-letter, cutting, nasty and final.

Dramatic exit time, like a bow in front of a curtain. I turned on my boot heels and stepped into the larger chaos of the riot. I've survived mosh pits at festivals, I know how to move through trouble unhurt. Not so the fan to one side of me, who stumbled, and got a kick to the head, dislodging his beanie. As the riot eddied around us, I pulled him upright, lest he be trampled.

He looked near-stunned, blood tricking down from his Mohawk, dyed in the team colours. I did what I usually did, when I had a client in strife, led him towards the edge of the riot, then out among the watching passengers, and towards a safe stillness. Somehow along the way we acquired a police dog. I looped a finger through its collar, and as a scuffle neared us took a step sideways, and down a flight of stairs. Perhaps the dog led, perhaps I did, as we step-stumbled down towards a local service platform, containing only a few scattered passengers and their parcels.

A train pulled in, and automatically we entered. It chugged away back in the direction of Bremen, as the looming clouds released their snow, and we passed through empty farmland, small station after small station. The track dived into woodland, and in its centre stood a deserted station, the smallest so far. The dog barked, pulled at my coat skirts with its teeth. I heaved my dopy charge upright again, and we disembarked in the swirling snow, nobody following us out into the cold. The fan bent, scooped up a handful of snow, and rubbed it on his head. It seemed to revive him, and he lurched towards the exit. I could hardly abandon him—so I followed, as did the dog, wagging his bristly tail.

Waiting under the overhang of the station roof was a large grey donkey, whom the fan embraced around the neck, then used, as he had me, as a walking support. So out we stepped into the snow, the four of us, through a village, decorations and Xmas candelabras at each window, like an advent calendar. Within a few streets the village petered out, and our paws, hooves, runners and boots stopped scrunching snow, instead fell silent among the rag-rug of damp pine-needles in the forest. The fan walked free now, but I stumbled on a tree root, went headlong, knocking the heel off my boot. The dog bent over me, panting, the donkey lowered its velvet muzzle as if in concern, and the fan lent me a hand upwards. I wobbled, and he scooped me up as easily as he had the snow, depositing me on the back of the donkey. This is not Nazareth, I thought, and I'm definitely not a pregnant Mary. Nonetheless I rode on donkeyback through the forest to a clearing, in which stood what looked like a converted stable, or barn.

I know the donkey nudged the door with its muzzle and it swung open, I remember that, but the next moments are unclear. Somehow I went from riding on a hard hairy back to being carried bride-style, in a man's arms, over the threshold. I got deposited in a hearthside chair, and there followed a flurry of movement, as a fire was lit. I pulled off my wet boots, set them on the ashy hearthstone to dry. The fire caught, streaks of orange shooting up the chimney, and I slid onto the hearthrug. It was littered with straw and pet hair, but I lay on it, luxuriating in the warmth. The dog settled beside me, sighed, and went to sleep. After a moment I closed my eyes too.

Hours later I woke after the first proper sleep in a week. The early winter dusk had come, and with it had come Christmas, celebrated on the Eve in Germany. The fire illuminated a table, set for the feast, and a Christmas tree laden with bling. I couldn't see the fan anywhere, but the dog still snoozed beside me, paws twitching. In the chair on the other side of the hearth sat the Rathaus guide.

"You are Esel," I said.

A smile and nod.

"Tell me what happened next with the story," I said. "So the Bremen musicians drove the robbers out?"

"And the four animals ate their feast and took over the house."

"Did the robbers ever come back?"

"They sent a scout, to reconnoiter. In the dark, only to get scratched by the cat, kicked by the donkey, bit by the dog, and near deafened by the rooster. So he ran off wailing of witches with long talons, men armed with knives and clubs, whatever his fears made believable."

"Unlike an animal insurrection," I said. The fire was furnace-warm now, too much for my woolens. I sat up, and as I did saw perched in the rafters a rooster, with—surely not—what looked like a band-aid on its comb.

"Donkey, hund, hahn . . . Vo sind die katz?"

"She has nine lives. She might go and live in another one for a while, but always comes back."

Reader, we spent Christmas together, snowed completely in till almost the New Year, in freak winter weather conditions for that part of the country. We talked, prepared excellent meals with Esel, drank glühwein, got to know each other. Nothing more, I wasn't leaping into anything rash again. We listened right through a large collection of vinyl and DVD, then the musical instruments emerged. Esel, could he play slide guitar! And I plunked away cautiously on bass. Hahn hung from the rafters and sang football songs in a mean imitation of Robert Plant. Hund was shy, some drummers are like that, but every now and then he would pad down to the cellar studio, from which would arise the sound of drums, played like a fury.

Just when all the food in the house was exhausted except for a box of chocolate mice, the villagers arrived with a snowmobile and dug us out. And, because I could leave then, cat-contrary, I didn't.

One upon a time the Grimm brothers collected an oral story, tidied it up for print consumption, but left the message intact. Strip it down, and the story is about finding a haven, or of being diverted from your path, most fruitfully. I went to marry a classical musician, and ended up living with a rock band. Nothing I hadn't done before, in my wild youth, an old life of mine, to which I had inevitably returned.

"Remind me how the story ends," I said to Esel, as we watched the New Year's sunrise, coiled up together under a geological strata of blankets. "So they lived happily ever after?"

"No, that's not what the story says."

"What, then?"

He lay back, thinking. "Everything prospered so well with the quartet."

"That's good!"

"That they did not forsake their situation."

"How very formal those Grimms were!"

"Not the very last line. It ends with: 'And there they are to this day for anything I know'."

There are two ways to write what happened. First is a romantic tale: on the way to what I thought was the love of my life, but in reality was a flingette, I met on the plane a gent more congenial to my tastes, musical and otherwise. Then I encountered him again, while he was doing emergency tour guide work, and found that I could survive a snowed-in Christmas with him and his bandmates. They could even use an experienced rock promoter.

Second is something stranger: life in a continuous Grimm's tale, as a musical shapeshifter.

It could even be both.

For anything I know.

THE REVENANT

How do you talk to a ghost? Just like you talk to anybody: a
smattering of the commonplace, some gratuitous observations,
information of varying use, and gossip. The latter seems to be
particularly appreciated—well, when I was talking to Mo, that
was what he seemed to like most. I just had to remember not to
question him, because he didn't like that at all.

It was Keith's annual twenty-ninth birthday party, as usual in
his little basement flat at No. 17, Esplanade Way. And as usual
everyone was there, mostly folk who'd lived in the rest of No. 17
or were still living there. Keith was stumping around the living
room on his calipers, roaring with laughter; musos were jamming
acoustically in the bedroom; in the little garden the shy were
communing with Mr. Wopperty, Keith's large and phlegmatic pet
rabbit. A boy dressed like Lana Turner talked to a girl in a 1960s
tux. A couple (indeterminate sex) were necking around the art
deco lampshade. In the kitchen the "you'll-always-find-them-in-
the-kitchen-at-parties" crowd were packed tight as sardines. The
bath was full of ice, and a couple of somebody's kids were sailing
little boats between the bottles of wine and reefs of tinnies. The
boats were made of corks, with cocktail stick masts and bright
sails cut from scraps of gift-wrap paper.

I frowned, without knowing why I was frowning. One child looked up: "We're polar explorers. Sir John Franklin and his men."

The other child, younger, said: "Cold hands." And demonstrated on my bare calf. I stepped back, out of the bathroom, feeling the small star of cold on my skin like a brand. As if looking for someone, I made another circuit of the party. Ruth, one half of the world's most poisonous ex-couple, was sitting on Keith's double bed, staring at a mandolin player. In the kitchen, Will, her other ex-loving half, was making punch. Good, they were being kept apart. The young S&M guys from the flat upstairs were chatting with Keith's incredibly straight twin brother: from the sound of it they supported the same football team. Another potential source of trouble: the bikers formerly from over the back fence were doing a drug deal with the yuppie couple currently renovating Harley Heaven, as was. Out in his hutch, Mr Wopperty was hoeing into a pile of vegetables, cut Thai-style into fantastic flowers and leaves.

The party was going well, adults, kids, even the rabbit all catered for, all sources of conflict miraculously averted. Keith's annual 29th birthday bashes inevitably mixed the oddest bunch of people together with no bloodshed. Or had, at their best, which was roughly three years ago. I rocked on my Manolo heels listening to the sounds of a happy, well-run party. It was too well-run, too harmonious, for a party without . . .

I didn't have to name him, even in my mind. I just turned, and saw him leaning against the wall, gangly and shock-headed as ever, that slow, wide smile on his face. The party facilitator, was what he was called by a surprising number of people, who had found him the perfect guest to soothe a fractious baby, make toasted cheese at 4 a.m., seek out the shy friends of a friend and introduce them to everybody, play DJ (or cupid), and make sure everybody had a good time. A man sorely missed, especially at the last couple of Keith's parties.

"Mo . . ." I breathed.

"Cat." His voice was just as I remembered it, and it sent a smile right across my face. We never were lovers—our sexual proclivities went in opposite directions—but he was the best male friend I'd ever had. Many other people shared him, I guessed—his funeral had been standing room only, with the door of the chapel open and mourners spilling into the foyer and onto the footpath outside.

We were all wearing bright colors and carrying streamers and balloons, as specified in the dear departed's last wishes. The dear, so dear departed . . . He shouldn't be here, I knew, and yet the party was going so well his presence was the only explanation.

"Those kids in the bathroom," I said. "You made the game for them. They're too young to remember you, and how Sir John Franklin was the subject of the history thesis you liked researching so much you never finished it. You got Son the chef, who can only talk work, to make the fancy veg for Mr. Wopperty . . . just like you used to do."

"Habit," he said self-deprecatingly.

"You mean life was a habit for you? Like a drug, something you couldn't stay away from?"

"No," he said, a look on his face that I'd known well: drop the subject. A guest looked up drunkenly at me—Alec, who'd houseshared with Mo once. I watched his face for the reaction, but there was nothing there, just puzzlement at Cat talking to herself, must be some sort of fancy mini-mobile . . .

"He can't see you," I said, stating the obvious.

"Most people can't. Those kids in the bathroom, they could, they acted like I was the tooth fairy. But then they believe in the tooth fairy, in Santa. Others, well they sense me somehow, I can influence them. Like Son, f'r instance. Or poor hate-filled Ruth, whom I led out of ex's way, and she went . . . no doubt thinking it was all her own volition."

"Still the party facilitator," I said lovingly.

"Habit," he repeated. "But one that's too much of a strain, always has been. Worse now. Shall we go?"

His change-of-scene line, that could lead to the strangest of adventures, like following the old disused Circle line tracks through the city at midnight, crashing a Young Liberals party pretending to be the press, or getting the worst hangover I ever had from the sake at the bar where the city's sushi chefs went to unwind—pandemonically—after work.

Automatically I reached for his arm, then hesitated. He made no move to offer it in my direction, and so, hobbling a little on my high heels, I followed him out the door, down the courtyard path and into the street. Outside as the cars of Esplanade Way hurtled past, I said: "The party may go to rack and ruin now."

"Someone else's problem," he said. I turned and looked into his eyes. From the look in them, he'd maybe gone to hell and back. Literally? I wasn't game to ask. As I pondered the problem of etiquette with a ghost, a thought came to me. I was so startled I almost stepped off the pavement. A car horn blared at me, and I swayed back.

"I had a great-great aunt who was a medium, I just remembered! She was a servant at a house when Conan Doyle came visiting, and he said she had a gift and should train."

"If Conan Doyle came visiting I'd have asked him to sign copies of Sherlock Holmes," he said.

"Well yes, anything else he did tends to look insignificant."

"And he took seriously fairies at the bottom of the garden."

"Agreed, but he was right. About you . . ."

"Me?"

"Well, what you are now."

"There's nothing right about what I am now."

"Er, yes, well it's against nature, of course." Oh gawd, that was tactless. If I said the wrong thing would he just disappear into thin air and leave me alone in this busy street, all my longing for him reawakened?

"But you have to admit he was right about my great-aunt Hortense. There really must have been a gift, and I've inherited it."

"Like a particularly ugly chandelier? Take it from me, Cat, there's no such thing as a psychic gift."

"Then why can I see you, when nobody else—the children apart—can?"

"I don't know."

There was a brief lull in the traffic, and he suddenly sprinted across the road. I followed, horns blaring as I made the opposite pavement in an athlete's leap, thinking: if he'd gone across when the traffic was thick, would he have just passed through the cars? Would some driver, with whatever you have that isn't—from the horse's mouth—a psychic gift have crashed, trying to avoid the spectral pedestrian? Maybe looking left, looking right, then crossing is another of the persistent living habits, like being a party facilitator.

He was moving quickly now, through the beach crowd, passing through all the bathers and boardshorts like a Moses amidst the red sea. I only caught up with him on the beach. He kept to the concrete barrier above the sand; I walked below, with my shoe-straps looped over my fingers. They'd cost all of the first paypacket in my new dream job, were something I'd once only dreamed of affording.

We'd always walked like that, down here on the beach: Mo hated sandy feet. At least it saved me the temptation of checking whether he left footprints.

"There were faces I didn't recognize at the party," he said. "And some faces I would have expected to see but didn't. Like Bren."

"In the country. With twin babies. And Sonja. They got married, too."

"But, but . . . she's a mad anorexic. Serve her a stir-fry and she'd thread bean shoots through the spring onion rings."

"Not any more. Moved on, apparently."

"Delilah?"

"Still trying to live down the famous right-wing father." By having sex with anyone who asks . . .

"The Bradfields?"

"Arsehole and Doormat? I don't know." And I don't give a damn, I nearly added. Why did he want to know about these people? I hadn't thought about them for ages, since the funeral, in fact. Even then I'd found no headspace for them. Like various of the partygoers, Alec, Will, and Ruth, people I'd known a long time, too long it seemed, since they were getting tedious now. The same quirks, the same jokes, the same ruts . . . even old Keith.

Mo, however, was continuing: "That surfie, the one everyone had the hots for. And he was completely oblivious. What was his name? Wayne."

"Don't you know?" I blurted out.

"Know?"

"Bali."

"Holiday?"

"No . . . he's dead."

"So are billions of others," Mo said. "Don't expect me to know every one of them, even if I did know them once. Anyway, how can you die on Bali, apart from an overdose of hedonism?"

"I'm not sure I can explain to you quickly." What I needed was a potted selection of the world's news highlights, to play to Mo on some convenient video recorder. Planes playing giant-killers with skyscrapers. Boatloads of refugees. The *Lord of the Rings* films. What else had happened in the three years that I . . . and so many others, had been bereft of Mo?

The sun was setting over the sea, a glorious sight. He stopped to stare.

"Miss that?"

"No."

"What, you watch it each night from your little white cloud?"

"Stop fishing!" he said.

"I can't help it, I don't meet ghosts everyday . . . that I know of. Although, when I come to think of it, every day I pass people who look more than otherworldly. Junkies on trains. Office workers fixin' to die at 9 a.m., Monday morn. Little old ladies, one foot in the grave."

"You can be dead, and feel alive," he said. 'Worse is to be alive, and feel dead.'

"That sounds like depression."

He nodded reluctantly, the last rays of sun gilding his hair.

"It was."

"Sorry, I thought you were such a happy person."

"Everybody thought that. Which made it harder to admit, and in the end, impossible."

He strode on ahead, and I had to run in the sand to keep up with him. Things were all of a sudden getting clearer in my memory, things I hadn't wanted to admit, either. Mo had made a will, in moral support of Goran, who had AIDS. Then together they'd sat down and planned funerals. Goran wanted Buddhist, and a flight of doves released over the harbor. He was still alive, though, thanks to a course of experimental drugs, but Mo was . . . dead.

"It wasn't an accident," I blurted. "You love classic old detective fiction. You know how to research. And you know how to facilitate things."

It was blindingly obvious, now I thought of it. The garden shed in his aunt Goldie's old property burning down—a barbie accident, Mo told everyone. Then his moving everything rescued from it into the cramped kitchenette, with hoes and spades cluttering up the walls, the table and bench space laden with rusty old tins containing godknowswhat. And his leaving them there, because everyone knew Mo was untidy. Until the night he came home late, drunk and high, in the middle of a blackout, and made himself a cup of bedtime coffee. And, the drunken klutz, knocking over the sugar tin and also another, unlabeled tin, which contained something known as "Rough on Rats." Both, the coroner had found, had got into his coffee. Who would have known that some old poisons didn't go off? Who would have known that, except Mo?

An alternate scenario grimly played through my mind: Mo picking his night, buying his grog, making sure people saw him in the pub, coming home with his slab. Having one last drink, one last joint, one last coffee, spiked with sugar and Rough on Rats. Leaving the table a suggestive mess of cups, spilt white granules and gaping, rusty tins. Leaving the windows and door open, with him seated on the couch by the door, as if catching the night breeze for the last time.

"You even arranged for a stranger to find you."

A Mormon missionary, a big, devout, lonesome Maori, whom Mo had invited around for tea and biscuits the next morning. Mo feeling sorry for someone again, we all said. Or not, as it happened. Elder Taniwha, or whatever his name was, had come to the door and found not a soul to save but a body.

"What a dreadful thing to do to someone, even if they were a god-botherer."

"I figured he'd have the consolation of religion."

"Maybe, but he was still upset. He came to the funeral and cried a river."

"Did he? I wasn't there."

"'No wonder you're unquiet," I said, exasperated.

"But I'm working on quietude," he said. He jumped off the concrete, on the land side, and strode into the gathering dark. I clambered up and stood on the pavement, hopping from foot to foot as I tried to get the sand off my toes and my expensive shoes on my feet. Then I followed him down Morag street, with its occasional waiting prostitutes, still as statues.

Some I knew: "Hi Shazz, hi Magnolia"—who had been Marcus, once. Not one said "Hi" to Mo, though being an Outreach worker, he'd known them well. All those people telling him their troubles; something of which I too had been guilty, I now realized. Mo could get my darkest secrets out of me on the strength of one cup of tea, if I was depressed enough. Nothing about his depression though: there was never any space in the conversation for *this* person's troubles.

"Mo?"

"Hmn?"

"I'm sorry." I tried to reach out for his hand, but hesitated, remembering; and as if flinching away from me, he made an abrupt turn, into the park. I followed, damning my shoes, which were not made for walking, just for standing around in, looking decorative.

"Sorry for what?"

"For being a lousy friend."

We were passing under a straggly rose arch, and I could barely hear his reply: "It doesn't matter."

"It doesn't?"

"Nothing does anymore. I think that's what I'm slowly starting to learn."

"What you're back here for?"

A shrug, barely visible in the gloom. We had now reached at the center of the park, dark between the lights of streets at either side— Morag street where we had entered and the main thoroughfare of Grosvenor Road ahead. He stopped abruptly, at the fountain, and sat on the parapet, as if waiting. Now he seemed to be staring into the watery depths.

"Nothing there but syringes, condoms, and sick goldfish," I said, into a new and unnerving stillness. What was I doing here at night? Everyone knew that the park after hours was full of dealers . . . and worse. In the gloom I glanced around 360 degrees and saw a heart-stopping sudden movement—three, no four shapes, hooded like New York gangs, the fashion for junkies and muggers. They were coming towards us . . .

"Mo," I whispered. He looked up, but all I could see was the pale oblong of his face. Was there any expression there?

From out of the dark came a low, nasty chuckle.

"Mo! Do something, say boo, anything!"

He made a gesture of what might be helplessness, then shook his head.

I kicked off the shoes and ran. School athletics championships were something I'd never thought would be useful in later life, but now I flew across the park, exiting in Grosvenor road. There a bus was standing, its door just closing as it prepared to pull away from the stop. I leapt up into it with a hop, skip, and jump, and it pulled away, leaving the sound of pursuing footsteps far behind.

The passengers stared at me, in my party dress but with grass-stained bare feet. Those shoes had cost me a bundle ... but some things you have to leave behind. Like Mo, I thought, palely loitering, not lifting a finger, as if he were come to lure me to my doom.

No, I thought. It just probably didn't matter to him anymore. With that far from comforting thought, I rode the bus to the shopping center. I disembarked into the bright bustle of restaurant signs, the usual late night munchies and nightclub crowd. So many restaurants, so many new faces, so many new apartments. And here I was living at the same place I had for years, above the second-hand bookshop in a side street, despite my new high-powered job, doing work I liked for the first time in my life ...

The shop lights were on when I arrived home, Richard the landlord farewelling some book fiend friend or client in the doorway. He held the door open for me, a book under his arm as usual. Richard never much noticed people, preferring books, but on this night he stared at me, then said:

"You look as if you'd just seen a ghost."

I stopped on the staircase to my first floor flat.

"Maybe I did."

"I always wondered what that would be like." He patted the book. "Sydney Smith—you wouldn't have heard of him—had a flight of fancy on the subject. In his letters, here. We were just talking about it, my outatown client and me. Listen." He opened the book.

"'I am living quite alone in a large gothic room with painted glass and waited upon by an old woman with only one gothic tooth. About six o'clock when it is dark the various ghosts by which this house is haunted come into the room and converse with me—dead deans the color of Rogers—'"

"Rogers? What color's that?"

"A book's, I suppose—'and ancient sextons of the cathedral, prebendaries now no more, elderly ladies who lived near, and came regularly during their lives to morning-service. I have very little pleasure in their conversation, they seem to be limited foolish people, much the same as people still alive—the deceased clergy are particularly inquisitive about preferment, and the elderly ladies enquire about patterns. When I am tired of their company I order tea and candles and they hobble away.'"

I nodded slowly.

"Lovely stuff," said Richard, misinterpreting the gesture. "Master of the English prose . . . and with such a delicate sense of anti-climax. 'Limited foolish people' indeed."

"Much as they were alive," I quasi-quoted. "Good night."

"Good night."

Upstairs in my flat I got out candles, lit them, and in the flickering dance of dazzle and dark made my best tea (Oolong). If it worked for Sydney Smith it would work for me. But the ghosts hadn't hobbled away, I had . . . leaving my Manolos behind, and lucky not to leave anything else. I opened the window, leaning on the sill, seeing in the street below the passers-by, hearing their (limited) conversation. The night wind stirred my hair, and I thought of Mo, waiting in the dark with his door open. His house was gone now, demolished for a dinky little development. Make Aunt Goldie turn in her grave . . . except that, as Mo had taught me, she probably didn't care anymore. I lifted my head, staring across the streetscape at the gabled old-fashioned roofs, and the bulky dark blocks of apartments, marching closer and closer, like lead-footed giants. The suburb had changed, so had I.

Time to move on, leave the ghosts behind. But for the moment, just as I had with Mo, I sipped my tea and enjoyed the sense of a lost time, briefly and happily returned.

ABSOLUTE UNCERTAINTY

1. HEISENBERG PROBABLY SLEPT HERE.

A blink of the eye, a quantum jump in place and time, to the island of Helgoland, off the coast of Germany, early twentieth century. Atoms coalesce, forming the silhouette, then the solid shape of a human, like a gradually colored-in picture from a children's book. For a moment the Watcher, still in jump-shock, is motionless; then he wraps his thin arms around his torso, feeling the cool wind from the sea despite the tweed jacket and plus-fours, suitable wear of the period according to the props department. He turns his head, assessing the surroundings. The little beach shack in which he stands, a perfect hide, is built of driftwood, the same dull color as the sand, its windows and one door gape open. Open to the elements, thinks the Watcher, all of them . . .

The prompt-chip in his head says: "List them. Recall the drill: to offset loss of equilibrium after a jump, try a rote exercise to test and restore memory."

Obediently the Watcher starts to list aloud: "1, hydrogen; 2, helium . . ." He continues, counting down through the periodic table: " . . . 92, uranium; 93, neptunium; and 94 plutonium, so-important plutonium." Then he comes to a dead halt. Has plutonium been discovered yet? the Watcher thinks, confused. This is 1925, after all.

"Plutonium was only discovered in 1940, during research on the atomic bomb, recall?"

"I do . . . now."

The Watcher takes several steps forward to the nearest window. Outside the sky is overcast, leaden as the sea, which surges sullenly in lazy little wavelets. Salt grass tussocks quiver in the breeze; sand-grit sloughs from the dunes in fine dry streams. Otherwise, the only movement is a dot, far down the arc of bay, moving at a slow, meditative, walking pace.

"The target. I trust you remember that now. Werner Karl Heisenberg, physicist, Nobel laureate at thirty-two, devisor of the Uncertainty Principle . . ."

"But at this moment just twenty-four, very brilliant but unproven, and without university tenure."

The Watcher stares at the nearing dot, not needing the prompt anymore. He thinks of the elements, no element of Heisenberg, its constituent parts or electrons. German nationalist. Admirer of nature. Sufferer from allergies. Gifted classical pianist. Chess wizard. These are the quirks recorded in the biographies, but who knows what else has eluded the official record?

The Watcher crouches and draws in the sand of the hut, recapitulating, partly as aide-memoire, partly from admiration, an intellectual journey into the secret world of the atom. He keeps glancing up as the beachwalker nears and details become clearer: the thick sweater, the knapsack, and above all the one spot of color in the entire dreary landscape, the young man's brush of reddish-blonde hair. Entranced, the Watcher abandons his scribbles in sand. Then, from behind the headland, lightning stabs and crackles, followed by torrential rain. The figure looks here, there, then makes a dash for the single shelter nearby—the hide.

The Watcher puts his hand to his mouth. "This isn't supposed to happen! We're just here to observe, right, nothing interactive, no chance of upsetting the course of history?"

"Yes, but the limits of a jump are not totally knowable. We can predict, but not in fine detail."

"Can we jump, like *now*?"

"Sorry, no. We'll just have to wing it."

Appalled, the Watcher cowers in a corner, as footsteps pound towards the hide. Werner Heisenberg, flame-headed, handsome and young, leaps inside, shaking the rain off him like a cat. Then he sees the movement in the corner of the hut.

"Birdwatcher?" he says, in early twentieth-century German.

"*Ja,*" the prompt replies (and lies), using its override to speak in the Watcher's voice. "Interesting migration patterns of stormy petrels here."

"Forgive me for intruding," Heisenberg says. "When the storm is over I will leave you to your birdwatching." He takes off his backpack and sits down on the floor of the hide. The body-language says: conversation-verboten, I want to think.

The Watcher stares at him unblinkingly.

"Max Born was right," says the prompt to the Watcher, in private, silent-to-onlookers mode. "He thought the young Heisenberg looked like a simple farm boy."

Or, thinks the Watcher, unnerved, the Hitler youth, not so far away now, in 1925.

Around the hut lightning flickers and thunder beats on the air loud as snare-drums. Heisenberg's gaze moves, wandering free as his thoughts, from this Herr Birdwatcher to outside, then back again. Suddenly he stares as the lightning flashes again, momentarily banishing every shadow from the hut. He bends closer to inspect the sand, as the lightning takes another flash shot of the bay. Then he looks up at the Watcher. "You have not completed this equation, sir."

The Watcher, unnerved, can only repeat the prompt's words: "*Ja.*"

"May I?"

The youth reaches out, draws in the sand.

The Watcher nods, and responds with another sandy calculation, also incomplete.

Heisenberg glances at it, smiles and solves the problem with a few deft finger lines. Another equation follows, then another, the pair talking the universal language of numbers.

"I had not thought to encounter, in Helgoland, a kindred soul, a brother in Physics," Heisenberg says.

More equations follow; the Watcher thoroughly enjoying himself, recapitulating the work of Heisenberg's predecessors,

Planck, Born, Bohr. With a flourish of his fingers, he suddenly goes too far, and the young man frowns.

"You are very up to date. Too up to date, perhaps. It's uncanny . . . Who *are* you?"

"A tourist," the Watcher says, knowing the answer is feeble.

"I know everybody in physics, everyone that matters, and now I think of it Helgoland is small—I should surely have heard if some Herr Professor Doctor or even a student had come holidaying."

He eyes the Watcher sharply.

"You are some researcher from America, the antipodes . . . surely not from the Bolshevists?"

His hand pats empty air at hip level, as though reaching for an imaginary gun.

The prompt butts in, answering the question. "What would the Bolshevists want with the interior of the atom? It is surely not in their collectivist philosophy . . ."

Heisenberg smiles, with a faint curl of the lip. "What would they want with atoms? Weapons, I suppose, so they could export their Red philosophy all over the world, not that anyone knows how you would derive weapons from theoretical physics, not yet . . ." He pauses, somber. "But the question still remains—who or what are you?"

The prompt says, to the Watcher alone: "Be careful. This is an abstract, logical, mathematical thinker in the extreme, not a spinner of fancies."

Even in his dreams? wonders the Watcher, and suddenly has a solution to this tricky situation. He thinks for a second, sure of his place in Heisenberg's personal time, then adds another set of symbols to the calculations on the floor. The young man goggles.

"But . . . but, that's something I've been thinking about, not published, not talked about to anyone, even to Bohr."

"You will," said the Watcher. "When you awake."

Heisenberg laughs, falls back onto the sand.

"Cute," says the prompt. "He actually bought it!"

Heisenberg lies on his back, chuckling. Then he raises himself on one elbow. "But you must answer my question, Herr Birdwatcher, even in a dream. I repeat, what are you?"

"Let me handle this," says the prompt. To Heisenberg it says: "You remember Herr Dickens' little story, 'The Christmas Carol.'"

"Yes, the miser, and all the visiting ghosts of Christmas, come to teach him a moral story. If you are a Physics ghost, maybe, you are not the ghost of Physics past, not Herr Newton with his long wig, not with the math you do . . . And your physics is right up to date. So are you perhaps the ghost of Physics present?"

His wide-set eyes look even wider.

"Not exactly."

"No, I've met Herr Einstein, and you aren't him . . . Ah, you are the ghost of Physics future?"

"Careful," says the prompt.

The Watcher eyes Heisenberg, seeing perfect calm and assurance.

"You don't seem surprised."

"No. Because it does not seem strange that I would have a visit from Physics future . . . because I think I am part of that entity."

He cranes closer to the Watcher's face, then subsides, disappointed.

"Though I see you are not me . . . that Physics future is not wearing the face of my older self."

"You seriously expect to be the future of Physics?"

A slight but perceptible nod. Really quite a handsome man, thinks the Watcher. Although an arrogant young shit.

"He's right, of course," says the prompt to the Watcher.

Yes, the Watcher concurs, he is right. He hesitates, unsure whether to voice the thought, but Heisenberg speaks first.

"Well, what have you to say to me, oh ghost from the future? I'm right, aren't I? Otherwise you wouldn't bother me with a visit. Because I wouldn't be important enough."

The young man smiles, triumphantly. The Watcher knows that something has changed, that his observation has now subtly influenced, and altered, the observed. What the real, the unobserved Heisenberg might be, cannot now be measured with any certainty. But Heisenberg won't think of that little idea for a few years in the future yet.

"I have nothing to say," says the Watcher. "Except in the form of mathematics. Which is most important to you."

And he reaches for the blackboard of sand again. The dialogue of ideas continues, while the storm rages outside. After a while Heisenberg's eyes begin to droop, and his hand falls to the ground. He sinks back and after a moment begins to snore, heartily and healthily.

"You dropped him, didn't you?" the Watcher charges the prompt.

"When he slapped at that sand fly, a few minutes ago. That was the stun."

"I thought that was strictly for emergencies."

"Well yes, but did we have any guarantee that he might not suddenly decide that it was a little odd to be solving higher mathematical problems in his sleep and that he might be awake, after all?"

"Killjoy!"

"No, just being cautious. Are you sure you weren't teaching him matrix algebra? For that was the achievement of his trip to Helgoland."

The Watcher stands and uses his foot to obliterate the sand lines of equations.

"Famously Heisenberg thought of it all by himself, during his sea bathing, long walks, and nights of solitary thinking, this form of mathematics so useful for describing the atom."

The Watcher says nothing, staring down at Heisenberg.

The prompt continues: "Need I remind you more? Although matrix algebra had been devised in the 1850s, Heisenberg had never been taught it. Discovered it independently, he claimed, just like Leibniz and Newton each developed calculus in Germany and England during the seventeenth century."

The Watcher only smiles. "Shall we go now?"

"Since our time here is up, yes."

A few moments later, the hut is empty except for Heisenberg, deep in drugged sleep. The wind completes what the Watcher had begun, completely erasing the equations written on the sand of the floor.

Welcome, class! Today in Biocultural Studies 101 we will continue our examination of moral ambiguities and the limits of biography. We will focus on a real slippery customer, I mean a prime example, in this session: Karl Werner Heisenberg, twentieth century physicist in what used to be called Germany, quantum mechanic, theorist of the uncertainty principle, and worker on the alternate atomic weapon of the 1940s, the 'Nazi' bomb. Using what is known about Heisenberg, an interactive template has been constructed. Now we will employ that template in a series of extrapolations, using the sim-module to examine aspects of Heisenberg and his times. Last session the class chose points in Heisenberg's life for observation and exploration. We have just experienced the first, from 1925, in which use was made of a time-traveller (™ H. G. Wells, 1895) going back to encounter Heisenberg as a young man. Do we have any questions?

. . . Yes, the prompt is a personal, portable, Artificial Intelligence, there to supply our Watcher with a limitless source of information and advice. Just what the time tourist needs.

. . . Well-spotted. Yes, that was stock sim-footage in the beach scenes. Helgoland is a barren lump of rock off the coast of Germany, without anything growing. Heisenberg went there because he had hay fever. And he came back cured and with matrix algebra, though nobody is quite sure how.

No more questions? On to the next observation, and this time, let's have some input from the class. I want to see you using your personal modules for some REALLY *creative interactions.*

2. "ON THE PERCEPTUAL CONTENT OF QUANTUM THEORETICAL KINEMATICS AND MECHANICS" BY WERNER HEISENBERG, 1927

The scene is night, in a prison camp: a bare, cleared space in the middle of a forest, the boundary marked by barbed wire, forest outside, wasteland of huts and dirt within. The night is cold; the breath of the guards in the watchtowers forms white mist on the air. There is no other movement apart from a slight scurry under one of the huts. A rat, maybe.

A logo comes up in the empty air, then fades. It reads: QUANTUMSTEIN

Digits appear in the sky, like neon stars, counting down. Then figures, their heads little more than dots, their bodies clad in striped prison pajamas, creep out from under the huts and run across the bare earth towards the wire. Dogs bark, an alarm shrills, searchlights sweep the enclosure, a machine gun chatters and spits. Yet, amidst the noise and confusion, the hit rate of the game seems very low; as a searchlight impinges on a figure, it immediately dodges and leaps aside into the darkness.

The Watcher, situated in an empty lookout tower, eyes the confusion, and—very occasionally—bloodshed.

"I don't think Heisenberg would ever have envisaged the Uncertainty Principle in these terms."

"Well yes, Hitler only came to power in 1933, some time after his formulation of the principle," replies the prompt. "But the analogy is not without merit. Theoretical physics had hit a blank wall trying to determine the exact position of electrons within the atom. Heisenberg pointed out that in order to observe the electron, you must illuminate it by short-wave electromagnetic radiation. But the illumination, when it strikes the electron, affects it, altering its position. Therefore, because the act of observation changes the motion of the electron, it cannot be measured with certainty. Thus are the limits to knowledge revealed."

Down below the Watcher, some figures lie still on the ground, some have doubled back to the huts, a few are still approaching the wire.

"Einstein hated the Uncertainty Principle."

"He also hated Hitler."

"Who hated Einstein and 'Jewish science.' But think what the haters had in common: a belief in absolute certainty, a god's-eye, Hitler's-eye, classical-physics view of the world, where all could be explained in terms of science or the 'Jewish world conspiracy.'"

A figure reaches the wire and simultaneously freezes, as do the other figures and the moving searchlights. A logo appears in the air, flashing GAME OVER!

The Watcher says: "A win for the inmates."

"Or their player," says the prompt.

The Watcher is silent a moment, musing. "Heisenberg was lucky the Nazis never realized the implications of the Uncertainty principle."

Above them the GAME OVER! sign vanishes, as does the QUANTUMSTEIN logo.

"They had better things to do," says the prompt, "like creating their version of utopia."

The scene changes subtly, the forest outside becoming more threatening, the guards in the towers more clearly delineated—

square-jawed, their uniforms bursting with muscle, their faces fair and achingly handsome. Another logo appears, simple and stark, a cross twisted on its axis, with starkly angled arms. The figures under the huts appear again, this time sporting symbols on their pajamas, little red hammer+sickles, or stars, or pink triangles. Regardless of the particular symbol each displays, they all have the same caricatured features—hook-nosed, weasel-eyed, and cunning. They bolt for the wire again, to the cacophony of dogs and guns, the sound-effects louder and accompanied by sweeping symphonic music. Yet this time each searchlight finds its victim unerringly, shots ring out, and the figure falls bloody. The score appears like a beacon in the night sky, the numbers constantly changing, tallying the carnage below. Red symbols are worth 20 points, pink triangles 10, and the yellow star 50. Within a very short time the score hits 1000, and the game is over, every prisoner still and dead on the ground.

There is a long silence, broken by the prompt: "Some have said that Hitler should have been a science fiction writer, expressing his anti-social urges in pulp utopias. I beg to differ. I think he would have been supremely happy as a sim games designer."

The Watcher sighs. "I don't think I much like this game of HITLERSTEIN."

"You object to the racial stereotyping? He'd have loved it. Gorgeous Aryans annihilating Jews, gays, communists: all Hitler's enemies caught in the searchlights and machine-gunned dead in seconds."

The Watcher steps onto the parapet of the tower, then into space. He floats down like a snowflake, landing lightly besides a stripe-clad body.

"Hitlerstein is too simplistic by far. And dull . . . There's no chance, no excitement. Every shot kills, every hit jacks up the score. Only an idiot would thrill to it."

He strolls among the still figures, finally stopping beside one, face down in a larger pool of blood than the rest. Is it his imagination, or does the close-cropped fuzz of hair have a reddish-blond tinge?

The prompt continues: "There weren't many theoretical physicists in concentration camps. The Jewish professors lost their jobs in the thirties and emigrated. So did the few women physicists, who also lost their jobs, though they were merely faced with *kinder* and *küche*. Others joined the exodus: even non-Jewish physicists, like Schrödinger of the famous cat, left. Heisenberg stayed, despite being an exponent of Einsteinian, 'Jewish' physics. That required guts . . . or an uncommon amount of sheer stubborn patriotism."

"Home is where the heartland is," says the Watcher. He kneels down, gently turning the figure on its back. The face, peaceful in death-sleep, is despite the bloodstains recognizably an older Heisenberg.

"To get here would have meant active resistance against Hitler. Real heroism . . . or martyrdom. Not many people have that."

He lays the figure down again, then gets to his feet.

"Instead people resisted in their minds only," says the prompt. "Hoping Hitler was just a temporary aberration, soon overthrown. They were afraid. Or passive. Even complicit?"

The Watcher sighs. "Prompt, let's get out of here!"

Own up! Who thought of Hitlerstein? That was really grotesque. Should have guessed it, Reet, of course. Might have known you'd drag your pet gaming in here somehow. On to the third observation, this time not using Heisenberg, but different, though related, templates. Not so much is known of these originals, although they had, via their connections, vital importance to this biohistory.

3. THE WHITE JEW OF LEIPZIG

In an immaculate sitting room, two middle-aged women take tea, surrounded by antimacassars, overstuffed furniture, a flower arrangement underneath a crucifix, and portraits of family members. Pride of place on the mantelpiece is taken by a framed photo of a bespectacled, pudgy man, the spitting image, though in drag, of the Frau playing mother, pouring the tea. He wears a swastika on one black uniformed arm, and next to him stands the Fuhrer.

Heisenberg's mother accepts the proffered cup and sips. She doesn't look much like her son.

Now she speaks: "I appeal to you, on the strength of our family friendship."

"Your father was acquainted with my late husband through their membership of a schools' hiking club," the older woman says with a tinge of frost.

"He always spoke highly of your husband," says Frau Heisenberg.

"They were men of German honor."

"As are our sons."

The other woman looks at the mantel photograph, smiles. "I am very proud of Heinrich," she says. "But I never interfere in his affairs."

"I am very proud of my Werner, too," says Frau Heisenberg.

The other woman lifts her hand. "Frau Heisenberg, I am not political, not like my son, and I know nothing of physics, which is what your son does. Why should I take note of an article about your son, politics *and* physics?"

"Because it appeared in *Das Swarze Korps*, the newspaper of your son's organization, the Schutzstaffel."

"He is Reichsfuhrer-SS, and far above such things as a mere article. Why does your son simply not write to the editor?"

"Because," Frau Heisenberg says carefully, "they called him a White Jew. It will take more than a letter to the editor of the SS-paper to refute that. Shall I quote it to you? They said he was a representative of Judaism in German spiritual life, who ought— along with all the other White Jews—to be eliminated just as the Jews themselves must be."

The other woman puts down her cup carefully, glances at the crucifix then back again.

Frau Heisenberg continues: "My son is a good physicist and a good German. I am not asking you much, just to take this letter, from my son, which is addressed to your son. If it is sent by normal channels, he fears it will not get there."

"And so the need for abnormal channels!" She looks affronted at the thought of being anything else than normal.

"What else am I to do? I am not political, but I know that my son is not a White Jew. We mothers know our sons, and we care for them. That is why I have come to you."

She reaches into her handbag, brings out the letter.

"We care for our sons, that is what a mother does," says the other woman. "You for your Werner and I for my Heinrich." She reaches out and takes the letter.

Heisenberg's mother says: "Thank you, Frau Himmler."

Strange but true, strange but true. Next to that little encounter, a time traveler and a Nazi sim game seem positively ordinary. When in trouble with the Nazi regime, send Mother to the rescue. Yes, Heisenberg's grandfather and Himmler's father really did go on school hikes together. And a letter sent by Mum-post prompted an extensive SS investigation into Heisenberg, at the end of which he was cleared of the charge of being a White Jew. He could continue with his research, just so long as he didn't mention who it was came up with the theory of relativity, nor any other Jewish theorists.

Ah, a question. Reet? Didn't see much input from you this time. ...You want to know what the fringed lampshade was made of? I think I know what this is about. Who did the lampshade? ... Ah, Matt. Stock sim footage again? Thought so. Reet, don't look so disappointed. Yes, I know Himmler is supposed to have owned a lampshade made of human skin, harvested in the concentration camps, but no images of it have survived. Thank goodness. And I certainly don't think he would have given it to his mother.

Next observation, out of sequence, but it continues with our attempts to create an alternate history of Heisenberg, as opposed to what, as in the previous observation, is verified by the historical sources.

4. RATTLING THE TIN CAN

"When I am by myself, I now easily fall into a very strange state, which belongs neither to the past not to the future and neither to you nor to Physics, and with which nothing can be done."
— Heisenberg to Elisabeth Schumacher, 1937

Leipzig in January 1937, wintry and cold. The Watcher wanders down the snowy streets, rugged up in comforter, astrakhan hat, woolen mitts, and a heavy military-style greatcoat. He passes hausfraus with baskets, students playing snowballs, children trailing sleighs. It would be impossibly Christmassy and nostalgic were it not for the occasional glimpse of a Nazi uniform, leaving a jackbooted trail in the fresh snow.

On a street corner, a solitary figure marches to and fro, stamping his feet to keep warm. As the Watcher nears, the figure edges towards him, proffering a tin can. A beggar, in the middle of the third Reich?

"Hallo, Herr Professor Doctor Heisenberg," says the prompt.

The beggar stares, his face tired and wan as candle wax. "You know me? You do look slightly familiar. A former student, maybe?"

"I am shocked to see you out in this cold, begging," says the Watcher with sincerity.

"Ah," says Heisenberg. "You think perhaps I have lost my position? No, Doctor Goebbels has decreed that all university staff shall assist in collecting extra funds, for the fourth anniversary of the Reich . . . which will be on the 30th of January. Even Professors must help in this great effort. Hence the tin can."

He speaks deadpan, without the slightest sign of irony.

"You have changed," says the Watcher. "From Helgoland in 1925."

Heisenberg starts, looks closely at the face under the fur hat. He speaks, half to himself: "I had thought, in this cold and snow, that I was drifting in and out of a dream state . . . and now I see a figure from a dream of twelve years ago, the mathematical birdwatcher from Helgoland."

He falls silent, staring at the Watcher for several minutes.

The prompt adds, for the Watcher's benefit: "He is indeed in a strange frame of mind, possibly caused by severe anemia. Years later he wrote that 'the houses in these narrow streets seemed very far away and almost unreal, as if they had already been destroyed and only their pictures remained behind: people seemed transparent, their bodies having, so to speak, abandoned the material world so that only their spirits remained behind.' Quite poetic, really, for a physicist."

Now the prompt addresses both the Watcher and Heisenberg: "How democratic of the new Germany, to have Nobel-winning academicians collecting for the Reich."

Heisenberg's face twists slightly, in bitter if unvoiced disagreement. "We have no choice," he says in an undertone. "Oh ghost of physics future, what I could be doing if I were not forced to stand on an icy street corner, collecting pfennigs from those as frightened as I am?"

"It seems utterly senseless and futile," says the Watcher.

"It is, and so is everything around me—Elisabeth apart. I am engaged now, Herr Ghost. Shall I show you a photograph of her?"

He fumbles with the buttons on his coat, clearly intending to reach into an inner pocket, but in the process drops his can into the snow. The Watcher retrieves it.

"No don't, I wouldn't want you to freeze . . . besides I've seen photos of Elisabeth, and she is a fine young woman."

"So . . . I remain significant in the physics of the future." The face assumes some of its old confidence. "That is something worth knowing at least."

"Significant because notorious . . ." mutters the prompt.

The Watcher ignores the little voice. He is trying to hand the can back to Heisenberg, but the physicist, lost in thought, ignores it. A man in Nazi uniform strides by; the Watcher automatically proffers the can with its little swastika and is rewarded with the tinkle of a small-denomination coin.

"I will admit I was worried. Is it still a truism of your time, Herr Physics-Future, that a man does his best physics very young? Planck was an exception, though, coming up with quantum physics at forty-two. You see I need, amidst all this madness, to know that I can still do something important for science."

"You will," said the Watcher. "You will."

"If morally quite deplorable," mutters the prompt.

Heisenberg shakes hands, in pure gratitude, with the Watcher, and in the process has the can thrust into his hand again. He smiles dazzlingly and approaches the next passers-by as if buoyed by extra hidden heat and life. While his back is turned, the Watcher takes a few steps sideways, into the shadowy shelter of an overhanging porch, and then into oblivion.

"Should you have given him hope?" says the prompt. "Without it, he might have dusted the snow of Nazi Germany off his shoes and headed off to a cozy professorship in the Americas."

"And the Los Alamos project, ultimately," says the Watcher.

"German bomb, Allied bomb, what's the difference? Still killing machines."

"But the German bomb never killed anyone."

"Heisenberg's reputation apart," says the prompt.

Yes, I know that observation was chronologically out of order. Heisenberg got called a White Jew and investigated by Himmler after his marriage, not before. The Nazis brought him to his lowest ebb, but when his patriotism proved impeccable, they gave him hope—a juicy scientific problem. Nuclear fission had been discovered by 1940. The question now arose, how could you harness this force into something uniquely destructive? The trouble was that others were thinking along these lines, too.

5. A COZY WALK IN DENMARK

The scene is a courtroom with, improbably, down the middle of it, a walk lined with northern, deciduous trees. A judge, lawyers, the jury of Biocultural students, all watch two men, wearing suits of the 1940s, pace down the walk, talking furiously, sometimes toppling over the brink into argument. At the end they freeze in frame, then reverse, going back to the beginning of the walk again in furious backwards motion, talking gobbledygook. At the beginning of the walk, Heisenberg, now balding, graying, and slightly thicker in the waist, looks confident, the other, an older man with thick lips and heavy eyebrows, wary. The sequence repeats, freezing again at the end; Heisenberg looks frustrated, his companion shell-shocked.

The Judge says: "Who is the counsel for the defense?"

The Watcher stands, peeking shyly from under the curls of his powdered wig: "I am."

He sits.

"And the counsel for the prosecution?"

Again the Watcher stands. "I am," says the prompt.

"Fine, so long as we know who is speaking. Call the first witness."

"Call Neils Bohr!"

The older man steps out of the freeze-frame and walks unhurriedly to the witness box, where he is sworn in. His voice is slow and very soft.

The prompt speaks: "In 1941, when Denmark was occupied by Germany, you received a visit from your former student and scientific collaborator, Werner Heisenberg. This was an official visit, on behalf of the Reich."

Bohr nods. "At that time the occupation was relatively benign: there was the illusion of self-rule, even cultural exchanges. Thus we had Heisenberg come to the Copenhagen Institute for Theoretical Physics, proposing co-operation between German and Danish science."

"For what purpose?"

"So that Germany could win the war; he was quite open about that."

"And how did you and your colleagues feel about this?"

Bohr looks miserable. "None of us liked the idea at all."

"You had personal reasons here, that I should like you to tell the court."

"My mother was Jewish. I knew what that meant, in Nazi terms. There were 8,000 Jews in Denmark, although no attempt was made to arrest us at first. It was not until 1943 that we had warning of deportations, and my family fled to neutral Sweden . . . along with nearly all the Jews of Denmark."

"A remarkable escape," says the prompt. "But we were talking of two years earlier, and Heisenberg's visit."

"Heisenberg was my friend. I invited him to dinner, though Margrethe, my wife, objected. Afterwards we went for a walk."

"What happened?"

"The end of a twenty-year friendship."

"Tell us more."

"You must understand that when fission happened, we physicists knew about it very quickly. I helped spread the news at a conference in the United States and published on the subject within months."

"Indeed, an important paper. But on the theoretical aspects only."

Bohr nods again. "Heisenberg wanted to talk to me privately

about fission. Applied aspects, this time. I soon realized he was trying to pump me for information. We all knew what fission might mean, in terms of the war effort."

"You refer to the atomic bomb?"

Another nod. "Then he changed tack. He asked me about what such a weapon might do, in the wrong hands. He knew I had contact with American scientists, even in occupied Denmark. Would not it be better, he said, for scientists not to work on this bomb and let the war be decided by more conventional, less catastrophic means? Whose scientists? I wondered to myself. Whose hands are the wrong hands?"

"And what was your conclusion?" the prompt asks.

"That there was a German bomb on the way, that Heisenberg was involved at an important level, and that he wanted me somehow to retard the development of the Allied bomb—as if I could!"

"Objection!" shouts the Watcher. "Witness is making unsupported surmises about the defendant's motives."

"But that was what I thought," Bohr says mildly. "And that is what I told my family, and the scientists at the Institute, and the Danish underground, who of course conveyed it to the Allies."

"What was your impression of Heisenberg's moral state?"

"Oh, he was as confident as ever. Blindly confident. He knew he was right. I wondered if he'd been tainted by that terrible regime and could distinguish right from wrong anymore."

The Watcher says: "There are two sides to every story."

"Indeed," says the Judge. "Thank you, Professor Bohr, that will do. Call Professor Heisenberg."

Heisenberg stalks out of the freeze frame and to the dock.

"Professor Heisenberg," says the Judge. "You heard the preceding testimony."

"I did, and I regret to say that my dear friend Bohr misunderstood me. I proposed, at the risk of my skin, a joint effort by Allied and Axis scientists to prevent the development of the bomb. All it would require would be twelve of us in agreement: myself, Bohr, Fermi, Oppenheim, for instance."

The prompt says: "A most unlikely agreement."

"Nonetheless I proposed it. And, moreover, I kept my part of the bargain. I headed the project for the German bomb, and it was never developed. I did not have the blood of thousands of civilians on my hands, like the Allied scientists . . ."

Bohr rises to his feet, protesting in Danish. Heisenberg answers, in German, shouting, and the court is in uproar.

Two sides to every story, eh? What did you, as jury, make of that? Still uncertain? Let's call another witness.

6. GOUDSMIT'S VERSION

An American army officer steps into the witness box. His voice is accented, his glasses round; despite the uniform he has the look of an intellectual.

"You are Samuel Goudsmit, theoretical physicist," says the judge.

"One of the few in America not working on the bomb." There is some nervous laughter around the courtroom. "Thus the uniform. I was selected to be scientific head of task force ALSOS precisely because I knew nothing about the Manhattan project. An ideal man, then, to send to Germany in the process of liberation."

The prompt says: "For what purpose?"

"To find out how far the Germans had got with their bomb project. To secure, first, their uranium and send it back to the Manhattan Project. To secure, second, all relevant information on the Nazi bomb. That meant also the scientists involved, including Heisenberg."

"Secure?"

"Out of the Ruskies' hands."

"So what happened?"

"ALSOS followed the occupying Allies to Strasbourg, where the German Physics Laboratory was. That gave us papers that said Haigerloch, in the Black Forest, was the place to go. Trouble was, it looked like the French, coming from one direction, or the Russians, from another, would liberate the area first. We put on a spurt, beat them to Haigerloch, where we found an atomic pile just short of going critical. We didn't find Heisenberg until a few days later, with his family in Bavaria. Colonel Pash went after him and had a helluva journey—climbing over snow passes, exchanging fire with the enemy, repairing bridges, trying to fend off German units who just wanted someone to surrender to. But at the end of it he arrested Heisenberg."

"You interrogated him?"

"Sure, when Pash brought him back to Heidelberg."

"Did you mention your parents?"

Goudsmit takes off his glasses, wipes then replaces them. "I thought you'd bring this up."

"Yes, so you can tell the court what happened."

"My parents stayed in Holland when I went to the States. I nagged them and nagged them, no Jews are safe in Europe, you gotta get out! They'd just managed to get their travel papers in '43 when . . . I heard they'd been rounded up and deported."

"How was Heisenberg involved in this?"

"Well, he'd stayed with me at the University of Michigan in '39 and was definitely the most influential person I knew in Germany. Friends in Holland asked for his help."

"I wrote a letter, as requested, on behalf of Goudsmit's parents," responds Heisenberg from the dock.

"Yeah, but it was too late. Two old people, never did harm to anyone, ended up in the gas chambers."

"Ahem," says the Watcher, remembering his role of defense council again. "You upbraided Heisenberg because of this, during the interrogation?"

"Not during. Informally, before."

"And you hold this against him eternally?"

A pause. "No, not anymore. Wasn't much he could have done, I guess."

In the dock Heisenberg gives a slight, approving nod.

"But I do hold other things against him. After the war he ran that line he used on Bohr again—how he tried to hold back the progress of the German bomb. That was a lie, at the beginning at least. Later I reckon he came to believe it was true."

"He didn't try to stop the bomb?" asks the Watcher.

"I know science jocks. Heisenberg wasn't any different from Oppenheim and the rest. You have a problem in applied physics, how to make the biggest bang in the world, ever. Now wouldn't you give the problem everything you had, so you could be first, and famous? Give me a break!"

"We will break," says the judge. "Before the next witnesses."

Hmn. Who programmed the Goudsmit template? Ah, Le. You forgot halfway through he came from Holland, not Brooklyn. The accent went all over the place. But, that apart, the sentiments were accurate, what he might, less colloquially, have said.

7. THE ENGLISH MANOR

A trio waits beside the witness box; an English major, armed and in uniform, a woman in a thick tweed suit and flowerpot hat, and a young, donnish man with tousled hair and thick glasses.

The judge says: "Major Cotton?"

"Yes, sir!" The major almost marches into the witness box.

"You are in intelligence?"

"All my army life, sir!"

"I understand you were responsible for Farm Hall."

"Yes sir! We had a problem: ten captured German bomb scientists. Some of the Yanks wanted to shoot them, but we knew they were valuable people. We just needed to keep them on ice, while certain things transpired . . ."

"The Manhattan Project?"

"Absolutely correct, sir. And it was quite nice ice, a little rural manor house with barbed wire around it, quite the cushiest internment camp in England. I got the idea from Bletchley Park, sir, where the cryptographers were. They'd talk shop, maths shop, all the time, and I said then, if Jerry ever got a mike in here . . . That gave me the idea. We'd save ourselves the bother of further interrogations, let our German friends do the interrogation themselves, talking politics and physics to the listening walls. Every room in Farm Hall was wired, even the latrines."

"Thank you," says the Judge. "You may go. Miss Margot Parkes!"

The tweedy woman enters the witness box nervously.

"Miss Parkes, you are a translator, and you worked on the Farm Hall tapes. Do you remember August 6, 1945, well?"

"Of course! Hiroshima. It caused quite a stir among the interned Germans."

"You transcribed and translated their words accurately?"

She says, levelly. "Upon my honour."

The trees in the center of the courtroom have gradually disappeared during the course of the trial, and now the dock enlarges, filling the space. It becomes a doll's house, one wall missing, with Heisenberg inside, setting up a chess game. A door behind him opens, and a group of men enter, one of whom sits opposite Heisenberg, joining him in the game. The rest lounge around the table or lean against the wall, smoking, drinking, talking among themselves. Their voices and stances are outwardly relaxed, but there is an underlying tension.

In the distance a radio plays the BBC news theme. The men listen, their jaws slowly starting to drop. Then hubbub ensues, in German.

Miss Parkes translates: "They could not believe the Americans could have beaten them to a bomb. It was inconceivable. How had they done it?"

Heisenberg grabs a pad, starts calculating furiously. Several others lean over his shoulder. The rest argue; Heisenberg grimly continues on. Finally he slams the book shut and speaks authoritatively: "He said the American bomb must have contained several tons of uranium . . . an amount we Germans would have had the greatest difficulty in obtaining. Of that I am absolutely certain!"

The don shakes his head. "The Hiroshima bomb only contained 15 kilograms of uranium. That was all that was needed, for a critical mass, chain reaction, and explosion. If the Heisenberg team had got several tons together, they'd have blown a sizeable chunk out of Germany."

"So the German estimate of critical mass was wrong?" says the Judge.

The don nods significantly at Heisenberg. "Biggest mistake he ever made, unless you count not getting out of Nazi Germany in the first place."

"The Farm Hall tapes don't lie, sir," says Major Cotton. "They don't show any reluctance about the bomb, nor regret . . . except that Germany had lost the war."

"Yes," says the Watcher, "But who would want to see their country defeated, trampled over by invading armies, no matter how hideous its rulers?"

Nobody answers, and in a moment the question becomes rhetorical, as from within Farm Hall one of the German scientist speaks. Whatever he says, it makes the internees looked as if they have been whipped.

Miss Parkes translates:

"He said: 'If the Americans have a uranium bomb, then you're all second-raters. Poor old Heisenberg.'"

Well, what have you decided, class-jury? Is Heisenberg guilty as charged, or innocent? Yes, I see you pause, a rich source of moral ambiguity, indeed. . . . What's that, you want to explore his uncertainties even further? But we're going on to President Chelsea Clinton and her moral ambiguities next session; we haven't time. Oh, all right, use the Berg template, I'd forgotten all about it. Just don't take too long.

9. "WHEN I HEAR ABOUT SCHRÖDINGER'S CAT, I REACH FOR MY GUN." STEPHEN HAWKING

The German scientists file out of the doll-house dock and sit among the audience. Heisenberg remains, head in hands, as the remaining wall of the dock slowly replaces itself, leaving only a doorway-sized space.

"Your honor," says the Watcher, "the jury have asked for a thought experiment. We will seal Heisenberg in this box, with a trained executioner. When the box is closed these two will return to Zurich, 1944, where they once met. The executioner is here today, he has heard all the evidence in the case. He let Heisenberg off once before; now he must decide again and execute capital punishment, if he so decides."

"Oh," says the don. "Schrödinger's bloody cat . . ."

"Or not so bloody cat," the Watcher continues serenely. "There is a 50/50 chance of it surviving. But we do not know that, because outside the box we cannot hear the executioner's gun. Therefore, to us, the cat—in this case a wily ginger tom—is, while unobserved both alive and dead, or neither, in a state of suspended animation."

346

"And the jury avoid coming to a decision, and thus abrogate any responsibility in the case," continues the prompt. "How well have they learnt their moral ambiguities!"

"But where is this executioner?" says the Judge.

The Watcher reaches into his pocket, removes a black handkerchief and folds it into a neat origami hat. "You may need this, or not, Mr Berg."

He hands it to the judge, who takes off his wig and black gown, revealing a forties-style suit underneath. He pulls out a pair of tortoiseshell glasses from a top pocket, puts them on, stares at the don, then ruffles his hair, in imitation.

"Moses Berg!" says Major Cotton. The Judge snaps to attention. "Your mission, should you choose to accept it—and I want to make clear there is no choice here—is to impersonate a physics boffin."

The Judge starts to protest.

"We know you have no physics."

"I'm a ballplayer, sir. Boston Red Sox."

"Yes, but you have excellent German and the knack of getting on with everybody. Very useful thing, in a spy. Your mission is to attend a colloquium in Zurich, December 1944. Your target, Professor Heisenberg, is giving a talk there. He is head of the Nazi atom bomb project. Find out whether he is a significant threat to the Allies, and if he is, shoot him."

He hands his gun to Berg, who puts it in his pocket, and strides to the dock-box. As he enters, it goes dark inside, showing starry night and city lights. The wall closes behind him and the court waits, staring at the box.

10. MOE BERG JUDGES

Two men walk through the dark of wartime Zurich, exchanging after-dinner talk, banalities for one, who is happiest talking physics, a smokescreen for the other, hiding his thoughts.

The spy business is screwy, thinks Moe Berg, but this beats everything. I told them, I told those guys back at the OSS in Washington, this is right outa my area. "Yes," they said, "but you're smart, a quick learner, and an excellent listener. We have every confidence you'll make the right decision in this case."

Moe sighs, feeling the weight of the gun in his suit pocket. One week ago, he had been sitting in a lecture theatre, among an audience of guys in tweedy suits with glasses. He had taken lots of notes, but there was nothing said about the bomb, only something called S-matrix theory. After the question time, which was equally abstruse, he'd gone down to the podium and mingled with all the people shaking hands and chatting to Heisenberg. Moe knew how to insinuate himself into a gathering, work it until he had met all the important people present. This colloquium was no different from a cocktail party, even if the conversation was uniquely rarified. And at the end of the gathering he'd gotten himself invited to a private dinner party for Heisenberg. Even sat next to him, in fact, gun in pocket. Was it proper etiquette to shoot dead a dinner guest, however morally suspect? Should you do it before the soup course and put people off eating, or over coffee and make them vomit up their meal?

"How fine it would be if we had won the war," Heisenberg had said. Well, that caused a hiccup in the table talk. There would have been spies from all sides at the table, besides Berg and the host, Paul Scherrer, Professor of Experimental Physics at the Zurich Poly and Berg's contact. Even now Berg suspected the information was speeding towards Roosevelt, on the one hand, and the Gestapo on the other, who would be furious. Such a defeatist remark bordered on treason to the German cause. Heisenberg could be shot for it . . . if Berg didn't get there first.

Conversation, though, in this short walk back to Heisenberg's hotel sticks to neutral subjects. After all, this is neutral Switzerland, crammed with refugees and also money, hidden in Nazi bank accounts or in those of their concentration camp victims. Three years earlier you might have passed the drunken James Joyce, blissfully unaware that a word he invented in *Finnegans Wake* would be attached to a sub-atomic particle, the quark.

Moe glances sideways at Heisenberg, tries to imagine that broad face with its freckles and clear bright eyes, under a Nazi uniform cap. It doesn't fit; but Moe still can't see this man wearing a halo either. Was he constructing a bomb? That was what the OSS wanted to know. Some of the refugee scientists back at Los Alamos were sure of it, had even offered to assassinate Heisenberg themselves—something Moe had chuckled over. As if they'd be allowed out of the US, let alone anywhere they might fall into enemy hands.

Moe had been in Rome, talking to captured Italian scientists; he'd overheard some pretty interesting stuff at the colloquium and the dinner party. Everybody had their own opinion, and now Berg had to decide about this man. One thing is certain, Heisenberg is a genius and either innocent (well, as innocent as you can be heading a weapons project in Nazi Germany) or as bad as the regime he serves. At the moment, though, he seems indeterminate.

Leaving good or bad aside, thinks Berg, the mission comes down to two things. If he is as brilliant as people say, then America's winning the war depends on his death, before the Nazis make their bomb and use it. Or else he has no importance, because what is he doing outside Germany, lecturing on a subject without military significance? The Americans sure wouldn't let their own bomb scientists do that. Moreover, Heisenberg has no bodyguards, so the Nazis clearly aren't worried about him defecting.

Berg turns his head slightly and sees for a moment, in the shadows, Nazi goons in greatcoats, armed to the teeth. Then they are gone, in the wink of an eye.

"A pleasant night for a walk," says Heisenberg.

"Yes," says Berg. Over this man he has the power of life—to leave him at the door of his hotel, ready for a good night's sleep; and death—from the metal warm under his fingers, that bright smile frozen in a rictus, that brilliant mind stopped forever. To kill or not to kill? He has run the pros and cons over in his own, far less brilliant mind.

And yet he is still uncertain.

MIST & MURDER

It began with a difference of opinion, between myself and my employer Madame la Duchesse Claudine Recherche Dubois.

"Ghosts and murders! Pepin, they do not mix."

We had just been to L'Odeon theatre to see the thrilling new mélodrame, *The Murder of Maria Marten*. The audience had hissed at the villain, as he murdered his sweetheart, and buried her in the Red Barn; dabbed tears at her grieving parents, as they searched for their missing daughter (little knowing how close her corpse lay); and shuddered deliciously as the ghost of poor Maria appeared in her mother's dream, an angry revenant. Now we were headed homewards in Madame's phaeton, which was where the argument ignited.

"But Maria Marten was based on a real case! From Old Earth."

La Duchesse made a gesture that loosely translated as: Pish! "No doubt the mother had eaten cheese at supper that night, and that, coupled with her maternal anxiety, translated into a phantasmickal dream."

"You ascribe a spectre to indigestion, Madame? Where is your sense of the sublime?"

"I find only horror in a man who cruelly murders his sweetheart. And nothing sublime in the unfortunate combination of Welsh rarebit and worry."

I leaned back against the satin upholstery, momentarily defeated. Then I had it: "Perhaps Madame, you as a detective object to a ghost trespassing on your territory, solving its very own murder."

I saw a sudden uncertainty creep across her impeccably powdered and rouged face.

"Peradventure. Or it may be that I merely have a very cold imagination, as Mrs Radcliffe says. I am a product of my times, Pepin, the New Eighteenth Century, where there is a rational, ratiocinative explanation for everything, no matter how uncanny. I prefer Radcliffe to Monk Lewis, detection to dream revelations. And I don't believe in ghosts, most definitely."

In the course of the argument the phaeton had reached the Hotel Exclusif. In my capacity of Secretary, I helped Madame out, sideways, given the width of her hooped skirt.

"Shall I summon room service and ask them to toast some cheese for us?"

A definite shudder. "No Pepin. I am in no need of scientific experiment tonight, rather an undisturbed sleep."

How very fortuitous that a visitor next day should serve to continue the argument, this time in actuality rather than theory. I was out posting the latest in my series (*Mémoires of a Lady Detective*), to the publisher, Mr Colburn, and returned to find the Abigails in a positive orgy of packing.

"Pepin, we are going on a country house visit. To a Mr Longmuir, whose name perhaps should be Marten."

"He has a Red Barn?"

"No, a mansion on the river, down from the spaceport. And he has a daughter living still. But if ever I saw a man who looked as if he had seen a ghost . . ."

One of the Abigails gave a decisive nod.

"Did you ask him if he sups on toasted cheese, Madame?"

"He says: not with his digestion. There must be some other explanation. I will not believe in ghosts, Pepin."

"But nonetheless we are going ghost hunting?"

"Yes, and what should I take?"

I pondered. "Flour, to test for tracks. Tripwires. And a blunderbuss."

"I meant to wear, silly."

An Abigail emitted a slight cough. "Nightclothes, given that hauntings occur after dark. May I suggest a peignoir or three, in some subtle, dark shades. And not too revealing, unless, Madame, you intend to set more than hairs upright."

Where had Madame got these Abigails? I wondered. From some agency specializing in the unshockable, it would seem.

"I very much doubt it. Mr Longmuir is rather a prissy example of manhood," said La Duchesse. "He pointedly looked anywhere but my décolletage. And begged that our visit be discreet. He has a schoolgirl daughter, apparently a paragon of purity."

The other Abigail emitted a slight snort.

"My thoughts precisely. Innocence of a schoolgirl is only in the doting daddy's eye."

"Not like Mrs Longmuir, then," said the first Abigail.

"Pray tell . . ."

Always ask a servant, they know everything. And they did, talking in turns, while they folded and packed clothes into trucks.

"Rowed away, she did."

"Down the river to the spaceport."

"In the company of a nautical gent."

"With twirling moustachios."

"Captain Jasper Sparrow, of the *Black Opal*."

"And *Adventures of a Space Pirate*."

"It was all the fault of her reading group, they said."

"Too many space operas."

"Like Horatia Hornblower."

"And she never, ever, came back."

Mr Longmuir was a man in a tightly buttoned suit, with a harried air, despite a fine house and gardens, landscaped down to the river. We arrived via his personal ferry, and were given a guided tour, firstly of the garden highlights: the folly, the avenue of blossoming trees, the hothouses and the ha ha. He was, quite frankly, a house and gardens bore. As our disguise was to be feature writers from *The Gentlewoman's Companion*, New Ceres' domestic bible, we were obliged to endure it. I took notes and tried not to yawn. Then, once inside, his flow of information shifted, from the details of décor to what was relevant to our investigation.

"I lock all the outside doors at nine o'clock sharp," he said, demonstrating on the front door, while a liveried footman looked on. "See, Reynolds?" To us: "New servant."

"A habit of long-standing?" La Duchesse inquired discreetly. Her dress for this occasion was similarly discreet: slate blue silk with barely a hint of sheen, let alone hoop, a frothy lace fichu covering her décolletage.

"A man of wealth can never be too careful. Nor a father of a daughter. The windows are shuttered at the same time. I also lock all connecting doors to the servants' quarters. Routine, Madame, the only way to run a household."

His tour encompassed in grinding detail every room in the expansive house, a warren of interconnecting rooms, from scullery to the library. The one exception was his daughter's quarters, where he only opened the door briefly, to give a glimpse of a white muslined back, with chestnut ringlets and a powder-blue sash, busy at a desk.

"My little petal."

Only when we were finished, and safely closeted in the master bedroom, a riot of flowery wood-carving covering walls, furniture and ceiling, did he drop the cover of genial host. He sank down on the tapestried four-poster as if suddenly drained of vitality.

"So," La Duchesse said. "To the business at hand."

"I would not have bothered you, Madame, but you are the doyenne of confidential investigations, and this is a matter I wish to be kept very private."

I sat down on the windowseat, nudging the trailing sun-blind away; La Duchesse remained standing, no longer the bluestocking journalist, but in clear control.

"Because you have seen a ghost," she prompted.

He mopped his brow, nodded reluctantly.

"Perhaps you can tell us precisely what happened."

He put his handkerchief away, composed himself.

"Always after lock-up, I do the rounds and see dear Rebecca safely tucked up by her nurserymaid. Then I go to bed, with a cup of cocoa." He sighed. "It began late last year. I fell asleep while reading an improving book. I don't hold with novels."

A quick glance from La Duchesse. It said: *Not like your wife.*

"When I awoke, the candle was still lit. And I saw a shadow on the wall, a silhouette, that shouldn't have been there."

"Where?"

He pointed at a patch of smooth wood by the bedside, miraculously free of wooden foliage.

"What did you do then?"

"I got out of bed and fled the room, so quickly the candle guttered behind me. I came back with a candelabrum for more light, but the silhouette had gone."

La Duchesse turned, inspecting the room.

"And your candle was?"

"On the chairseat."

"Which was in this position?"

"No, the back was turned to the wall."

La Duchesse sat down in the chair, a relatively plain item of lathe-turned wooden furniture, given the rest of the room.

"Did the silhouette return?"

"No, but three months later the apparitions . . . escalated. Always the same form. He closed his eyes, remembering. "I will confess I had given up reading in bed, I merely kept up the cocoa. I woke—and saw a white light in the window, where Mr Pepin is. And a figure, but standing rather than sitting."

I glanced around involuntarily.

"What did you do?" La Duchesse again.

"I admit that I cowered. I couldn't scream, it would have woken dear Rebecca. Trembling, I got out of bed, neared the window, almost too scared to move, and lunged—but in my hands clutched only the curtain fabric."

I touched it—a heavy white opaque silk.

"And the light vanished. I could feel the closed shutter through the fabric, but nonetheless opened the window, put my head out . . . and saw light again, the figure down near the folly. Pointing, pointing . . . then it disappeared again. I jumped out of the window and rushed around the grounds. Nothing, except the lights of the distant spaceport, a vessel falling to earth like a star."

He curled up on himself a moment. La Duchesse waited, then said, "You knew the figure. No random apparition would produce this effect."

He uncurled, nodded. "It was a face I had not seen in five years. The woman whose name I swore I would never utter again. She—once my own dear wife. Firstly as a mere silhouette, then manifesting in her wedding dress, but . . . but . . . soaked red, from her heart's blood."

If we had posed as being from *Cookery New Ceres*, we would surely have been exploded like a firecracker. Dinner that night was appalling—to the gourmand. Reynolds the footman served meagre portions of plain chicken, without its skin, and a selection of overboiled vegetables, for the sake of the Master's digestion. Rebecca, who might possibly have made things interesting, if only by pert schoolgirlisms, was relegated to her schoolroom, a tray taken in by her nursemaid. The desultory conversation elicited only that Longmuir had always been a martyr to indigestion, even before the nervous shock of the apparition and Mrs Longmuir's departure. I began to think the woman had left out of sheer boredom. Given such dreary domesticity, piracy had an undoubted attraction.

Longmuir gazed moodily out the window. "Not much of a sunset tonight," he murmured. "Fog's coming off the bay."

Indeed, it rolled up the river and into the grounds like a greedy grey beast. Which was much like I felt. As we zigzagged through the passages to the guest apartment in the far wing, La Duchesse went into a huddle of whispers with Reynolds the footman. Gold coin met the outstretched hand, to result, some fifteen minutes later, in a large plate of melted cheese on toast.

I waited until the door had closed behind his livery, then said, "You're experimenting on me!"

"Precisely. You are the subject, myself the control. If we both see ghosts, then I will believe in the supernatural. Eat up!"

The Abigails began to unlace La Duchesse's gown. For any man it would have signalled a change of appetites, from the comestible to the carnal. But I was not a man, and I kept eating, too hungry to ignore the cheese. Once again, I blessed the disguise that breeched me, safe from the perils of stays and corsets: undressing my mistress was like dining on lobster.

Some half hour later, a hesitant knock sounded at the door. I opened it, to reveal Mr Longmuir, in dressing gown and nightcap; he blinked at La Duchesse, who was resplendent in beribboned mob cap and a plum-coloured satin peignoir trimmed with deep lace ruffles, a gown outrageously lavish but indubitably modest. I picked up the folding bed and blunderbuss, and followed Longmuir as we tiptoed to his bedroom.

"Good night," he murmured. "Sleep well."

"I doubt it," I muttered, queasy already. Then Longmuir was gone, to sleep in our apartments, while we kept watch in the haunted room.

"Not a comfortable bed," said La Duchesse, bouncing up and down on it. "Pepin, have you set the trip wires?"

"Set, Madame."

"And the flour?

"Sifted and scattered."

She lay back on the bed, a draught setting the candle flame dancing madly, a carnival of shadows. But none that looked like a silhouette, save of us. I reached out my hand, made a shadow mouse; La Duchesse responded with a cat.

"Good night, Madame."

"Good night, Pepin"—and she blew out the candle.

Three things woke me: a mouse-scratch in the panelling; the cheese, rolling uncomfortably around my digestives; but most significantly the white light that poured into the room. I sat bolt upright on the folding bed, staring at the figure that had appeared on the windowseat as if standing on it, a vision insubstantial, that rippled with the curtain behind it in yet another of this room's infernal draughts.

I cursed the cheese, then withdrew the anathema. La Duchesse also sat up, staring: at a woman in her wedding dress, tall and handsome, with a veil of blood stretching down from her coiffed head, the length of the dress to her satin slippers. For a moment there was complete silence, the only sound the rustle of the curtain. Then I forgot my assumed manliness and screamed.

La Duchesse reached down and gripped my shoulder—that stopped my panic, and at that moment the figure vanished. Shaking

I got out of bed, fully dressed as was the plan, and reached for the blunderbuss. A match struck, as behind us in the wainscoting it seemed as if even the mice scrambled for safety. My mistress lit the dark lantern, and shed mob cap and peignoir to reveal a neat plait instead of her elaborate daytime coiffure, and a plain dark man's suit, the double of mine.

"Pepin! Is that window secure?"

I pushed the curtain aside.

"Shuttered and latched, Madame. Nobody could get in from the outside." My hands were still a little unsteady, but I opened window and shutter, leaned out, with La Duchesse craning behind me.

Cool night air met me, laced with fog, which was beginning to clear in the faint dawn breeze. It currently resided at just above head-height, creating an eerie grey effect reminiscent of some Gothic grotto. I heard a distant lapping from the river, as though it supped on land. Behind us came a waking commotion, the servants and Master arising, consequent to my scream. It seemed too peaceful outside to allow of any unquiet spirit, but then, near the folly, the figure reappeared, again luminescent white save the slash of red blood, but now pointing . . . at what?

"Follow!" said La Duchesse, and we leapt out the window, not something ever to do in my mistress's high-fashion hoops, but easily performed in breeches. We landed in a soft-dug flower bed, and went racing down the lawns. The figure stood as if waiting for us, absolutely still, except for that disquieting ripple. Now we faced each other across an expanse of geometric shrubbery, waiting . . . for what?

"The blunderbuss, Pepin!" La Duchesse whispered.

"But what if it is some person? An actor, the lady herself?"

"I am assured it is not. Fire!"

And I lifted the huge ponderous weapon, fired. It sounded like a cannon in the stillness, and the recoil knocked me over and into a box hedge. As I extricated myself, spitting leaves, I heard an unearthly scream, and from the house, shouts as Longmuir chivvied his servants outside.

I stood up awkwardly, to see the light gone, and La Duchesse standing where the figure had been, apparently pulling strips of mist from the air, which fell like wafting grey blossoms.

"An apparition! That wears silk!"

I neared, to be handed a strip of torn cloth, as light and soft as thistledown.

We searched the grounds, as the mist rose and the sun followed, without discovering anything—except that when someone falls down the ha ha, they injure themselves. In this case it was Mr Longmuir, who inflicted upon himself a broken leg, and several cracked ribs, to judge from the angle of his foot and the way he clutched his chest. La Duchesse immediately took charge. The private ferry was commandeered to take Longmuir to the nearest infirmary; Rebecca and her nursemaid, who had joined the search just in time to fuss over the invalid, accompanied him.

Once the ferry and its cargo were dispatched, La Duchesse clapped hands.

"I think what we need at this point is a breakfast . . . a good one, in the kitchen. No standing on ceremony at this hour!"

And no mistaking who was wearing the pants, either.

At the back of the house we sat at the scrubbed pine table with La Duchesse's Abigails and the Longmuir servants, while the cook and scullery maid produced a breakfast quite unsuitable for a man of delicate digestion.

"Eggs Lincotte," said La Duchesse. "Pain perdu. Devilled kidneys. My compliments to the cook."

"I'm Hannah, Ma'am, and it's a pleasure to cook properly again."

When in doubt, ask a servant, and this gang slipped easily into gossip mode, while I took notes. The maids were devoted readers of *Mémoires of a Lady Detective*, and had recognized La Duchesse immediately. So much for our disguise!

"Never a spread like this since the Missus went."

"She liked her food rich and spicy."

"And parties, noisy ones."

"Masks and fancy dress themes."

"Like Pirates."

"Then she heard a real pirate had just docked at port, on a flying visit for repairs."

"Captain Jasper Sparrow, author of *Adventures of a Space Pirate*."

"The Missus' favourite series."

"She sent him an invite, as a lark. And he larked back."

"What a rager he turned out to be."

"So was she."

"Couldn't blame her for running away with him, with the master so pale, dull and abstemious . . ."

"And all his routines."

"Getting worse they were."

The gardener, a tall husky man seated at the far end of the table, had been silent. Now he cleared his throat.

"*If* she ran away with him."

"Oh," said Hannah, "Wilberforce, not that again."

"We're helping Madame and her secretary with their queries, aren't we? So it's only fair I say that Captain Sparrow was a dashing fellow, but not one for the womenfolk. Don't ask me how, but I *know* for certain."

"Thank you Wilberforce," said La Duchesse. She opened her purse, began tipping handsomely, with most I noticed to Hannah, and also Wilberforce.

After breakfast, we made a full tour of the premises again, in the absence of the owner, ascertaining that the trip wires and flour were intact, and that nothing had entered from outside. La Duchesse scrutinised the sites of the hauntings, tapping the panelling of the bedroom, with tweezers removing what seemed like ordinary rubbish from the garden: fragments of old coloured window glass, espalier wire, and more of the mysterious grey silk. She also instructed me to make quick sketches. That done, we inspected the house again, leaving until last the only rooms we had not seen earlier, Miss Rebecca's.

As we neared her bedroom door it opened a crack, to reveal a liveried rear-end, bent under the single four-postered bed.

"Ahem!" said La Duchesse, entering and closing the door quietly behind us. "Mr Reynolds, I presume? I knew you were no servant, however new-employed."

He crawled out backwards, stood, and gave a slight bow.

"Well-spotted, Madame. May I ask how?"

"Your thumb was in the toasted cheese."

He sighed. "Not the sort of thing we learned in the Lumoscenti."

"You had a report of new-fangled, forbidden technology?"

"We had a report of a phantasm, idle servant's talk in a pot-house, but intriguing."

"You too do not believe in ghosts?"

"Only as illusions presented within the time-frame of our New Eighteenth Century. A phantom in a Phantasmagoria, an invention of the 1790s, but not a Zoetrope, or Dr Pepper's Ghost, illusions which date from the Nineteenth, and forbidden, Century. We license the spectacles in our theatres most carefully, and a report of an amateur performance merited investigation."

"Performance, but by whom?" I asked.

"That remains to be seen. Consider these books"—with a nod at the tomes on the bedside table. "Christian Huyghens! *Hamlet*! We have here not romances, nor conduct books, but a bluestocking child."

"I was much the same at that age," said La Duchesse. Sotto voce, to me: "Before I discovered the distractions of love."

"Then consider this"—and he led us to the connecting playroom, a higgledy-piggledy treasure trove of juvenile achievement, from the easel to the workbox, junior alchemy set, prisms, kaleidoscopes, telescope, astronomic charts, woodworking tools, and not a doll in sight. A school hat hung from a hook, and La Duchesse gave an approving nod.

"The Madame de Stael Memorial Academy for Young Ladies, my alma mater. Nothing forbidden there, except a girl left fallow, with no cultivation of her natural abilities."

"To judge from this mess," Reynolds says, "Miss Longmuir has no ability for housekeeping. But for everything else, it would appear. Woodworking? I had no notion that was the latest craze for young ladies."

"The Academy prides itself on its bluestocking tradition, and also on providing practical careers for girls. Wood-carving, locksmithing, even the stage, but props-management rather than actressing. New professions, instead of the oldest."

"In my opinion," Reynolds said, "Miss Longmuir is the cleverest person in this house."

"But sufficient to cause the Lumoscenti concern, at 12 years old?"

"How clever is or was her Mamma?" I asked. They both turned and stared at me.

"An excellent question, Pepin. Here we find a guide to the character and interests of the daughter. Her mother, on the other hand, is a blank. Nothing I have seen in this house suggests the personality and possessions of the absent Mrs Longmuir."

She paused, finger to mouth.

"Which makes me wonder. A woman in a midnight flit does not usually pack anything but lightly. She must have left something behind, which her husband no doubt shut out of sight and thus remembrance."

"There is an attic, Ma'am," said Reynolds. "I had yet to concoct a reason to inspect it."

A sudden movement out the window, which like the master bedroom opened onto the garden, caught my attention. The private ferryboat had returned, and was docking at the riverside jetty. But something about it was different.

"Madame, is it usual for a boat to carry the flag with its owner's arms half-mast?"

The ferryman's dress was subtly different too, with a band of black on sleeve and hat, clearly distinguished from the green of the household livery.

"Oh!" and La Duchesse stood beside me, Reynolds craning over both our heads. "I fear that poor Mr Longmuir's injuries were more serious than expected, that he has . . . died."

"Or was murdered," said Reynolds.

Servants were running from the house to the ferry, just as two figures, tall and short, in long black cloaks disembarked: Miss Rebecca Longmuir and her nursemaid.

"There will be an inquest," Reynolds said. "At which, as investigative agents, we will be summoned to appear. To present our conclusions."

La Duchesse looked from him to me.

"And the conclusions of an investigative agent, whether of the Lumoscenti, or a Lady Detective, can only take one form: to bring the mystery to an end."

Coronial inquests are generally convened *in situ*, and quickly, but it was a week before my mistress, I, and the Abigails, all clad in sombre mourning, took the ferryboat back to the Longmuir estate. It was crowded: with the Coroner, doctor, and witnesses, all wrapped up in cloaks against a biting sea breeze. We disembarked, and hurried up to the house. In the library, the largest room, was where the inquest would be convened. Miss Longmuir sat there already, on a couch and veiled in black, holding hands with her nursemaid.

The Coroner seated in the late master's chair, a jury of neighbours empanelled, La Duchesse nodded to the servants. A series of exhibits, shrouded in dustcloths, were brought in and lined against the near wall. Then the Coroner opened the proceedings, in a droning voice to which I found very difficult to listen. La Duchesse had kept me hard at work the last week, dictating letters, taking record of interviews, conducting experiments, and what with one thing or another I had very little sleep. I drifted into a light doze, then awoke with a start, as my mistress took the floor, in black velvet and matching pearls.

"Mr Coroner, the function of an investigation is to be reconstructive, and I had to reconstruct first a recent sequence of events, then an older one, of five years back. That was when Mrs Longmuir notoriously eloped with Captain Jasper Sparrow, never to be seen again. Except, perhaps, in Exhibit A, published late last year."

With a curtsey, a housemaid pulled the dustsheet away from an occasional table containing a prosaic business ledger and pile of pamphlet-sized booklets, their covers adorned with bright, gaudy engravings. I recognized the familiar format of my publisher, Mr Colburn & Co, whose popular memoir series included . . .

"*Adventures of a Space-Pirate*. Not originating with Colburn, but licensed for distribution in New Ceres. A series with a substantial following here, even if the author is somewhat dilatory in his instalments, given his busy career in piracy. He is, at present, running several years behind actual events in his career. But last year, a new volume did appear . . . and sold out almost immediately. Mr Colburn was obliged to provide me with his personal copy to read. Alas, he was quite unable to provide an actual interview with his author, who is rather elusive, natural given his profession."

She took out a jet lorgnette, and quizzed the topmost booklet before her.

"Captain Sparrow, like others in the memoirs trade, does disguise facts and figures to prevent too close a recognition. And exaggerates, no doubt. In this one volume alone he escapes a sunspot storm, rams a space-whaler, and also . . . attends a Masked Piratical ball, as himself. At a riverside mansion, on a planet that bears an unmistakable resemblance to New Ceres."

The Coroner painstakingly noted that fact.

"The highlight of this particular narrative is a card game, with the officers of a Naval vessel, unsuspecting old adversaries of Sparrow. The fake and the real pirates play for high stakes—he cleans them out completely, and most comically. Yet, curiously, there is no mention of running off with his hostess. Indeed, the more I read these books, the more I noticed an exclusively masculine cast of characters, with no apparent need of feminine company."

Wilberforce, seated besides the ferryman, received a visible nudge.

La Duchesse closed the book, opened another, the ledger.

"Mr Colburn kindly provided me with his list of subscribers. In which I notice the Madame de Stael College."

She passed the books to the coroner.

"Next, Exhibit B." The housemaid gave her curtsey again, and pulled the dustsheet from Mr Longmuir's bedroom chair.

"Mr Coroner, honourable juryfolk, consider this chair. A rather plain, lathe-turned item, but which with certain modifications could take part in a scientific experiment: to determine if a man was merely a deserted husband, or something much worse." She put one hand on the knobs, finials on either side of the high back. "See, one unscrews . . . and the other most decidedly doesn't."

An anticipatory silence filled the room.

"May I request the curtains be drawn . . . Not now, when I signal! And for a candelabrum to be lit. Also, if I may borrow the Chinoiserie screen, by the fireplace."

It was arranged behind the chair, the dustsheet draped over it, the candelabrum lit and placed on the seat.

"If I may humour the audience with a shadow play. In this house's schoolroom, I observed woodworking tools, among them some lathe-turned knobs. They appeared innocuous, but in certain lights, they bore a remarkable resemblance . . . to the Headmistress of the Madame de Stael College, its janitor, an unpopular figure, and to this lady, Exhibit C."

364

She produced from her hanging pocket a miniature portrait.

"Mrs Longmuir, a silhouette, done from life and concealed in the family attic. Now draw the curtains."

The room, save for the flickering candle, plunged in darkness, illuminating the knobs on the chairback and throwing their shadows against the draped dustsheet. They appeared unexceptional, at first. Then light, or rather shadow, dawned. One knob had been cunningly turned so that it formed a face in silhouette—the counterpart of the one in the miniature.

"Jouets séditieux, seditious toys, a trifle from the Old Eighteenth Century, but surprisingly effective when used here, as an agent of justice. But not as effective as Exhibit D."

La Duchesse nodded to the maid, who removed yet another dustsheet, to reveal two metal boxes.

"A word on provenance here. The coastguards, acting on my suggestions, dragged the riverbed within a narrow radius of the jetty. They unearthed, or rather unwatered these, the insides smashed, the delicate glass scattered. Fragments could be found in the garden, including a shard of mirror. I had repairs made, but a vital component was missing."

She removed one candle from the candelabrum, opened a hinged flap in the nearest box and inserted it. A stream of light emerged from the front, and hit the dustsheet draped over the screen.

"Ah," said Reynolds, now in his Lumoscenti robes. "A Magic Lantern."

"Or Lantern of Fear, as some call it. It projects: pretty panoramas, images of foreign potentates, anything that can be painted in miniature, on glass. I have here only a view of New Copenhagen, which will have to suffice. See the square of painted glass, in my hand, see me place it in the Lantern, behold on the dustsheet, the image magnified. Pepin!"

"Yes Madame?"

"Perhaps you can describe the phantom you saw in Mr Longmore's bedroom."

I stood before the assembly, all eyes on me, and tried to describe what I had seen. "A lady, tall and stately, in her wedding dress, satin à la Polonaise. She was very pale, with chestnut hair, and she stood perfectly still, though she rippled slightly."

La Duchesse took hold of the dependant dustsheet.

"Like this, pray?"—and shook it. New Copenhagen trembled as if in an earthquake.

"Your phantom was projected onto the silk curtain. Probably from the next room, via a hole drilled in the wall and concealed among the wooden foliage."

"I did hear a scratching sound, Madame, but thought it mice, attracted by the smell of cheese."

"Thank you, Pepin. Wait here a moment, while I present my final exhibit . . ."—a tall rectangle underneath its shroud.

From the audience Hannah the cook spoke: "We think we know what your next exhibit will be, Ma'am. It used to hang over the fireplace, till Master banished it to the attic."

"Hannah, you are perfectly correct." The last dustsheet fell to the floor, and I beheld the spectre, to the life, or rather paint: a full-length portrait of a tall, chestnut-haired woman in white, a bride à la Polonaise.

"Madame, she was much less realistic when I saw her."

"Because she had been copied, in miniature, and a crude swathe of red blood added. That was one image, the other was for the garden, with an arm crudely upraised, pointing . . . at what? And why?"

Silence fell, broken from the other side of the room, by the sound of two hands muffled in black silk mittens, clapping.

"Well done, Madame," said a high, girlish voice. "Open the curtains, extinguish the candlelight. You have exploded me quite."

Rebecca Longmuir stood, pushing back her black veil. From where I stood I could see the intelligence in her face, but not, I thought, any particular malevolence. She walked slowly over to La Duchesse, an effortless upstage.

"You were wrong in one matter. My inspiration was not the new instalment of *Adventures of a Space Pirate*. That was secondary. Certainly when I read it I found no mention of Mamma's elopement. To him she was no more than Mrs Longbottom, as he called her, a merry but gracious hostess."

One of the jurymen stood up. "As she was, that night. I was a guest, and went as Captain Sparrow. So did several others, including the genuine article. Which one of us rowed Mrs Longmuir down the misty river? I didn't, but I can't say who did."

"A confusion to be exploited at a masked ball," said La Duchesse, "for amours or worse. Especially next morning, when everyone except the host is hungover, and the lady cannot be found."

"Ahem," said Rebecca, and the juryman subsided. She turned, held out one hand, and the nurserymaid joined her.

"From Captain Sparrow's narrative, and from certain hints dropped by my dear Nursey, I acquired the dreadful suspicion Papa had been telling me fairytales. He seemed to think my apex in life was to be his housekeeper—when I could read Mr Hughyens on Optics, could paint, carve wood, and shine as props lady in the end of year school mélodrame! So I resolved to test him, as Hamlet did his Uncle. I copied the silhouette, transferred it to a jouet séditieux, and substituted it for the knob on his bedside chair. It took several nights, before the angle of shadow was correct, but assuredly he reacted like the guiltiest of men."

She turned to La Duchesse.

"I have read all the *Mémoires of a Lady Detective.* In my innocent teatime prattle, I inserted into Papa's mind the notion of your discreet investigations. Who better to expose his guilty secret? And so you came, to witness a Magic Lantern show, myself inside, Abigail outside, with a second Magic Lantern in the folly, projecting onto a gauze curtain hung between two trees. A Phantasmagoria, Mr Reynolds, not a Zoetrope nor Dr Pepper's Ghost. Oh! such fun we had, until you shot your blunderbuss, Mr Pepin. Nursey and I took fright—we concealed the Lanterns beneath our shawls, then dropt them, their mechanisms smashed, into the river. Where I fear Papa dropt Mamma, when her desire for a noisy, spicy life conflicted too much with his desire for bland peace. But, I assure you, I did not drop Papa in the ha ha, that was the least of my intent. I only wished that justice would be done."

The doctor, scheduled to give evidence last in the inquest, suddenly stood.

"I must interrupt. Death was consistent with a heart attack, there is no doubt about it."

"Twas Nemesis, the agent of justice, pushed him," said Hannah. "Or maybe the ghost of Mrs Longmuir herself.'

"I don't disbelieve in ghosts," said Rebecca.

"Indeed," said La Duchesse, "and why not, pray?"

"You never asked me what my inspiration was, to first try Papa, then expose his guilt before you. Why it was the ghost of dear Mamma appearing in my dream, wordless and imploring, dripping water and seaweed!"

And La Duchesse turned to face me over the veiled chestnut head and mouthed two words: Toasted cheese!

Back at the Hotel Exclusif, my pen scratched, as I wrote the final words of the latest *Mémoire of a Lady Detective*:

"To solve the problem seemed to be impossible, and so the case of the dream revenant, à la Maria Marten, has remained a mystery to this day—a mystery to which the Lady Detective carried the closest investigation, without being any wiser by the inquiry."

"Very good," said my mistress, reading over my shoulder. "Have you thought of a title yet? I fancy: 'The Lantern of Fear'."

"It suggests horror, Monk Lewis and his shuddering ilk. Also it gives the plot away, something never to do with mystery narratives."

"'The Phantasmagoria'?"

"Likewise, Madame." I was the writer, and as such I had authority. So I turned to the title page, and wrote, the pen sputtering slightly:

"MIST AND MURDER."

RED OCHRE

Fogarty's Animal Show had just crossed that invisible border up north beyond which people are strange. The first signs were dark looks and mutterings in front of the snake cages. Ian Limrock watched, intent as if he were tracking game, then padded off to tell his boss. "They don't like the Python Plus."

Old Frank Fogarty was counting takings in his caravan, a glass of gin within easy reach, and was none too pleased by the interruption.

"Who don't like my snake?"

"The locals."

"I don't care, so long as they pay. Look at this lovely money! You'd think they'd never seen wild animals before."

Ian persisted. "They mean trouble."

Fogarty snorted. "Garn, you black bastard."

There was a splintering crash, and a shout from Eileen, Fogarty's most valued employee (after Ian Limrock).

"Frank! Ian! They're smashing cages!"

Fogarty abandoned cash and gin and bolted out the caravan door, one second after Ian. In the interval before a beer-bellied yokel threw a punch at him, he noticed a ring of Queenslanders around the Python Plus, armed with pieces of the snake's cage.

The blow connected, and as Fogarty staggered back, the Python feinted, then shot between a pair of legs in sawn-off jeans. Ian suddenly ran away. Fogarty swore at him, ducked a second blow, and charged into the melee. In the centre of the fight Eileen was standing on top of a flour bin, clouting methodically. Another cage smashed, and something small and rat-like emerged from the wreckage, shook itself and sped off. The locals parted for it as if they were the Red Sea. It was the Snakecatcher. Fogarty grabbed a hick by the hair and reached with his free hand for a weapon. Then Ian screamed.

Typically, while the rest of the staff fought, Ian had looked to the animals. He'd followed the Python along the line of the caravans, where the creature obviously hoped to find some peace. As it happened, it found the Snakecatcher, a mortal enemy, and the precious pair took fang and claw to each other. Ian intervened and got bitten: the Snakecatcher nearly severed two of his fingers.

"Well," Fogarty remarked as he tied the tourniquet, "look on the bright side: you might have been munched by the Python."

The Plus was poisonous.

Ian's screaming stopped the battle. Some of the marauders ran off, and the rest were outnumbered enough to surrender. Fogarty had the captives brought up to where Ian lay, to keep them quiet until the police arrived. It was a sight: torches, Ian in shock, the Python writhing inside a tied-up sack, and the Snakecatcher making sepulchral noises from inside Eileen's handy flour bin. Then the prisoners started their dark looks and mutters again, this time at poor Ian.

"Shaddup!" yelled Fogarty.

Somebody said "Mutie" loudly, then the order took effect. They were silent even when the police arrived, all draggle-tailed and sleepy-eyed, quite unfit for handling half a dozen charges of assault and malicious damage against their drinking mates. Fogarty thoroughly enjoyed that part of the evening. Then a big blue van took away Ian and his fingers. Fogarty gave him his bottle of gin to sip on the way.

"You can't say Francis F. Fogarty doesn't stand by a good employee," he announced to the staff. "Well gang, show's over— let's clean up this mess. Yes, Diz?"

"Mr Fogarty, I got me head kicked and it hurts."

"Show Uncle," said Fogarty and the boy parted his lank locks. There was no lump or bruising, but Dizzy looked worse than usual, usual being useless.

Fogarty sighed. "Okay, you're exempt."

The next morning Fogarty woke up late, cut a big bunch of bougainvillea, and went down to the infirmary. He was met by a woman, in police uniform.

"I'm Sergeant Muddiman," she said.

You don't look it, thought Fogarty. Her uniform was immaculate. "Well, ma'am, er, Sergeant, pleased to meet you. I'm Frank Fogarty. You busy interviewing Ian about the spot of affray last night?"

"Mr Limrock isn't here." She stepped aside to reveal a rumpled bed with an empty gin bottle beside it, but no Ian.

"Where is he?" Fogarty suddenly remembered Ian lying in pain, and the townspeople looking evil at him. "If my Ian's been harmed I'll . . . "

"Relax, he's safe."

"Safe where?"

"The Mutie reserve. Your Ian was ferried up there by aerial ambulance, this dawn."

"Oh!" and Fogarty sat down on the bed, still clutching the flowers. Muddiman stood there looking at him, not without sympathy. Fogarty felt a sudden temptation to offer her the flowers, but then decided against it. Might take it as police bribery, he thought. Then he pondered her words, running them around and around in his head, but getting nowhere.

"Ian told me Queensland had reserves for his kinda people, but that's past, innit?"

"It's past."

"And no way is Ian a mutant. Jesus, what happened?"

"I was off-duty last night," she said, "and out of town. When I got back, your employee was out of my jurisdiction, Mr Fogarty. I don't condone what the staff here did, but I can't blame them for panicking. Not with a patient who'd been bitten by a Mutie animal."

"He wasn't. What bit Ian had a set of perfect chromosomes—the Snakecatcher, alias Mongoose, alias Herpestes Edwardsi." Muddiman gave him a dirty look. "But since that's Greek, er, Latin to you, I'll say it's a small furry carnivore from India."

"An enemy animal?"

"No, no," said Fogarty. "Not Indonesia, India. They've never invaded Oz, well, not yet."

"Mr Fogarty," said Muddiman, "the Indo army got within fifty kilos of this town. We don't forget that, not with the Muties to remind us. Okay, so Mr Limrock wasn't bitten by your pet snake, but you had no business bringing such an animal up here. Don't you realise that where people are scared stiff of the DNA plague, even a Mutie serpent is a threat?"

"I've been trying to tell you. The Python isn't a Mutie. Mutated sure, but not by Indo bad-loser germs. There's a notice on the cage, if your mob had bothered to read it. I bought the Python from a bunch of gene-splicers with a funding crisis. It's poisonous—the extra genes come from the Indian cobra—but not plaguey."

She was silent. "Point took?" he asked after a while.

She nodded.

"Then get me Ian back!"

"I see no reason for that. Ian'll get proper medical treatment at the reserve—in fact the Mutie hospital is the best equipped in the North. And it isn't far off the main Cape road. You can continue your tour, and pick up Ian when he's recovered."

"Hospitals, they're 'xpensive."

She sighed. "You won't have to pay a cent, I'll tell the reserve doctors to bill this town. It was, after all, our mistake."

"Very good," said Fogarty.

"Now about the six respected citizens charged last night . . . "

"More got away. But me 'n' the staff could identify."

"I'm sure you could. Hmn. How would you like replacement cages for your animals? And a police escort to the next town? One condition: drop the charges and keep your mouth shut."

"That's two conditions."

"Here's a third—when you come down Cape York on your way home, don't pay us a return visit. You've caused quite enough trouble already."

They bargained a bit, while the bougainvillea wilted in the early-morning heat. It put Fogarty in mind of a wedding bouquet, with him the bride and Muddiman the groom, as they concluded the marriage between his and her conditions. Knot tied, Fogarty sauntered back to the camp, and found Dizzy waiting outside his caravan, as welcome as a mum-in-law.

"Mr Fogarty, me head still hurts."

"Okay, take sick leave and fly back to Sydney. One condition: take that Mutie snake with you."

Fogarty was still in Muddiman mode.

"Gee thanks," said Diz.

They fed the Python three whole cans of meat substitute, so it wouldn't do much more than burp for a couple of months. Then Fogarty sent Eileen down to the airstrip to book a seat on the next flight south.

"They pay," he instructed.

Eileen raised one eyebrow.

"Diz got a kick in the head, din' he? Only fair the locals cough up for causing his . . . "

"Percussion," Dizzy said helpfully.

"You said it. Now get packing . . . your bags."

Eileen still looked quizzical, and Fogarty leant towards her. "Reckon meself it was the midwife dropped him. But nobody here'll know he wasn't percussed yesterday."

She grinned.

Next morning Fogarty saw Diz off at the airstrip, with his luggage and a travelling cage marked "goanna" in large red letters.

"Eh, what's that?" said the airstrip groundsman, pointing at the cage.

"Bloody big lizard," Fogarty said quickly, waving to Dizzy as he stepped onto the aircraft. The plane took off, but Fogarty lingered around the green corrugated-iron terminal. He felt at a loose end, and knew he was missing Ian.

"You play poker, mate?"

It was the groundsman again, shuffling a pack of dirty cards.

"Haven't you got anything useful to do?" said Fogarty.

"Not with the traffic at this strip. C'mon, give us a game."

"Or two," said Fogarty. At the least it would stop him thinking about Ian being alone and sick in a strange place, and locked up with Muties into the bargain.

"You must practise every day," he said to the groundsman, five games later.

"Used to, mate. But the folks around here went off the game. Dunno why—I think it's great."

You would, thought Fogarty, eyeing the untidy pile of his money in front of the groundsman. Then he noticed the other had put his head on one side.

"Work to do," the groundsman said sadly. Fogarty could hear it too, now—the sound of a light plane heading up from the south. He wandered outside and watched as the aircraft circled the strip, then landed. It had a little row of wayang figures painted on the fuselage.

"What's with the decoration?" he asked the groundsman.

"War surplus. The shadow puppets mean Indo kills."

"Who's the pilot, then?"

"Doctor from the Mutie reserve."

"Yeah?" said Fogarty, thinking, how very interesting.

The plane puttered up to the terminal, like a tropical wasp heading for a big green banana plant. Fogarty narrowed his eyes at it, a plan forming inside his head.

Looks like there's room for a passenger, he thought, and followed the groundsman over to greet the pilot.

"Can you do me an intro?" he asked, catching up.

"No worries, mate . . . Gidday, Doc Jon. Frank Fogarty here wants to meet you."

That done, he ambled off to see to the plane, leaving Fogarty and the doctor shaking hands.

"Actually, I'm Jon Blackmore." Unlike Muddiman he suited his name, for the hand in Fogarty's was dark. "What can I do for you?"

"I was hoping I could get a lift up to the reserve, to see a mate of mine." Fogarty launched into the whole silly story. At the mention of animals the doctor gave him a strange glance, not hostile, like the townspeople at the Python and Ian, but as if the zoo man had touched upon a private thought.

"Can I take a look at your animal show?" he asked, when Fogarty at last fell silent.

"We charge," said Fogarty.

"Not if you intend to bum a ride off me."

The two walked back along the dusty airstrip road, Fogarty now and then glancing sideways at the newcomer. Reminds me of someone, he thought, and after a few more steps, Fogarty's noisy and Doc Jon's quiet, realised that it was Ian.

At the camp, he escorted the doctor around, showing him the animals in their old and new cages (the town carpenter and his apprentice had visited in his absence, courtesy of Muddiman). Doc Jon said nothing, but gradually the line of his mouth softened, and he began to smile. By the end of the show, which finished with drinks in Fogarty's caravan, he was almost affable.

"When you pick up Ian—" he began, then drained his glass before continuing. "Is there any chance of you putting on your show at the reserve?"

"Ah," said Fogarty. "What kinda audience would we get?"

"Muties."

"That's what I thought."

"They'd really love to see it," said Doc Jon.

Yeah, but could they pay? thought Fogarty. "Maybe," he said.

"Think about it. OK, I'm off to the pub to rent a room for the night. I'll see you on the strip tomorrow—at dawn."

Fogarty spent the rest of the day getting the show all packed up and ready for Eileen and the police escort to take up the road to the next town. Next morning, he went off to the airfield dark and early to find the groundsman still wearing his sarong, the North Queensland equivalent of the dressing gown (despite the war, some Indonesian influence persisted). Doc Jon stared at Fogarty, without acknowledgement. This morning he put Fogarty in mind of a marsupial: he had pouches, under his eyes.

"Bit tetchy today," murmured the groundsman. "They had community singalong at the pub last night. Got a bit out of hand, and by the time ol' Muddy read the riot act to them, it was three AM."

With that warning Fogarty didn't say a word to the doctor—except "Morning", without the prefix "good", in case he disagreed—and was repaid in kind. It was not until they had been in the air for half an hour that Doc Jon's vocal cords creaked into action.

"There's no wild animals left on the Cape."

"That so? I heard they were scarce . . . Well, they're scarce everywhere, that's how I make my living."

But Doc Jon was talking right through him.

"Population pressure, a war, pollution—maybe something else."

"Like what?"

"I'll show you!"

The plane suddenly swooped sideways and down, and Fogarty closed his eyes. When the flight seemed more or less stable, Fogarty peered through his eyelashes, and regretted it, because they were zooming down the middle of a narrow valley. There was a big wall of rock at the end of it, coming up fast.

"Look to the right," said Doc Jon, and Fogarty reluctantly obeyed: the doctor was using the tone you say "Yes sir" to. He glanced sideways and into a hollow halfway up a sandstone bluff: there was a red streak on the flat stone, the shape of something that looked like the Python's great grandaddy. Then Fogarty slammed his eyelids shut again, because the plane had shot upwards as if on kangaroo legs, over the rock wall and into a clear blue sky.

"Did you see it?"

"Red," Fogarty said blindly. "A sort of snake."

"That's Serpent Dreaming Shelter. I went there once, on foot. It's a place where the poor old people, Murri, the local Aboriginals, made rock paintings. A lot of those paintings were of animals, and they were magic, to ensure a continued supply of game."

Fogarty opened his eyes again, and looked at the doctor closely. Now he could see traces of the people that Doc Jon talked of, diluted like the blue in much-washed jeans.

"Come the white invasion, the painting stopped. The artists were dead, and their descendants detribalised. Like me. Without the increase magic, the wild animals died out."

Fogarty could not think of anything to say, so said nothing.

"Make of it what you will," said Doc Jon, then shut up again. Fogarty dozed a bit, and dreamed his pilot threw him off the plane, straight into the maw of the Dreamtime serpent. He awoke with a start, and found they were circling an airstrip. Beside it was a big white hospital building: pre-fab housing, each with a chunk of garden to it; and red desolation.

"Funny place to put a hospital," he said.

Doc Jon swore at the distraction and the plane landed with a thump. The pilot-doctor put the brakes on, and they lurched to a full stop in the middle of a cloud of dust. Now that they were earthbound, Doc Jon replied.

"You ever hear of lepers?"

"Long time back."

"We've brought the Indo disease down to the same level of contagion—bloody low—but still nobody wants Mutie neighbours."

Fogarty stared out the window and saw figures walking towards the plane, through the veil of red. They were only silhouettes, like the wayang puppets, but it did not look like a freak show to him. The doctor sighed.

"The Muties won't want to see you, Mr Fogarty, they've met too many brutes like your cage-smashers. So please only go where I tell you."

"Sure," said Fogarty, his mouth dry in a way that had nothing to do with the dust. But he forgot all that when he saw Ian. The injured man had a little room to himself and was sitting up in bed.

Fogarty grinned like a melon.

"Hi, you black bastard."

"Hi whitey," replied Ian, as always. There was a little pause, and then Ian said, "This is my fault."

"Aw, it could have happened to any of us."

"Yeah, but I had the idea to go up the Cape in the first place."

Fogarty looked at him sharply. Come to think of it, Ian had pushed for this trip.

"I didn't only have your profits in mind," Ian confessed.

"Treason," and Fogarty waggled a finger at him. "Go on, tell Uncle, what was your real reason?"

"Roots."

Fogarty thought back. In the tautologous city of Townsville Ian had said something about . . .

"I thought you said your folks came from an island south of here."

"Not to start with. That island used to be a prison for bad blackfellas from the mainland. The ones that wouldn't die quietly."

He almost spat at his boss, and Fogarty said, "Easy, Ian."

"Detribalised folk have short lives and shorter memories," Ian said, in distress. "They forgot where they came from."

"You reckon it was the Cape?"

"I thought one day, Limrock, that's a bloody odd name. I've never seen it on any but me relatives. I wondered if it was a translation of a Murri name. So I went to the record office—"

"And looked up the family gum tree!" crowed Fogarty.

Ian nodded. "Me old tribal ancestor, who went to the island in chains, was called Jacky Limnrock, L-I-M-N-R-O-C-K. I sat around with some of me family trying to work it out. Cousin of mine, she works in a library, said 'Limn' was an old whitefella word, meaning to paint. Jacky the rock-painter. And where could he come from but where there's the greatest collection of rock art in Queensland? All those big cliffs around here, they've got paintings on them."

He laughed.

"Funny, I didn't mean to come to the Mutie reserve, but it's slap in the middle of rock art country."

Fogarty thought of a swoop into a skinny valley, the glimpse of a painted snake.

"What a way to come home," said Ian, leaning back against the pillow, one black hand fiddling with the white bandage on the other. Then his eyes changed. It was not that the pupils dilated, or that he opened the lids wide; he did not move a muscle but Fogarty became suddenly aware that Ian was looking not at him but at something in the open doorway, a metre from his unprotected back. Fogarty twisted round, and whoever it was reached for the handle and slammed the door shut in his face. Bare feet ran away up the hospital corridor.

"Your first Mutie," said Ian.

Fogarty nodded, thinking of what he had seen, just for a second, with the corners of his eyes. There had been the white uniform of a hospital orderly, that was only to be expected, but the rest was not. The head and hands had been all—wrong.

"I saw him before," bragged Ian. "When I was coming out of the anaesthetic, a whole bunch stole in to look at me."

"Christ!"

"They're curious—natch."

"I got told the Muties wouldn't want to see the likes of us normal folk."

Ian pursed his lips. "Who said that?"

Fogarty told him about Doc Jon, and all that had happened since the flight.

"The Doc sounds interesting," said Ian. "Must have a chat to him, if he knows about the paintings."

"You do that, kid. Make the most of your time here. We'll swing around the Cape and be back for you when they've grown your fingers back on."

"Thanks," said Ian absently, from the look on his face thinking of the near future, and the far past.

To snap him back to the here and now, Fogarty said, "Eh, Ian, what did that orderly look like? What about the others you say, the delegation at your bedside."

"They look like—" began Ian, then stopped. "Never you mind."

One month later, Fogarty was sitting in his caravan, counting takings, and feeling pleased with himself. The Animal Show had travelled up the east side of Cape York and down the west side, skirting only Bamaga at the tip, where the twain met. The DNA virus had been released there and Fogarty thought it best to follow local practice and avoid it like the plague.

He took another swig of Weipa's poor attempt at gin, and began reading Dizzy's weekly Python report. It was always short—what could you say about a sated snake?—and as he came to the end a knock sounded at the door.

"Enter at your peril!" he yelled, expecting Eileen or someone else on the staff. There was a horrified pause, and Fogarty realised the person on the other side of the door was unaccustomed to his jokes. Then Doctor Jon Blackmore came boldly in.

"Oh hi," Fogarty said awkwardly. "Siddown and have a drink."

"No thanks. I'm flying later tonight."

"Shame. Well, what brings you to Weipa? Surely not to see dear little us."

Doc Jon's dark face twisted in a grimace. "No. The reserve got word of a mutant baby on an island north of here. When I arrived, everyone swore blind it had never existed, which means that it's been disposed of."

After saying that, he looked in need of a restorative, and Fogarty stroked the gin bottle, wondering whether to re-offer its contents to the visitor. Somebody had to drink the stuff. Then he pictured the little war surplus plane swatted like a mozzie against a rock wall and let the bottle go.

Doc Jon looked at him levelly.

"But I was looking for you as well."

"Wassamatter? Ian eating the reserve out of house and home?"

"Certainly not. He volunteered to help around the place, as a way of saying thanks. That flummoxed Admin—they didn't know what to do with Ian. But then he started taking the Muties out to see the rock paintings, and that fitted the guidelines for occupational therapy." He paused. "Ian even got the Muties copying the paintings."

"Yeah, he's good that way," said Fogarty. "Hempathic, that's the word. Nobody I ever had got on so well with the animals."

"Good with animals," Doc Jon repeated, and gave Fogarty an odd glance. "Well, the art classes were a great success, and Admin even got the idea of putting the Muties' work on the market."

"So what's the trouble?"

Doc Jon looked uncomfortable.

"Ian's been giving the Muties ideas."

"What sort of ideas?" asked Fogarty suspiciously.

The Doctor hesitated. "Murri ones. The Muties are treated as if the old Queensland Aboriginals and Islanders Act were still in force. It's okay to be paternalistic, because the poor brutes are sub-human. You see the similarity, if you're Murri."

"You saw it before Ian," said Fogarty. "But you'd never stick your neck out."

Doc Jon shrugged in reluctant agreement. "All right, I encouraged Ian, from atavism, and the ideal of Mutie rights. But it's gone beyond identification with the likes of Jacky Limnrock . . . too weird. I don't want to talk about it. The word is, Mr Fogarty, that you come and get Ian pronto."

"Hmn," said Fogarty. "Are the Muties rioting?"

"No."

"Not burning down the hospital or bashing out the bureaucrats' brains? Then there's no hurry. I'll keep to my schedule, thank you, and come when I damn well please."

The Animal Show still had a couple of communities to visit before the jaunt to North Queensland became cost-effective (or as Fogarty said to Eileen, "Before we've covered all the hicks").

"Admin won't like that answer," said Doc Jon.

"Tell them to get stuffed!"

Doc Jon laughed. "I'd love to. But seriously, Frank, don't leave it too long. See you soon."

"See you."

Fogarty knew that Ian could look after himself, and if he had the Muties on his side, so much the better. So it was two weeks before Fogarty's Animal Show turned off the main road and onto the dirt track leading to the reserve. The caravanserai blazed a big trail of dust which said "We're coming!" better than a smoke signal in the baby-blue sky. Given such notice of their arrival, Fogarty expected a red carpet, if not a firing squad, out to meet his show. But the only reception committee was Doc Jon, sitting alone on the hospital doorstep.

"Ian's not here," he said.

"This is getting to be a habit," said Fogarty. "They dispose of him, did they?"

Doc Jon winced.

"Kicked him out, three days ago."

"So where is he?"

The doctor opened his mouth to answer, but at that moment a louvred window clanked open behind him.

"Split Rock," said a husky distorted voice, and the louvers slammed shut again. The slats of glass were tinted against the tropical glare, and it was dim inside the hospital, but the white smock of an orderly could be glimpsed, in strips.

"Thanks a lot, Gideon," Doc Jon shouted over his shoulder. He turned back to Fogarty. "They're all his mates now."

He shut his mouth and simmered down.

"Split Rock is a painting site just outside the reserve. Ian's there with a bunch of Muties right now. Tell your crowd to wait, and I'll take you down in the staff jeep. It's not far."

"Hold on a mo'," said Fogarty, and dashed back to the first truck, opened a cage, and took out a certain something (warm and sleepy). He put it down the front of his shirt and rejoined Doc Jon, who had driven the jeep round to the front of the hospital.

"Ready to go," said Fogarty, and clambered aboard. The doctor stared at the bulge in his shirt, seemed about to ask a question, then put his energy into the accelerator. The jeep bolted down the road. There was a pierced strip of metal beneath the windscreen of the jeep, through which air gushed, cooled by its passage. It was a poor man's airconditioner, and Fogarty, refreshed, looked alertly round him.

The land demanded his attention. They were driving between sandstone bluffs like those of Serpent Dreaming Shelter, each with a sparse cover of blue-green trees on their lower slopes, then the steep exposed rock face, then a layer of trees again on the flat hilltop.

"Old wise hairy people, that's what they're like," said Fogarty.

"Are they?" said Doc Jon. "Look again."

Fogarty did as he was told, and after a moment nodded. There was nothing human about those hills, rather something else, as pervasive as the red of the road dust, the earth between the mesh of spindly trees and the cliffs themselves. He tried to think how to describe it, and after a while gave up.

"There's something about this place. You can't pin it down, because it's like words won't fit it."

"You can't anthropomorphise the land."

"What's that you said?"

"Anthro: man. Morph: form. We can't force our terms on this country. It won't let us."

They fell silent again, as the jeep neared a hill from which great chunks of rocks had straggled, in a line from just below the crest to mid-point. The landslide must have been ancient, for the rocks were well entrenched.

"This is Split Rock," the doctor said unnecessarily. He parked beneath the megaliths and started to get out.

Fogarty said, "No, wait here Doc. I'd like to see Ian on my lonesome."

The doctor sat back, looking as if he wished he had a good book handy. Fogarty got out of the jeep and stared up at a sixty-degree slope, with a little trail leading up it. He cursed, but started up the track, more climbing than walking.

He was just below the first of the giant rocks, when something moved in its shadow. Fogarty squinted and saw a wild black man, near-naked, with unkempt hair and a stubby beard.

It's the ghost of old Jacky Limnrock! Fogarty thought, then, that's my Ian. He waved, but the gesture froze on him. The other had given no sign of recognition, indeed was looking out over the valley as if Fogarty was invisible, as if there were no road there, no sign of the white gubba men, just the land as it had been since its formation in the Dreamtime.

Far below a jeep door slammed: Doc Jon was going for a walk. Fogarty started, slipped and sat heavily on the ground. He looked up to see Ian's eyes focused on him.

"Hi."

"Hi."

"What the hell have you got in your shirt?"

Fogarty stood up awkwardly. "Hold out your hand."

Ian did, displaying the scars at the base of his fingers, bright pink on the inside of his hand, charcoal outside. The doctors at the Mutie hospital had done a good job. Fogarty felt a very brief qualm, then put the Snakecatcher into that healed hand. Ian flinched, but the mongoose ran up his arm and sat on his shoulder, making long-time-no-see noises.

Fogarty swallowed. "Just checking to see if you still had your nerve."

"You white bastard," said Ian. He lifted the animal off his shoulder, gave it a hard look, then replaced it.

"Glad to see you Frank, I'm even glad to see Biter here."

He led Fogarty around the rock and there was a little camp, with a rubber mattress, a gallon drum half filled with water, and tins of food. Everything had an institutional look to it.

"The Muties been looking after me."

"So I see."

"They're up at the main painting site. You can't see it from here, there's a bloody big rock in the way."

He dipped a mug in the water, handed it to Fogarty, then filled one for himself. The Snakecatcher crawled down his arm and lapped delicately at the water.

Fogarty wiped his mouth. "Now, suppose you tell Uncle how you came to be camping out with Muties."

Ian stared into his cup.

"Doc Jon reckoned you'd been telling the Muties about the bad old days, sorta consciousness-raising."

Ian looked up.

"Bet he didn't tell you that was his idea. Then it misfired." He paused, frowning. "I was taking the Muties to the rock paintings, and telling them about massacres, which they just listened politely to. The old tribal legends they liked better."

"Ian, you ain't tribal."

"There's books of legends, written down by white blokes." He spat into the dust.

Fogarty changed the subject, fast. "What happened then?"

"The Muties found out what a"—he fumbled for the term—"totemic ancestor was. You see, in all the Dreamtime stories, the animals started as people. Then they . . . mutated. I'll show you."

He put down mug and mongoose and started towards the next rock, Fogarty following reluctantly. The old zoo man was not in the mood for climbing. Ian skirted around the monolith and there was a scuffling noise, muted panicky cries. A voice hissed, "Stranger!"

Fogarty stopped with a foot in mid-air. Ian answered, "It's only me old boss, he won't bite you."

The noise continued. "Frank, wait!" called Ian, then in a different tone, "Oh all right, run off then."

There was silence. For lack of anything else to do, Fogarty followed Ian's path to the rock. By the time he reached it he was panting heavily, and he leaned against the bulk for a moment. Then he followed the curve round, keeping one hand always against the monolith. Behind it, coming more into view with each slow step, was a very large fissured rock, shaped like a cube.

There seemed nothing remarkable in the sight, yet he felt unease, a creeping sense of intrusion. It was very quiet by the rock, the only sounds his breathing, and his boots against the hard-packed earth. At the edge of his eyesight he caught a sudden flurry, as if a Mutie dived into a welcome shadow. Ian, where are you? he nearly shouted aloud. Why'd you leave me alone in a creepy place like this? It was so hard to go on, with Ian out of sight, perhaps forever, but he forced his feet forward. One step, then another, and the whole of the rock was visible. One side was overhung and in its recess was vivid, sacred colour.

Layer upon layer of figures. Some were red, some ochre, some chalkwhite, some charcoal—and all were piled on top of each other as if Ian's people had more respect for that lump of sandstone than for their own artistry. It was like looking into a starry sky, that same feeling of time and clutter.

Fogarty, experiencing visual overload, glanced away and saw Ian standing among a number of small lengths of hardboard, slabs of masonite, even a sheet of bark. All had copies of the animal figures painted on them. Ian cocked his head at Fogarty and wandered through the open-air scriptorium, halting when he came to the rock face. He pointed at one of the greater magnitude figures, a squat shape in purple-black and white.

"Frank, what's this like?"

"Hmn. Echidna, alias Spiny Anteater. Seen from above."

Ian nodded. "Jacky Limnrock would call him Bulinmore. In the Dreamtime he was a man, who had no stone axe to cut a honey-bee nest from a hollow tree. He tried to borrow one from his tribe, but everyone said no. So in revenge Bulinmore drank the waterhole dry. The tribe asked him for water, they were thirsty, but he just grunted. Then they threw all their spears at him, and when he was dead, they cut him open and their water gushed out. The waterhole was filled again."

"Don't understand that story, Ian."

"Bulinmore had to keep wearing those spears, as a reminder to the Murri that they should share everything."

"Oh. Well, Ian, it's your culture."

"My secondhand culture, got from gub books," Ian said sadly.

Fogarty was looking at the figure of Bulinmore again.

"You said downhill that the Muties got interested in those animal stories."

"Yeah. They think they're going that way too, 'cept that they seem to be mutating by degrees rather than all at once."

"They think they're some kind of . . . whateveritwas?"

"Totemic ancestor. And if you look at them, there's something in it. I've seen Muties like snakes, lizards, turtles . . . "

"Kee-rist!" said Fogarty. "Do you believe that?"

"It happened before," said Ian.

Fogarty shut up and looked at his feet, rather than look at Ian. The dust around the shelter was deep, and pressed into it were many-shaped footprints, as if his Animal Show had been wandering loose up here. Just then, there was a scrabbling sound behind them and Fogarty turned, half-expecting a Mutie. But it was only Doc Jon who came round the rock, red and panting.

"Can't . . . you two . . . hurry up?"

"We're coming," said Fogarty. Ian had walked a little distance off, and stood looking away from them. The doctor sat down beside a masonite copy of Bulinmore and wiped his face.

"I heard the whole story," Fogarty said softly to him.

Doc Jon rolled his eyes in answer. He said nothing for a few minutes, regaining his breath, then got up and remarked, seemingly to the rock paintings, "I don't believe it was the virus. You did this!"

That was all he would say, and the two made their way down the hill, Ian following a distance behind. When they got to Ian's camp site, Doc Jon took a long drink from the drum and said, wet-mouthed, "The whole of your camp's reserve property. This could be construed as theft."

"You gonna charge the Muties?" said Ian. The doctor glared at him and for a moment they threw mental spears at each other. Fogarty frantically pondered some peace-making gesture.

"The Muties still like to see my animals?" he said.

"Of course," said Doc Jon, still looking at Ian.

"Well, you tell them, and your bosses, that in gratitude for the medical treatment Ian's had, it's freebie night at the show."

"Have it here," said Ian. "S'nicer than the reserve. There's a good flat space down in the valley." He pointed. "Everyone could walk out. I'd like to see Admin get some exercise."

The doctor laughed.

"Very well. I'll get the zoo to drive down. Anything else I can do?"

"No," said Fogarty. "Just come back to see the show, seven o'clock should give us time to set up."

"See you later, then," said Doc Jon, and headed down to the jeep. His departure raised a great sheet of dust from the road, which slowly drifted up to Split Rock.

"Did you hear that?" Ian shouted. He added to Fogarty, "For the painters. Rocks have ears in this place."

A handful of sandstone flakes landed at their feet.

"Message received," said Ian. "Frank, come down and take a look at the site."

They collected the mongoose, who was nosing among the tinned food, and slithered down the slope. As they crossed the road Fogarty said, "You and the Doc don't seem to like each other much."

"He's lovely," Ian said bitterly. "Half Uncle Tom, half anguished white liberal. He reminds me of the gub who said the Queensland Aboriginals and Islanders Act would 'smooth the pillow of the dying race'. They thought we were gunna die out. Well, we didn't, and neither will the Muties."

After some time a snake composed of caravans and trucks came into view, people leaning out of the windows of the head vehicle. Fogarty gazed at the angle of the sun.

"Bugger it! This show will be a real rush job!"

During the frantic work that followed, Fogarty did not give much attention to Split Rock. The tropical dusk came down like a shutter, and they worked on under lights. Once he glanced up and saw the red of a camp fire, as if the painting class were cooking tea. At least there was a breathing space, a little time to relax before the visitors from the reserve arrived.

Fogarty got up onto Eileen's flour bin.

"Ahem, may I have your attention? Shaddup! Okay gang, two things. First, a big hand for Ian, great to have you back again. Thanks. Thank you. Secondly, a few words about some of the people coming here tonight. They're Muties, and they don't look like you and me. But they're Ian's mates, and I want them to feel like very special guests. Got that?"

There was a general murmur, then a resounding, "Yeah!"

Fogarty jumped off the pedestal, with thoughts of his caravan and its liquor cabinet. Then he saw Ian walking towards the outskirts of the camp, carrying a torch.

"Where you going?" he called.

"To get the painters. They won't come down on their own."

"I'll keep you company."

Ian lowered the torch so that it shone into Fogarty's face.

"Frank, you near gave yourself a heart attack climbing up there last time."

"Well Ian, I'd sooner have that than you going up there and never coming back."

"Yeah?" said Ian, but they walked on together. Negotiating Split Rock by torch and starlight was not particularly easy, but they climbed up, following the path by touch more than anything else. As they went, they lost sight of the camp fire, for the first large rock blocked the view from below, the obscured flames giving it a red corona.

"Did you mean," said Ian, "that I'd go bush?"

"Maybe," panted Fogarty.

"Oh I was tempted, when I first came here. But that's over now."

They felt their way past the rock, and came to Ian's camp site. The fire burned in tatters from the night breeze, shining on silver metal, torn open jaggedly. The Muties had been feasting on the tinned food.

"They must be up at the shelter again," said Ian.

"Painting by torchlight," said Fogarty. "How dedicated."

Ian gave him a look that had knives in it, and Fogarty moved away, walking through the camp to the other side of the rock. He gazed down into the valley and for a moment he thought he had double vision, for the cluster of lights from the show appeared to have twinned. Then he distinguished the line of torches, yellow stars, winding along the road from the reserve. "Looks like the guests have arrived," he said.

Ian turned uphill and yelled, "They're here!" There were answering cries from the main painting site.

"Come on," said Ian to Fogarty. "Let's bring the painters down!" They scrambled up the slope, and around the great rock again, moving towards clamour. This time Fogarty was not afraid; he felt curious and excited.

Long branches had been ripped from the thin trees, set alight at the leafy end, and propped against the unadorned areas of rock. The red light shimmered and danced, and the ochres of the ancient paintings glowed back at it. Beyond the rock face was a swirl of movement, the strangest people.

A woman leapt, twisting her distorted body into the air, with a great inarticulate "Aagh!" of greeting. Her head was long and flattened, her features recessed, and although Fogarty could not be sure in this red flickering, her skin looked grey-green. She landed and bent to pick up a painting, with fingers that were clubbed at the tips. She hoisted the picture, grinning widely.

Beside her, another Mutie imitated the gesture, with difficulty, for he had short limbs and a squat round body. A figure waving a short length of flaming bough, hard to see because it moved so wildly, almost bowled this artist over. He staggered, but stood fast. Fogarty looked at the sheet of bark the Mutie held. It was a careful if naive copy of an image from the rock, also short-limbed and rounded. He searched among the jumble of the painted recess for the original and found it—a dark-red and white turtle. There were two copies of it before his eyes, one living and breathing.

Fogarty gazed at the Mutie woman, at her painting, then at the rock face again. She was a lizard. And the others in the firelight, staring at Fogarty warily yet with welcome, each corresponded to a figure painted on the rock wall. There was even a Bulinmore, lurking half in and half out of the shadows.

Fogarty turned towards Ian, and saw his face was expressionless, as if several emotions had cancelled each other. He said, "I found my roots, Frank. Fine new growth they've got."

THE QUEEN OF EREWHON

"Hey you! Story-eater! Devourer of lives! Leave us alone! GET OUT!

Those are the first sounds on the tape: Idris spitting at me, refusing to be interviewed. I wind on a little, until I hear a different voice—Sadry speaking.

Sadry: . . . ghosts. The house at Erewhon could have been full of them for all anyone knew, for there was only our family of three and the hired hands rattling around the building. Erewhon had followed the Rule for generations, not that I knew that. I was only a child, I think three. Things hadn't got explained to me yet. I had no idea how odd my upbringing was, for the High country, with only one father.

One night I thought I heard crying, so I got out of bed, curious. I wandered along the upstairs corridor which all the sleeping rooms led off. When I got a little older, I learnt why this space was called "Intrigue", in all the Rule houses. It kinks and curves, with crannies for people to hide and overhear—hence the name.

Me: A public space?

Sadry: Or a private one. I followed the sound to the outside wall, to a window with a recessed ledge. The shutters were closed and the winter curtains drawn, but between both was a space where someone might sit comfortably and that was from where the sound came. Now it sounded human, and female. I heard soft words, a male voice responding. Two people were hidden there! and curious, I stood and listened. But it was bitter frost weather, and rather than give myself away by teeth-chatter, I retreated until just round the corner I found a basket. It was filled with rags, either bought from Scavengers or our old clothes (Highlanders never throw anything away). So I climbed into it without making a sound, for it was an old Tech thing, of *perlastic*, rather than wicker. I curled up warmly in the contents and listened in comfort, not that I could understand much. Eventually I fell asleep, and woke in dawnlight to find my mother bending over me. And unthinkingly I blurted out the last words I had heard, which were: "I only want to be married to the one I love best, not all the others."

My mother said: "Where did you hear that?" and so I pointed at the ledge.

"The two lovers, there, last night."

She looked at me hard, then flung the curtain back. It wasn't me who screeched, it was her—at the sight of dust thick and undisturbed on the ledge. Then she scooped me up in her arms and went running down Intrigue, to the room she and my father shared, a small room, his younger son's room.

Idris: What did *he* do?

Sadry: Took us both into bed, calmed us down, for now I was hysterical too, and then very gently questioned me. What did the voices sound like? Could I imitate them? When I was as dry of information as a squeezed fruit, he said:

"It could have been any unhappy Queen of Erewhon."

And then he told me about living under the Rule, of his first wife, his brother, and their husband-lover.

Polyandry. The first time I heard the word I thought it a girl's name: *Polly Andree*. The misapprehension, though instantly corrected, stuck in my mind, so that I persistently thought of the woman at the centre of these group marriages as a Polly. And here I was in Polyandry Central, as anthropologists called it, the Highlands of Suff, and I still couldn't shake my personal terminology. It was a bad slip to make when trying to convince Bel Innkeeper to find me space, in a town already filled to bursting for the Assizes.

"We call them *Queens*," she said.

I'd listened to tapes of Suff accents but the actuality was something else, my comprehension of it being delayed, with embarrassing pauses at the ends of sentences. When I finally understood, I replied, too hastily:

"I know. Like bees."

All the while we had talked on the inn's back verandah a steady stream of fat brown bees had zoomed to and from some nearby hive, so this comment was both dead obvious and instantly regrettable.

Bel snorted. "You Northerners! Think you know everything, with your new-Tech ways! Ever seen a hive, ever seen a Rule House? No, that's why you're here, to find all about the funny Suffeners, isn't it?"

I said, carefully: "Okay, I'm what you call a story-eater, an anthropologist. But I can understand you've had a gutful of being studied and written up. I'm not here to sensationalize you, but to observe the court case."

Bel stopped folding the inn washing and gave me her undivided attention. "Why?"

"Because it's important."

"It's brought everyone down from the mountains and into this valley! How'm I supposed to house 'em all? And you, too."

She rocked on the balls of her feet, thinking. "Well, since you're here, I'd better be hospitable. And teach you about queen bees, too." She pointed at an outbuilding. "That's the honey-hut, and the one free space I've got. Take it or leave it!"

The hut was tiny: between pallet and beekeeping equipment there was barely any room for me. Above the bed was what I at first took to be a Tech photoimage, but it proved to be a window looking onto the mountains, made of the glass and wooden surround of a picture frame. In fact the whole building was constructed of scavenged oddments from the days of affluence: flattened tins, scraps of timber, and other usables slapped together in a crude but habitable mess. I was used to recycling, even in the neo-industrial North, but I had never seen such a higgledy-piggledy assortment before. It was to prove typical of much of the town itself.

I lay on the pallet and dozed for a while, lulled by the soporific hum from the nearby hives. When I woke, I tested my tape recorder—a precious thing, not because it was a genuine Tech artefact, but because it was a copy, its workings painstakingly rediscovered. Of course, it wasn't as good; nothing was, for we would never be as rich, nor as spendthrift, as our forebears. For over a century now, since the Crash, we had been adapting to an economy of scarcity. It was the adaptations, rather than the antiques, or the neo copies, that interested me—particularly the Rule Houses, and at their centre, the Queen Polly Andree. How would it feel, to have multiple husbands? And what would happen if you grew tired of them?

Sadry: My father said, "Nobody knows how the Rule began, just as nobody knows who bred the mountain Lori to be our herd animals. A Northerner, a story-eater, once told me the Rule was a pragmatic evolution, practiced by other mountain peoples. He said large populations cannot be sustained in marginal highland. One wife for several men—who are linked by blood, or ties of love—limits breeding, and means the family land can be passed undivided through the generations. It made sense; more than what the Lowlanders say, which is that we Highlanders deliberately chose complicated sex lives! Yet he spoke as if we were specimens, like a strain of Lori. That annoyed me, so I wouldn't give him what he had come for, which was my history.

When I was the age you are now, my brother Bryn and I were contracted to marry Nissa of Bulle, who would grow to be our wife and Queen of Erewhon. When I was twelve and Bryn fifteen—the same age as Nissa—we travelled to Bulle to "steal" our bride, as is custom. When we got back Erewhon celebrated with the biggest party I ever saw and afterwards Nissa spent the night with Bryn. I was too young to be a husband to her, though we would play knucklebones, or other children's games. That way Nissa and I grew friends, and then, after several years, husband and wife.

But we lived without passion, all three of us. So when love did strike Nissa and Bryn, it did like a thunderbolt. And the lightning cracked through this house, destroying nearly everybody within it.

Market day in the Highlands is a spectacle, even without the added excitement of an Assizes and a sensational lawsuit. I woke early, to the sounds of shouts, goods being trundled down the main street, the shrill cries of Lori. When I came downstairs, the meal area of the Inn was full. Bel was cutting buckwheat bread; she handed me a slice, spread with Lori butter, at the same time jerking her head at the open door. I took the hint and went outside.

Immediately I found myself in the middle of a herd of Lori, who assessed the stranger intelligently from under their black topknots, then parted and pattered around me. The animal was a miracle of genetic engineering, combining the best of sheep, llama and goat, but with three-toed feet causing less damage to mountain soils than hooves. Like the other Highland animals it was dark, resistant to skin cancer; a boon in an area cursed with thin ozone, even so long after the Crash. Various studies had posited that the Lori designer might have been the social architect who engineered the lives of Highlanders with the Rule. If so, I wondered why human genes had not been manipulated as well, given that these people had insufficient protective melanin, varying as they did from pale to brown.

Suffeners met by sunlight would be shrouded in the robes of Lori homespun that served all purposes, from formal to cold-weather wear, wide flax hats and the kohl that male and female daubed around their eyes in lieu of the precious Tech sunglasses. But inside, or under protective awnings such as those strung over the market square, hats would be doffed, robes flipped back like cloaks, displaying bare skin, gaudy underobes and the embroidered or beaded or tattooed emblems of the Highland Houses. It was a paradox: outwardly, dour puritanism; inwardly, carnival.

I stood on the fringes, observing the display of goods and people. Nobody in sight was armed, well not visibly, but I had read too many accounts of bloodshed and the consequent bloodprice not to sense the underlying menace in the marketplace. The most obvious source was the young men, who tended to ostentatious ornament, an in-your-face statement of aggressive sexual confidence. The women were less showy, but had an air of defensibility, as if being hard-bitten was a desirable female trait in the Highlands. Small wonder, I thought, recalling the mock kidnap in the marriage ceremony, and how common real raids had been until recently.

I felt a little too conspicuously a vistor, so bought a second-hand robe, the wool soft but smelly, and draped it over my shoulders. Thus partially disguised, I wandered among the stalls. A one-eyed man watched over Scavenged Tech rubbish, cans, wires, tires; a nursing mother examined the parchments of designs offered by the tattoist; a group of teenage boys, herders from their staffs, noisily tried on strings of beads; and two husky young men haggled over a tiny jar proffered for sale by an elderly woman. Hungry for overheard talk, information, I lingered by the tattoos, my interest not feigned, for I was particularly taken with one design, a serpent eating its own tail. Conversation ebbed around me, and I learnt the one-eyed Scavenger had found a new site, that the herders weren't impressed by the selection of beads, that the mother wished to mark that she now had children by all three of her husbands with a celebratory tattoo, and that the men were buying a philtre or aphrodisiac, for use on a third party. Now I was slipping into the flow of Suff speak, I quickly comprehended the old woman's spiel:

"If Celat had tried *my* potion on Erewhon, none of this would have happened."

All within earshot involuntarily glanced up at the bulk of the biggest building in the town, the Courthouse/lockup. I had, in my wanderings through the market, seen many emblems of greater or lesser Houses, a distinction the Highlanders made by the size of the landholdings. The signs were displayed on people and also the stalls, signalling the goods that were the specialties of each House. I had been making a mental checklist, and had noted two emblems unseen: the blue swirl of Erewhon, and the red swordblade of Celat. Those entitled to bear them currently resided within the lock-up, while the merits of their respective cases were decided. On the one hand, unlawful detention and threatened rape; on the other abduction, arson and murder. No wonder the town was packed.

Sadry: The place of graves at Erewhon is a birch grove and as we walked through it, hand in hand, my parents named each tree: "This is Bryn's, this Moli the trader's, by chance at Erewhon that night and for ever after". It was a peaceful spot, even with the new thicket of saplings, Nissa's work. I could believe that any ghost here would sleep and not walk—which was precisely why I had been brought there.

Idris: Nissa and her lover were buried in the snow, weren't they? Or at Bulle?

Sadry: I don't know . . .

[A clattering interruption at this point, the turnkeys bringing in that night's meal, the sound also coming from below, as the Celats, housed on the ground floor, were simultaneously fed]

Sadry: On that day, or one soon after, I saw above the birches a line of pack Lori winding their way down the mountainside. Their flags had the device of a bee: Westron, our nearest neighbours. And that proved to be the first of many visits from the local and not so local Houses.

Me: Including the Celats?

Sadry: *[nods]* The message would be always be the same: Erewhon has been decimated, and you need an alliance. That meant, me + whoever was the highest bidder. But my father said to all and sundry that they had made such offers before, when he was the sole survivor of Erewhon House. And had he not responded by a second marriage with a lowland woman, outside the Rule? I, as his only child and heiress of Erewhon, also should have the opportunity of making a choice, when I was old enough.

Me: They agreed to that?

Sadry: With grumbling, yes.

Ever since contact was re-established between North and Suff, nearly a century after the Crash, anthropologists had been fascinated by the Rule. Much of their interest was prurient, with accounts of giant beds for the Queen and her consorts (a lurid fantasy, given the Intrigue configuration). I had in my pack a report positing the mechanisms by which Highland men could apparently switch from het monogamy, albeit with a brother or brothers involved in the marriage; to bisex, when an additional unrelated male entered the House, a partner for both husbands and wife; to homosex, with the Queen relationship purely platonic. It was not exactly light reading, but I persisted with it, lying on the pallet, the hum of bees filling my ears. In the end the graphs and diagrams were too much for me, and I simply stared at the wall and thought.

On, for instance, how easily the complex relationships in a Rule marriage could turn nasty, Nissa of Erewhon being merely an extreme example. Yet divorce, with people "walking out and down", ie to the Lowlands or to join the itinerant traders, was uncommon. Highlanders had a vested interest in conciliation, in preserving the group marriages: that was why many houses contained Mediators, skilled negotiators. The ideal was embodied in a toy I had bought at the market, that little girls wore dangling from their belts: a lady-doll on a string, with a dependent number of men-dolls.

Why, I wondered, dandling the puppets, did sexual options not exist for women as well as men, with, say, linked girl-dolls? Were the Queens simply too busy with their men? Feeling frustrated I wandered outside and found Bel attending to the hives.

"Come see!" she said, and so I donned over my Highland robes the spare veil and gloves hanging behind the hut door. Bel had lifted the roof off a hive, and I stared over her black shoulder at the teeming mass of insects.

"I think I understand," I finally said, "why a hive is unlike a Rule House."

She nodded, invisible behind her veil. "Ever see a Hive where the drones bossed the show? Or without any other female bees? It would be impossible . . ."

"As a House with two Queens?" I finished.

She straightened, holding a comb-frame in her gloved hand, staring across the valley at the Courthouse roof.

"You're learning, story-eater."

Sadry: Highlanders say, when you die, you go downriver and that is what happened to me. My life at Erewhon with my parents, then my father only (after my mother went, as the Lowlanders say, underground) that is upriver to me. Everything since is the next life.

[She spoke with such intensity that I almost reached out and touched her, to bely the words]

I went out alone after a stray Lori, the best yearling we had. Our herders had given up searching and my father was ill in bed, but I stubbornly kept looking. Most likely the animal had drowned, so I followed the Lori paths along a stream raging with snowmelt. Almost at its junction with the great river that runs from Erewhon to the lowlands, I saw a patch of colour in an large thornbush overhanging the torrent: a drowned bird, swept downstream until it had caught in the thorns. But though it was shaped like the black finches of the Highlands, the feathers were white-gold-red: a throwback to the days before the hole in the sky opened. I wanted the feathers for ornament, so leant on the thornbush, to better reach out—but the bank collapsed beneath me.

The water wasn't deep and the bush cartwheeled in its flow, taking me, my robes entangled in the branches, into the great river. Up and down I was ducked, alternately breathing and drowning, torn by thorns, or dashed against riverstones. All I could do was grab at air when I could . . .

[She paused and I again noted the fine white lines on her exposed skin, a tracery of thornmarks. Worst was the scar tissue in the palm of one hand, where she must have clutched at the bush despite the pain, in the process defacing and almost obscuring her birth marker, the Erewhon tattoo.]

I think miles went by, hours—for the next thing I recall was the evening moon. I gazed up at it, slowly comprehending that I lay still, out of the helter-skelter race of the river, and that something wet and sluggish held me fast. From the taste of silt in my mouth I knew that the bush had stuck in the mudflats where the river widens. In the moonlight I saw solid land, shoreline, but when I tried to struggle towards it I found I had no strength left. But I lived! and surely my fathers' herders would soon find me.

Idris: You'd forgotten . . .

Sadry: On whose land the mudflats were. So I shivered through that night, until the morning sun warmed me. I had no protection against it, so covered my face with all I had, which was mud. Then I waited for help.

Idris: The next bit is my story . . .

Sadry: [laughing] Tell it, then.

Idris: The river had lately brought we Celats a fine young Lori, fresh-drowned. So in hopes of further luck, I scavenged in the mudflats again. The bush sticking up like a cage, I noticed that first. Next I saw a faint movement like a crab, a human hand, then eyes looking at me out of the mud. I had to use the pack Lori to drag her out, she was stuck so fast, half-dead as she was. And the bird too, the one that had brought her to me, I found that when I washed the mud from her robes."

[She pulled from beneath her underobe a thong, pendant from it a love-charm fashioned from tiny feathers, white-gold-red. Sadry almost simultaneously revealed a duplicate charm. I wondered again at the mixture of toughness and sentimentality of the Highlanders, then at the strength of this pair, one to survive near death from drowning and then exposure, the other to save her... In my cosy north, teenage girls are babies, but these two had a life's hard experience.]

In the courtroom, they looked tiny, my quarry, against the black-clad might of the Highland Rule. The tribunal hearing this case consisted of a Judge from Chuch, the Suff capitol, a Northern Government representative, and the only empowered woman in sight, Conye of Westron. This Queen had been the subject of a classic study, so I knew her story well— but still boggled at the fact that this dignified old lady with the multiple tattoes had seven husbands.

I bent towards Bel, sitting beside me in the public gallery. "Now *she* is like the Queen of a Hive!" I murmured.

"Only because she outlived all her drones!" Bel replied.

Around us, Suffeners commented too, court etiquette permitting this background buzz, along with eating and the nursing of babies or pets.

"—I ain't disrespecting new dead, but old Erewhon was mad to say no to Westron—"

"—had a bellyful of the Rule, hadn't he—"

"—but risking all that House lore being lost—"

"Excuse me," said a male voice, from behind me. "You're the anthropologist?"

I turned to see a fellow Northerner, nervously holding out an ID. It read: Fowlds, journalist.

"I'm normally posted in Chuch, so I can't make head or tail of this mountain law," he said.

"And you'd like an interpreter? Meet Bel!"

The Innkeeper grinned, speaking slowly and precisely:

"The two girls in that dock are one party; the two men another. They tell their stories, and the judges decide who are to be believed."

"Ah," he said. "And who is likely to be credible?"

Around us Suffeners sucked sweets and eavesdropped happily.

"Well," said Bel, "on the one hand we have a House wealthy and respected, but eccentric—maybe to the point of having gone just too far. That's Sadry of Erewhon, second generation Rule-breaker. On the other hand, Idye and Mors of Celat, a lesser House. Now they are Scavengers, but once Celat were mercenaries, hired trouble, before your North outlawed feuding."

It had been a condition of autonomy, I recalled, which had incidentally obviated the need to have a concentration of fighting men in the fortified Houses. And thus the need to create bonds between them, a prime function of the Rule?

"But the other girl is Idris of Celat? What is she doing with Erewhon?"

"That's what the tribunal is trying to establish," said Bel, as thunderous drumrolls sounded through the court, signalling the formal start of proceedings.

Sadry: I knew that somebody found me, but merely thought I had crossed into downriver, this life revisited, with a ghost Lori carrying me on its back to a ghost House. Somebody washed me and bandaged my cuts—I asked her if she was an angel spirit, but she only laughed. I slept, ate buckwheat mush when it was spooned into my mouth, slept again. The next time I woke, the room seemed full of men, all staring at me.

"Idris, do you know who she is?" said one, in a voice soft and smooth as a stroked cat.

"How could I?" said the angel.

"She looks like rotting bait," said another, so big and hairy I thought him an ogre.

"Idris, has she been instructing you how to treat her wounds?" asked the first.

Mutinous silence. Of course I had, for sick as I was, I was still an Erewhon healer.

"Only one way to find out!" said the third, twin of the second, but clearly the leader. He unwrapped the bandage on my right hand, to reveal the palm, which he inspected closely, picking at the scab with his nails.

"Blue! The missing heir of Erewhon!"

Big hands lifted the pallet, carrying it and me out the door and along the Intrigue space. Somewhere along the way my raw hand struck rough stonewall, and a red haze of pain washed over me. Even the jolt as the pallet met floor again, in a larger room, I barely noticed.

"Where's that girl? Idris?"

"Here!"—but spoken as if through clenched teeth.

"Get her good and better, and soon, okay?"

And with that they left. The pain had cleared my head: now I could see that the angel crying as she re-bandaged my hand was only a girl my age, in a room too stuffed with Scavengers' rubbish to be ghostly.

"Which House is this?" I asked, after a while.

"Celat."

"Oh," I said. "Trouble."

"The thugs were Idye and Iain, my brothers; the smoothie Mors, Mediator of this House, and their lover."

"No Queen?" I asked, trying to recall what I knew of Celat.

"This is her room."

Idris stared into my face, as if expecting a reaction. Something was wrong, I could tell that.

She sighed, and added: "Our mother is years downriver." Her words and tone were like a trail, down which I chased a hunting beast.

"We've been too poor and disreputable for any marrying since."

The trail was warm now, and I guessed what I would find at the end of it would be unpleasant.

"Until you came along," Idris finished. "That's why they moved the bed. Don't you understand? They want you for Queen of Celat *and* Erewhon."

Indeed, an ogre with three male heads, ferocious game. I knew I had to fight it, or marry it, but how? More thinking aloud than anything else, I said:

"I'd sooner marry you!"

Idris: *[triumphantly]* "And I said: Do you mean that? Do you really mean that?"

The hearing began with a reading of the various charges and counter-charges, then a series of witnesses appeared. I began to get a sense of Suff law, as the bare bones of the case, what was not disputed by either side, was established. But the mix of ritual and informality in the proceedings disconcerted me, as when Bel waved wildly at some witnesses, a married trio from Greym House. They waved back, before resuming their evidence: that they, being river fishers, had found a hat with blue ties in their net.

"At least there's no argument she fell in the water," Fowlds commented.

Mors of Celat rose and bowed at the judges. I thought him a personable young buck, not as loutish as Idye beside him, with a feline, glossy look—if you liked that sort of thing. An answer to a virgin's prayers? Not from the look of black hatred that passed between him and the two girls.

"Can he address the court? I mean, he's an accused," Fowlds murmured.

Bel had gone rushing out of the gallery, leaving me to interpret as best I could.

"As a Mediator Mors is privileged to argue points of law."

"They're marriage counsellors, right?"

"Among other things," I said. "Things get fraught, you need someone like that. Otherwise you might end up like Nissa's Erewhon."

"Oh, the case people keep on mentioning," he said.

"They're similar, that's why."

"But wasn't that a mass poisoning . . ." he began, but I shushed him as Mors began to speak.

"I bring the attention of this court to the law of the Scavengers . . ."

"Cheeky beggar!" somebody muttered.

"Huh?" said Fowlds. I was feeling confused myself.

"Er, I believe it's basicallly finder's keepers."

"But it's not been applied to living humans since feuding days," Bel finished, from behind my shoulder.

"But there's a precedent?"

"Oh yes. Oh my!"

Idris had leapt up, shouting:

"I found Sadry, so she's mine! Not yours, not anybody else's."

Conye of Westron rose, and moving effortlessly despite her age, placed herself between the pair, her arms stretched out, invoking quiet.

"Another Mediator," said Bel. "She'll adjourn the court now, and let people cool off. It's getting late, so I guess they'll call it a day."

"See you in court tomorrow, then," said Fowlds. He bent towards me. "You're an anthropologist, so is it true that these mountain guys are hot trots?"

"Why don't you find out?" I said.

"Oh I will!"—and he wandered away.

Bel said: "Come and meet a non-bee Queen."

Sadry: Idris' brothers left us alone, but Mors would bring some small comfort, like fresh milk, sit on the end of the pallet, and talk, playing mediator.

Idris: The thin part of the wedge.

Sadry: The thick part being your brothers. I put no trust in him, but he was too engaging for me to keep sulking. It became a game, to talk and parry his flirtation. That way courtship lay, I knew.

I asked: "What brought you to Celat?" and he looked rueful: "Love. Or a potion. Or perhaps both."

Idris: [sarcastic] "Men are such romantics."

I said: "And you've stayed here?"—looking pointedly around the Scavengers' mess.

He said: "I mediate when Idye and Iain get into trouble."

"Like now?" I said.

He sighed. "This wasn't my idea. But as a challenge, I find it—seductive."

"As opposed to rape?"

He said, lightly: "You know that is the last resort."

I must have gone white, for he added: "But that would mean I'd failed. And I'd hate that."

When he had gone, I said to Idris:

"I suppose he's not too bad."

On the wall hung the one precious thing I had seen in Celat, a Tech mirror. Idris abruptly lifted it down and set it on my chest, holding it with both hands, so all I could see was my scratched face.

"You think, you really think pretty Mors courts you for love, when you look, as Idye charmingly said, like rotten bait!"

"No," I said, sobered. She touched my cheekbones.

"I can see under the surface, but *they* can't. That protects you for the moment. But when you heal . . ."

I said: "Get word to my father!"

She hesitated, before replying: "Mors came from the market with the news your father's dead. Of sickness or worry, they say. And so Erewhon is vacant and everyone's looking for you."

I cried at that, and she kissed away my tears. After a while I said:

"Then we must get out of here all by ourselves."

The Queen proved to be the fisher-girl from Greym, whom we found, together with her husbands, in Bel's private attic rooms. The trio were replete with honeycake and a keg of the weak Highland beer. Close to they seemed painfully young, in their mid-teens at most, the two obvious brothers and the girl touchingly in love with each other. Bel introduced them as Milas and Meren and Jossy, saying of the latter:

"Pregnant, she tells me, but she won't say by whom . . ."

Jossy grinned with gap-toothed embarrassment. The boys were more forthcoming:

"Aw, she's just kiddin' you, Cos."

Indeed, I thought, the Rule was strict regarding sexual access, precisely to prevent squabbles over paternity. Then I did a delayed doubletake at the last word spoken. Cos meant *cousin*...

I stared at Bel. "I thought you were a lowlander."

"Not always," she said. "Once I could have been a Queen."

Milas coughed. "Aw, that's old history now."

I was starting to catch on. "You walked out and down from Greym? Why?"

Bel replied with a question. "You like men?" she said, looking at Jossy. "You like lots of sex with men?"

Jossy giggled; the boys exchanged glances, tolerant of their eccentric relative.

"I'll take that as a yes," Bel said. Then, more to me: "But if you don't, then there's no sense living in misery. I had a pretty young cousin, who would never question the Rule. So I gave my husbands to her."

"Our mam," said the boys proudly.

"These are her twins. I had no children, so I walked free."

She smiled at them, on her face the lines of a hard life, lived good-naturedly and without regret.

"What did you do?" I asked.

"Came down to the village and this Inn, where I asked for work as a kitchenhand, anything. And here I stayed, with Bel, who owned the Inn. When she went underground, I took her name and carried on the business."

She poured out more beer, and sliced the remaining cake. As she did, I noticed a tattoo extending from the palm of her hand to the wrist: an oval enclosing two stylized bees, under a gabled roof.

"Two Queens in a House?" I asked softly, as she passed me the cake.

"No," she replied, "Two worker bees in their Inn."

I took her hand, to better examine the device, and then noticed the pigment of one bee was faded, and that it was drawn differently from the other. It also looked vaguely familiar—and I whistled softly as I recognized a birth marker, the bee of Westron modified into an emblem that was all Bel's own.

"With your bee-skills, I should have guessed you were born at Westron."

I released her hand.

"As you're a relative, I wonder if you might get me an interview with Queen Conye. She's an interesting woman."

A guarded nod. Press on, I thought.

"I'd like that," I said. "Almost as much as I'd like to talk to Sadry and Idris."

"Easier said than done," she said.

"Well, yes."

"Conye's cranky on me, for letting the House down." She paused, and what she said next nearly floored me. "But I can get you into the lockup." She turned to the Greym three: "And you didn't hear that, did you?"

"No, Cos," muttered one of the boys, and I began to realise the powers of this extraordinary woman.

Sadry: "Erewhon's symbol is a blue swirl, the river of life, for it is knowledge of illness that is the strength of our House, just as Dusse has botany, herbalism, and Westron the secret of mead.

[I nodded, thinking that it was as if when setting up the Rule someone had determined that the precious Tech knowledge and goods be apportioned equally between Houses]

Sadry: In our cellars, cut deep into the mountainside, we hoard the artefacts of Tech medicine.

Me: I heard you had a pharmacopeia.

Sadry: Yes, a book of the coloured beads that the Tech people didn't wear but ate, to keep themselves well. That we salvaged ourselves, other books the Scavengers bring us. Our oldest book, though, isn't medical—it's called Erewhon, but it's not about my House, but a dream, a nowhere place. In this book things are reversed: the sick are criminals, and the criminals regarded as ill.

Idris: Are we criminal, or ill?

Bel: Both, probably, in the eyes of the men.

Sadry: The book-Erewhon seemed strange, but not much stranger than the Rule. Or the way I would live in my home, with Idris, if the court permits us.

[I thought, but did not say, that while Bel could live in the Lowlands, a happy impossibility in Highland terms, two Queens in the same mountain House was probably intolerable for the Rule-followers. Sadry was Queen of Erewhon by inheritance, but if this case went against her she could end up Queen of Nowhere.]

The Greym three had had a big, exciting day and they drooped like flowers with the dusk. Bel brought them blankets, letting them doze on her private floorspace. After she blew out the candles (Highland style, of rush and tallow), we two retired to the downstairs bar, where she ejected the last drinkers. Now we had the place to ourselves I wanted to interview this runaway Queen, but instead Bel went out. Alone, I stretched out on the hearthrug and watched the fire, thinking of the Houses and their troubles. As I lay there, unbidden came to mind the memory of an interview tape I had once heard, with an anonymous woman of Bulle.

Bulle woman: "The Rule is: share and share body alike in marriage. That's why Queens seldom have a night to themselves once they wed. It's best if you're stolen by brothers, because they're like beans in the pod, so you treat them the same. But if you've got one you like less, or one you love most . . . that means trouble. Poor silly Nissa!"

Interviewer: It was the lover that was the problem, wasn't it?

Bulle woman: His name was Yeny. I met him once, and wasn't surprised that Bryn Erewhon was head over heels, why he brought him into the marriage. The trouble was Nissa fell for Yeny too, and she wanted him all for herself, like a Lowlander. The sensible thing would have been to let those two walk out and down, but Bryn was stubborn, I guess, like Erewhoners are. He called in a Mediator, but that didn't work. So Nissa took the matters into her own hands."

Slowly, imperceptibly, I slipped into dream-sleep, images appearing and disappearing before my slitted eyes. First I saw the blue sign of Erewhon, the river twisting into a figure eight, an infinity symbol, then the self-devouring serpent I had admired at the tattooist's. A log collapsed in the fireplace, and I opened and closed one eye, importing the flamescape into my dream, for now I flew above red mountains. Below my eagle-I were Houses, and I zoomed in and somehow through the thatch roof of Erewhon, to see Nissa (who looked amazingly like Sadry) zig-zagging through Intrigue. She went down a flight of stone steps to the courtyard where a Scavenger waited with goods for identification and sale: sheets of dirty foil, on one side covered with symmetrical white studs. The dream-watcher followed Nissa into the cellars, where she consulted a tattered book. When she came out again, she paid the Scavenger, and tucked the drugs into her underrobes.

I felt her cold hand—then realised it was Bel, shaking me awake.

"Come on! I've bribed you an hour's talk!"

"Wh . . . ?" I started to say, then received a spare robe full in the face, and with it the realisation of where we were going.

"Hurry! Wrap yourself up!" she said.

Doubly shrouded we slipped into the darkness of the street, the mountain air chill even in summer. The village at first seemed asleep, with the mountains looming over it as if over a cradle, the gleam of snow at their peaks like watchful eyes. But as we moved swift and silent as Loris, I noticed cracks of light under shutters, heard babies' cries or soft talk, and saw distantly, in the gap between two buildings, a group of men carousing around a bonfire, among them Fowlds.

"He'll get slipped a philtre and good and proper fucked," Bel commented.

"That's what he wants," I said.

After what seemed an age Bel finally led me into a dark doorway I slowly realised was a back entrance to the Courthouse. Inside, someone waited for us, their robe thrown completely over their head, almost like Bel beekeeping. The apparition led us up stairs of scavenged Tech concrete to the second floor, where a door was unlocked for us, then locked behind us.

Sadry was awake, spinning Lori wool on a spindle, the Highland cure for fidgets, or using up time. I could see for the first time her scars, and her composed, indeed, queenly mien. Idris slept, her head on Sadry's knee; she stirred as we approached, knuckling her eyes. For a long moment there was silence, before Bel fumbled under her robe and produced delicacies: fresh Lori cheese, fruit, cured meat.

"Greetings Bel Innkeeper, greetings Northerner," Sadry said, her voice neutral as she accepted the gifts.

I had nothing to offer, but nonetheless pulled out my tape recorder from under my robes. Idris goggled at the device, then said to Sadry:

"What, our words to be set down and used against us?"

"For an interview," I said, alarmed, "It's standard practice."

"I didn't agree to a Tech toy," Sadry said. She looked at Bel. "Your intermediary never mentioned it . . ."

Idris reached forward, as if to snatch away the device, and I clutched it, inadvertently activating Record. She spoke, her voice a snarl, rising . . . until Bel clapped a hand over her mouth.

"Hush," she said. "Would you wake the guards? When the Northerner is like me, and like you!"

Idris' eyes rolled.

I said, my voice trembling, now I was so near to my goal, and yet not there yet: "I . . . we . . . my friends . . . we monitor . . . looking for . . . breakers of the rules . . . even in such a male-dominated society . . . you see, it's so important that you exist, we need a record . . . of women loving women . . . that's why I want your story!"

The gaze of these two girl lovers met, considering my plea.

I started the interview story-eater style, using the polite Highland opener of recounting my latest dream. One dream demands another, and so Sadry responded with her ghost story, continuing the theme of Nissa, which recurred as if haunting the conversation:

Sadry: My father said he got sick of it, Bryn moping, Nissa storming, and Yeny in the middle (who was not *his* lover) unable to make up his mind. So he went off herding . . .

Idris: It saved him from a dose of worm-cure!

[I thought of my dream again. If Bel had not shaken me awake, I possibly might have continued the dream, with Nissa-Sadry one snowy night serving her in-laws a Bulle herbal remedy, but combined with what from the pharmacopeic texts in the library she knew to be sleeping pills. Presumably she wanted everyone in the House to sleep long enough for she and her lover to elope.

*Murder meant feuding, and mass murder surely a civil war. Her
bad luck then, or her curse, as the Highlanders said, that the pills
were contaminated, or when combined with the herbs, toxic. Ten
people died at Erewhon, two more when Nissa's flight ended in an
avalanche—incidentally saving, as the Bulle woman had noted,
that House from a ruinous bloodprice]*

Me: What saved Mors?

*[They eyed me. This I knew was the nub of the case, whether
the story of Nissa had repeated with Sadry.]*

Idris: He was called away to Mediate, in a dispute over some
Lori.

Me: And with only two men left in the house, you acted.

Idris: They got drunk as pigs.

Me: On pissweak Highland beer?

Idris *[defensively]*: Maybe they had mead.

Me: That's a luxury. You said Celat was poor.

Sadry: What is this? An interview or an interrogation?

Bel: It will help you! And you need help.

[Long pause]

Me: What happened?

Idris: I cooked for my brothers that night, and then went
upstairs with sop for Sadry. We could hear roistering below, and
I barred the door of the Queen's room with what I could find and
move . . . without Mors to mediate, Sadry wasn't safe.

Sadry: The House went quiet.

Idris: I went down to see what was going on, and found my
brother Iain passed out at the table. Idye was the same, sprawled
in the courtyard. Without losing a moment, I went out to the field
where our two best and biggest Lori grazed. I brought them into
the courtyard, found halters and saddlecloths, then tied them by
the door, while I went into the house for my queen.

Sadry: I could barely walk, so she near carried me downstairs,
and got me onto the Lori.

Idris: I went upstairs to get extra robes against the night air, but
having a sudden idea, grabbed rags, and a haybale I had been using
to re-stuff a pallet. With them I formed a mock Sadry under the
blanket in the Queen's room.

Sadry: That done, just like that! we stole away into the darkness,
heading for Erewhon.

Idris: [hesitant] We don't know what happened next.

Me: I hear Idye was too drunk to remember a thing.

Idris: I was right to take her! Iain went into the Queen's room!

Me: He was fuddled.

Sadry; He meant harm.

Idris: But in igniting the dummy Queen, he harmed nobody but himself.

Me: And the House.

[I thought again of the Inn fire, of the log imploding in a shower of sparks. Celat House and its flammable rubbish had burnt like Bel's kindling, leaving ashes—in which Mors and a party from a neighboring House had found the charred form of Iain, a metal candleholder and long-bladed hunting knife by his side. Idye had survived, simply because he had slumped in the courtyard, out of the flame's reach.]

Sadry: We defended ourselves.

Me: I understand that, but to the extent of doing a Nissa?

Idris: That is for the court to decide.

Bel: We should stop now. The guard's shift ends soon, and I could only afford one bribe!

And she turned the recorder off. End of conversation, with the two defendants, but not with Bel, for when we got back to the Inn she stoked the fire and poured out beer for us.

I took a couple of mouthfuls, and said: "This stuff really is feeble. I reckon Idris nobbled her brothers' beer!"

Bel shrugged. "All the village thinks so, but with what?"

Now it was my turn to shrug. "I've seen a pharmacopoeia book in a museum. It described everything the Tech culture took for their ailments. So, if something drastically increased the effects of alcohol, Sadry would have known it and told Idris."

Bel pulled off her outer layer of robe. "Maybe."

"But how did they get hold of it?" I wondered.

"The House was full of Scavenged goods, remember?"

"Good point. Anything could have been stored there." I rolled out on the rug again, watching flames.

Bel hunkered down beside me. "Well, if we are play judges, and have solved the mystery, what do we do now, given the important difference between this case and Nissa's? Idris and Sadry survived, and that means they are answerable for bloodprice."

"Even for an accidental death," I replied, with a sinking feeling.

"And the fracticide makes it worse. Not to mention burning the House, and stealing Idris, the one thing Celat had to barter on the marriage market."

I supped more beer. "Extenuating circumstances. Sadry escaped enforced marriage."

"But she also broke the Rule."

"Into little pieces," I finished, putting down the mug. "They don't stand much of a chance, do they?"

Bel put her hand on my shoulder. "That was why I took you to the lockup, to collect their story, and disseminate it over the North."

I turned, and her grip grew firmer, kneading me.

"And, because I wanted you to be grateful to me."

I laughed and quoted Idris: "'Do you mean that? Do you really mean that?'"

I had come to the mountains a detached, dispassionate observer, with a story to eat. But, almost despite myself, the case study of Sadry and Idris, and the other like-minded women of the Highlands had come to involve me. Taking Bel's hand in mine, I touched her bees and felt them slightly raised—a cicatrice. Tonight, we would play Queens of the Inn, and the two bees would crawl all over my skin. And tomorrow, to celebrate, I would go to the market tattooist and mark myself with the snake—for now this mountain herstory was part of me, and I was a serpent eating my own tale.

RUNAWAYS

"10, 9, 8 . . ."

Counting down the New Year is always something special for us Runaways. We have a big bbq, the whole of the family staying up till midnight, even the babies. However, we don't hold our New Year's parties at anybody's house, but out in the open, in the hill country, because that's our home, every stone of it. And we don't recognise new-fangled calendars like the Julian, or the Chinese, because we have our own New Year's day.

"7, 6 . . ."

Great-Gran Mowra stood on a big stump, leading the countdown. We had the lookout and its picnic ground to ourselves, just like we wanted it. The sheer volume of music coming from the boom boxes, the sight of the beat-up utes and the milling crowd of Runaways, in plaid shirts, jeans, barefoot, or in moccs, showing their (missing a few) teeth and tatts, with dogs and kids running riot, the general message being don't-you-mess-with-us . . . well that scares others away. Nobody wants to picnic with trailer trash, nobody looks too closely at trailer trash. It's useful camouflage.

"5, 4, 3 . . ."

To one side the kids were ready with the home-made firecrackers. Just in case, I took a firm hold of the rope that held the Handies, though they should be used to fireworks by now, with all the training I'd given them.

"2, 1!"

The night exploded with light, dogs barking and Runaways from all generations yelling at the top of their voices. The rope jerked a couple of times—Dimmey, of course—and then was still. We kept up the pandemonium as long as we felt like it, and then Great-Gran Mowra waved for silence.

"Ahem," she said. "Now for the Runaway family's New Year's resolution."

She paused, as if listening, although the only sound was the crackling of the flames, the wind in the trees, a soft Handie snort.

"Well!" she said. "Tough times, indeed, at the mo'. From the news you'd believe the end of the world was coming, or maybe just the end of *their* blessed economy. We've got trouble to either side of us, just like the days of the river family and the plains family all over again. Under the circumstances, the resolution has to be . . . the same as ever. Lie low, prosper discreetly and above all, *survive!*"

The family cheered, every one of us. We weren't expecting anything different, just the Runaway family 40,000-year-old plan, but it was always nice to hear it again.

And with that, the celebration was over. We Runaways had work to do, some of us, and the rest needed our sleep. The boom boxes were switched off, the fire doused, dogs, kids, oldies packed into utes and vans, and we gradually and quietly disappeared into the night. We Runaways are good at disappearing, running away, that's how we got the name.

I sat, holding onto the rope and saying goodbyes. When I was the last Runaway at the picnic ground, I stood up, and whistled: Work time!

Six large pairs of eyes reflected the moon's full light back at me, six pairs of ears pricked. I had prepared earlier, for the night's run, and each Handie carried a pack. I fixed the rope to my harness and said:

"Hey ho, let's go!"

There was silence all around, apart from the sound of Uncle Tich's muffler, a receding roar. The nearest non-Runaways were ks away and there was nobody to witness a slightly rough looking citizen leading—how cute!—six shetland ponies into the bush.

And immediately down a steep incline, enough to make any watcher think their eyes had been playing tricks, and that they'd mistaken the ponies for shaggy and agile mountain goats.

The bush is full of tracks, if you've got the right knowledge. Go off the dirt or macadam and you'll find the roads for the creatures of the bush—wombat, wallaby and the Runaway family. Some, like the wombats, are well-marked, like the tracks of a mini-tank, if a tank left square turds behind. Others, well, they're invisible unless you're a Runaway. We can follow them with our eyes closed. It's like an old and much loved tatt—you can follow the curves of it around in your mind without looking at or touching it. Don't ask me how. If I live long enough to be an Elder, then one day Mowra'll tell me.

Some of the Runaway tracks lead to secret places, plantations and workshops for small illegal things. Couple of the Great-Uncles dig for gold somewhere down that left fork and over the hill; I've seen another uncle, who's got a sideline in seasonal produce, wild magic mushrooms, on that track sometimes. But if you take the right fork for five k or so, and climb over the fence to the water catchment area, that's where the younger cousins grow their ganja crop. But if anyone's snooping, it's for private use only, Mr Officer sir! Mr Mafia sir! We Runaways always stay on the good side of the powers that be, official or not.

"Lie low, prosper discreetly and above all, *survive!*" It was a good motto, dreamed up who-knows-when, when the Runaway family first found themselves in the hills, squeezed between larger, fiercer families—what the anthropology types would call tribes—on richer, more attractive chunks of land. So we made do, adapting anything that came along to our use. If that meant trade goods, fine, if that meant the occasional couple from another family, eloping in a wrongheaded marriage, fine—we don't mind new blood! If that meant runaways pale like blossom and wearing bracelets hard as meteor stone, walking to some place they called 'China' . . . well, they too joined the family, and shared what they knew with us.

Course, things got tough when the rest of the Blossom family arrived with their suitcases, chattels and guns. However, we were on land nobody saw much value in but us (unlike the land of the poor old plain and river families). So we learned a lot of new skills in a hurry, lied a lot (specially to the missionaries), and stayed around the hill country. When it became a problem that we weren't pale in colour, we found Blossom family members who had the Runaway sort of attitude, and *intermingled* with them. Now, couple of centuries and a lot of sex later, we were olive-coloured, with skinnier legs and darker eyes than the norm. But nothing anyone could get personal about.

Next fork in the path I went left, following a thread of track along the side of a hill, the Handies padding behind me. This was an old, old route, where Runaways went carrying goods to trade with the other families. Some things don't change—it's just the goods and the value put on them that does. Once a shell from the distant seashore was worth its weight in . . . something or other. Now a shell was worth nothing much; I carried gold dust, mushrooms, ganja, and other stuff, valuable to various people. Call me a courier, call me a black marketeer, call me a smuggler, if you must. Just don't call me girlie . . .

In a gum tree just above, a possum let out a territorial roar. Hi, fellow Survivor! I thought, then, Ohshit! From behind me came a fearful whinny, then a frantic scrabbling. I turned to see the line of Handies kinked: the second last Handie was half on, half off the path, and teetering.

Dimmey! Might have known it. When Aunt Gidj had passed on the Handies to me, I'd assumed the naming, which tended to simple descriptors: Sturdy, Shagpile, etc. Most folk couldn't tell the Handies apart, but I could see the subtle differences, in looks and personality. All of them had sound horsesense or better, except for one. Dimmey was trouble, which nearly became his name with a capital T, until I decided he was just Dim. Anything that could go wrong, would, if he was involved. Now the Handie on either side was supporting his weight, stopping him from sliding any further down the hillside.

The rope was Smart, being liberated from a bungy-jumping business in one of the gorges. It had all sorts of interesting properties, but hadn't been made with sheer brute Dimness in mind. Worse, there was no room for me to edge back along the track, unless I climbed over the intervening hairy backs. I called to the hindmost Handie: "BigGrrl! Stay put!" Then I patted the muzzle of the leading Handie, Trusty (because unlike Dimmey, he was reliable) and took a couple of paces forward, leading the line of Handies with me, except for BigGrrl. The Handies pulled, BigGrrl stood fast, and we dragged Dimmey safely onto the track again.

When we got to the nearest open space, on a small hilltop, I paused, thinking what to do. If Dimmey was going to be a scaredy-shier all the trip, then I might as well leave him behind hobbled, to be retrieved later. On the other hand I had a full load of packs, and an eager client. I sighed, and went on into the night.

Coming down the hill, I saw moonlight in front of me, reflected off the window of a small mudbrick house. I knew the people living there were squatting illegally; and if they knew I sometimes went walking by their parsnip patch at night, they didn't show it. Them that asks no questions isn't told a lie, I thought, and then came the rest of the words, long forgotten, read aloud from a picture book by some teacher:

Watch the wall, my darling, while the Gentlemen go by!
Four and twenty ponies
Trotting through the dark—
Brandy for the Parson,
'Baccy for the Clerk;
Laces for a lady, letters for a spy,
Watch the wall, my darling, while the Gentlemen go by!

Well, I wasn't carrying grog, smokes or spy info—not this night. And if there was any lace around then it certainly wasn't on *my* knickers. Nor were there any gents involved, nor twenty-four pack carriers, only six. Maybe, if the business expanded, one day. If wishes were Handies . . .

Shooting star overhead, something else to wish on, if I'd wanted to. I followed the speck of light with my gaze, until it dropped behind the steep rockface, just ahead. The little valley with the squatters was some distance back now, yet I waited for a minute, listening to the night sounds around me. It never pays to be too careful; but all seemed clear. "Hup!" I said to the Handies, and we started the short climb up the rockface.

The steep slopes on this track were the reason for the rope; that and Dimmey's fondness for wandering off. Mostly the Handies would follow you like dogs, though no dog could climb like this. The old rhyme was running through my head again, I just couldn't seem to get rid of it. Not four and twenty, nor pony either, not entirely . . .

The Handies didn't look unusual, just short, shaggy little horses, though a bit out of proportion, with a bigger head, ears and eyes than the pony-norm. But it was the feet that were the giveaway. If you bothered to look under the long footsocks of fetlocks, there was no hoof, just a bunch of toes, with little stubby claws. We Runaways hadn't bred them, we'd *acquired* them, or rather their mamas, two pony mares in foal. Acquiring, Runaway style, meant usually outside the official economy—from trade, fencing, favours owed and done. It wasn't that the mares had fallen off the back of a horsefloat and Aunt Gidj just happened to be passing by, but . . .

After the foaling was over, at Gidj's little farm, she needed a lie-down. Six live young and mutants to boot . . . I mean, to foot. Then she summoned the Runaway's animal experts for a conference. There were four of us, Great-Gran Mowra, Gidj, me and Uncle Tich, who'd once been a jockey.

"And just where did you get those mares?" he'd asked Gidj.

"I guess . . . it was middlemen I dealt with."

"Middlemen?"

"The body language said the goods'd been liberated from somewhere. I smelt a bit of fear, too. But not enough for me to look some cheap horseflesh in the mouth, well, no closer than usual."

The heap of blanket on Gidj's lap had stirred then, and she'd stuck a feeding bottle into the little mouth that appeared between two folds. The runt of the litters, had to be revived, needed special care. Dimmey, of course . . .

Uncle Tich thought a bit. "I heard some talk about the Ag College over the hills. They got all sorts of money from the racing industry, to *experiment*, I heard."

"On ponies?" I'd asked.

"Starting small . . . Just like horses did, with Eohippy."

Gidj looked at me. "Movies, you ever seen anything like the foals before."

"No, not even in Hollywood."

Runways are good with animals, that's how I'd blagged myself into a job with a film crew doing a wildlife documentary. At first it was opening cages and picking up poo, then serious animal training for commercials and features. Film work had taken me around the world; until I got homesick for the hills, and fellow Runaways, even if they'd taken to calling me Movies. But better that than Girlie.

"Sorrow," Tich'd said. "That's the word—sorrowgacy. The foals aren't with their mamas, not that these mamas know."

"Blossoms is just too clever for their own good," Gidj had muttered, rocking her bundle gently.

I'd gotten up at that and walked over to the stalls, looking at the mares and the foals, teetering on their long legs, just like any other equine baby. They didn't look like children of sorrow.

Tich had rubbed two fingers together. "Sorrowgacy means money, maybe big money. Someone might pay to get their property back."

"I'm not sure I'd want to deal with the folk who did this," Gidj had said, pulling out a small foot from the blanket, and displaying it in her palm.

Tich had rocked in his seat like it was a saddle. "It'd have to be racing folk did this. What's stopping horses from going any faster? Mostly foot design. So maybe they spliced in some greyhound genes, or a monkey's . . ."

We had talked and talked about it for hours, until Mowra, who hadn't said a word all night, settled the issue.

"Family rule: big money usually means big trouble. Don't let's go looking for it."

Gidj had added fiercely: "Nobody's taking these babies away for experiments."

Tich had sighed. "Well, in that case looks like we're keeping 'em. But I only work with horses I can ride. So I guess that leaves Movies."

There was a long silence.

"OK, Movies?" said Mowra.

"Er . . ." I said.

"OK, Movies." It wasn't a question now, more an order.

OK. I lifted up my hand and made the sign, forefinger and thumb meeting for the 'o', the rest of the fingers splayed like the top of a 'k'. It was the way I'd learnt on the film sets, when what with all the bells and whistles going off, the signals for the trained animals, you could hardly hear yourself think, let alone speak.

"Guess they'll come in handy somehow," I said.

Gidj had stroked the little foot in her palm. "Hand-ies." And the name had stuck . . .

It wasn't long before I found out just how handy the mutant foals could be. A pack of feral dogs had gone on a rampage through my farmlet one night, and in the general mayhem I didn't notice at first that the Handie paddock was empty. Gate was shut, the fence was too high, surely, for them to leap: so where were they? I walked around the paddock in the dawnlight, clutching my shotgun, now and then coming across the results of my sharpshooting—a dog-corpse in the grass. Then I noticed the windbreak trees looked cankered and craned my neck upwards to see, in the branches, seven dark lumps, the foals and one really pissed-off cat, hair on end.

Hmn, good night vision for a horse, hmn, good climbers. At that time I was going up this cliff regularly, though not with Handies, but tourists. Adventure Bushwalks, my business was called, and I led parties along tracks that weren't special, or secret to the Runaways. For a while it was a nice little earner, nothing like the film industry, but OK. Shame the world economy had to go pear-shaped, for suddenly people didn't have the yen, or dollars, for holidays anymore.

We were nearly at the top of the rockface now, a line of climbers and ropes. Another metre, and I clambered onto the hill saddle, followed by Trusty & Co. At this point in the tour I'd have been handing out water bottles but Handies were a tougher breed. I began to jog, and they trotted behind. The ridge was flat and wide enough for an ATV (as the tourists never failed to remark) . . . except that jeeps and the like weren't leaving the city much, what with the fuel supplies alternately dribbling or droughting.

The first big fuel drought saw the Ganja cousins on my doorstep. Could I help them out? They needed to get supplies to market, and they'd lucked onto someone who could help, who lived on a tributary to the city-bound river, and had a boat. Trouble was, he was leaving tomorrow and he lived on the other side of the hills.

"C'mon Movies, you climb, and you know all the routes . . ."

"Yeah, but carrying that load?" Then my gaze fell on BigGrrl, a yearling now, like the rest of the foals, and a hefty filly indeed. I did some weightlifting experiments. It nearly killed the cousins laughing, the sight of walking haybales with a Handie underneath. Hmn, strong little beggars. First trip I took BigGrrl and Trusty, for obvious reasons. They did just fine, which set me thinking, and then training my charges hard as I could. They responded well to commands, good as a dog, they were brighter than the average equine (Dimmey excepted) but still I had the feeling I'd only scratched their hairy little surface.

Next drought, I was ready, and started tendering for business, as you might say. Of course, this meant dealing with folk outside the Runaways, from all the Blossom families that had come and settled among us. We had Survivalists in one valley, busy hoarding everything they could lay hands on and guarding it. Next valley along were ferals, and a little further down the tax lurk winery mob, alias *The Mob*. Someone had burnt down a bridge? Fine, I'd circumnavigate it. Somebody had some hot property they wanted moved to a safe place without anyone knowing? No worries. Some consenting married adults were having a long-distance affair? Fine, I'd play post-box Cupid.

Of course, this meant people outside the family would see the Handies and might start noticing they left some odd tracks. The best Runaway minds brainstormed, then made, galoshes, as we called them, to fit over the little feet and make them look like hooves. It was a devil of a job getting the Handies used to them, but by sugar bribes, bullying and cajoling, we managed it. Even though Dimmey still kept losing his . . .

I called Gidj round for tea, and to show off the troupe in their nice new galoshes.

"They might look like ponies now," she said. "But don't you forget they're something more."

"Yeah, but what?"

She shook her dreadlocked head. "I don't know yet. We can't tell what they can do, because they're still babies. You take a baby, a helpless whinging lump, give it a few years, and you'll find it teasing the hogs or going out rabbiting. Runaway babes, that is."

"Handies ain't interested in hogs or rabbits."

"They will be."

OK, I signed at her. Have it your own way . . .

We were over the ridge now, heading down again into land that I'd have preferred to avoid, as the family here wasn't you-mind-your-own-business-I'll-mind-mine. But that was where the handover point was, agreed in advance, so I had to stick to it. I was just the messenger, no need to shoot me, no need to think about what was a pretty lucrative load. Even if I didn't know what the recipients were going to do with it. "Them that asks no questions . . ."

I took a wombat's track down to the road, which was silent and empty—it had been blocked and guarded, some ks ahead. No chance the Handies and I'd run into Old Man wombat, for he strolled this section of his track at sundown, keeping to his own regular body clock. My rendezvous point was the old graveyard on the other side of the road, something that unnerved me a little. Trust the Blossoms to be blind to the bad vibes.

Down to the macadam now, on which a horse's hooves would have clip-clopped, but a Handie just pad-padded. And there, in the graveyard, shone a torch, the signal, the beam shaking slightly as it turned on and off. Nervous of Blossom ghosts, I decided—but then the nearest Handie gave a sudden soft snort and stopped still in its tracks. Each one of them halted with their ears up and their nostrils dilated, as if they didn't like what they smelt or heard. I got a whiff of it too . . . there was a whole group of folk waiting for us, when the understanding was that this was a small, private deal, between me and my client only. If he wanted a load of guns ferried over the hills to deal with his uproad neighbors, then that was my business only until the goods were delivered and I got paid.

"Movies?" That was my client, all right, but with a strangled sound to his voice, as if he had a knife at his throat. The smart rope was still attached to my harness, with its control pod: I tapped the code that broke it into sections, and felt it part and retract, each Handie stepping free. Then I whistled at the top of my lungs, the command that meant: Scatter! And go home fast!

One Handie charged up the road, another down—a third and fourth went crashing into the undergrowth, and what the other two did I don't know, because I bolted for the wombat track. Yells came from behind me, a shot cracked in the darkness, but I was moving at speed on the smooth-trodden earth of the track. I didn't stop until I was over the hill, and then only momentarily, because feet were pounding up the slope after me. I glanced at the starry sky, checking my bearings, as a volley of shots spat into the night. There was another path leading off the wombat track, special to us Runaways, invisible to anyone else. If you weren't an elder like Mowra, it was for emergencies only, like *now*! I hightailed down it, moving as quietly and quickly as I could.

The interference being run by the Handies was spot-on. I guessed the ambush had been for the load of guns in the packs . . . and the Handies had all gone in different directions, divvying up the pursuit. Smart work that, smart as their troublespotting; without the early warning we'd have been surrounded soon as we entered the graveyard. "Teasing the hogs or going rabbiting," was what Gidj had said. Well, they weren't doing *that* yet, but they were certainly going up the learning curve like it was a rockface.

I could hear the crashing and swearing behind me reach the hill-top, see torches sweeping through the bush. Moving as silently as I could, I looked for cover, and found it: a feral blackberry bush. I crawled under it, biting my lip at the thorns. Then I just laid low and watched the pursuit head off in another direction. When their racket had passed, I extricated myself slowly and painfully from the spiky embrace.

Once out, I moved on down the track, ears and eyes at the alert. A leaf cracked behind me, and I froze, listening, my heart pounding and adrenalin surging up and down my body. Inwardly I counted to fifty, then again, but nothing stirred. I went on, after x paces pausing again, then after another x, stopped for longer, listening or sniffing as hard as I could. Hell, I was being so careful it was almost paranoia, though after this night, paranoia might just seem sound good sense.

Who had gazumped my client? The bunch blocking the road, I guessed, his Survivalist enemies. I stopped again, holding my breath, but all that happened was that a frogmouth swooped overhead, chasing a large moth. Teach me to traffic in guns; but I'd carried all sorts of illegals before and nothing had happened. Ten paces on and I froze once more. Was that a faint vibration on the track behind me? Again a long wait, for nothing, not even wildlife.

Hell, I was getting worse than Dimmey for scaredy-shies—at this rate I'd take years to get home across the hills. Better to ignore the paranoia and just keep walking on.

I was following a curve now, the corner of the hill, a rock outcrop jutting out. I stopped, realising why this route was elder-only. There was old, old story stuff here, the rock being something else, once. If I lived long enough, if I lived past this night, Mowra might tell me all about it. I touched the outcrop, paying my respects. Though it was still and cold under my hands, from somewhere within it I had the sense of something like a beat, maybe the artery thump of Runaway country lifeblood, what had kept us here all these eons. I connected to it . . .

When I lifted my hand my inner duststorm of fear and stress had settled; and I had also the distinct sense that I'd been read a lecture, as elders do to the silly young. Now I could think of something else besides the big Me, Movies. Like what it might be like to be a little horse, running through the night, guns on my back, guns behind me. Were the Handies scared, wounded, even dead, because of the error of judgement I'd made, in carrying a dangerous cargo? I'd tried the scatter command a few times in the bush; the Handies had responded well, but never with real danger after them.

Just because my family are runaways, doesn't mean we're cowards. We help each other, in a fix. I hoped the Handies would have had had the wit (just how much wit, was something I'd probably have to revise upwards) not to get themselves in a fix. But at least I should try and find out whether they'd all got away or not.

From the outcrop I could sense the path ahead. A little way on it met another, quite well-travelled, an everyday Runaway route. If I kept to this track I'd have a long walk home, curving around what the Survivalist family thought was their land, but was really Runaway country, as it had been long before and would be long after them. The other way curved back through old growth forest, towards the folk who'd tried to kill me and my horses. I took it.

In the forest was a super-gloom, the only light from snatches of starry sky seen through the leaf canopy overhead. And that was how I got myself in a right mess. My boot met something which gave, flesh over bone, and living flesh at that. Next moment I grappled in the dark with something, no someone, waking from sleep with grog on his breath, but nonetheless wiry and strong. We rolled over and over, bumping into tree roots and what felt like the metal and wheels of an all-terrain motorbike. I did what I could, wrestled and bucked, but still ended on the ground, him sitting astride me, as if we were doing a spot of *intermingling*. A torch shone in my face.

"Girlie Runaway!"

First girl born for several generations in my branch of the family, and what did my parents call me? Yep, you guessed it.

The voice sounded familiar, vaguely.

"And who are you?"

In answer he shone the torch up at his chin: a local.

"Well, Girlie, after all these years."

I knew the face, but not the name. "What are you doing here?"I said.

"Well, I'm with the Survivalists now." As if that explained everything. "And you're with the Runaways, as always. I usta be friends with a coupla them, we dealt in ganja. They'd take me walking through the hills on the Runaway tracks—until we had a little argument about the proceeds. Your cousins owe me."

"I'm not my cousins' keeper."

He ignored that. "Fact, when I heard about this little op, I figured they were doing the gun-running, right down their alley, it would be. So I started wondering how I might get my dues. Survivalists are new around here, they don't know that it's hard to catch a Runaway. They didn't ask me and I wasn't going to tell them that graveyard ambush was daft. I've seen your cousins do the scatter and scarper trick."

I was going to have words with them, if I ever got out of this mess, for being indiscreet . . .

"Now, your cousin Wombat, know how he got the name?"

I knew, but wasn't going to tell him. It was for Runaways only, even if he trotted out that tired joke about eats, roots, shoots . . .

"Sticks to certain paths, he does. And he's fond of this stretch. So, I thought, lemme volunteer for outer sentry duty, then get lost . . . on Wombat's fave trail, so I could get my dues either coming or going."

He belched, the smell of a home-distillery thick as a fog. "While I was waiting I passed the time with a little tipple. Musta overdone it, because next thing you fall over me. Nothing coming, but something going?"

"I'm not Wombat."

Long pause. "Runaways stick together, everyone knows that."

Yes, drat it.

He sighed. "It's not much I'm owed, not really. But is it worth your value to the family?"

"I won't be worth much if you keep crushing me."

He hiccuped. "Point took. But Girlie, you aren't gunna do a bolt on me, areya?"

I could feel something in his pocket, digging into me, and no, it wasn't because he was pleased to see me, either. If this was what I thought it was . . .

"No tricks," he said, rising slightly. Immediately I twisted beneath him. The torch went flying and I aimed a distracting blow with one fist, with the other hand trying a spot of pick-pocketing. Damn, not a gun, but still better with me than with him . . .

It was safely underneath me when he plumped down on me hard, knocking the breath quite out of my lungs. For a little while we just sat there, me panting, he sitting there on my back like he was Uncle Tich, out training his hopeless racehorses.

"I said, Girlie: no tricks."

One of his hands reached down, fiddling in his pants. Oh gawd, he wasn't getting randy, was he?

"Where's me bike key?" he said.

Underneath me, buster. He felt in all his pockets, reached over and retrieved the torch, using the beam to rake the surroundings. I saw, close by, a disused wombat hole, almost overgrown . . . but also a faint movement, something ducking out of sight.

"Musta dropped it." He thought some more. "Oh well. Changa plan. I'm not carrying you Girlie, you ain't skinny no more. And I gotta make sure you stay put. Since I can't ride me bike, I gotta walk. I need something like yer little ponies, to carry you back to this hidey hole I've got. And there you'll stay until your cousins pay up."

His fingers gripped the harness on my back and all in one movement he got up, pulling me with him. The torchlight skidded wildly, my feet ruffled up the leafmould . . . and with that noise as cover, I threw his precious key down the burrow. You'd need an earthmover to get it out now, or a tame wombat.

"Rope attached, hey. That's useful." The torchbeam shot all over the place again, then he focussed it. "Oh, one of them clever ropes. Know how to deal with those." He held the torch in his teeth, grabbed the rope's control, and squeezed it flat as a roadside tinnie. "There. Now it's just ordinary rope."

He wound the rope around me and also the nearest treetrunk, not a forest giant, but still thick and strong. My hands were trussed in front, the remaining rope then tied at the back like an apron. I tensed, testing the knots—they felt sloppy. When he'd finished he frisked me, and I blessed the instinct that had me dispose of his key. But he took everything useful to me right now: knife, torch, matches. The rest, like the sugar cubes for the Handies, he strewed at my feet.

"Never was a boy scout," he said. "And I know how you Runaways get outa things. I also know how they can't hold their liquor either—'specially you, Girlie. Sorry about this, but business is business."

He held a bottle in his hand; now he took hold of the hair at the back of my head, and pulled my head back hard. I gasped, and the lip of the bottle slid between my teeth. Foul-tasting pot liquor cascaded into my mouth—it was swallow or choke. It burned a trail down my throat and into my belly. When the bottle was empty, he released me. Ever feel the bite of the snake, and know that you have only a few minutes to save yourself, before the poison takes effect? That was how I felt, and there was nothing I could do.

I watched as the beam of his torch receded, growing fainter, then finally disappearing around a turn of the track. Cursing was something only Mowra did, and then reluctantly, but nonetheless I sent a nasty wish after him. Break a leg, or better still, your neck.

I tried to think, before the grog fuddled me, what the hell to do. How to get out of here . . . *with or without help.* I had seen movement in the torchlight: there was something out there. Now I could hear, very faintly, sounds approaching me. No wild animal would do that, and a human, unless they were a Runaway, would make too much noise. I didn't know what was coming, but I'd chance that it was friendly. I stood and waited, all I could do, while the liquor burnt its way through the walls of my belly.

A dim shape neared. I held my breath, listening hard to: a scrape against tree trunk, a long exhaled breath, then, when it was less than a metre away, a snort. A moment later rough horsehair, covering iron-hard muscles and flesh, rubbed against me. A Handie! but in the dark I couldn't see which one. Its head lowered as it scoffed the spilt sugar at my feet. I reached out a hand as far as the rope would let me, felt the leather of the pack saddle, but no load. Well, after tonight I wasn't trafficking in guns again, but they could have been useful now, assuming I could have got one out, loaded it, and shot my bonds off before the grog hit.

"Do you a deal," I murmured, when the crunching of sugar had stopped. Shit, I was slurring my words already. "Get me out of this tangle and it's double sugar ration. *Zhu-ga, Zhu-ga*, you know what that is."

It was whistling in the dark . . . but the Handies responded to whistles. I felt it sniffling upwards, following the sugar trail back to my empty pocket. It brushed past me, following the line of the rope around the tree. Silence. Then the rope jerked, even the tree shuddered, as the Handie began a determined onslaught on the knot.

Smart rope wasn't just hemp, but all sorts of other things, mostly not the stuff you'd chew on or even sever easily. But I couldn't blame the Handie for trying; they had a vicious bite on them, as Cousin Wombat had found out when he teased them. Serve him right. I'd have the Handies more than bite him when I got out of here . . . if, that is. Yeah, when the Handies took up rabbiting, maybe.

Or maybe they would, real soon now! The rope pulled, cutting into me, then started to give. I flexed my arm muscles, then next moment the ropes dropped loose from the trunk, and I stepped away, and free. First thing I did crouch over and stick my fingers down my throat. I vomited hot bile, but not much of it. And now my head was spinning, my wits dulling with nausea. I worried the loops of rope around my hands, but they wouldn't give and I couldn't see to work out the knots. Nevermind, I still had my feet free. I stood, took a step—and fell over.

Beside me the Handie snorted again. I grabbed at its tail, pulling myself up, then collapsed half across the small wiry body before I could—sort of—stand again. I had just enough sense left to loop my bound hands over the pommel of the pack saddle. The shaggy head turned and I felt hot horse breath on my face: it was smelling me.

"Yeah I'm sick," I muttered, "real sick. And that means that for once, you're the boss. Get me out of here, any way you want." Then, very softly, I gave the whistle for home.

We started off, me half-crouched over, half-supported by the Handie, concentrating on keeping on my feet, keeping my feet moving. All I could hear was the sound of leaves crushed under our footsteps, the faint creak of leather and rope. All I could smell was dried horse sweat, all I could see was the dark mass beside me, ears pricked, as if pleased with itself. The horse boss took us off the Runaway trail, going cross-country, following a maze of different animal tracks, wallaby, wombat, and smaller. I barely comprehended them, so grimly determined was I on keeping my body under control. The night had contracted around us, just me and the Handie, all alone in the universe.

I know I passed out at least once. The consciousness flicked off, and next moment I was kneeling on some hard and nubbly tree roots, dangling off the Handie by my bound hands. One hurt like buggery, and I felt blood drip down my wrist. The Handie nudged me with its muzzle, hard: on your bike, mate! I knew then it had bitten me awake, but better that than drag me like a stunt man in some western. I pulled my feet under me, forced myself to stand, and on we went again, the constant ache from my hand like a strong and horrid coffee, keeping me walking wounded.

It was a hell of a journey, measured only by the different terrain under my feet: leaf mould, dry earth, tussocks, and rock. The only way I knew that hours had passed was that very slowly the nausea, the discombobulation, turned into the mother of all hangovers. But I was getting my brain back, even if it hurt. I started to see shapes more clearly, although they were all a shade of dusky grey. Now, in the pre-dawn light, the first dawn of the new Runaway year, I could get the sense of the land around me. We were moving out of the old forest, and into the beginnings of the serious hills. Soon, we'd be out from the canopy, soon it would be light enough for me to see and sort out the knots.

The trees thinned, became scattered, and finally fell behind us. We were climbing now, on exposed pastureland littered with rocks. Ahead I could see an outcrop, one I knew. From it you could see my house, but better still was that part of the outcrop formed a bowl, where rainwater collected. Beneath my feet all sorts of tracks converged, for the rock pool was dry only in the worst droughts. When we reached it, I knelt and the Handie lowered its long head to drink. The water might be brackish, and with little wiggling things in it, but it was the best thing I had ever tasted.

When I had drunk my fill, I hunkered back, wiping my mouth. I tasted blood again, and inspected the wound. Vicious but fair, under the circumstances. Then I stared at the ends of the ropes. They were not chewed, like I was, but neat. Somebody had gone and *untied* the knots. I stared at the Handie again, seeing now that it wasn't big, not like Sturdy or BigGrrl, nor hairy like Shagpile, nor . . .

"Dimmey!"

He looked at me from under his straggly forelock, ears still pricked. Then he lifted one foreleg almost to my eye level and lowered it. It was naked, the hand plain to see—he'd lost his galoshes again. The toes on it flexed, then touched. Well, I'll be, opposable digits. No wonder he could get his galoshes off so easily, or get rid of his pack, which had been securely fastened. Or untied the rope. The runt of the litter, who'd always got special attention, always played up, played stupid, as when he got lost (exploring?), or fell off the track (a pretence to test the smart rope?).

The outermost toe of the Handie touched the next one in. "Yes," I said. "I know you're clever, I know you untied me."

Then my hair stood on end as the three remaining toes straightened, splaying like the arms of a K. OK, my OK. For all I knew the Handies had not only picked up the sign from me, but were also aware of its meaning.

It repeated the gesture. OK—and there was only one answer. With my good hand I made the O and the K, showing I understood . . . that you're more than I thought you were, that I was in a fix and you got me out, that I owe you. OK? OK.

Wait until Gidj heard about this, I thought, or Mowra. We'd got used to the other families, and their little ways, even the Blossoms. Now here came along another family, not even human, but with funny agile feet and even more agile brains. Well, it'd be a learning curve for us, but I figured the Handies already had some of the

Runaway attitude, which was what was most important. Give it time, and we'd all go rabbiting together, just like Gidj said. Even though I wondered if the boot, I mean, the galosh, was on the other foot, er, Hand now.

But in the end, we'd probably lie low, prosper discreetly and survive together quite well.

Then I held out my hands in supplication to Dimmey-no-more, waiting to be untied.

THE PARISH AND MRS BROWN

The trouble with moving home three times in one year is that I have difficulty remembering where I am. This happens especially in the early mornings when, half asleep, I have the choice of three locations: a semi-detached house in a London suburb with my mother; a house in the far north of Queensland shared with difficult artistic Russ; and the log hut I am currently sharing with dependable Nic, in the middle of the Victorian bush.

The confusion is also emotional. Each morning I have to think hard to remember who I am living with. Different people; similar relationships. Let me explain.

A long while ago, although it could have been yesterday, I took tea to Mother in the garden. It sounds like a nice filial gesture, but it was a feint. She almost never went into the garden, for that was my domain. I wondered what she was doing there now.

There was a ritual in our tea making. I filled a chipped Spode cup with Earl Grey tea, added a cumulus of milk and a pellet of saccharin. Then I set the cup on a matching saucer. So artificially genteel.

She was standing by the rose bushes, eyeing the blooms. They looked almost as bad as the flowers in her hat.

"Thank you, dear," she said, accepting the cup. I waited. There is an element of subservience in this relationship.

"See anything in the teacup?" I asked casually.

"You make me sound like a vulgar gypsy," she said. All the same, she bent over the cup, her hat seen from above momentarily resembling a funeral wreath.

"The leaves are whirling round and round," she said finally.

"That probably means a storm," I replied.

She eyed me sharply. "You sound hopeful."

"It would make a change."

"Hmn. You know, dear, I've never believed that tea leaves can foretell the future, but . . . you aren't planning to do something with that Australian, are you?"

"No, Mother."

She lifted her cup. Well-mannered English ladies never slurp.

"Australian and an artist," she said after a moment. "I frankly don't know which is worse."

"We had this conversation before. I told you I wasn't going to end up on the walls of an art gallery. Russ wouldn't want me to paint me nude. He's an Abstract Impressionist."

"Means nothing to me!"

"He eschews realism. My naked form has not the slightest artistic interest for him." I took a deep breath. "As opposed to non-artistic interest."

She looked at me over the rim of the cup.

"I don't want to hear. If you must pick up men in pubs . . ."

"We met in a wine bar! Russ doesn't drink beer. He's not a stereotype Australian."

"But he's terribly coarse!" She handed me the cup and saucer.

"He's not a prude, you mean."

"Russ is having a bad effect on you," she said. "I suppose one can't order one's daughter . . .

Oh you do, you do, I thought.

"But I wish you'd stop seeing him."

I evaded giving a direct answer.

"He's going back to Queensland next week," I said.

Mother clasped her hands in a little exaggerated gesture, no doubt for the neighbours' benefit. There is little privacy in an English suburban garden.

"I'm so pleased!"

She smirked at the roses. There was something avaricious in her gaze, and I remembered my suspicions.

"What are you doing out here?" I asked.

"It's my garden, isn't it?"

No, it's mine, what little there is of it. I escape here.

"You don't spend much time in it," I said, conciliatory.

"I leave the gardening to you. I must say you're very good at it. I love the roses."

"They're poisoned by pollution," I said, deprecating myself.

She wasn't listening.

"Can I have them, dear?"

"What?"

"Flower arranging. At the Women's Institute. I put my name down for the course."

"You love me," I said. "Yet you don't cut my head off and stick it in a vase."

She stared at me.

"What a horrible thing to say. I'm *glad* your Russ is leaving."

Yes, he was leaving, and at that moment I decided to go with him. The roses settled it. The next week, when Mother trotted off with the severed roses in a basket, I took two suitcases in a minicab to Russ's studio-flat. That evening, we were on a flight out of Heathrow.

Six months later, I took refreshment out to a garden again. This time, it was a tropical garden, and Russ was trying to paint it in the heat. He had his easel just outside the back door. In the time I'd lived with him, he'd dropped the 'abstract' and become 'impressionist'. It was then that I discovered that he couldn't draw.

He shifted the brush to his palette hand, and took the glass of chilled white wine. There was no thank you; the taking-for-granted was overt.

"This is lousy hock," he said.

"Sorry, the good wine's expensive."

"Getting at me again for not selling paintings?" he asked.

"No," I said meekly. Russ is volatile.

"Just you wait," he said. He looked like the flame tree; his hair was the colour of the flowers and there was a streak of bright green paint on his face. He continued: 'They don't appreciate Art here. So I'll give 'em Reality. Pictures of the back yard."

"They may be hicks," I said, "but they're not stupid."

"Who says?"

I was quiet.

"Nic," he said. 'Well, he's not that bright himself."

"He works for IBM."

"In accounts. That doesn't require an IQ."

"He's giving up full-time work," I explained. 'Going to work part-time for the Victorian branch and live in the bush."

"When?"

"Soon."

"Great! I'm sick of coming home from sketching the beach and finding him drinking all the coffee in the house."

"Coffee costs less than wine."

"What do you mean by that? Don't make me jealous, woman; I'll never sell pictures if you do."

"It's childish to burn your paintings when you get miserable."

"Artistic temperament, my dear."

He seemed inspired by that remark, and turned to the canvas again.

"Take this damn glass."

"You aren't very gracious," I said

"Compared to Nic? Look, run away with him if you like. See if I care. I will. I'll probably have a nervous breakdown."

He was enjoying himself. I took the glass, and paused.

"What are you waiting for?" he demanded.

"I want to do a bit of gardening. The fruit bats dropped mangoes on the lawn last night. They're beginning to smell."

"I don't want you in the picture. Get back inside."

I obeyed, but inside I started packing my bags again. Now and then, I paused and looked through the wooden window lattices. Russ was painting away, with great strokes of the brush. It wasn't Art, and it certainly wasn't Reality.

Now, four months later, I'm ensconced with Nic, in a log hut surrounded by bush. The garden is the biggest of all so far, nearly an acre, on the edge of Crown land. It's beautiful, and yet . . .

Mother's favourite saying was "Never leave the parish because of Mrs Brown; you'll meet her in the next." Geographic location may change, but I don't. Maybe I'm naturally subservient. Why then do I so resent it?

I took a mug of coffee to Nic. It was late, and he sat beside the fire, still wearing his business suit. He's six foot four of pinstripes.

"Ta muchly," he said. I waited. As he didn't volunteer a subject for conversation, I started.

"I got a letter from Mother today."

"Oh."

"Nothing in it, as usual. There was the usual gossip about the London neighbours, and yet another lecture on my lack of morals. She says she wants to visit."

"Bloody hell."

"You sound like Russ," I said.

"From what I hear about your mum, she'd be about as welcome as he would." He paused, then asked suspiciously:

"You don't write to Russ, do you?"

"After what he threatened, I didn't dare leave a forwarding address."

"Good. Can I have some more coffee?"

I put on the jug again. Nic stared into the fire and said: "I'll tell you a funny."

Nic couldn't tell jokes.

"I was in the microcomputer department, and Leroy—he's boss there—was trying to sell someone a word processor. This man was some sort of hack writer. Leroy told him—with a word processor you can churn out space stories, Westerns and Gothics just by reprogramming the nouns. For Black Bart read Ming the Merciless or Baron Darkeville. And the customer said 'What if the computer gets confused and I get Bug Eyed Monsters in the Purple Canyon? Or rockets blasting off from the Haunted Castle.'"

He stopped, looking expectant.

"I don't get it," I said irritably.

"Computers aren't muddled like that."

I handed him the second mug of coffee, in complete silence. He seemed hurt.

"You coming to bed?"

"No, I want to think. I always have insomnia after one of Mother's letters. So I'll sleep in the spare room tonight."

Another feint. He went away, and it occurred to me that there was nobody to escape with now. Even if there were, I could only expect more of the same. Oh garden, my refuge . . .

I slept soundly in the spare room, and woke with the habitual confusion. Was I in London with Mother, North Queensland with Russ, or Victoria with Nic?

I got up and started to dress, listening to the small scratchy noises of the bush waking to a new day. Nic had kept the property feral by not clearing it.

I looked out of the window, at acacias grey-green in the half-light. The spare room leads directly into wilderness. Possums nest close to the hut. I opened the door, and stepped out.

Straight into a blaze of vivid tropical colour. I blinked. Ahead was the clash of a flame tree, orange-red and viridian; Windsor and Newton paint unmixed from the tube. The clash continued onto the grass beneath the mango tree, where rotting fruit lay. I could smell them; sour-sweet. A fruit bat, like a demented umbrella, took off from the mango tree and fled from the dawn.

I looked towards my feet. The scene was repeated, ineptly, on a canvas left out to dry. In North Queensland, there are six months without rain. The time I'd spent trying to help Russ become an artist! Russ?

The heat was already oppressive, and I was dressed for a Victorian winter. Inside! I thought. This gaudy garden didn't belong to me now. I lived in a low-key stillness, with the bushland and Nic.

I slammed the door shut. Then I looked hard at the walls, papered with chintzy roses. I'd joked to Mother that her wallpaper was like her garden. Nic's hut had only bare boards as room dividers. This was my English home. The garden I could see from the window was prissy and small, overlooked by neighbours. All the flowers were dusty; they could have been made out of fabric.

Appearances deceive, I thought, and pulled the window open. The catch was stiff, since it was never unfastened during the long London winter. I stuck my head out, and smelt mist, damp trees, and eucalyptus from the redgum just outside this log hut; no, this box of a suburban house, all mod cons . . .

Give me a choice between indoors and outdoors, and I will usually bolt for the garden. The bush stayed where it was as I ran out of the house. Clearly, I thought, there are rules to this business. Interior and exterior are in two different places, although the view through a glass window is consistent with the house. But why do they shift and change? I leant my head against bark, and stared down the garden. Mist disentangled from the trees. I felt calmer, and decided to stay outside.

Then something flew over my head. Rosella? Late owl? I glanced up for a better look.

It was furred, yet it flew. I would not have screamed at a sugar glider, but this was a tropical fruit bat, with great leathery wings. I yelled for Nic, shouting secret feelings; that I'd thought he was possessive, like the other two, but I took that back. Be here! Then I forgot, and ran back up the garden to see a house in front of me; familiar and like a birdcage; latticed for ventilation against the tropical heat. Russ's canvas of mango and flame tree leaned unsteadily against the red gum. The Queensland house stood in the Victorian garden. I stopped running.

I haven't dared move since then. Half an hour has passed, and house and garden have gone through a series of metamorphoses. Three locations have been merging.

The fruit bat reappeared, looking bewildered. I was inured to it by then, and watched it fly past silently. Beds of pallid roses made their way across the bushland like a lot of apathetic early settlers. I didn't scream again; not even when the red gum sprouted mangoes and flame-coloured flowers.

Now I can see someone standing by the picket fence which divided my English garden from the next back yard. I can't see clearly; whoever it is seems to be shifting as if seen through a heat haze. He's coming closer. He? There is a confusion. I think I catch a glimpse of Mother's flowery hat; no, only Nic can be that tall, but Russ has all that red hair.

GOD AND HER BLACK SENSE
OF HUMOUR

I could have been famous, I see that now. Me, Cecily Chaucy, second-rate feminist journalist. I could have had my fifteen minutes in the spotlight. Visions of it recur at intervals, of my middle-aged face beaming from the covers of magazines, and from TV screens from Manhattan to Middlesex to Mittagong, Australia, my home town. Oh megalomania! Oh bliss!

Instead, here in my seedy upper New York flat (sorry, apartment) I think about bills, deadlines, the word processor, and the golden opportunity knocking at my door and me never answering it. I always wanted a Pulitzer prize . . .

When, alone in my double bed, I recall my one stupendous scoop, and how I blew it, I come back to the groupies. I use the term loosely, extending it from lewd ladies to fame hounds in general: all those seen around stars with their tongues lolling, wanting a little reflected glory in their dogs' lives. I couldn't have borne them in my company—not with what I know.

It began with me choking on my breakfast as I read the latest issue of *Ms*.

"Oh no! They couldn't!"

What had stuck in my craw was the feature article reclaiming Marilyn Monroe for feminism. There she was, an America, a new-found land, with the *Ms* flag proudly set atop her.

"Boy, have *Ms* laid themselves open! I could send that article right up to the ceiling!"

The immaculate conception of a parody, celebrating the most unfeminist heroine I could discover, popped into my mind. But who? It would have to be somebody over the top, to top Ms Marilyn.

"Mom!"

"Mum," I muttered. Dwayne, my contribution to the patriarchy, came into the kitchen clutching a white profoundly phallic object.

"It's my art project," he said, brandishing it under my nose. "A lighthouse, in plaster of Paris."

I smote myself on the forehead, nearly knocking my glasses onto Dwayne's, er, erection.

"I've got it! The Plastercasters!"

For those not versed in sixties sleaze, a footnote. The Plastercasters were three lasses who collected the penis imprints of rock stars. They worked together: while one prepared the ingredients for casting, another would prepare the subject, and the third would take notes. There was even an exhibition of their handiwork. Three more unlikely candidates for feminist sainthood could hardly be imagined.

I had my subject, and now I had to cast words around it. First take your source material . . . and I found there was sweet FA on these FAs, except in books with titles like *The Hundred Most Embarrassing Moments of Rock and Roll*. I began to warm towards the Plastercasters—like other women, their achievements had been neglected.

Then I felt chill, as I realised the long, hard slog of interviews in front of me. I was blowing hot and cold indeed.

My recipe for interviews is basically to grill over a portable tape recorder, after catching your interviewee, of course. I needed the original soundtrack on the Plastercasters, and for that I had to get me some contacts. Way back, I used to drink with some rock journalists, *Rolling Stone* staffers. They were an enviable lot, if you envy a lot of interviewing lunkhead hunks who played one-chord rock at a volume to stun mullets. I unearthed my address book of the time (bound in embroidered denim, a period artefact), from under Dwayne's old baseball gear, and started dialling.

"Hi there. Remember Cecily—the only Cecily in the US of A?"

The intervening years being interesting ones, in the Chinese sense, I expected few of my old beer bibbers to be traceable. In fact, about half were still on this planet, but they were definitely off it, mentally. Jim was bibbing full-time, Patti was in a drug induced coma, Bob would not get off the subject of UFOs, and sweetwise Suellen, my favourite, had somehow metamorphosed into a Buddhist nun.

"Hey!" I shouted to Dwayne. "I think I have positive proof that rock n' roll rots the brain."

I was talking to a brick wall, wall of sound actually: he was wearing his Walkman.

When one tack fails, change tactics. Noeleen Ryan, now a high-powered Hollywood PR, had once been . . . Noeleen Ryan, married to a Sydney dentist who wanted her to quit her job and keep the house 'hygienic'. I lent Noels *The Female Eunuch* and she threw it at him, literally a parting gesture.

"I raised your consciousness, got you to your current giddying heights," I said.

There was a crackle on the line from Hollywood, maybe Noels laughing.

"I'm on the fourth floor, dahling. Okay, Brucie was the pits. Okay, I owe you. So whadderyouwant?"

I told her: an interview with Frank Zappa, whose appreciation of junk culture had led him to some involvement (I had heard) in the Plastercaster's exhibition. He had also edited the unpublished *Groupie Papers,* a compilation of several sixties sexual diaries.

"He won't be easy," she said.

"I still want to talk to him."

"Okay, I'll interface for you. But only in my spare time. It'll take a while, dahling, you hear me?"

I heard, and put the project on hold, devoting my attention to my bank balance. Unlike expense-account journos, I finance my wild ideas by hackwork, and this one looked as if it would be costly. Also, the rent was due, and ringing Noels had not helped the phone bill much. I opened my 1980s address book, a sombre little leather number, and dialled some editors.

Serendipity is one of my favourite words, and I happily discovered the concept, by chance, at a collector's convention. The collectors talked continually of it.

"Waal, ah just bent to tah up mah shoelace, and ah saw it under the chiffonier—genuwaan Minton."

That quote came from an interview I recorded with an elderly couple who collected thundermugs (potty about potties, I nearly wrote, but the commissioning editor was sudden death on foreign slang). Later I wandered into a seminar on investment opportunities.

" . . . the collectors who are gonna strike it rich are those collecting tomorrow's antiques today: forties, fifties, *sixties* memorabilia."

The emphasis was mine. When the lecturer, a sleek Wall Street type, had finished, I started a conversation.

"Sure there's sixties collectors," he said. "I can give you addresses. But they're weirdoes."

I bit my tongue: he had just told me he collected Kewpie dolls.

First name on the list he faxed me was Scooby Doo, no moniker but a legal changeover. It denoted a male emotionally stopped at New Year's Eve, 1969.

"I was a surfer, hung out with Kesey and the Pranksters, roadied for the Dead, y'know, then got into the anti-war movement, but that did nothing for my inner self, see, so I got into TM, then Sri Chimnoy . . ."

The cat had lived enough for nine lives in one decade, and now devoted his time (and a bequest) to collecting anything that reminded him of his youthful glory.

"Plastercasters? Yeah, I knew 'em. Warm and generous . . . but not nice gals."

I repressed a feminist snort.

"Any mementos, Scooby?"

"Only the clap, haw, haw."

Women's Lib being a seventies event, he was oblivious to my mega death glare. He wheezed at his own wit for about a minute, then said, "I had stuff some place. Seattle . . . Washington?"

I put my head in my hands as he explained. Every time his sixties squirreling filled his apartment to bursting point, he put his treasures into storage. And, like any squirrel, he would forget where he put them.

"Can't you remember?" I shouted.

"Not so well after '69," he said.

Only Scooby Doo's comments on my collectors list stopped me from feeding him squirrel bait. One name he knew: Smith. Everyone knows a Smith, but this was Zebedee Smith, whom Scooby said owned several of the Plastercasters' casts. Smith, when I phoned him in Outer Magnolia, Georgia, said he didn't. He protested too much to be true, so I checked on him and found that Z. Smith, Inc., had just contracted to reorganise the computers of Liberty Baptist College, home of Jerry Falwell. Smith also deserved squirrel bait, I thought.

Back chez Cecily, I found an example of Noeleen's business stationery—fuchsia pink—enclosing a note on prosaic PC paper from Frank Zappa. He was just off to Alma-Ata and couldn't spare a minute—but would send me someone who could.

"Mom! Mom!"

"Yes, Dwayne."

"There's a trailer home out front."

A tiny head crowned with grizzled dreadlocks peered from the cabin at the total lack of parking space. Old hippie, I categorised: that's my messenger!

"Dwayne, your mum is about to get into a motor vehicle with a strange man. Come along and be my bodyguard!"

I hustled Dwayne downstairs and into the cabin of the trailer home.

"You Ms Cecily Chaucy? Frank sent me," said the visitor in an accent stuck somewhere between the isles of Manhattan and Dogs. "Where the blazes can I park?"

"There's a really bad fast food franchise several blocks up . . . always room in their car park. I'll direct you, Mr . . . ?"

"I'm Grubbs."

My first impression of Grubbs as small was no trick of perspective: he was not much bigger than Dwayne, and something of a mannequin beside my overweight self. The bodyguard being therefore unnecessary, I sent him off to the really good fast-food franchise. Grubbs and I sat in the cabin, drank beer, and talked.

"Oh, you met Scooby. I remember him. Too many psychedelic munchies. One was enough for me, even if it was an Owlsley original. I mean, after I had Owlsley's bathroom cabinet read me aloud its diaries, I just knew there were better ways of having fun. Like people.

"When I retired from the music biz, I bought this trailer. I went off the road, to get on the road. Now I just drive around the Americas, seeing all the nice people I know."

"Nice people include ex-groupies?" I asked. He caught the irony.

"I don't care what people do, so long as nobody gets hurt. Those chicks hurt nobody . . . but themselves. You'll see."

He patted his address book, which was the size of a minor telephone directory. "All sorts of people in here. Anybody in the counter-culture, I knew."

Just talking to Grubbs I could see my article changing direction.

"If you don't mind me saying, Cec," (the beer was talking, a little) "you should talk to more than the 'casters. They were part of a movement, even if they were its weathermen."

"Explain," I said. Dwayne was walking back across the macadam, looking replete.

"They were extremists. The other girls didn't get a memento of the guy, 'less they got pregnant."

Had Grubbs sniggered, like Scooby, I would have stormed out of the cabin, but he didn't. He was, I was realising, that rare find, a genuinely nice person.

"We'll talk about this later," I said, as Dwayne clambered into the cabin, smelling of fried oil. I put my notebook in my dilly bag and stared at Grubbs.

"You're a godsend."

"Nah, Franksend . . . though they're alike, at times."

Grubbs had many friends in New York, but between visits he compiled a list of likely interviewees, with attached word-sketches. In my spare time from earning my multifibre wholegrain and Dwayne's Wonderbread, I made a lot of phone calls. And I had one phone call made to me.

"You don't know me, Scooby said I was to get in contact. We were bidding at the same garage sale."

"What for?" I said, inane at nine a.m. on a Sunday morning.

"Woodstock scrapbook with autographs."

My eyes opened wide as a daisy.

"Who are you?"

"Penneman Wexford IV."

The name had been bottom of the collectors list, which now I recalled had been in alphabetical order.

"You can call me Wexy," he added hesitantly.

"Well, Wexy, do you collect anything to do with sixties groupies?"

"Oh yeah, I did. It's kinda embarrassing now . . . the shrink my family sent me to said it was sexual frustration. He was right—I stopped collecting in that area once I got laid."

"How old are you?" I asked, incredulous.

"Twenty."

Wexy was young, rich, and almost incidentally, black. I drove over to his home later that day and found a mansion, one floor of which was devoted to Wexy, the heir, and his collections. The family's puzzlement at Wexy was almost a physical presence in the house. They had spent the sixties with their heads down, earning their first million, only to have their only son relive the decade they had ignored.

"Every now and then I sell something I'm bored with for two hundred per cent profit, and they think, well maybe we've got a chip off the old block here, and leave me alone for a while."

He laughed, leaning up against the big glass case containing his civil rights ephemera. The lad was decidedly creepy, but he had sorted and classified the display behind him to near-museum standard.

"I don't see anything to do with groupies."

"In the safe. The maids, they're Church of the Nazarene. They found some of the photos, and that's how I got the shrink."

It was a sordid treasure trove, a Pandora's box of pure sleaze.

"Can I borrow some of these, Wexy? They look just the thing to jog old rusty memories."

"Go right ahead," he replied, and I selected a bagful. "Come back if you want any more."

"Thanks."

On the way out we encountered his parents, sitting in a stationary golf cart on the huge front lawn. They brought to mind lumpy soft toys, stuffed into a model car by a child and then forgotten. Golliwogs, I thought, then suppressed the image on grounds of extreme ideological unsoundness.

The Wexfords looked at their son, then at me—I was wearing sneakers, overalls and my 'Sisterhood is Powerful' sweatshirt—and then at each other. I fled.

"Cor!" said Grubbs. We were sitting in the trailer which, in contrast to its nondescript exterior, was a cave lush with exotic textiles and travel souvenirs. He had spread the photos over his large Moroccan carpet, and grainy or blurry depictions of soft pornography contrasted oddly with the tufts of richly coloured wool. "That's Suzy Creamcheese (crummy shot of her), Cynthia Plastercaster, the Butter Queen . . ."

"The goods," I said dryly.

"How in heaven did he get these?"

"I chose not to ask. With these, and your nice friends, we're ready to go."

"You betcha," he said.

In the next few weeks, without venturing out of New York State, I met some of the strangest women it has ever been my hap to interview. There was a housewife who grew telepathic sunflowers, she said; the two hundred-pound den mother of a Christian bikie gang; a health fanatic, orange from eating carrot cake exclusively; a winner in the 'Matron' section of a Tattoo America contest (flayed, I thought, she would have made a floor covering as ornate as Grubbs' carpet); and the mother of the reincarnated Jimi Hendrix, whom Dwayne played video games with and pronounced to be 'Just a kid, y'know'. All were weird, but not wonderfully so, in my eyes if not theirs.

"I feel like a researcher for Mondo Bizarro," I complained to Grubbs. He smiled benignly, as he had through all my interviewees' psycho babble. I realised that Grubbs also was a collector: of slightly used, damaged human beings.

Dwayne went on his annual holiday to his dad in Tuskegee, so I made the most of the child-free time. My heap of interview cassettes mounted. When the New York groupies were covered, I begged for out-of-state assignments from my editors. I took anything going, which is how I came to cover a stand-up fight at a Daughters of the American Revolution convention (on the way to see those Daughters of the Youth Revolution, the Plastercasters). My original subjects seemed relatively sane, in comparison with their other sisters in sleaze and I recorded four hours of chat with them. Then I caught a home bound flight. The plane grazed a thunderstorm half-an-hour out, which tossed the passengers like flapjacks. I got off the flight sick to the stomach, from the trip and from my project.

Let me explain. What had begun as a campy parody, then mutated under the influence of Grubbs into sociopop history, I had always intellectualised. I had never anticipated a gut reaction to what I, as a good feminist if not a good woman in the old-fashioned sense, would naturally find nauseating.

The first danger signs had appeared during the interview with the Tattoo Queen.

"Ah've nevuh been intah women," she said reflectively. I blinked. This statement had concluded a sordid tale of sex with another girl in the middle of a Blood Sweat and Tears tour party.

"Then why did you do it?" I asked.

"Get usselves noticed. Get some action."

I bit off the end of my pencil, savagely if not symbolically. Now it was her turn to look surprised.

"You hafta unnerstan'," she said. "The boys in the bands were the heroes of the revolution. It was a honnuh and a privilege to do them."

An honour and a privilege. These flower-powered frolics had not signalled the dawn of a new age, rather continued the long night of women linking themselves to men for their wealth, their fame, their transferred status. Camp-followers are as old as the oldest profession. The only difference had been the lie of sixties liberation through rock and roll, Dionysian sex, and hippy love. "Instead of saying, 'We're part of the love scene,'— they're actually doing it," Jimi Hendrix had said of his faithful servants.

Behind this romantic façade, like a lace curtain concealing a show of arms, was male chauvinism rampant. I heard too many tales of debasement, of men like spoilt toddlers venting their frustrations on the perennial scapegoat, the promiscuous woman. Hendrix, who had praised the doers, not talkers, of the love generation, treated them brutally. One girlfriend he had kicked in the face, breaking her nose in three places. When I heard this I longed for my old Aussie pressing of *Band of Gypsies,* to kick and kick again.

I sat in Grubbs' trailer and cried, tears dribbling down my nose and onto the Moroccan carpet.

"There now," he said. "I thought this might happen. When we met I wondered what's a nice feminist like you doing with the groupies?"

"I'm sick," I said, choking, "of writing about the nastiness of men. I want to write about positive women."

"What?" he said. I had been unintelligible through sob. Calming, I repeated myself.

"You could just write up the 'casters," he said. "They got something actual

"Tangible."

"—from it."

I thought about this suggestion. The Plastercasters had seemed oddly admirable, precisely in their turning their sexploits into pop body art. And there had been talk of others, who had used rather than be used, been active rather than passive. Two names had recurred in the interviews.

"—not like me. Christa and Tessie never took no shit—"

"—I really hated all those haughty aristo groupies, those moonlighting countesses jetting over from Bavaria with Daddy's millions. I hated Anita Pallenberg, and those sisters, Christina and Theresa—"

"—so the security guard wanted his piece of the action, and grabbed this foreign chick, Chrissie or something, and that girlfriend she hunted with, Terrie just floored him. I mean we fell about the place, this big fat dude, knocked cold by this skinny chick—"

"—all the supergroupies partied till dawn, we was real nightbirds, me, Devon, that Christie and her friend—"

"Two girls," I said to Grubbs. "Maybe sisters, maybe titled ladies from Europe. They did everything together and did everyone, looking down their noses the whole time. They crop up in interview after interview, but nobody can get their names straight. They agree on one thing—those girls were never humiliated."

"In your bag," he said.

"Eh?"

"With the photos you got from your spade pal." I pulled out the sachets containing Wexy's photographs. We had divided them into two groups (of groupies): those depicting my interviewees, which I would show to them, and those I would not. He took the latter and shuffled through them. "I meant to say you had a rare thing there, 'cos Theresa and Christa were anti-paparazzi. Theory was their families didn't know about the company they kept. Here."

It was a scene taken through a motel doorway, of a man lolling drugged or dead beat in a chair, watched by two women seated on the double bed. One was fair, one dark.

"That'd change," he said, stubbing a thick forefinger at the two sleek heads. "I'd see them on tour after tour, and the blondie would have gone dark, and the brunette peroxide."

"Confusion," I said. "They were creating confusion about themselves."

There was a knock at the trailer door.

"My date," said Grubbs, aborting my half-formed hope of a comforting fuck. Amiable as Grubbs was, with my figure I could hardly be his type. He was probably into jailbait. My gaze on my sneakers, I headed for the exit.

"Talk to you later," he said, as I opened the door to reveal the jailbait—a husky earringed male. What a relief, I thought, it's not just me he's not attracted to, it's my entire gender.

I went home and watched MTV with Dwayne. Just as a Jimi Hendrix clip began, causing me to become depressed all over again, the phone rang.

"Hi there, Wexy. What are you collecting now?"

"Anything to do with psychedelic horror movies." He laughed. "The maids think it's Satanism. How's your collecting, of information?"

I gave him a progress report, up to and including the two women in the photograph.

"Grubbs said they hated having their picture taken. So how did that shot happen?"

"Read me the accession number. On the back."

I reversed the photo and saw a string of numbers in precise handwriting.

"Hold on," he said. I could hear his footsteps echo away on the polished floor of his museum, then echo back.

"I got that from the estate of a photographer who liked to play candid camera. There's some great shots Little Richard doing a J.

Edgar Hoover impersonation, a food fight at the Fillmore, Pigpen spilling beer down some girl and lapping it up."

"Yuk!"

"You don't like those guys," he said.

"Nor a lot of their women. But it's an occupational hazard, getting fed up with an assignment before its end."

He wasn't paying attention, for the next sound down the line was his thin, slightly maniacal laugh—like a hyena on an icy night, I categorised.

"I was just 'membering how I got the photos. I'd argued a full hour with the widow, and she was holding out, until this Southerner, collector of sixties porn, showed up waving his chequebook. I said: 'You win, ma'am,' in a hurry."

"Not Smith?" I said.

"You heard of him? Seems everybody knows about that guy."

"Except Jerry Falwell," I said.

We chatted about this and that, and at the end of this conversation I had a date, in the purely platonic sense, to accompany Wexy to an exhibition on the history of the horror film. It was research for him and leisure for me—or so I thought.

In exhibitions, I like to whiz around from frame to frame, then return to gawk at all my favourites. Thus I was no companion for Wexy, who seemed to have an inner clock directing him to halt for ten minutes before each exhibit. He didn't appear to mind. I glanced back at him once, and saw that he was the centre of attention for several young women. He looks good, I thought; he looks rich. Then, with a pang: they must wonder what he's doing with this hag. Tears started to fill my eyes again, and I blundered out of the exhibit hall, into what I thought led to the wash room. It turned out to be an annexe devoted to a photographic pioneer.

He had collected scenes of the low life, brothel pictures as bad as anything in Wexy's safe. Anger banishes tears, in fact it practically turned them into steam, I became so heated. How little things change, I thought. Why, those women even look much the same as the ones in the sixties snaps, they . . .

I was standing in front of a sepia shot of two girls, one fair, one dark, in a room full of Art Nouveau furniture. Then I fumbled in my bag, eliciting a furious glare from a museum guard, who maybe expected some act of feminist vandalism. Instead, I withdrew the photo of Christa and Theresa and compared it to the exhibit, my gaze flitting from one to another. All four figures had in common slightly Slavonic features: rounded faces, high cheekbones and Cranach eyes. And, allowing for different hairstyles, clothes and face paint, these twin sets were as alike as matched pearls. Even the groupies' reported hauteur was a constant, for the pair in the brothel posed defiantly for the man behind the lens, their gaze reflecting him for the louse he was.

The caption underneath read 'Courtesans, Paris, 1899'. How very odd.

"Hey Wexy, come and look at this!"

He followed me, to much amazement from the looming young ladies. I gave them a Christa and Theresa look back, my self-pity subsumed by my collecting mania, for knowledge. However, Wexy disappointed me.

"Now ain't that strange," was all he said.

"Grannies? Great grannies? Or do courtesans run to type?"

He shrugged and sidled back to the chamber of horrors. After some minutes I did likewise, still baffled. My mind was so busy with the problem that the exhibits in the main hall could have been framed blanks. It was a good half hour before I was jolted back to the here and now, and it was almost as great a puzzle to realise why. Before me was a series of stills from an early vampire him, of Dracula peering through an open window at a girl bursting out of her sheets and nightgown. There was something familiar, disturbingly so, about the subject matter, and again it concerned the photo in my bag. I took the image out once more, and saw the factor in common. Dracula's gaze was focused on the girl's neck, and the unknown musician sat with his head thrown back, so that only his throat and prominent Adam's apple were visible. Christa and Theresa's expression was the same as Dracula's. Bedroom eyes, I had loosely categorised it as earlier, but in fact it was pure naked greed.

I stood, in the middle of the exhibition crowd, hearing beyond the spooky muzak the words my interviewees had used: nightbirds, aristocratic, unusually strong, predatory and fascinating. Now they were apparently also immortal. I hiccupped a slight laugh: the 'Hendrix' mum, who had hated any competition, had referred to the pair as 'vamps'.

I turned my head and saw Wexy, leaning back against a pillar, watching me. Should I tell him? No—amidst these illusions of terror the possibility of real vampires was too damn crazy.

We went to our separate homes, his palatial and mine humble. I slept on the problem (and also on my Garfield pillow). The next day I awoke still feeling I was bats, but with the hunger to know, for certain. Grubbs I wanted to consult, but he was saying his goodbyes. Come winter this migratory mouse travelled down from the north to visit his friends in Arizona and New Mexico. I only managed to catch him at his farewell party, held appropriately at a trailer court, way out of town.

What with his friends, their spouses or lovers, children and dogs, several hundred souls attended. I was told that as a goodwill gesture, the whole of the largely deserted trailer court had been invited as well. There was a bonfire big enough for Beltane eve, dope, alcohol in many forms, including a punch that seemed to be chopped fruit plus vodka, and trestle tables like cityscapes from the mounds of health food piled on them. The band comprised four tubby old hippies who, like Scooby, seemed to have no musical memories beyond 1969.

I spent much of the celebration dodging behind trailers, either seeking Grubbs or avoiding the loopier of my interviewees. Quite late in the day I found the party boy, off by himself admiring a smouldering heap of fallen leaves. Brown became red-gold became soft grey smoke.

"Hi there."

"Hi, Cec." He poured cheap claret the colour of beetroot blood into my plastic cup. "How's tricks?"

"I'm not turning any."

He gave his benign and (I realised) evasive smile.

"Well, how's that article going?"

"It's not. Christa and Theresa's why. I want them."

"Not in my book," he said, smiling again. I looked at him hard. "I never much liked them," he finally admitted.

I made a round fish-mouth of amazement: amiable Grubbs, confessing dislike for somebody!

"Cec, I don't know why. We talked . . . you could have a good natter with them, if they wanted. Once we got onto the subject of Napoleon. Now I used to read everything 'bout Boney, he was a hero for a little tich, but those girls matched me fact for fact. Even on troop manoeuvres. It was . . . uncanny. They spooked me."

He swilled some wine, a drop trailing red from the corner of his mouth.

"What became of them?" I asked. Leaves skittered across the asphalt to the fire, blown like moths to a light source.

"They spooked other people, very important people. I don't know if those two had a nose for downers, but it seemed like every guy they did had bad times after. Rumour had it they were the last to see Brian Jones alive, f'r instance."

I thought: the bite of the Lamia, the kiss of the belle dame sans merci, either weakens or is (femme) fatale.

"Word was they stole your karma. Somebody got sloshed at a party, actually accused them . . . and they lit out."

As they must have, I thought, so many times before, moving from population to population, like conmen in search of new suckers. In their case, suckees.

Grubbs shook his head, his dreadlocks wagging in disorder.

"I saw them once after. This was at a filling station, my first year with the trailer. A stretch limo pulled up alongside, chauffeur, tinted windows, and when the door opened I could see what looked like real tiger-skin upholstery. The door opened for Christa and Theresa to go to the powder room. They hadn't aged a moment, it seemed. I might have said: 'Hi, how's tricks?' but then I saw their sugar daddies. They'd moved on to the Mob."

"When was this?" I asked.

"Late seventies. There was a Mafia feud on . . . I'd seen those hoods in the papers. Few months later, I saw them again."

"Christa and Theresa?"

"Nah, their godfathers. Shoot-out at some spaghetti parlour—there was blood, guts and pasta all over the evening news."

Bad times after, I recalled.

There were cries from the main body of the party, behind us: "Where's that Grubbs?" and "Grubbs, baby, where you hidin'?"

"Now I come to think of it, I did see those girls again, sort of. Friend of mind in LA, his mother died, and I helped him pack up her things. There was a photo of the old lady in the twenties, one of a bunch of girl extras cuddling Rudy Valentino. The two at the back were Christa and Theresa, to the life."

I opened my mouth to spiel my discovery, but a pseudopodium of the party surrounded us, yelling "Grubbs, speech!", "Come 'n' cut the cake, man!" Two robust young men in headbands grabbed Grubbs by the elbows. "See you, Cec," he said, as he was hustled away. "Next time I'm in New York"—which hasn't happened yet.

I collected Dwayne from the vicinity of the punchbowl, and drove home, feeling languid. Dwayne, who was very quiet, went to bed almost immediately. I followed soon after, relishing the thought of sleep. Around midnight, I awoke in a huddle, to see a figure creeping towards my bed. I drew a deep breath, for my scream like a fire siren, but then heard the intruder whimper.

"Dwayne! What the bloody hell!"

"Mommy!" and my grown-up of nine stumbled into my arms, weeping.

"Hush, hush. What happened?"

"Bad dream . . . like the videos me and this kid were watching . . . in his dad's trailer."

Dwayne had copped an eyeful of video nasties, each boy trying to toughen the other out. Machismo! I soothed him, and he went to sleep beside me, while I stayed alert as a ferret. Deciding not to waste my wakefulness, I turned on the light, and took pen and pad from the bedside table.

Earliest sighting of Christa and Theresa, I wrote, Paris, nineteenth century. Before that, maybe back as far as the Napoleonic wars. Then, Hollywood in the roaring twenties, the rock world in the swinging sixties, and in the seventies they became mob molls.

What's the common factor? Grubbs said they knew a lot about Napoleon, from personal experience? They were described as courtesans in the fin-de-siècle photo -bet they never thought it would adorn a museum wall, to trip the wire of Cecily's suspicions. Courtesans are the upmarket end of the strumpet scene, catering for the rich . . . and famous. They're starfuckers! It fits: film stars, rock stars, gang stars, they flit around the hippest, hottest men.

I sucked the end of my Biro and thought: never in any mythology have I read of vampires with such specialised tastes. Then I drew a big fat question mark on the pad, my lips twisting as I tried not to laugh aloud, thereby alarming the little boy who slept peacefully beside me. As a dark refinement of the Lamia fear, the theory was the stuff of male nightmares: supernatural women targeted on men only, and those famous. If I accepted it, I could also conceive of vampires as furies, Christa and Theresa as a feminist punishment for man's inhumanity to women. I could believe that there was a god, and that she had a black sense of humour.

Dwayne began to snore softly. Stop it, I thought, not to him but to myself. Cecily, this search leads right into the looney bin, along with all the other quests for self-enlightenment via telepathy, tattooing and karotin. Turn back, you've gone too far—but in truth I could go no farther. The trail of the vampires was cold, as cold as my bedroom on this autumn night.

I put the pad into the privacy of my bedroom drawer, switched off the light and snuggled down beside Dwayne. Breathing into his face stopped his snoring; now I could go to sleep. I had a male in my bed, neither Grubbs, nor Wexy, nor any man to have sex with—nonetheless the presence was comforting.

In the morning, I put the pile of tapes aside, opened my address book, and dialled an editor. I might not be a fearless vampire hunter, but I could still stalk the mighty dollar.

Months passed in this fashion. The mounds of tapes became a collector too, of dust, and the pad stayed in my bedside drawer. Then one day the phone rang during a snowfall.

"Hi, Wexy. Is this an early Christmas greeting?"

Moments earlier, I had stood up from the word processor, and opened a window to catch some flakes. They had glittered on my sleeve, each one briefly like the view down a monochrome kaleidoscope, before dissolving into shapelessness, conveying no image.

"I got the photos," he said (I had mailed them back to the mansion the morning after the nightmare). "You ever write that story? I keep looking in the magazines for it."

"Oh, it's still in progress," I white-lied. There was a deep female voice in his background, and he paused as though listening.

"Then I can help you out again. Remember those girls who had doubles on the museum walls? I—we've found them."

"Where?"

"The big AIDS conference," and I turned my head away, spluttering with noisy laughter. Where else to find vampires, in these sordid days?

"Ms Cecily? You there? Static sure is bad on this line." The voice in his background spoke again. "They're delegates from some European university," he said.

Vampires from the Ivory Tower. Wexy's tale was getting weirder and weirder.

"Where are you?" I said, and he gave the address of a plush hotel, by coincidence the same that had housed the collectors' convention. "I'll be there in a jiff," I said.

This way madness lies, said a small inner voice as I replaced the receiver, but I ignored it. Pausing only to ask Ms Next Door to look out for my child, I dashed down lunacy lane.

Wexy was waiting in the marble hotel foyer, wearing a sleek leather jacket with fur lining. Beside him was what looked like a psychedelic barber's pole, which in propinquity proved to be a girl the colour of indigo, swathed in layers of bright woollens. She had wrapped a long knitted scarf around her head, securing this turban with her convention badge.

"Meet Kathy, my girlfriend."

Wexy might be odd, but he was one of the eligible rich, I had seen that from the girls in the gallery. I wondered if this dark lady was what his family considered suitable.

"She's a doctor," Wexy said proudly, and Kathy gave him an amused glance. "Not yet," she said in a voice deep and rich as a treacle well. "Just now I'm only an exchange student, from Rwanda."

She extended a hand reminiscent of a bunch of liquorice straps, it was so black, long and thin. I put my pink mitt into it and we clasped, linked for one moment. Then Wexy spoke, interrupting our silence.

"I was telling Kathy about you, 'n' I showed her the photos. Next thing she got me down here to—"

"Confirm the sighting," finished Kathy. In repose her face was as flawless and daunting as a Benin bronze. What's in your mythology? I thought. Do blood drinkers prey in the night of deepest Africa, and how do your people deal with them? Then I looked away from her dark impassiveness. What could I say to this woman here to exchange knowledge about life and death, about the bat in my old belfry?

"They're in room 401," said Wexy.

"Thank you," and I walked away, among badges and foreign languages. The elevator was close, but for the good of my mortal weight, I decided to take the fire stairs. By the fourth floor I was winded, my heart beating with exertion as well as anticipation. I leaned against the door out of the stairwell, retrieving my breath. When it was back, I checked the contents of my bag—notepad, Biros, tape recorder, cassettes, all the tools of the newshound trade were there.

I opened the door a crack. It was silent, well-oiled, so I caught a glimpse of movement, stealth at speed. A man came out of a hotel room, glancing anxiously around him. He closed the door and went to the next, crouching to examine the lock. Then he pulled a ring of keys as thick as an Egyptian necklace from his overcoat, and began testing them, one after the other, on the door.

Hotel thief, I thought. Then I began to estimate the number of the room, counting down from those numbers visible through my eye slit. I checked on my fingers—he was breaking into 401.

A key turned, and he slipped into the room, shutting the door behind him. He knew that room was empty, I thought, maybe he had a tip-off from the hotel staff. I left my hide and stole down the passageway in my rubber galoshes, sinking soundlessly into the thick carpet. Just before 401, I half knelt, listening to the soft noises of his intrusion.

It was in this position that I was discovered, minutes later, as the elevator doors opened, opposite me. Two passengers alighted—I looked slowly upwards, from their high heeled boots, cut intricately from costly leather, to their tailored fur coats, and finally at their heads. One woman was fair, one dark: my mind's eye blinked and I saw that they were in reality two different shades of ginger. But they had rounded faces, high cheekbones and slanted eyes . . . oh thank you Kathy, I thought.

For a second I froze, but then I put finger to lip. The nearer raised an arc of eyebrow and in answer I pointed to the door of 401. The sounds within had stilled: the man was listening. "Intruder," I mouthed.

There was a pause, then they nodded and walked quickly and noisily down the corridor, to the fire exit. I followed silently in my galoshes. When the fairer one reached the fire exit door, she felt within her handbag, a lozenge of leather as colourful and shiny as a glazed lolly, I mean candy. She withdrew a room key and rattled it. The other opened the door, then slammed it shut. They were pretending to be other guests on this floor, for the burglar's benefit, I realised.

I pulled out my notepad, so as to communicate.

Hotel thief, I wrote.

The darker of the two took my humble Biro in fingers tipped with red varnish. She wrote *Gun?* Then she handed the pen back to me.

I closed my eyes, trying to recall the intruder. He was thick-set, Hispanic, and when he had turned in my direction his coat had swung open. Shining at his belt had been a —

Knife

They looked at each other and I saw the stiffening that means resolve. I recalled, with a sudden thrill, that they never took shit from anyone.

We returned down the hallway, they padding on tiptoe, their stiletto heels never stabbing the carpet. The fair woman was holding the keys carefully now, to prevent them rattling. I saw the other reach into the suede heart—it was hot pink—that was her handbag. She pulled out something that gleamed metallically as she concealed it in her hand.

At 401 there was a touch on my shoulder, and I was handed the key, with a mime of throwing the door wide open. Swallowing, I bent over the lock. I inserted the key, then quickly turned it and the door handle in concert, throwing my weight hard against the door.

I caught a glimpse of the thief, as he rose, startled, from a pillaged suitcase. Then I was knocked sideways, as the women rushed past me. The force was such that I somersaulted, coming to rest against the legs of the dressing table. I got up, unsteadily, and beheld fur, heels and overcoat in a snarling heap on the other side of the double bed. Seizing the nearest blunt instrument, a table lamp, I leapt on and over the bed, tearing the lamp plug from its socket. But I was too late—the scuffle had resolved itself into a man, face down on the carpet, with two women astride him, back to back. The dark woman held his wrists and the other his feet.

"Put that down!"

Those were the first words they had spoken to me, and though they were but three they were spoken with a detectable accent. I set the lamp on the bedside table, beside two laminated convention badges.

"Where's his knife?" I asked nervously.

The fair woman looked back over her shoulder at me, and I saw she held the knife between her teeth, the painted lips drawn back from the metal in a rictus.

"We need to tie him," said the other, and again I noticed the accent, the 'w' close to 'v', like a stage spy. I glanced around frantically, and saw the suitcase, its contents higgledy-piggledy. The uppermost item I grabbed, and found it was a silky item of underwear, with a French label. I held it up dubiously, but she nodded.

Then the man twisted, bringing his head round to face me. He goggled at the lacy shackle and bucked like a bronco. The dark woman raised one hand as she ascended, then brought it down hard on his head. He collapsed, his eyes hurt and puzzled.

"You pack quite a punch," I said, and she held out her palm to reveal a tiny but murderous pistol, of the colour and sheen of platinum.

"Take it. Point it at his face."

I did, giving in exchange the silk, which was quickly and expertly trussed around his wrists. Keeping my gaze on the prisoner, I felt in the suitcase with my free hand and withdrew another lacy unmentionable.

"This is kinky," I said, but threw it towards the trio. It was caught and used as a foot binder.

The hog tied, they arose, dusting themselves down. One retrieved her gun from me, the other spat out the knife onto the bedspread. She wiped her mouth, then dialled three digits on the hotel phone.

"Management? Room 401 here, we have surprised a thief. Can you send security?"

There was a pause, tiny excited sounds coming from the receiver.

"No," she said. "We had help, he's no danger now."

She replaced the receiver and said, "They're on their way."

The man writhed, swearing in an undertone. The dark woman stepped back, kicked him *there,* then sat calmly down on the bed. She took out her makeup kit and, together with her twin, began to restore her face to pre-fight immaculacy.

That shook me. My bag was lying under the dressing table, where it had rolled with me earlier. I sat down and lifted it onto my lap, wrapping my arms around it. Just then, I needed something to hold.

Security guards came and went, carrying the moaning intruder and his knife with them. It was all a blur to me. I was roused finally by the clink of glass against the marble of the dressing table. Looking up, I saw a tooth mug from the bathroom, and the fair woman pouring brandy into it from a chased silver flask. She moved back, leaving the glass behind—it was intended for me, I realised. I took it, and after several mouthfuls had enough courage to look clearly around me.

The room had been tidied, the suitcase repacked and stowed. Christa and Theresa were seated on the bed, in poses almost identical to those in the photograph of more than twenty years ago. They had shed their fur coats, throwing them over a bedside chair. The outline suggested the form of their sixties companion, the man with his throat exposed.

"Who are you?" said the dark one.

"I'm Cecily Chaucy, journalist," I said, and drained the glass. I set it down, then fumbled in my bag for my Press card, in the process emptying pens, pad, tape recorder holus bolus onto the shag carpet. My hands were shaking, and when I finally located the card it shot out of my grip, landing on the floor between them. I lunged for it, and found myself lying between sleek, streamlined legs. The boots that had kicked the intruder were close to my face, and I noticed that paste pearls were impaled on the tips of the heels, pearls big as the Ritz.

I smiled broadly, and held up the card for their scrutiny; they eyed it without emotion.

"What were you doing outside the door?" said the owner of the pearl boots.

I sat up, drew a deep breath and got logorrhoea. Wexy, Grubbs, Scooby, the photos, it all came out at speed, with me barely able to impose intelligibility upon it. While I spoke, they exchanged glances. Finally I ran out of words and just sat there with my mouth hanging open.

"Well," said one. "You dress like a bag lady and come out with that!"

"Clever," said the other. The ambience had suddenly become very tense. I reached back to my bag of tricks, and picked up a paperback book, holding it up so that they could see the title. It was Anne Rice's *Interview with a Vampire*.

"I want that. Please."

"You blow us," said the fair woman.

"I'll write you up like a mob informant, dates, details, names all changed."

"Too risky."

I had become uncomfortably aware that they were both bending towards me. Almost I fancied I could feel breath on my naked neck.

"I'll blow you if I don't get the interview!" I said wildly.

Did I hear the dull percussion of toothbone against toothbone?

"You can't treat me like that intruder, there's people know I'm here."

"A man café *au lait* and a girl *café*?" It was spoken close to my ear.

"No!" I said with unnecessary force, my negative too positive to be believed. I saw, and almost felt, a nod pass from one to the other. Then the little common-sense voice that had warned earlier, that this path led to madness, returned to me. I repeated its words, like an autocue.

"The man *café au lait,* as you put it, is not someone to waste without the world's notice. If I go, he'll raise Cain; if he goes, his family will."

They both leaned back.

"Bargain," said the dark woman.

I nearly laughed. Images from Dwayne's story-books crowded on me, all warning the dire consequences of haggling with the supernatural. They'll do me down, I thought, but better that than them doing me in.

"All right," I said.

"We talk, but—"

"No publicity," finished the other.

"Hey!" I said. "I want my kudos. It was hard work tracking you down."

And also luck, but I kept that to myself.

"You want your kudos more than talking?"

I thought about it. They had me there, by the neck. "No," I replied. "My curiosity is worst. I could kill for it."

They exchanged words briefly, in a foreign tongue, then the dark woman stood up.

"We talk, but no pens, paper, tapes—nothing."

I walked back on my knees to the bag, which gaped flaccidly. Gathering up my tools, I dumped them into the cavity, zipped the bag shut, then handed it to her. She opened it, to check that the recorder had not been activated, then placed it on the dressing table.

I stood, facing her, and she frisked me, coolly and asexually. With the touch, much of my fear evaporated—here was no graveyard ghoul, but a living being, albeit the strangest I had ever encountered. She sat down on the bed again, but I moved away, seeking the interrogator's distance, and found it in the coat-decked chair. There I sat, lapped by luxuriant fur, feeling momentarily like an empress. The composition of the original photo was near complete.

"Now," I said. "Which of you is Christa and which Theresa?"

"Krysia," that was the lighter haired.

"Tesia," from her dark companion.

I mulled over the names and accents: 'You aren't, not really, from Transylvania?"

They didn't laugh.

"Borders change in that part of Europe."

"We lived in a village and spoke a dialect of a little language."

A toss of the head. Evidently that defined them.

"What happened, to bring you from Little Upper Yew Tree—I mean the village—to the here and now?"

A pause. Then Tesia said lightly, "Men."

Troops had sacked the village, taking, among the booty, twin sisters.

"How old were you?"

"Oh, babies."

"No," said Krysia. "Women. Just."

I tried, mentally, to strip off their sophistication, to see two peasant girls crying in their shifts on a chill spring day. Red uniforms; red wine from forced casks, the peasant's hoard; flames. It was a picture informed overwhelmingly by European art movies. The original scene would not have been strikingly composed, with an accent of red here, an accent of red there, but haphazard and nasty, like real life.

"We fucked our way up the ranks," said Tesia. As if to mitigate the brutality of that remark, Krysia added:

"The only . . . career path."

They were both looking wry.

"A woman became Empress of all the Russias that way," Tesia said.

"Catherine the First," I said. "You knew her?"

"Before our time." That was Krysia again.

The experience had been less ugly because of their prettiness, which had won them protectors. It was an old story, one I had heard before, usually with a sentimental gloss to suit the victim-narrator. Told starkly, it jarred—particularly with the nature of these storytellers.

"You're not victims," I said, "but hunters."

Oh they looked it, curled up on the bed like a pair of leopardesses.

"We didn't know it then."

"Not at first. Girls wore out fast in that work. We thought we were just lasting well—like Diane de Poitiers."

I nodded at the name, recognising the mistress of a young French king, as pretty at fifty as her portrait by Fouquet, now some five hundred years old. Then I shook my head, as a unit of information struck home.

"You didn't know! Now I can see you don't fit the vampire stereotype exactly—you don't haunt crypts, you never died and you don't shun the day. But are you telling me you didn't think it odd, to suck blood?"

"We don't."

My mouth snapped open, as if a spring had been triggered by my own surprise.

"But . . . what are you doing at an AIDS conference, like a bad joke in the *New Yorker?*"

"The AIDS virus," said Krysia, "is not only transmitted via the blood."

I considered that remark, tried to close my mouth, but instead let out a moan.

"Seed? That's disgusting!" Then: "No wonder you don't attack women."

"We can use blood."

"We experimented."

"But it's so obvious."

"Indeed," I said ironically. "Pardon me, but your teeth are in my neck."

Again, they didn't laugh. To a real vampire, I thought, the distorted media image might not be amusing. Yet they had exploited it earlier, when they had breathed down my neck.

As if through bushes I could perceive information evading me. I circled it, tried a shot from another angle.

"*Did you* know Napoleon?"

Here they did laugh.

"No. We got as far as his marshals."

"Ah. I thought you might have caused his downfall."

They looked at me opaquely, but I pressed on.

"Grubbs said you have a Lamia effect."

Krysia looked at me disdainfully.

"You, Miss journalist?"

"Ms," I muttered.

"—who think you know so much about vampires, tell me something. Why does Dracula suck blood? What does he get from it?"

I looked into the white and green of her eyes. "Immortality, I reckon."

"But what is in the blood to do this?" asked Tesia.

I hesitated. "The life force?" Metaphysics, like an eccentric neighbour, had entered the chase, and I did not care for its presence. A text from my first year at university, Sydney in my dark ages, came to mind.

"'Their blood is their life and when they are dead they are completely ended. That was some cleric on why animals don't have souls."

"You're getting off track," said Krysia.

Pat, pat, they were playing with me. Well, three could take part in that game. I began, mentally, to flip through my old anthropology textbooks.

"Blood mysteries are a constant in primitive and *peasant* societies." Then, thinking of the conference downstairs, "There are traces of that reverence for blood in the AIDS hysteria."

A pause, while I returned to the textbook.

"Ditto for sperm in the macho societies. The ancient Greeks thought it alone gave life to a child . . . hence the meaning of the word 'seminal'."

Krysia leant back against the quilted headboard; Tesia crossed and re-crossed her dainty boots.

"You imply that there really are mystical powers in the body fluids?"

"We don't imply."

"We prove it."

Never argue with absolute certainty, I had adopted that rule after I experienced a crash landing in the company of a Baptist choir. They sang 'Nearer my God to Thee' as the fire trucks chased the plane down the runway, and meant every note of it.

"Remember Warhol?"

At that, I gave up trying to compete in their cat-and-mouse game, and just played deadpan.

"Yes, I remember." Then I twitched: "Was he one of your sixties conquests?"

They stared at me disdainfully. At one time I had interviewed the imprisoned Valerie Solanas, for a teensy feminist rag, and from her gained the impression that Andy Pandy was utterly asexual. This pair seemed to confirm it.

"He said," Krysia continued, "that in the future everyone would be famous for fifteen minutes."

"Meaning that fame would be distributed equally," I said. "Instead of just a few somebodies amongst the mass of nobodies."

Like me, I thought. The room was lit only by the soft pale light of the snowfall, but suddenly a vehicle in the car layer-cake next door shone its yellow headlamps briefly upon us. It lit up the red dye in the hair of my interviewees, and above them on the wall a print of Van Gogh's *Sunflowers*. Before, the picture had been standard hotel ambience, but now it transcended the mundane. The yellow and gold glowed at me, intense and vital.

"There was a somebody," I said, pointing. "What did he have?"

"Abundance of the life force," said Tesia.

I looked down from the picture, at them.

"Oh." I was in some muted state, beyond shock, beyond surprise. "You prey on the talented and famous because they have more life force, thus maximising your returns. And you choose men because you can collect from them, *unobtrusively*. Starfucker, starfucker, star. You really were bad karma for those musicians."

Cecily the huntress stood, one foot on her prey, the information. The chase was over, but nonetheless I pursued some pups of knowledge, in a mopping-up operation.

"A few details. Why were you with the Mafia goons? They had no genius."

"As a learning experience."

"False passports, false signatures ... they keep ahead of the technology."

"Of identity," said her twin.

Something had occurred to me: in the brothel photo the Cranach slant of their eyes had been more pronounced than in the sixties shot, and now. "Plastic surgery?"

"Yes. Much more, soon."

I supposed that their distinctive beauty would be cut away, to be replaced by an anonymous Hollywood cuteness. "Shame," I said.

"Necessary," said Krysia. She got up from the bed on one side, glancing at her gold watch; Tesia did likewise on the other side.

"We have talked enough."

"You must go."

I stood up also, and moved slowly towards the door, prolonging the interview as much as possible.

"Has the conference been a 'learning experience'?"

"We know the current state of AIDS research. There are no miracle cures; not yet. People will still be scared."

"The new celibacy is hard for us," said Tesia.

"You'll get round it, I feel sure."

They laughed, for the last time in my presence.

I hefted my bag and said: "One last, teensy-weensy question. What was the original colour of your hair?"

"We can't remember!"

Seconds later I was in the corridor, and Tesia had shut the door behind me. The elevator journey was a blur. In the lobby I glanced round, wide-eyed, and saw Wexy and Kathy on a couch, canoodling. Not wishing to disturb them, not wishing to be disturbed myself. I walked out into the street. The snow was still failing. Before me on the sidewalk was a black man dressed as Santa Claus, something so mundane that I leaned up against a wall and laughed hysterically.

Krysia and Tesia had learnt more than the manufacture of fake IDs from the Mafia. When I got home, and was unpacking my bag (with a stiff whisky handy) I found some of the contents missing: my Press card, my leather address book and a photo of Dwayne in his baseball clothes. Tesia must have stolen them when she checked the tape recorder. There was a warning in these losses—they knew who I was, where I lived, and where I was vulnerable.

Okay, I thought, you win. But their victory had been much earlier, when they had prevented me from making a record of the interview. I could still have sold the story, but without evidence only to the kook press, thus destroying whatever credibility I had as a journalist.

A first-rate newshound, I considered, pouring another whisky, would have been prepared, with another recorder hidden in the lining of the bag. Cecily, you screwed up badly.

But you wanted to, said the little common-sense voice.

"Oh shut up!" I said aloud.

No, I won't. You wouldn't have done anything they didn't want. They were wonderful, to you.

I flicked a hair out of my eye, a grey hair, I noticed.

"They were so beautiful, ageless and free," I said.

You hero-worshipped them. Groupie yourself!

"All right," I said. "So I did. I'm ashamed of myself. Now what do I do?"

Make the best of a bad job, said the voice.

I listened to the groupie tapes again, and began sorting the material into articles. The Plastercasters, and some of their more notorious friends, I used in a 'Whatever Happened to' piece, which sold to *Rolling Stone*. For the good of my feminist soul, I wrote a considered and angry analysis of groupiedom, and placed it with *Ms*. Then I was left with the slightest, but still interesting part of my documentation, the sixties collectors.

Deciding to beef it up, I interviewed the rest of the names on the original list, including a suddenly cooperative Z Smith. His ex-wife had denounced him to Falwell, and he was suing under the discrimination act for the loss of his contract. Anxious to appear a 'regular guy', he forbade any shots of the collection and posed for the photographer in a three-piece icecream suit. Scooby Doo had no such qualms, but it proved impossible to pose him in front of his collection, there was nowhere in the apartment the photographer could work unimpeded. Since I had last visited the collection had grown, and was crowding him out of house and home.

"Storage time again!" he said.

We finally shot him outside the front door, wearing all of a job lot of Peace badges he had just acquired, stuck on jeans, work shirt, baseball cap and thick beard. He looked like a psychedelic Pearlie King.

The final photo session was at the Wexford mansion. The photographer grouped Wexy and Kathy in front of the civil rights collection, and as they struck various poses (generally involving cuddling) I noticed that Kathy wore a large diamond ring.

"Wedding bells?" I said, half to myself, but a Wexford maid overheard. She was a big flinty woman, apparently present as the guardian of the polished floor, but now a smile stole over her stolid face.

"That's a good girl," she said emphatically. "A good Christian."

The photographer was changing film, and Kathy disengaged from Wexy and came over to us.

"What sort of Christian?" I asked her.

"Russian Orthodox. Lord knows how the missionary got to Rwanda."

"That's right," said the maid. "The Lord knows, He knows indeed."

The article on the collectors sold to a glossy magazine, then was reprinted in various odd spots of the globe, including dear old Oz. It wasn't the stuff of journalistic prizes, but it brought in some gourmet bacon. I asked the little common-sense voice what to do with the money, but it had apparently gone on holiday. Deciding to do likewise, I booked Dwayne and me for a trip down under, since the folks back home—I mean the rellies—were all excited at seeing my by-line in their local paper.

It was a windy spring day for our departure, with equal amounts of rain and apple blossom in the air. At the John F. Kennedy airport, Dwayne burrowed into his stack of comics. I had some improving literature to read on the flight, but felt too idle and anticipatory to begin it. Instead, I read other people's newspapers, until I was arrested by the headline 'Nobel Sperm Bank Robbed'.

I jumped up and bought a copy of the paper for myself, scanning frantically even as I handed the kiosk girl my change.

"Nobel Sperm Bank, that's for the rich folks that want some famous scientist's kid," she said.

"Yeah," I said, "IQ groupies," and she gave me a gap-toothed grin. I sat down beside the oblivious Dwayne, reading the words over and over: 'professional job . . . entire stock stolen . . . Police have no leads.'

So Krysia and Tesia had circumvented the new celibacy, just like I said they would.

SAGITTAIRE

Call it sixth sense, intuition, someone walking over an undug grave, whatever. Jos got off the plane in Madagascar, and almost as soon as he sniffed the tropical air of Antanarivo, the capital, a mental alarm bell started ringing. There was something strange there, the sort of strange that said: 'I'm going to get you . . . '

Jos wanted to voice those thoughts, but it was hard to find a suitable ear. Not the UN Peacekeepers, simply doing their job. Nor his fellow election scrutineers, and certainly not the delegations of politicians and their minders. None of these struck him as sharing his sense, so strong that it was quite overwhelming, of imminent weirdness. It hardly helped that, day after day, Madagascar kept living up to his uneasy expectations. Take the old man with the suitcase, for instance, in Nowheresville II . . .

THE TRAVELLING OF BONES

The UN *vazahas* (which was what the Madagascans call foreigners) knew they ought to be polite, politically correct. They really shouldn't nickname every backblock settlement Nowheresville, except that it was hard to get the tongue around such complex

475

names. When it came to writing down the Malagasy language, French vowels and English consonants were used, and they fought for national supremacy or at least parity: long multi-syllabic caterpillars sprawled all over the map.

Nowheresville II was at first only notable for the stinking heat, even at 10 a.m., which only the *vazahas* seemed to mind. It didn't deter the gawking kids, nor the prospective voters, their parents. Outside the town, people had congregated from the outlying villages and farms, at night sleeping on the ground in their flowing *lamba* wraps, so keen were they for democracy . . . or blood. Either could happen, with this knife-edge election.

An old man approached the UN contingent. He wore the Malagasy uniform of t-shirt, shorts and lamba, topped by a four-cornered hat. One arm was weighed down by a large battered suitcase, which he carefully put down before engaging Gaston the interpreter in machine-gun Malagasy. After the initial volley, Gaston translated:

"He's a Betsileo on his way back from a trip to the North."

They all eyed the old man. He didn't look like trouble . . .

"Betsileo are great travellers. Walk all over the island," said Gaston.

"Peaceful?" asked a Peacekeeper.

"Good citizens, family men . . ."finished Gaston.

"What does he want?"

"He's worried he won't get home in time for the election."

"Absentee vote, that's what he's after," Jos surmised. "Has he got ID?"

More machine-gunning.

"He says yes, and his voter registration papers."

"Let him through to the tent then."

The Peacekeeper growled: "Let's check out the suitcase first."

He bent over the case's rusted metal snaps, as the old man protested, too late! The case fell open, spilling large grey lumps, one of which rolled to Jos' feet. The empty eyeholes of a skull wrapped in torn newspaper stared up at him. He stepped back aghast, the sun beating on him, his head spinning . . .

A pair of firm small hands caught him as he wavered, kept him from falling. Then several Peacekeepers carried him into the shade of the registration tent. He was laid down by the entry, a damp towel placed on his forehead, with the coolest thing to hand—a coke can—resting on top. From a great distance away he heard the conversation with the Betsileo resume:

"What do we have here?" said the first Peacekeeper. "A murderer?"

Gaston explained: "It's his brother. Betsileo wander, but if they die far away, their ghosts can get homesick. Air Mad even has a special service to carry the remains, but this man decided to save the money and do it himself. He's been walking for days, carrying his brother in the suitcase."

Yet another volley from the old man.

"He says he's very sorry he upset the young *vazaha*, but his brother appeared in a dream. And insisted that he be brought home . . ."

"How do you feel?" said a woman's voice, behind Jos. She had an accent, but he couldn't identify it immediately.

"Better."

"You've gone an interesting shade of pale," she said.

"I'm not surprised."

"But you were surprised out there. So much you nearly fainted."

"It's this place," he said, too shaken not to confess. "It weirds me out."

"I remember coming here as a child," she said. "The heat, and the foreign language, and chameleons everywhere. It terrified me. But you get used to Madagascar."

"I hope," somebody said outside, "that Mr Betsileo doesn't want an absentee vote for his brother as well."

"You never know, in Madagascar," murmured the woman.

He turned his head, dislodging the Coke, to see one of the invited political observers (or junketeers, as the election workers call them). She looked a girl, with her chestnut hair cut short, but had an unmistakeable air of authority to her, as if her loose white linen shirt were a suit of armour. All he could remember is that she was a Senator from Australia. With an unusual name: Jeannith.

"*You* caught me."

She smiled: "No worries."

A Nowheresville child approached them, holding a baby lemur, the Madagascan monkey, for petting or sale. The little primate clambered into Jeannith's arms and clung to the silver pendant around her neck. He wondered why nobody had warned Jeannith about the risks of wearing jewelry in a Third World country. He checked her hand (no rings) while the monkey nibbled at the pendant. It would be a cute scene were it not that Jos recalled what lemurs were named after—the Roman spirits of the dead.

I'm too damn suggestible, he thought.

A WILD MAN WITH BACKWARDS FEET

With the next day came a change of plan and scene. Extra teams were needed for the Madagascan West, and so Jos and his fellow workers boarded a Hercules. With them went the attendant political observers, a squad of Peacekeepers, and some of the more hard-bitten journalists (not a good sign). After a cramped and earmuffed ride, the passengers disembarked at a big Nowheresville: the western provincial capital. Waiting at the airstrip were the local authorities.

Instant photo-op: the press and politicos scrambled into action! The welcome party wore western suits and ties, while the civilians on the plane were dressed for the rainy-season, in lightweight cottons and sensible sandals. The contrast gave Jos a sense of inversion: what if we whites were the Third World, and these elegant dark faces were the Firsts, the masters? Cameras whirred as observer met the officially observed, the leader of the political delegation shaking hands with the provincial Governor. Jos remembered, irreverently, Bob Geldof telling the UN General Assembly that they were either scoundrels or the representatives of scoundrels; and applied it to both ends of the handshake. But the Malagasy did have the nicer smile . . .

A convoy of jeeps took them to the town centre, dominated by a Catholic church and, to one side and surrounded by a strip of parkland, the Governor's residence, a compound behind high concrete walls painted bizarrely, in a half black, half pistachio-green stripe. Jos's hotel was on the main square, where stall-holders were packing up after market day. As night fell, loud *salegy* music was heard, and the square metamorphosed into an informal dancehall. Tomorrow the election workers would head for the Zone Rouge, the most Western and lawless part of Madagascar, but tonight they felt like partying. Look, even the priests and nuns were there—odour of sanctity, odour of safety.

"*Salut vazaha!*" said a dancer, proffering a bottle. "Thanks," Josh replied, sipping the universal language of beer. After that the night got hazy. He danced with some pretty Malagasy girls, he drank more beer, he got into an argument (in French) with a young Catholic priest called Jean-Paul.

"You *vazahas* don't know what we're up against!" the priest (nicknamed JP) kept repeating.

"The ballot or the bullet, I guess," Jos replied. He was tired and tipsy, he knew he shouldn't be talking like this to a complete Malagasy stranger, priest or not.

"There's worse things than bullets," JP muttered. "Shall I show you?"

Suddenly Jos had somebody's lamba wrapped around him, becoming the centre of a group heading away from the party—men of the cloth didn't do kidnaps, or did they? They darted through the streets, then over grass, finally hiding in the park bandstand, from which they peered cautiously at the front gate of the Governor's residence, the bottom half of the wall inky black, the green top seeming to pulse in the irregular streetlight. Clambering into a UN jeep were the politicians and journalists. Huh! Jos thought: sneaked away to a snob party, did you? Bet it wasn't as good as *our* party. He saw from between the disguising folds of the lamba the Governor lifting Senator Jeannith's hand to his mouth, a courtly, lecherous goodbye. She bent towards him, spoke—and he dropped her hand unkissed.

JP interrupted his reverie. "The main door, for his official guests," he whispered. "And now the private entry."

They doubled back, circumnavigating the wall into darkness thick as tar. Mud or worse squelched under Jos's feet, but he smelt the pungent sweetness of a rotting mango. Above them stretched the branches of a huge tree, through which shone a chunk of moon. He saw a fan of light coming from a smaller door in the wall, half open, and out from it sneaked men in dark lambas. They watched as the group dispersed into the dark, and the door closed behind them.

"See that? His unofficial, more important guests," said JP. "*Mpanandro*—sorcerors."

"What can they do?"

"What they always do here. Influence."

"The vote?"

In the dark, JP was little more than gleaming eyes, but they moved: a nod.

Someone else broke in, an urgent babble of Malagasy, in which Jos could distinguish the word *kalanoro*, repeated, in fearful tones.

"What's kalonoro?"

A sotto voce babble ensued, everyone anxious to speak.

"A hairy wild man," translated JP. "Telepathic, and with backwards feet. Does the governor's dirty work."

Further babble.

"Kalanoro love pistachios and the colour black. That's why the residence is two-toned up to kalanoro height."

"You believe that?" Jos was trying not to splutter.

"C'est la pays Malgache."

"You make it sound more like a horror story."

He remembered, then tried to forget, the newsprint-wrapped skull, its empty eyeholes.

"A horror story? In which the hero stops scribbling when the monster bites his head off? Maybe you prefer a travelogue, like your Lonely Planet writers, of a hero traveling happily through a strange land, dancing with friendly locals, drinking their beer and eating exotic food?"

Well, yes, Jos thought uncomfortably.

"And then you go home, while we live with what the election brings. We've had colonialism, monarchy, despotism, communism . . ."

Somebody in the group spoke again, empathically: the others echoed the words.

"What was that?"

"We survive. And if you watch out for the *mpanandro* in the Zone Rouge, then you will too, *vazaha*."

Somehow and sometime he got back to the hotel clutching a gift bag of locally-grown nuts, and flops into bed. He woke hungover in the pre-dawn, his alarm shrilling for an—oh gawd— 5 am departure. Standing up, something crunched under his feet . . . pistachios, or rather their shells, scattered wildly around the open window.

He took an aspirin with some bottled water, tried to think calmly and rationally. The Governor's kalanoro could be a pet lemur. A very weird one and previously unknown to science, maybe, but stranger things had happened in Malagasy zoology. Take the aye-aye, for instance, a lemur resembling Nosferatu, whose front teeth never stop growing, all the better to gnaw coconuts with . . .

He took another swig, shaking his head, but the thought of Nosferatu had brought to mind an image from the film, of swarming rats. The night thief could be a rat, and bubonic plague persisted in Madagascar.

Hang the horror stories, he thought. I'll settle for being a bloody tourist.

THE RULES OF POINTING AT TOMBS

Plague . . . sorcery, what else? You get used to Madagascar, Jeannith had said. Next day he encountered her again, waiting for the convoy to the next Nowheresville. An apology for fainting on her, graciously accepted, turned into a conversation. When the UN party left, she joined him in the hindmost jeep.

They sat in the flatbed under fierce sun, watching clouds of red dust boil up from the dirt roads in the jeep's wake. Slowly they gained privacy as the other passengers either donned their Ipods or slept off the street party. Now Jos had Jeannith's one-on-one attention, flattering even if mere political behaviour, working a room. Oh well, make the most of it, he decided.

"So, how did you get used to Madagascar?" he asked.

"I spent five years here. My parents were aid workers. I still understand Malagasy, if it's spoken slowly. And it was useful to know more about Madagascar than the rest of the Australian parliament."

"That got you in the delegation?"

"Yes, despite my being a junior senator."

"Most politicians I see are . . . more senior," he ventured.

"So the Governor pretty much said to me last night. He called me a bébé,—babe or baby—it's equally demeaning. So I said to him: 'Sainte Jeanne'!"

"Sainte Jeanne?"

"Joan to the Anglophones. She was a teenager *and* a politician. The original tough chick in chainmail."

"So you hear voices and want to save France?"

"Only on my iPod, and why stop with France?" she shot back. It might be said with a grin, but he sensed an underlying seriousness. He could say something really inappropriate here, about getting burnt at the stake, but a passenger on the other side of the flatbed started to snore.

"Looks like they went to a better party than I did," Jeannith said. "All official, all stodgy, at the Governor's. Apart from the colour scheme."

"This Catholic priest I met last night said the official residence is painted like a peppermint liquorice throughout."

"It *is*, like the interior designer took acid."

"The colour is supposed to appeal to the Governor's kalanoro," Jos ventured.

She sighed, clearly familiar with the term. "No, it *suggests* that he has a kalanoro. They don't exist."

"The priest seemed very sure they did."

"He believes in the Father, the Son and the Holy Ghost. So he shouldn't believe in kalanoros too, but this is Madagascar. There's twenty tribes, thousands of taboos, and the natural's all tangled up with the supernatural. Which means things get pretty weird at election time. Those politicians we meet, they might wear suits and ties, but they've got a *mpanandro* on the payroll."

Sorceror, he recalled with a chill. "I saw some last night, outside the Governor's."

"No surprise. He's placing a bet both ways: temporal and magical powers, spindoctors and witchdoctors."

"He had a small army of them. Enough to influence the ballot."

She made a face. "God, I hate superstition! And God too, for that matter."

Jos gaped. He knew the junketeers have been acting as if they were on holiday, wearing silly straw hats and partying hard, away from official scrutiny. But still the candour astonished him. "Hey, you're a politician!"

"So? I can still be honest about being an athiest. I'm from Australia, where even the Tories are called liberals." She leant back against the jeep's side. "Now don't look so shocked. I know you're Canadian, from the maple leaf. They're sensible people, as a rule. So tell me you're sensible too."

"Not quite. I mean, I don't know. That's what I believe. I guess you can call me an agnostic, I know that I don't know what strange things are in the universe."

"So you're placing a bet both ways. Keeping your options open."

"Not like a Malagasy politician, if that's what you mean," he said, nettled. "I simply don't know. And until I do, if I ever do, I'm keeping my mind open."

"Just watch out that nobody closes it for you then, a swami on a street corner, or a bible-basher in the next plane seat. They're out to get fence-sitters like you."

They fell uneasily silent. Around them stretched fields of green savannah, marked here and there with the lyre-shaped horns and humpbacks of grazing Zebu cattle. A nearing hill had a block-like shape on its top, and she gestured with one arm, her fingers bent down. "That's a tomb."

"Why'd you do that?" he said, imitating the gesture.

"*Fady*. It's bad luck to point at the dead."

"Fady?"

"Taboo."

In her certainty Jeannith seemed, despite her poise and position, like a rebellious teenager. He tried a dare, as he might with an ordinary girl, to stretch the moment of honesty, see how far she would, in terms of social intercourse, go: "Well, if you don't believe in superstitions, prove it. Point at the tombs."

All around them the land seemed empty of people, but she hesitated. He checked for Gaston the interpreter, in the front of the jeep, and saw the dark head lolling, apparently asleep. She followed his gaze, nodded.

"If I'm going to be sacreligious I prefer not to have Malagasy witnesses." She reached out again, this time pointing with all five fingers. "There!"

The sun beamed heat, but not on Jos at that moment. The sense of being just a happy traveller in Madagascar had vanished.

THE NOOSE IN THE WATER

Nowheresville III and its polling booth were hours away, and they stopped for lunch under the trees shading a small river. Gaston got out, eyed the mud on the bank:

"No swimming! Crocodiles!"

Lunch was fruit, baguettes and tinned fish: picnic fare, and like a picnicker he took a stroll along the riverbank afterwards, bending under overhanging boughs. Lost in a green dappled-shade daydream, he did not see Jeannith until he almost stumbled upon her. In her hand she had a length of rope, tied at one end to a tree, with the other end disappearing into the dark water. She hauled on it, remarking: "In Australia this'd be a yabbie trap. That's crawfish to you. Here . . . "

The river end of the rope splashed free of the water, and she held a dripping hangman's noose.

"Oh . . . For crocodiles?" she said after a moment.

"I don't think so." The muddy knot was intertwined with loops of plaited grass dangling small bones and seeds: a macabre necklace.

"Throw it back!" and she did, plop! Next moment they heard a rustling in the grass, got a glimpse of something dark, the size of a large lemur . . . though it could also be a Fosa, the Malagasy puma. They turned and fled back to the circle of jeeps, pausing after the initial panic to get their breath back before returning innocently to the picnic. There, they found an old man distinguished by an indigo lamba and, at the end of stick-thin legs, glittery plastic sandals. Though he chatted politely to Gaston the atmosphere was tense. In the Zone Rouge the visitor could be Dahalo, the local bandits, or their spy.

"There might have been somebody else lurking upriver," Jos breathed to the head Peacekeeper present, a Belgian lieutenant, who nodded, said to Gaston: "Give him a mango, show we're friendly, then *nous allons, tout suite!*"

The old man took the mango in one wizened hand, and bared teeth verdant from the local *qat* narcotic. Jos had never seen anyone look more like a sorceror, even with the plastic shoes. A sight for the Lonely Planet Guide, he thought.

THE COLOUR OF MISCHIEF

Half the convoy took the first fork in the road after lunch, then further sections peeled off, until only three jeeps drove, under a blazing sunset, into Nowheresville III, a town of mud and thatch houses perched on a small hill above a gurgling, pebbly river. This was the end of the line, the road into the Zone Rouge finished here, tomorrow being election day. As they drove up the hill, they saw the surrounding flats bright with lambas: the waiting voters.

Jos, via low cunning and deft manipulation, had swapped destinations, ending up with the half of the Australian delegation which included a Shadow Minister, and also Jeannith. However, there was no chance for further intimate talk, and the chat in the jeep stuck strictly to electoral business.

During the unloading he found Gaston temporarily alone and made the most of the opportunity. "What does a noose in riverwater mean?"

"To my tribe, nothing." With mild hauteur. "Here it could mean anything."

"Can you ask the locals?"

Gaston looked indignant: "You don't ask about other people's fadys, vazaha." Implication: bad manners or worse . . .

"Would a mpanandro decorate a noose with bones and grass?"

The interpreter paused, the silence a qualified yes.

"I saw it at lunchtime, like a trap for something."

"The old man! He wore indigo, which is a mpanandro colour all over the island. It can mean mischief."

What mischief can a noose in water do? thought Jos. Affect an election? If I can entertain that thought, then Madagascar is really getting to me.

STAR SIGNS

Dinner was with the délégué (headman/mayor) and the advance party of Peacekeepers, who had been here for days setting up the election booths. It comprised boiled rice, flavoured with scant flakes of dried saltfish, washed down with Whisky Malgache, which disappointingly proved to be water boiled with burnt rice from the cooking pot. Children and adults stared through the open windows, watching how vazaha ate. Most of the attention went to the Australian Shadow Minister, a man who looked like a bank clerk, but had a farmer's big hands, and bigger, slouchy hat. Despite Madagascar's history of powerful (even psychotic) Queens, thought Jos, remembering his Lonely Planet potted history, Jeannith was secondary—as if she were merely a political wife, seated beside Mrs Délégué and her small daughter. The child had stared at Jeannith all meal long, but now she advanced upon her, smiling. Jeannith responded, and the child stood on tiptoe, catching at her pendant. She crowed, one word: "Bibyolona!"

The room, and the watchers outside, went quiet.

"It's only my star sign," Jeannith said. "I was born under Sagittarius." She held the pendant up to the one electric light, showing an engraving of a man-horse.

Gaston squinted at it: "Ah, *Sagittaire* in French, like in the newspaper horoscopes."

"Bibyolona . . ." repeated the headman. There was an earnest colloquy with Gaston.

"He wishes to respectfully enquire if your Sagittaire is an ody?"

"Oddy?" said the Shadow Minister.

"A lucky talisman," explained Gaston.

Jeannith opened her mouth, as if to say no, and then paused. The balance had changed in the room: the Zone Rouge Malagasy were eyeing her with new respect, even outright awe.

Jeannith looked pleased. "Tell him, if he wants it to be, then yes."

And Jos thought: so now you do play along with superstitions, to get the respect. Politico!

HALF MOON RISING

After dinner the evening seemed so cool and peaceful that Jos strolled down the main street of Nowheresville III, then, emboldened by the not accidental company of several Peacekeepers, including the lieutenant, wandered beyond the town limits. The crowd of voters had settled down for the night, small cooking fires dotting the landscape. Jos was reminded of a scout convention, or an outdoor rock festival, though again he felt that niggle of Malagasy weirdness.

"We have no way of knowing which are good citizens, which are Dahalo," said the lieutenant. He indicated a circle of white stones, marking the landing spot for the helicopter, which tomorrow would take the filled ballot boxes for counting in 'Tana. "The voting, and the lift-off, that's the priority. After that, we vamoosh and count the votes. And hope we don't get another Timor."

Above them shone a half moon, and it glinted off several vazahas coming towards them, Jeannith and Gaston, with their own Peacekeeper escort.

"We just saw the old man from the river! Down among the voters," Jeannith cried.

Gaston qualified: "We saw an old man in a dark lamba and glitter sandals."

"Plastic shoes are high fashion in the Zone Rouge," said the lieutenant.

Jeannith looked momentarily abashed. "We couldn't get close enough to see if it was the same man. But people acted scared of him."

The lieutenant sighed. "That's not an offence. Even if he is Dahalo."

They moved on again, Jeannith attaching herself effortlessly to their party and walking slightly ahead with the Lieutenant. They made a handsome couple in the moonlight, Jos noted enviously, though the conversation was initially electoral. Then the lieutenant asked:

"So what brings you here, Mademoiselle Senator, to this island at the end of the world?"

Yes, thought Jos, what motivates you, Ms Materialist Girl?

Jeannith smiled: "To do good, help people."

Like me. Help if only in a small way, thought Jos. Then her next words made him realise how unlike him she was.

"That's the conventional answer, and one I believe in. But there's more. *La Gloire*. My mother's fault, I'm afraid. She wanted a strong woman's name for me, but she couldn't decide between Saint Jeanne d'Arc or Judith, the battle-maiden, or the charmer who beheaded an enemy générale. Finally she decided on a double-whammy, so I became Jeannith, after two heroines. And the name, it seemed, had an influence, because I developed a yen to do good, but *gloriously*. And thus I took to party politics, as Saint Jeannith might have done, in another time and place."

Jos understood then that Jeannith's sudden semi-intimate and intense focus, the moments of apparent artless candour, were for everyone, part of a bigger picture, an ever-upwards path. If flirtation was a tool, then she would use it, even on a nobody from Montreal, like him. Although his erotic castle in the air was a tentative construction, it still tottered alarmingly on its foundations . . .

To be followed by splashing from the river, screams and panic in the field of voters. It started on the riverbank and spread like locusts. The mass of lambas heaved, twisted, divided.

"*Le Diable*! The Dahalo!" said the lieutenant. "*Au village!*"

Jeannith stood her ground, watching the uniforms and Gaston recede. Jos, simply because she stayed, did likewise. The Peacekeepers shouted for reinforcements; the voters screamed, one word intelligible:

"Bibyolona! Bibyolona!"

"Which is, I think, the translation of Sagittaire . . . whatever that is," Jos said.

"I don't know, I never was in the Zone Rouge before." For the first time since Jos had met her, she looked uncertain.

"Can you understand what they're shouting?"

She listened intently. "Some of it. 'Half moon' . . . that's when Bibyolona walks . . . 'if he sees you he'll kill you'."

From the direction of the village the lieutenant yelled: "*Get back here!*"

Jeannith ignored him, staring avidly across the flat at the lambas fleeing in all directions. They looked as filmic as extras but this was reality, not an action or horror movie. Down by the river, a dark shape moved: the silhouette of a man leading a horse, no a man on a horse, no a man-horse.

"A centaur!" Jos tried to remember about centaurs, they liked girls, they couldn't hold their drink . . . no, that was the white man's centaur, the Malagasy version was surely different.

"Madagascar's not *that* weird. It's a trick, disrupting the election."

"Then it's working . . ."

"It's only popular delusion and the madness of crowds," she said. "Like far too much else in the world. Come on!"

She clutched her hand to her chest, went running towards Sagittaire. What can she do? he wondered, but followed, heart thumping. As they neared, the shape resolved itself into the sorceror or his double, sandals gleaming in the light of the bad half moon, leading, by a noose around its neck, a monster. Its feet were splayed, its heavy body covered with matted hair, where a horse-neck should be was a human torso, stocky and muscular, the head deformed, the hands clawed. It dripped river and mud, it smelt like stagnant water and flyblown meat.

Jos had known fear in his various elections, but not this stark, sensual terror. Maybe he cringed, for Jeannith grabbed his shoulders, shouting: "Don't you know what it is?"

Faced with her certainty, the Malagasy collective madness or critical mass of superstition momentarily deserted him and he saw through her athiest's eyes. The noose merely led a horse, shivering and swaybacked, with riding on its back a huge black lemur. A kalanoro? In the dark he could not check if its feet were backwards or not.

Then the mpanandro jerked on the rope and he saw Bibyolona again. The saw-toothed mouth opened, bellowing earsplittingly, weirdness in crescendo. The monster reared, towering over them, front legs lashing out. Jos ducked, avoiding a hoofstrike, and fell headlong, hitting his head hard against a rock. The visions spun, but for a moment he saw something else: on the other side of the river moonlight glinted off gun barrels. The Dahalo, the mpanandro's reinforcements, superstition *and* brute force.

Jeannith was still standing, facing Biblyolona. She reached down, into an abandoned yet smouldering cooking fire, and extracted a branch. It flared as she lifted it, illuminating her Sagittarius pendant, the man-horse star sign, held out in a gesture of command. He realised that she was countering superstition with a horoscope charm, a pretend ody against a pretend centaur. A lie against a lie, he thought, but she doesn't see as I do, that the lie has reality, and can kill. Her power game can only work if she has miraculous—or frightening—strength of will. But she has, the politicians' self-belief, equally delusory and dangerous.

He closed his eyes temporarily, a cop-out, but he could not cope anymore. When he opened them again, the flame and half moon made a shadow dance in which the magical flickered in and out of existence. Two fantasies imposed upon him, the menacing Malagasy centaur and the girl who would be a modern Saint Jeanne. Which was the stronger? He would believe in her, he willed it, but his agnostic balance got in the way. I know that I don't know, he thought; I do not know if I can believe, in either of them, Sagittaire or Sainte Jeanne.

He sat up shakily, and with that the two sides, the two realities, settled into balance, as if he was the fulcrum on the fence. A traveler might run away; but neither could he lie there and hope that Bibyolona would not bite his head off, as if he was stuck in a horror story. He reached around, and curled his fingers around the rock. It came out of the ground readily, the size and roughly the shape of the Betsileo's skull. Light enough to throw; heavy enough to inflict real damage.

A nobody no more, he lunged forward, into horror or a traveller's tale, he could only find out, though he died in the attempt.

MATILDA TOLD SUCH
DREADFUL LIES

What's that you've got in your lap? I know you're doing more than contemplating the billabong, sitting there with your back against the big river gum and your straw hat bent over what, since you're one of the womenfolk, I'd say was a mirror—except no mirror goes tap tap tap tap. Seen a lot of new things I have, mostly recently, yet what you're playing with has me mystified. But not for long, I reckon.

I can see it's got keys on it like a button accordion—now that brings back the memories. *Da-dum-de-da-dum* . . .

You stopped just then, didn't you, thinking your ears were playing tricks. I'm good at mimicry, that's how I learned to talk, from the various visitors. I can do all sorts of voices, from parrot to chainsaw to what I'm speaking now, Old Bush Bloke. Once heard, and I store it away, like the snatch of button accordian you just heard, playing *the song*. That's from the night a mob as called themselves the Communist Folkclub of Brisbane held a bushdance here. Commemorating the centenary of the song, you see, by having a knees-up where it all started, beside the bloody billabong.

I could have told them a few things about the song, like how the poet chappie sat, not where you are, but two trees along. Wore white like you do, and a big hat, but without flowers on it, being a fella. He had a little notebook and a pencil and he just sat there swatting away the blowies and scribbling. Whistled while he worked, too. Took me some time to figure out what he was up to, till I did my old trick and wormed my way into the back of his head, letting the thoughts run over and around me until they made sense.

Trying to fit words to the tune, he was. He had a story in mind, but he couldn't get the words to suit. So I thought I'd give him a helping hand. Course, some things got lost in the translation, but he got his song down in the end. Did all right with it, too, seeing as it ended up as the unofficial national anthem. Now and then I think I shoulda had a share in the royalties, but then I've not exactly got a use for money.

Still, that damn song's brought me extra visitors, like the commie folkies and their centenary. And now you, with your hat and your . . . excuse me, the curiosity's just killing me, to hear that tap tap tap and not know what you're up to. Ah, that's better. Hmn. Thought so. In the storytelling game, are you? Just like the poet chappie.

I like a good yarn, though it's not something I encounter often. For a while the number of stories I heard could be counted on a double bunch of dactyls. No, I don't mean fingers—I'm not one of your speciesists, could hardly be, given the circumstances. These days when I think back the line between paw and claw, digit and hand, seems a bit blurred. Ask me about the missing link, and I'd say something like: well, it's not that easy to pinpoint. But I do remember the first yarnspinner, like it was only yesterday.

Being of the stationary kind of persuasion, I usually have to wait until the tale, or rather its teller, comes to me. So that meant I didn't know about stories for . . . oh . . . must have been millenia, and I mean thousands of years, mate. Not that I was bored, given the visitors. Sometimes it seemed that you could blink and they'd be gone forever: goodbye, diprotodon, procoptodon, thylacine. Ever followed a roo's tracks, or seen from the mud around a waterhole who's come a-drinking? I had quite a visitor's book, though it was only temporary. Cast of thousands, no plot, unless it was who ate who. Yep, that was something you could certainly read from the footprints, until the next rain came and washed it all away. First time I saw one of the storytelling mob, he chased an old man emu through the billabong, catching it in the claggy dry season mud at the shallow end. Well, that wasn't unusual, nor was the rock he used to dispatch the emu, though I have to say it made a rotten axe. He dragged the carcass onto dry land quickly, showing a proper regard—not like some have—for the local water supply. Up on the bank he lit a fire and singed off the feathers. The meat was just starting to cook when the rest of his band—missus, littlies, coupla greyhairs, caught up with him.

Their eyes just bulged at the food, and that's when he started, singing out at the top of his voice, waggling his backside like an emu, miming axe blows. Had me flummoxed at first, till I thought of dingos dozing in the sunlight with their paws twitching and mouths slavering, dreaming about the chase. Yet he was awake, not asleep and telling a story about Emu and Mr Great Big Hero Hunter. Since he hadn't got the audience there for his big kill, except me, and I don't count, he was letting them know what happened. And embellishing it too, I could tell—he made that little barney go on for thrice the time it actually did.

Liar, liar your pants are on fire, I could have said, not that I knew what pants were, because he wasn't wearing *any*. Indeed I wouldn't see any nether garments, as the parson chappies would say, for thousands of years. In that time I got to hear a lot of stories, though. Emu and Hunter went through a few changes over the centuries, all sorts of stuff about totems mixed up in it, also ancestors . . . because it became the Hunters' family history. Lost count of the number of descendents he had, but they kept telling the story. They'd visit once or twice a year, have a good party with lots of dancing and bush tucker, and yarn to each other in the firelight.

Other stories they told were Kookaburra and the three sexy sisters, Greedy old Auntie who became a fruitbat, and bit by bit I thought I got the hang of this storytelling business. It had a beginning, middle and end, and also a moral. Don't steal someone else's tucker, don't go fornicating with your grandma, or something bad will happen. It may sound old-fashioned, but then I am. Old-fashioned and unashamed of it. You notice I used the word fornicate, instead of the modern equivalent . . .

Well, like I said, I thought I'd got the hang of yarnspinning, but then along came another mob of storytellers and moved the bloody goalposts. It happened on a peaceful kind of day: sunny, warm and so still the gumleaves hardly stirred from sunrise to sunset. Just like today, in fact, and if you'll look around you'll see the scene of the crime's hardly changed. I don't care for change much. That was why what happened came as such a surprise.

One moment there I was, minding my own business and next half a doz of the Hunter family came haring across the plain, as if they were closing in on a big roo. When they got nearer, I saw from the look on their faces that something was badly wrong. What's eating you, I thought, though a better phrasing might have been: what's gunna eat you? I wondered if the thylacoleo, our local attempt at a lion, had made a comeback, since I could hear something coming, big and noisy.

It went: thud-ker-thump, thud-ker-thump. I could see the Hunters wanted to run, but they were utterly bushwhacked. Through the trees I saw something bigger than the local fauna had been for—oh, for several eons. It was misshapen too, with two heads, one a bit like the Hunters, but the colour of a ghost gum, the other long-faced, with flaring nostrils and great staring eyes. The creature stopped under the paperbark, and blow me down if it didn't split itself through the middle, Ghostgum leaping off Longface, like a littlie from off ma's back. At the sight all the Hunters threw themselves into the water, there being nowhere else to hide but under the overhanging banks. But they didn't stand a chance, for Ghostgum lifted what looked to me like your standard digging stick and pulled thunder out of the air.

It deafened me, and the Hunters, who were swimming and wading into the billabong as fast as they could, they stopped with each peal of thunder, one by one. Happened so fast there wasn't a damn thing I could do, not even when I saw the red blood seeping into the water. Longface put its head down and ate grass, not interested; and that told me just who was the herbivore, who the carnivore. Ghostgum, on the other hand, he cuddled his stick, spearthrower, whatever, and smiled at the bodies floating in my billabong.

Pleased with himself he was, I could tell that, despite the contents of his mind being largely alien to me. I read snatches of his story, though none of it made sense for a good long while: something about him and a lot of other ghostgums on this big canoe, a few of them chiefs with thunderkilling sticks and bright red ochre all over them, but most locked below, tied together and feeling pretty sorry for themselves too. He sat there in the darkness running through his memories, mostly one of a dead ghostgum girl, her throat cut. That was why he was travelling over the water, being *transported*, and he was pleased about that too, the alternative being him hanging neck first from a big bare tree.

It was a nasty place, that mind of his, and it all got too much for me—the crowding of the ghostgum faces, more than all the Hunters I'd seen over the millenia, the words I'd never heard before, the sense that things were changing in my nice quiet billabong, which was now dyed red with blood. I got out quick and just let Ghostgum ride away, on Longface, whom he called Horse. He called himself an Englishman, an Explorer, though when I understood more of his thoughts, I knew he was only an explorer's servant, hired to do the dirty work. Which meant, slaughtering the Hunter people, just because they had a bit of spirit in them and weren't going to be walked over . . .

Now, I'm the contemplative type, not a big hero. I let bygones be bygones, arrange things my own quiet way, which means no showing off, no getting physical if I can help it. But I had to do something, the fish and tadpoles were already gagging on the blood, and I knew the usual mob of roos, etc. would show up for drinkies at sunset. No way was I going to let the local water supply stay polluted. So I just rolled up the Hunters in a sheet of paperbark and pushed them through the clay bottom of the billabong and deep into the rock shelf below, which was ammonite era. Completely confused the geological record, not that anybody's ever going to make a scientific paper out of it. They'd have to get past me first.

It's a pleasant spot, the billabong, just the place for a village, but you'll notice that nobody's ever done more than camp here, temporarily. Wonder why? See, I don't mind the occasional company, but no way am I gunna be in anyone's backyard. Sure the idea entered the various visitors' minds, but I just reached in and nipped it in the bud. Just like I got rid of the ghostgum's tucker, those bloody great wallopers of cattle, and worse, those stupid woolly sheep, with their hard hooves crumbling the banks and muddying the water. It was dead easy, all I had to do was take the idea of the slaughterhouse from out of the ghostgum's minds, put it into those herbivore brains, and then watch the stampede, whee!

After a while I got used to the new mob of visitors, who weren't all bad. Once I got to understand them, I found they had some interesting stories, quite my sort of thing. They believed in beginnings and ends, and morals too—that's why their evildoers were punished by being chained up and shipped to the other side of the world. Convicts, that was what my first ghostgum had been, and I saw a few like him, though none with such a nasty little history. Others came visiting, squatters, gold prospectors and drovers, though in the case of the latter, they tended to find themselves chasing a trail of dust and dags across the plain.

There was a governess from one local station, whose head was full of tales about love and romance, and the overseer from the next station, who thought a lot about a lass with quite a history, *Fanny Hill* by name. They used to ride out for trysts here, and told each other stories, so to speak. Then they didn't show for quite a while, and when they did they had half a dozen steps and stairs, come to get christened and watch ma and pa get married. See, a parson chappie had trekked out to this district, which was back of beyond those days, and found himself work for a week.

Up on the far bank, that space I keep clear in case the visitors feel like a spot of dancing, he set up his travelling altar and font. The latter was for the ghostgum littlies, and a bunch of the Hunters, the women in floral smocks, the men in *nether garments* and calico shirts, come to be baptized too. Wasn't their idea, they weren't keen on Christianity except for the bit about 'Thou Shalt Not Commit Murder!' But they cheered up mightily when they realized that some things didn't change at this particular waterhole. See, when the parson got carried away with his casting out of the baptismal demons and actually sloshed holy water into the billabong, the Hunters danced for joy, because at the end I was still bloody there. The parson reckoned it was conversion enthusiasm; I just had a good old laugh. Then, while I had a chance, I picked his mind about the big black storybook he carried. It had some interesting yarns in it . . .

Now, I'd had bit parts in some of the Hunter's stories, which is why they kept visiting. Still do, the last time being only last month, with several lawyer chappies in tow. Figure they must be planning a land claim, which is fine, so long as they don't forget about yours truly! I suppose their claim's maybe what brought you here, though you've got the song in your head, I can tell by the rhythm of your tap, tap tap. One catchy little ditty, innit? Whitefellas' dreaming, that's what the Hunters reckon, but they know there's more to the story than what the poet wrote down in his little book. Like the swagman, f'r instance.

Now I've seen swaggies over the years, and never a one's been what you might call jolly. Jolly skinny, maybe, and jolly shabby, but never cheery. Life's hard for roving farmworkers, which is the polite way of putting it, the impolite way being tramp. That summer was tough for everything in the district: heatwave, dry, and all sorts of trouble among the ghostgums, that I never quite worked out, except that it had to do with sheep. Jumbuck, that's the word the poet used, though nobody says that now. Funny how the name came about, from the Hunters mishearing 'Jump Up!', and thinking it was the proper noun. Knowing the way drovers swear, it's lucky we didn't have flocks of *fornicators* all over the place.

Anyway, early one evening I got a visitor, creeping through the trees, a big heavy swag near bending him double. When he dropped the load I saw he was a skinny old fella, bald as an egg on top, with a long stringy grey beard. He had a way of looking around, as if someone were after him, and I knew why. That bag of his smelt of someone else's tucker.

He got his breath back, and then he unrolled the swag, to reveal a mass of dusty curls. Dead sheep, but not any old hunk of mutton, because the kink and thickness of that wool said pedigree merino. Madman, I thought, or too starved to care, or both. He got out a big knife, and started carving up the carcase like a butcher. The blowies of course made a beeline, but he just stopped, dug a deep hole and buried the innards, being tidy, or covering his tracks. The hide he hung over a bough, for drying later. Then he started a small fire, banking it up so it got hot enough for a roast. He was so peckish by this stage that he was fair drooling.

Some galahs up in the treetops were having a screeching match, so he didn't hear, like I did, the sounds of a party of three or four on horseback, coming up quietly. He was just sitting there, staring into his fire, and I caught the topmost thoughts in his mind. They were mostly about roast lamb, but there was other stuff, recent too, about a couple of young lovers lying dead and bloody by the roadside. Been to a bushdance, they had, going home happy as lizards until they met this jolly swaggie. He grinned at the memory, and I started to get an odd feeling about him. The word's at the back of your mind, if you don't mind I'll borrow it. Yep, *déjà vu*.

I got distracted from what he was thinking then, because the next lot of visitors were nearing, as close to tiptoe as a horse can get. There was tracking going on, the sort of thing the Hunters do better than anyone else, but it wasn't a roo hunt, more a manhunt. That must have been one prize jumbuck, I thought, and sat back to witness the music, not that any of us knew the song then. The horses stopped for a while and there was a bit of whispering. Then they CHAAARGED!

It wasn't true that the squatter rode up on his thoroughbred—I reckon that was just the poet putting himself in the story. He did get it right about the three police, for what came galloping through the trees were two young constables, both new chums, and a black tracker, one of the Hunter family. The old swaggie jumped like he'd been shot, which he hadn't, it being damn hard to hit anything from a speeding horse. He let out a screech, as though he'd just seen one of the parson's demons. See, the jumbuck was weighing on his conscience, as were the lovers lying dead in the paddock, and a lot of other bad stuff too.

The swaggie had no place to run, as the coppers were coming up hard and fast, so he threw himself into the billabong. As he hit water I caught a thought of his, that maybe that wasn't a good idea, because he was starting to remember the place. I got the picture then, clear in his mind, of young Ghostgum when he was clean-shaven and had a full head of hair, aiming with his shotgun at the black bodies splashing away from him. Fifty years ago, it had been, and now there came more evil memories, the lass back in England with her cut throat, and a whole bunch of others, all of them unable to fight for their lives.

Like I said before, I think a story should have a beginning, middle and end. I like a moral too, and this filthy coward never had a proper one made of him, because transportation only gave him more places to get away with murder. Also, it had been a long time since I'd been in a story. So, when he surfaced he found me, getting physical just for him, which meant large as life and twice as ugly. He got such a shock he went and p-ed himself, and because he'd polluted my billabong *again*, I spat the dummy. I just grabbed him in my jaws and drowned him in the mud at the bottom of the waterhole. Then I threw the body twenty or so feet up in the air, and it came crashing down in front of the coppers.

I can do the police in different voices: the Irish bloke said *"Uisge-each"*, the Scots bloke said *"Kelpie"*; all translations for what the black tracker thought, but didn't say, because you don't talk about some things with the uninitiated. As they'd good and got the point, I disappeared into the water, making it look as if it was boiling, just for effect. Oh, I know I was showing off, but it only happens once in a blue moon, orright? They exchanged glances, and then, because they had evidence of sheep-stealing and the culprit had been banged to rights, against the ground in fact, they made the most of the opportunity. Gathering up the remains of jumbuck and swagman, they loaded them onto the spare horse, and skedaddled.

Course, back at the station questions might have been asked, about the guilty party's broken bones, from the fall, and his drowning in a waterhole the locals knew was only a foot deep during the dry season. But he was just helping with police enquiries, see. I reckon that if I hadn't interfered, they'd have had the pleasure of beating confessions out of him to decades of unsolved homicides. Ah, but then all those books saying whodunnit, fictions the lot of them, would never have been written. Nor the song, because the poet didn't want to write about a murderer, he wanted a working class hero, even if it was a swaggie. He was slightly commie at the time, but soon got over it.

I knew the black tracker wouldn't talk, so it must have been one of the others, over a few beers in a shanty, maybe. Coupla years later the poet heard a wisp or shred of the story, and showed up one day on his thoroughbred, seeking inspi-bloody-ration. He thought he'd write a nice little song about a haunted billabong. Course it wasn't haunted, except by yours truly, but I just couldn't seem to get that through his head.

You've gone all quiet now, no more tap tap tap. Well, just then I went quiet myself, as you do when the silence of this place gets to you, and you just want to listen. Oh, tap tapping again, are we? I've got the feel of your thoughts now, I know that what you've got there is a new-fangled notebook, a machine for storytelling. Mind if I sneak a look over your shoulder, see through your eyes a mo'? I do like a good yarn.

Well, blow me down, if all those lines and squiggles there aren't your story, but *mine*. And all the time there I was thinking I was talking to myself as usual, with nobody listening. Psychic, are you? Part Hunter? Gotta say one thing, you're good at taking dictation, much better than the poet. That's word perfect, faithful. Good as your other little stories, that you write in this notebook? It's only my second attempt at storytelling, you see.

What you're gunna do with it, though, now you've got the real story behind the ballad? A yarn's made for spinning to others, you know. Think you got a sure little earner there, good as "Waltzing Matilda", by Mr A. B. Paterson and A. N. Other? Like I said before, it's not as I've got any use for money, bunyips don't, on the whole. So take it and good luck to you.

AFTERWORD

Currently there are several memes circulating around the Net, to be posted on Facebook pages. You can choose from a variety of 30 day challenges, such as favourite songs or favourite movies. So, given that there are 25 stories here, written over that many years, and adding up to some 150,000 words (gulp, have I really written so much?), perhaps some of the form could apply to this afterword. With inspiring soundtracks, when I can recollect them.

I.
YOUR FAVOURITE STORY?

I have been known to say that it is the one I happen to be working on, even if it is proving a little bugger to write. Yea verily, for every sentence that writes itself easily, there are many more that dribble out like blood out of the proverbial (heart of) stone. I get a buzz out of chasing words down a page, I have also been known to say, and when that happens, it is better than the most expensive drugs.

The story that others like best? Well, I have been nominated for awards and won them, also made reprint anthologies and Year's Best anthologies. The most translated story is "Absolute Uncertainty", the by-product of reviewing a book about the history of physics, and incidentally the late Peter McNamara's Australian favourite, as cited in *Wonder Years*. But if I had a personal best it would be "Matricide", a story that is, well, personal. It appeared in SCIFI.COM, and then sunk without trace, except for an appearance in Bill Congreve and Michelle Marquardt's *Year's Best*. Like most authors, I am always hoping to better myself with each tale, but this marriage of technique and emotion is not something I could ever write twice.

(*Soundtrack:* "Absolute" gets Tom Lehrer, "Element Song"; "Matricide" gets Nico's "The Fairest of the Seasons".

2.
YOUR LEAST FAVOURITE STORY?

"Montage", I regret to say. Good atmospherics, entirely the result of walking along Wilson's Promontory beaches, but I've have done it differently now. Russell pointed out it had to go in, as it was shortlisted for an award. Okay.

(*Soundtrack:* Hunters and Collectors, "Talking to a Stranger")

3.
A HAPPY STORY?

My mother Marian said "Runaways" was a "warm story", and cheered her up. That in my book is very high praise. I could also revisit my pre-teen obsession with horses, and the landscape around Skyline Ridge, Yarra Glen, where my family lived for while in a log cabin. It was destroyed in a bush firestorm, Black Saturday, 2009. In retrospect a suicidal place to live, but it gave Marian art, and me stories.

(*Soundtrack:* Martin Carthy's version of the folk song, "Skewbald")

4.
A SAD STORY?

Quite possibly "The Lottery". "You wiped out all life on earth!" someone said to me after I read the story aloud in a New York bookshop. Umn, so I did, all vertebrate life. But I don't feel sad about it. Think what the other possibilities could have been!

(*Soundtrack:* Saint-Saens, "Carnival of the Animals—Fossil section")

5.
A STORY THAT MAKES YOU ANGRY?

"Kay & Phil", for misogyny, wilful literary neglect, and people who cannot tell the difference between a writer's actions in life and in their books.

(Soundtrack: Do Re Mi, "Man Overboard")

6.
A STORY THAT REMINDS YOU OF SOMEONE?

'Does the character in "The Revenant" have anything to do with Roger Weddall?' I got asked. The only reply was yes, but it was qualified, as with any depiction that goes through the fiction mills of the mind. It is good manners, and good sense, given the libel laws, to do as the novelist Frances Trollope did, and mince a character up finely: "for you would never recognise a pig in a sausage!" That said, the story is less about the actual Roger, nearly twenty years dead, than it is about regret.

(Soundtrack: Joni Mitchell, "Amelia")

7.
A STORY REMINISCENT OF PLACE?

"Red Ochre" for Cape York Peninsula, Queensland. Erewhon station in New Zealand, for "The Queen of Erewhon", drawn from a childhood memory. Franz Josef glacier, for "Albert & Victoria". From direct experience comes landscape, setting . . .

(Soundtrack: Wire, "Map Ref"; The Chills "Pink Frost").

8.
A STORY THAT REMINDS YOU OF YOUR PAST?

All of them, for memory, the sum total of what you are, informs everything you write, either dreams or actuality. But I choose to remember "The Parish", for it was the first story to be sold, and it was literally a life-saver. Even now, I see virtues in it, chiefly the dialogue.

(Soundtrack: The Go-Betweens, "Cattle and Cane")

9.
A STORY REMINISCENT OF AN EVENT?

"A Tour Guide in Utopia", for being invited to submit to the *Bulletin* twice in two years (the other being "The Lottery"), and being thrown out twice. And then selling the story to an Oxford University Press anthology. I believe in revenge, and always get it somehow.

(*Soundtrack:* Mission of Burma, "Academy Fight Song")

10.
YOUR FAVOURITE CHARACTER?

Funny how I seem to go in for bloody-minded and irreverent characters. Of which, the loudest and most fun is Raffy, from "My Lady Tongue". I used to encounter a woman who loved the story, and pestered me to write more tales about Raffy. I replied: "I can't do that until she takes me by the scruff of the neck!" Whereupon she walked behind me and, I swear, came very close to doing just that.

(*Soundtrack:* The Flaming Groovies, "Shake Some Action")

11.
A GUILTY PLEASURE?

"God and Her Black Sense of Humour" because I'd never do anything like that again. I don't know how I thought I could get away with it.

(*Soundtrack:* PJ Harvey, "Good Fortune")

12.
THE STORY THAT DEPICTS YOUR LIFE?

They all do, through a filter.

(*Soundtrack:* Lucinda Williams, "Car Wheels on a Dusty Road")

13.
YOUR FAVOURITE HORROR STORY?

"La Sentinelle". When sometimes the only way to depict sexual violence is to make it really, really grotesque.

(*Soundtrack:* Doll by Doll, Self-titled)

14.
FAVOURITE ACTION?

Walking through the forest at night in "Runaways"; or Germany in winter in "Something Better than Death", where what did happen melded seamlessly with what didn't happen.

(*Soundtrack:* Liz Phair, "Strange Loop")

15.
YOUR FAVOURITE ROMANCE?

Bet and Larissa in "Ardent Clouds"—explosive, volcanic, never consummated and never expressed. Or "Albert & Victoria" for resignation, the long haul unto death us do part.

(*Soundtrack:* Bernart de Ventadorn, "Can Vei la Lauzeta Mover")

16.
FAVOURITE MYSTERY?

"Mist and Murder". My homage to pioneering crime writer Mary Fortune, and a subversion of her story "Mystery and Murder".

(*Soundtrack:* The Sonics, "Strychnine")

17.
YOUR FAVOURITE SF STORY?

"Robots & Zombies Inc", for the opportunity to turn political leaders into androids.

(*Soundtrack:* The Only Ones, "Another Girl, Another Planet")

18.
THE STORY THAT MAKES YOU LAUGH?

"Duchess", for the fun I had creating lists of increasingly improbable garments for the Duchess to wear.

(*Soundtrack:* The Kinks, "Dedicated Follower of Fashion")

19.
A STORY WHICH YOU WISH YOU HEARD ON THE RADIO?

I want John Clarke to read "Matilda" on ABC radio. He is also a transplanted Kiwi, and the line "Being of the stationary kind of persuasion . . ." I can hear in his deadpan ironic voice.

(*Soundtrack:* Eric Bogle, "The Band Played Waltzing Matilda")

20.
A STORY FOR HOME RENOVATORS?

"Frozen Charlottes".

(*Soundtrack:* Gillian Welch, "Tear my Stillhouse Down")

21.
A STORY YOU CAN DANCE TO?

"Merlusine", set to Cajun rhythms, or "Oh how she dances!", either the Panther Burns or Jimmy Dickinson versions.

22.
YOUR FAVOURITE STORY FROM LAST YEAR?

"Sagittaire", for I was still trying to work out the ending.

(*Soundtrack:* David Lindley and friends, *A World out of Time*, music from Madagascar)

23.
A STORY THAT DOESN'T FIT ANY OF THESE CATEGORIES?

"The Lipton Village Society", which got me my first ever fan letter, from an editor who thought I should try writing for children. And that, dear reader, was how my first ever book occurred. If we count editions, bibliographies etc, I now have a score, but if it is all my own work, then *Matilda* is the eleventh book. It will be shortly followed by the twelfth, *Thief of Lives*, from (appropriately) Twelfth Planet Press. Somehow I think my best is still to come. I hope so.

ACKNOWLEDGEMENTS

"Merlusine" copyright © 1997 Lucy Sussex. First published in *The Horns of Elfland*, Penguin 1997.

"Kay & Phil" copyright © 1997 Lucy Sussex. First published in *Alien Shores*, Aphelion 1997.

"My Lady Tongue" copyright © 1988 Lucy Sussex. First published in *Matilda at the Speed of Light*, A&R 1988.

"The Lottery" copyright © 1994 Lucy Sussex. First published in *The Lottery*, Omnibus 1994.

"A Tour Guide in Utopia" copyright © 1995 Lucy Sussex. First published in *She's Fantastical*, Sybylla 1995.

"Robots & Zombies, Inc" copyright © 2008 Lucy Sussex. First published in *Dreaming Again*, HarperCollins 2008.

"Lipton Village Society" copyright © 1985 Lucy Sussex. First published in *Strange Attractors*, Hale & Ironmonger 1985.

"Duchess" copyright © 2006 Lucy Sussex. First published in *Absolute Uncertainty*, Aqueduct 2006.

"Montage" copyright © 1985 Lucy Sussex. First published in *Urban Fantasies*, Ebony 1985.

"Albert & Victoria/Slow Dreams" copyright © 2010 Lucy Sussex. First published in *Baggage*, Eneit 2010.

"Ardent Clouds" copyright © 2008 Lucy Sussex. First published in *The Del Rey Book of Science Fiction and Fantasy*, Del Rey 2008.

"La Sentinelle" copyright © 2003 Lucy Sussex. First published in *Southern Blood*, publication 2003.

"Frozen Charlottes" copyright © 2003 Lucy Sussex. First published in *Forever Shores*, Wakefield 2003.

"Matricide" copyright © 2005 Lucy Sussex. First published in SCIFICTION, scifi.com 2005.

"Something Better than Death" copyright © 2009 Lucy Sussex. First published in *Aurealis* #42, Chimaera 2009.

"The Revenant" copyright © 2006 Lucy Sussex. First published in *Eidolon I*, Eidolon 2006.

"Absolute Uncertainty" copyright © 2001 Lucy Sussex. First published in *Fantasy & Science Fiction*, 2001.

"Mist & Murder" copyright © 2007 Lucy Sussex. First published in *New Ceres* #2, Twelfth Planet 2007.

"Red Ochre" copyright © 1990 Lucy Sussex. First published in *My Lady Tongue & other tales*, Heinemann 1990.

THANK YOU

The publisher would sincerely like to thank:

Elizabeth Grzyb, Lucy Sussex, Delia Sherman, Deborah
Klein, Jonathan Strahan, Peter McNamara, Ellen Datlow,
Grant Stone, Jeremy G. Byrne, Sean Williams, Garth Nix,
David Cake, Simon Oxwell, Grant Watson, Sue Manning,
Steven Utley, Bill Congreve, Jack Dann, Stephen
Dedman, the Mt Lawley Mafia, the Nedlands Yakuza,
Shane Jiraiya Cummings, Angela Challis, Donna Maree Hanson,
Kate Williams, Kathryn Linge, Andrew Williams, Al Chan, Alisa
and Tehani, everyone I've missed . . .

. . . and *you*.

www.ingramcontent.com/pod-product-compliance
Lightning Source LLC
Chambersburg PA
CBHW030236030726
47493CB00022B/76